A Kovak & Quaid Mystery

DOUBLE EXPOSURE

Toni Leland

Double Exposure
©2012 Toni Leland

ISBN 978-0-9855309-3-8

Printed in U.S.A.

A Parallel Press Imprint

Equine Graphics
Publishing
Group
http://www.equinegraphicspublishing.com

Acknowledgments

As always, I want to thank the behind-the-scenes people who believe in my work and make this solitary job of writing a little easier: my advance reader and plotting partner, daughter Katie, and my final first-draft reader, husband Bob, who gives me the encouragement to take it to the next level.

For all the technical and factual details: K-9 Officer Michael LaFond of the New Milford (CT) Police Department for information about police dogs and their handlers; photographer Diane Horton for a glimpse into the world of equine photography; CW3 Steven Abernathy of the 3rd U.S. Infantry (The Old Guard) for details about Arlington Cemetery's Caisson Platoon; and Kurt Schemmerling in the Flight Standards District Office of the Federal Aviation Administration.

Last and most important, my wonderful Beta readers who read the manuscript not once, but twice! Your input is worth its weight in gold: Robbie Huseth, Holly Azevedo, Marilyn Fisher, and Katy Lindh-Wilson.
Thank you, everyone.

Toni Leland is the author of six equestrian novels, a paranormal romance, two juvenile chapter books, and a young adult novel; some of her short stories have appeared in *Arabella Romance Magazine, True Story, Bylines Writer's Calendar, From the Heart* anthologies, and *Horse Tales for the Soul.* Visit Toni at http://www.tonileland.com

Delaware, Ohio

"Where the hell is my horse?"

At the harsh tone, Kim Kovak jerked and punched the shutter button. Irritation skittered through her head and she spun around to glower at the person who'd just ruined a perfect shot.

The culprit strode across the grass, his dark eyebrows forming a slash across his forehead. Kim glanced back at the woman standing beside a big chestnut mare that was the subject of the photograph.

The woman frowned. "Jasper, can't you see we're in the middle of a photo shoot? You should have let me know you were coming."

The man stopped about five feet away and shoved his hat back. "Spur of the moment trip. Where's Talisman?"

Teri Fortune gave Kim an apologetic smile. "Sorry, could you give us a few minutes?" Without waiting for a reply, she turned back to the man. "He's in his stall, but we moved some horses around. C'mon, I'll show you."

They headed toward the barn and Kim looked up at the sky, annoyance treading on her patience. The light would be all wrong in another half-hour and she'd have to reschedule to finish the session. Much as she loved her work, dealing with the foibles of fussy owners and prima donna trainers took some patience, a virtue that seemed to dwindle as she got older. Shouldering the camera, she walked toward the barn to retrieve the rest of her gear.

As Kim stepped through the door, Teri's confused tone drifted on the air.

"Jasper, I can't imagine how... Are you *sure?*"

"Jee-zus, do ya think I don't know my own horse? How could you be so oblivious? He's been here five months!"

Kim hesitated, feeling guilty about eavesdropping, but also intrigued by the exchange.

Teri's voice took on a defensive edge. "Listen, you sent the horse here and he looks just like the pictures. Why would I question it? And maybe if you'd come to check on him sooner—"

"I don't know what kind of scam you're runnin', but it ain't gonna work."

Hearing boots thumping through the barn, Kim shrank back from the doorway and moved to the corner of the building. Jasper emerged, his face dark with anger. A minute later, he climbed into a silver Lincoln and gunned it down the lane, a spray of gravel playing off the board fence like gunfire.

The sound of horse hooves on concrete echoed inside the barn, then Teri appeared in the doorway, her features pinched. The chestnut mare took advantage of Teri's distraction and dropped her head to snatch a mouthful of lush grass growing next to the building.

Kim composed her features as though she'd heard nothing. "I think we've lost the light, Teri. I can come early tomorrow and finish up...hey, is everything okay?"

The young woman's eyes suddenly glistened. "Not even close."

Kim gazed at her for a moment. Fortune Farms had been a client for several years, so Kim didn't think she'd be overstepping her bounds by asking.

"What happened? He seemed pretty upset."

Teri's shoulders sagged. "With good reason. Apparently, somewhere along the line, someone replaced Jasper Martin's champion show jumper with a double." Her chin quivered. "He thinks *I* did it."

Kim thought for a moment. "How is that possible? Finding an exact match seems a little unbelievable to me. Besides that, how can he tell? What proof did he give you?"

"He's adamant that the horse in my barn is not Talisman, something about a secret mark of identification. Said he'd be back later to show me."

Kim pondered that. Why wouldn't he just show Teri *now?*

"I'm sure there's a logical explanation."

Teri let out a long sigh and stroked the mare's neck. "I sure hope so. In this economy, I can't afford any scandals to scare away what little business there is." She offered a thin smile. "Could you come tomorrow after lunch instead of in the morning?"

"Sorry, but I'm leaving for Kentucky around noon, so I'll have to either be here very early or reschedule for next month."

"Okay. I'll have her ready by eight. You certainly do get around. What's in Kentucky?"

"A big Egyptian Arabian event. Happens every year. One of my clients wants brochure photographs."

"You sure don't discriminate. Thoroughbreds, Arabians, and what else?"

"Anything I can take a picture of. The recession has affected us all, my friend."

Chapter 2

Driving through the lush Ohio farmland on her way back to town, Kim thought about the puzzling situation at the farm. It didn't seem possible that a horse could be switched out easily. And when would that have happened? While he was stabled at Teri's? Before he even left wherever he came from? If the animal had arrived five months ago, why hadn't Jasper come sooner to see that the valuable show horse had arrived safely and settled in? Kim snorted. Jasper Martin was a well-known and talented trainer in the national horse community, and a self-centered big-shot. He'd probably just assumed that everything was fine. Having built a strong, successful world for himself, he might never imagine that someone would try to bring it down. Kim sucked in a sharp breath. Is *that* what happened? Was this someone's vengeful act toward Jasper? Or simply a case of mistaken identity? Most likely, some barn helper had handed off the wrong horse. If they were identical, it *could* happen.

Kim pulled into the parking lot of the first motel she saw. Still pondering the mystery, she stared out the windshield at the landscaping along the front of the drab building. The shrubs were brown and crisp from lack of water, and rubbish littered the sun-bleached mulch. Neglect seemed to multiply in hard times. She thought again about Teri's problem. If this was a case of mistaken identity, what were the odds of having two identical horses in the same barn? Ridiculous odds, that's what. For a horse as valuable as Talisman, surely there were other ways to positively identify him. Freeze brands, microchips, DNA. Even that new-fangled iris identification system. And all those would be included on the horse's registration papers. How could such a glaring error have occurred? She clucked her tongue and climbed out of the car. It wasn't her problem, but it was certainly intriguing.

An hour later, she towel-dried her hair and stared in the mirror. The garish glow from the fluorescent bulb gave a sallow, unhealthy look to her skin. Even her dark red hair had a strange tint, almost green. Other than that, she didn't look too bad for just-turned-fifty. She smiled. Youth was wasted on the young. Since she'd gotten her act together, the past three years had been good. Successful. Independent. In charge of her own destiny. A murmur ran through her chest. A little lonely sometimes, but neither of the careers she'd chosen were good companions for the standard home life that included a husband and kids.

Her cell phone chimed and she hurried across the room. Her best friend's name appeared on the screen.

"Hey, Dixie, what's up?"

"Where are you? Your car's not in front of the condo. I was gonna see if you wanted to get a beer."

"That would be a little hard. I'm in Delaware."

"How'd you get way out *there?*"

Kim laughed. "Delaware, Ohio. You off duty tonight?"

"Yeah, for the next two days. Department is cutting back on hours, but not laying off. Thank God."

"I wish I was going to be home so we could do something, but I'm headed for Kentucky tomorrow."

"Well, crap. Guess I'll have to go see my mother."

"That would be a good thing. You need some diversions occasionally to help balance the nasty stuff you deal with at work."

"Yeah, it does get old. Sometimes I wonder why I became a cop, but the answer's always the same. I need to be part of the solution."

"I know."

Kim shivered, not so much from the air chilling her bare skin, but more from the memories trying to take over.

She pushed it away. "Listen, let me pass something by you. This doesn't make any sense to me, but maybe you'll see something I don't."

She outlined the scene at Teri's, realizing she didn't have much information and was probably expecting too much based on too little.

Dixie's tone grew serious. "Horse theft is big right now, but it seems crazy for the perp to go to the trouble of replacing the horse. Maybe it's more than just one person or specific instance."

"You mean a theft ring?"

"Could be. Where'd the horse come from originally?"

"I don't know. Maybe California. I can find out tomorrow."

Dixie's voice softened. "Listen, hon, don't get too involved. Folks who do this stuff aren't to be messed with."

The first light of dawn crept around the edges of the heavy drapes, tinting the walls and ceiling with a cool glow. Kim lay still, savoring that brief moment of morning before life set in. Dixie's sobering observations echoed in Kim's head, followed by warm thoughts about her best friend. With her petite body and tousled blonde hair, Dixie was the last person one would expect to be working as a sheriff's deputy. Kim stared at the ceiling. *And who am I to talk?*

She'd been drawn to Dixie Davis the first time she'd laid eyes on her. Maybe it was her infectious laugh, or those incredible blue eyes that drilled right through you, seeing all your raw secrets. Or maybe it was that subtle hint of something different, a sense that Dixie carried her own deep mystery. Kim thought about the moment when she intuitively *knew* about Dixie. Why hadn't they ever talked about it? She sighed. It wasn't up to her to bring it up.

She turned off the thoughts, climbed out of bed, and focused on her day. She had just enough time to return to Fortune Farms and finish the photographs of the mare before she headed for Lexington.

The zipper on her chinos stopped about an inch from the top. "Damn, I have *got* to lose some weight."

She stepped in front of the mirror and turned sideways. A bit of a tummy and a pleasantly round butt didn't exactly make her obese. Then she grinned.

"Big boobs make up for a lot of sins."

A few minutes later, she entered the motel's small breakfast room. The place was empty at that hour, but the complimentary doughnuts, pastries, cereal, fruit, and juice were neatly laid out on the counter. She filled a foam cup with blistering hot coffee, then chose a box of Cheerios and a banana to start her day. Cream moderated the temperature of the coffee and she sat back to take a sip. Jasper Martin's horse popped into her head again.

What would be the logic in stealing a highly-recognizable show horse? He couldn't be used in competition without the risk of being discovered. He was a gelding, so breeding value wasn't a motive. If Dixie was right about this being a professional operation, where was the money angle? Kim's stomach lurched. Slaughterhouses paid by weight, so a fourteen-hundred-pound Dutch Warmblood would bring a tidy sum, but it would be paltry compared to the show value of the horse. And why bother to find another horse to take his place? Just steal him and be done with it.

She tossed the plastic cereal bowl into the trash, dropped the banana into her bag, and headed for her room. This wasn't her fight and it only upset her to think about it.

لا

Fortune Farms lay in the hilly region of Delaware County. Teri Fortune's holistic approach to healing and boarding had built a healthy clientele of some of the wealthier horse owners in the nation. Teri's barns were spotless and the people she hired to work for her were carefully screened.

Kim drove slowly up the lane toward the big white barn. She was early, but she had an idea. Parking the car, she glanced toward the far end of the barn. Teri was leading a horse toward the pasture gate, but she looked up and waved. Kim grabbed her camera and hurried into the barn.

A handsome dark brown head appeared over a stall door. The name plate read "Talisman". The horse nickered and Kim chuckled.

"I'm not the one in charge of food, buddy."

She removed the lens cover and, with a quick glance toward the back barn door, let herself into the horse's stall. The big gelding opened his nostrils, drinking in her scent, then came forward and nosed the camera. Kim gave him a minute, then moved back and snapped off five shots of different parts of his body. What kind of marker could be hidden to keep it a secret? She'd just moved back into the aisle when Teri appeared.

"Kim, I'm so sorry to keep you waiting. I still have two horses to turn out, but there's coffee in the office, so help yourself. I won't be much longer."

"No hurry, I'm just slobbering over all this gorgeous horse-flesh."

Teri haltered a palomino mare and headed for the back door again. Kim waited until she was alone, then stepped back into Talisman's stall.

The horse chuckled deep in his throat as Kim stroked his neck, running her fingers along the base of his mane, then up toward his poll. Her fingertips explored, searching for telltale scarring from an implant. She found nothing. Maybe it was in his ear. She slowly moved her fingers up the velvety edges, grasping it gently between her thumb and fingers. He jerked his head away and snorted. She examined the ears visually, but saw nothing. She rubbed the gelding's jaw, working her hand slowly toward his nose. He seemed to like her touch. Teri's hands-on philosophy must agree with him.

She stroked his velvety muzzle. "Who are you, buddy? Will we ever know?"

Twenty minutes later, Kim looked up at the sky as she adjusted her camera. High, thin clouds diffused the light.

"These will look different than yesterday's shots, but we don't have much choice."

Teri positioned the chestnut mare. "Don't worry about it. The owner wants to sell her, so whatever we get that makes her look good will be fine."

Kim worked for almost an hour, kneeling, moving, changing settings, capturing the essence of the aristocratic-looking horse in the viewfinder. Between sets, she noticed the strain on Teri's face.

"Okay, I think we're finished. I checked yesterday's shots last night and I think the owner will find something he likes."

Teri did not smile. "I hope so."

She looked so forlorn that Kim felt compelled to say something. "Are you okay? I know you're worried about this thing with Jasper Martin, but I can't believe it's more than a mistake on someone's part."

"A county cop showed up here yesterday after you left."

Kim moved quickly to Teri's side. "What happened?"

"The officer said he couldn't launch an investigation without some proof that a crime had been committed, but he had to at least make an effort to follow up on Jasper's call."

Teri's eyes suddenly glistened and Kim slipped an arm around her shoulders. "See? If Jasper can't come up with anything other than a thin accusation, you shouldn't have to worry."

"I know, but it has more to do with his ability to cast doubt on my reputation. God, I've spent so long building this place and gaining trust in the equine community. He could destroy it all with just one ugly rumor. He swears he loaded Talisman onto the trailer himself."

"Tell me, why would Jasper place his top show jumper here for the better part of the season?"

Teri's face paled. "I'm not supposed to tell anyone, but the horse had a bad tendon pull at his last show. Jasper wanted me to quietly heal him so no one would know he'd been injured."

"And?"

Teri hesitated. "I couldn't find anything wrong with him."

Kim's astonishment left her speechless.

Teri looked away. "I know—I should have told him. But I needed the money. It never occurred to me that it might be a different horse."

Kim frowned. "This really stinks. I think Mr. Martin might be orchestrating an insurance scam."

Chapter 3

The four-hour drive to Lexington gave Kim plenty of time to think, and some old skills surfaced. If Jasper was trying to commit insurance fraud, the long time between Talisman's departure from his home barn and the discovery of the switched horse would give the trainer plenty of time to cover his tracks. With no urgency in the investigation, he'd not have to worry about chance comments by barn help or other people who'd been involved. As long as he could prove that the horse in Teri Fortune's barn was *not* Talisman, he would have a theft claim. Clever. But would Teri be the focus of the investigation? Would Jasper claim the horse was switched at Teri's barn? Kim shuddered. The girl was right—it would only take one incident to cast a cloud over her integrity and destroy everything she'd worked so hard to build.

Feeling despondent, Kim stared out the windshield at the mound of high clouds on the horizon. Whatever was going to happen, she could do nothing about it.

๛

After checking into a hotel, Kim headed for the Horse Park. Rush hour traffic was heavy on the bypass north of the city and she had to watch closely to avoid missing her exit. Thirty minutes later, she drove along the wide road toward the famous sprawling facility. Excitement danced through her head. Some of the most beautiful horses in the world were in residence and she planned to immerse herself in the charisma of the Egyptian Arabian Horse. There was no way to get a bad photograph of one of these creatures.

She parked as close to the barns as possible, then opened the event program. Shareen Van Khoten's elegant handwriting scrolled across the top of the cover: Sahara Riih Arabians, Barn 3, East Corner. Kim checked the facility map, then gathered her equipment and headed for the barns.

Excitement and anticipation electrified the atmosphere, punctuated by the loudspeaker calling classes, making announcements, and telling someone to move their truck or be towed. Rounding the corner of one of the buildings, Kim came to an abrupt stop as a small stallion, white as a cloud, danced at the end of his lead. He pricked his ears and snorted. Kim could barely breathe. Such fine legs, a deeply dished face and huge dark eyes. A feathery plume of tail arched over his back, then he turned away, fairly floating over the ground. The stallion was like something from an artist's brush. She watched him prance away, then let out a soft breath and continued on her way toward Barn 3.

Shareen had set up stalls as though she intended to stay for months. Her corner of the barn resembled a small estate, the entire stall block enclosed with heavy red and gold canvas drapes. A tent-like canopy rose above. Kim approached an arch hung with glittering beads, over which a sign lettered in fancy script read, "Sahara Riih Arabians." Below the name, *"They spurned the sand from behind them, They seemed to devour the desert before them."* Huge oil paintings of bejeweled and tasseled Bedouin horses racing across the sand hung on either side of the entrance.

"Oh, good, you are here!"

Shareen's aristocratic accent drifted on the warm afternoon air.

Kim turned. "I wouldn't have missed this for the world."

Shareen embraced her, brushing a light kiss across both cheeks, then stepped back and gestured expansively. "I would like photographs of our set-up, as well as the horses."

"It's beautiful. That saying over the entrance, what does it mean?"

Shareen's dark eyes sparkled. "Sir Walter Scott wrote those words in 'The Talisman' over 150 years ago. He was describing Saladin's horses who kept Egypt from being conquered by Richard I of England." Shareen's voice softened. "The desert Arabian is the fastest, bravest, most beautiful horse in the world, and has been so for centuries."

Kim started a bit at the mention of Talisman, a curious co-incidence on the heels of Teri Fortune's situation. But how amazing that these animals had survived the tests of time and had remained as pure as the foundation horses from which they'd sprung. At least, those that were under the care and conservation of Egyptian Arabian

15

purists like the Van Khotens.

Shareen took her hand. "Come, we'll have some tea and I will tell you what I need."

They moved through the beaded curtain, setting off a delightful chorale of tinkling. Two swarthy men sat on either side of the aisle, holstered guns clearly visible at their sides. A familiar ripple of nerves ran through Kim's stomach and she felt the urge to reach for her hip. Old habits died hard.

They walked down the aisle toward a small canopy at the back and she peered into each stall, her breath captured and snatched from her chest at the beauty of every horse. They all peered back at her, interested and alert, curious about the newcomer. These animals were valuable, so it would be reasonable to have someone on guard. But guns? It seemed impossible, and quite improbable, that anyone would try to steal one of these horses in the midst of a big event like this.

Under the canopy, Shareen motioned Kim toward a chair, then filled two glasses from a jug nestled in ice. Kim accepted the drink and waited for Shareen to sit.

"Thanks, I didn't realize how humid it is here."

"I, too, suffer when we come here. Arizona is so much more like my home in Egypt."

Kim took a long drink, then set the glass aside.

"I noticed you have some significant-looking guards up front."

Shareen's face clouded. "Yes, we do not travel anywhere without them anymore. There have been too many instances of theft and vandalism at shows and to horses left unattended. I follow the stories closely." Her gaze drifted toward the aisle and her soft features hardened. "I will not allow anything to happen to my children."

Kim shifted in her chair. "What kinds of things have happened? I hadn't heard."

Shareen lowered her voice. "With the terrible economy, people do things to make money. You can find it anywhere on the Internet. But I do not wish to encourage Fate by talking about such things." She rose from her chair. "Let's go to the arena. I will also show you where I would like the other photographs to be taken."

Kim followed, now barely noticing the elegant horses that watched with interest as she passed. A heaviness settled into her chest. In view of the situation with Talisman, Shareen's fears were not to be taken lightly.

Kim's practiced eye absorbed everything around her, and she made mental notes about the general show shots she'd take for future use. Shareen gestured as she talked about the schedule and her good luck to secure stalls so close to the covered arena.

"In years past, we've been stabled so far away that we needed the golf cart to get around." Her brilliant smile flashed. "This time, we are blessed with only a short distance to walk."

Kim gaped at the huge building that housed the new indoor arena, remembering the last time she'd been to the Horse Park. At that time, all events were held outdoors, but when Kentucky was tapped for the World Equestrian Games, the magnificent $45 million structure was built. She'd naively thought she would be able to attend those games and take wonderful photos, but all the hotels had been booked at least a year in advance.

Inside the arena, riders exercised their horses in the ring, a mélange of English, Western, and hunter disciplines. A few spectators dotted the banks of blue and gray seats that rose toward the roof. Trainers and owners hung on the rail, barking instructions to the riders in the ring. Kim looked up at the massive windows in the upper walls, then at the huge lights suspended from the roof. The light would be good enough to get decent exposures.

Shareen thrust a program into her hand. "I've marked our championship classes in red. I'd like shots both during the class and, of course, of any placings."

Kim tilted her head. "I'm curious as to why you aren't just using the show photographer."

"I like your work better than anyone else's." She brushed a strand of dark hair off her forehead. "Follow me. I'll show you the spot I want to use as a setting for the outdoor portraits."

Kim nodded, pleased by the compliment, but also aware that she was infringing on the professional photographer who'd been hired for the show. She would need to find that person and check in.

Shareen led the way across the road and between some

buildings, stopping in a grassy area bordered by towering Pampas grasses.

"I'd originally wanted the horses photographed at the edge of the water, but I think the grasses provide a better background, don't you?"

Kim turned to see what the view might be toward the water. Across the placid lake, the full expanse of the back wall of the stadium jumping arena had been painted with a mural of brilliant blue skies, rolling white fences, beautiful horses, and the proclamation of the FEI World Games 2010. The image reflected on the lake, doubling the impact.

"Yes, the mural would be distracting."

"Good. Now I must get back to the horses." She smiled. "Please plan to join us for dinner at Amalfi's this evening."

At six sharp, Kim pulled into the crowded parking lot of the Italian restaurant. As she walked toward the door, her phone chimed and Dixie's voice came through.

"Hey, Girl, where you at?"

"Just getting ready to join clients for dinner. What's up?"

"Call me tonight when you get finished. I have some news."

"What is it?"

Dixie chuckled. "No, you call me later."

"You brat."

"Me too. Love ya."

Kim pocketed the phone. Dixie was always full of surprises. What could she be up to now?

The hostess led Kim toward the back of the restaurant to a quiet private dining area where Shareen and her husband sat. Albert Van Khoten rose from his chair and greeted Kim with the traditional two-cheek buss.

"So good to see you again, my dear."

Kim made the appropriate responses, wondering how the effusive, dark-skinned Shareen had paired up with this fair-skinned, somewhat reserved Dutchman. They were as different as two people could be, yet they always seemed to be in tune with each other. Albert's steely gray hair defied taming, and his electric blue eyes could bore a hole straight through Kim's chest. But when he smiled, his entire face lit up.

She glanced at Shareen, seeing the love and respect in her eyes for this man who'd crossed cultural and religious barriers to be with the woman he cherished. *That's the way it should be,* thought Kim. *Why is it so hard to find?*

Albert's eyes twinkled. "We should get you to the farm in Egypt. It has been many years since we took photographs there."

"I'd love that! I've always wanted to see all those ancient wonders and, of course, the foundation of the Arabian horse."

Shareen laughed lightly. "You would be disappointed to see the 'foundation' horses in my country. They are not fat and sassy as we keep them here, but they are, indeed, the true blood of the breed."

Dinner arrived and Kim immersed herself in the most glorious Fettuccini Alfredo she'd ever tasted. The thick rich sauce—a perfect blend of butter, cream, and Parmesan cheese—coated every strand of pasta and curled around the bits of ham and mushroom. Shareen and Albert each had baked manicotti smothered in thick red sauce and glazed with melted mozzarella. Conversation suspended while everyone enjoyed their food.

For some reason, Kim thought again about Shareen's comments concerning her armed guards. She'd seemed genuinely frightened by whatever events had instigated the upgrade in security. Kim glanced at Albert. He might be more willing to talk about it, if she could find a way to bring it up in an offhand manner.

"That was fabulous. I can't believe I ate the whole thing." She took a sip of wine and grinned at Albert. "I'll start my diet tomorrow."

He chuckled. "You certainly need not worry about such things. American women are too thin. You are just right." He turned to his softly-rounded wife. "A man likes something to hold on to."

Shareen looked embarrassed and slapped his arm playfully. "Albert! Shush, do not talk of such things in public."

He leaned over and kissed her cheek. "As you wish, my darling."

Kim could barely watch the exchange, so envious of that

special bond that had eluded her.

Albert turned his attention back to Kim. "We will return to Cairo in November. Would you like to come in December? The weather then is wonderful, fairly cool and dry."

"That would be perfect. Winter is my slowest time and I don't have anything scheduled yet."

"Good. It is settled. We shall discuss the details before you leave Kentucky."

Kim took a deep breath. This was the perfect opening.

"Tell me, Albert. Do you need such heavy security for your horses in Egypt?"

Shareen gasped and Kim felt a tug of guilt for side-stepping the woman's desire to not discuss the subject.

Albert sat back in his chair and scrutinized Kim for a moment, making her squirm.

"Not so much as here, but still we must be alert. The international market for valuable horses is quite strong."

"Is there much insurance fraud? Or mostly just outright theft for resale?"

He glanced at his wife. "Insurance fraud seems to be more prevalent in this country. What we've been seeing is theft, especially horses in the U.S. being stolen and sold to wealthy buyers in Europe."

"But with all the identification precautions, wouldn't that be difficult?"

"Chips can be removed, freeze-marks obliterated, hair coats dyed, et cetera. If a criminal is determined, they will find a way." Albert shook his head. "Such a bad state of affairs."

Kim decided to go a step further. "Something strange happened back in Ohio earlier this week. For the life of me, I can't figure out the reasoning behind it."

She told them about Jasper and Talisman, adding her own thoughts about how it could have been done.

Albert nodded. "Buying time to let evidence fade and possible witnesses disappear would be a good way to facilitate an insurance scam. And if the stolen horse were sold overseas, that would be additional monies in the owner's pocket. Very clever, indeed."

Shareen spoke up for the first time. "Someone would have to go to a great deal of trouble to find an exact twin to the horse. And how could the two be switched en route? There would have to be other people involved. It sounds risky to me."

Albert patted her hand. "Yes, darling, but desperate people do desperate things."

Chapter 4

Kim crawled into bed and snuggled under the covers, thinking about the lovely evening with the Van Khotens. A hum from the bedside table interrupted her thoughts.

"Hi, doll." Dixie's smile came right through the speaker.

"Hi, yourself. I just got back. Now tell me your news."

"I've been accepted for the K-9 Unit!"

"Dixie, that is so fabulous! You must be over the moon."

"I still can't believe it. No more cruising the streets for speeders."

Kim chuckled. "There aren't enough cops in the whole state to control *that* problem!"

"Tell me about it."

"When do you start?"

"Monday. I'll be in training for nine weeks."

"What does your mom think?"

"I haven't told her yet. She'd only be happy if I quit the department completely and came to live next door to her."

Kim nodded, but didn't respond. Dixie had a lot on her plate with a high stress job and a demanding elderly mother.

"Listen Dix. I have to be up before the sun. I'll see you when I get back and we'll go out to celebrate."

"Okay. I'll check your cat in the morning. 'Night, sweetie."

Kim turned off her phone and lay back, a hard knot forming behind her breastbone. The time had come to tell Dixie about her past.

◦❧◦

The following morning, Kim immersed herself in what she loved and did best: capturing the essence of the horse. She felt blessed to be able to earn her living doing something so creative and enjoyable. Arabians were breathtaking and exciting, but she held no bias for the other breeds. The majesty of the big Warmbloods, the refined elegance of Thoroughbreds, the great attitude of hard-working Quarter Horses, the friendly and versatile Morgan Horse—

each held a magic for Kim that showed in her photographs. Even the mutts like Red. She closed her eyes for a moment, swept away by the familiar sorrow.

A horse whinnied somewhere and Kim turned away from the past to the work at hand.

At the end of the session with a small gray mare with large dark eyes, Shareen glowed. "I cannot wait to see your pictures, but please excuse me now, for we have a class in one hour."

She walked away with her horse and Kim gazed across the small lake. A breeze ruffled the surface, distorting the reflection of the bright mural. The sounds of the day faded and she suddenly felt very alone. Where was she headed? She'd met her professional goals and now stayed busy and content with her work. Was this all she could look forward to? The independent streak that had steered her through the landmines of life had been her undoing at times, though she usually came out on the other side unscathed. Why did she have these moments when it all seemed not enough? Had turning fifty been a bigger defining moment than just numbers? She looked away from the water, wondering if she'd have been happier if things had worked out with Peter. Those thoughts hadn't surfaced in a long time and she wasn't pleased by their appearance now. She'd managed the shock and pain, and moved on with her life. She'd gotten what she wanted. Hadn't she?

Annoyed by the uncharacteristic detour into the past, she strode toward the outdoor jumping arena. A lone rider practiced the course, his mount sailing over the obstacles as though lifted on invisible wings. Kim removed the camera lens cover and focused on the horse, feeling his rhythm, pressing the shutter just before the action. It had taken her a while to learn how to time jumping shots, but it had been worth it. Some of her better work had even appeared on the covers of one of the equestrian magazines.

She strolled around the perimeter, concentrating on the action. After about fifteen minutes, the rider trotted toward her.

"Hi, are you the show photographer?"

"No, just getting some general shots for my portfolio. I'm Kim Kovak from Ohio."

"Clark Jennings from Pasadena, California." He leaned down

and handed Kim a business card. "If you get anything good, I'd be willing to buy prints."

His bay gelding snorted and pawed the ground, impatient to get back to the barn.

"Thanks, nice to meet you," said Kim, offering her own card. "I'll post the proofs on my light-box when I get back."

The rider nodded, then turned his horse and trotted toward the gate. Kim looked at the card, idly wondering if he lived anywhere near Jasper Martin. Her mental scrutiny of the Talisman mystery returned and she strolled toward the indoor arena, mulling over the facts as she knew them. She didn't have much concrete evidence, but something wasn't right about the whole thing. Her investigative skills smelled a rat.

Kim settled into one of the seats in Shareen's front row box, glancing briefly at the growing crowd. During the early part of a horse show, when qualifying classes were held, family and staff usually comprised the spectators. But on stakes days, the audience swelled to near capacity for popular breeds like Arabians. Kim glanced at the program. Shareen's horses had qualified for two championships today and two tomorrow and, in a few minutes, one of Sahara Riih's beautiful three-year-old colts would compete against other equally magnificent horses for the futurity title. After the dinner break, the exciting and entertaining costume class would be the highlight of the evening, being one of the most popular spectator classes of the entire show. Kim looked forward to photographing the dazzling outfits and fantastic trappings each owner put together for that class.

Setting the program aside, she adjusted her camera for light and distance, then panned across the arena to get a feel for the setting. A moment later, a line of exquisite colts pranced into the ring, floating at the ends of their leads like fantasy mirages, each one as beautiful as the next. They were all legs and attitude, but the fine bones were clearly visible, a promise of the future. Kim spotted Shareen's trainer, a handsome young man of obvious Middle Eastern blood. He focused on the colt at the end of the lead, moving with the animal and making it appear that the two of them were one. Many of the other contestants were clearly having a tough time controlling their young charges, but Shareen's colt was the picture of obedience.

Kim captured him in frame after frame. She lowered the camera and studied the field of thirteen animals. How hard it would be to choose the one that would win thousands of dollars for his owner. Twelve other breeders would lose their futurity investment at the end of this class. The idea seemed more risky than Kim would be willing to undertake.

Forty minutes later, Shareen's colt was named futurity champion. Kim gasped and stood up quickly, capturing the horse's almost slow-motion trot toward the ring steward who held the winner's rosette and sash. A minute later, Kim hurried along the rail toward the exit. Her step slowed when she spotted the security guard standing with Shareen, who was clearly taking no chances. The colt would never be out of sight for even a minute. A heaviness settled into Kim's chest. Such a depressing concept.

د

Back in her hotel room, Kim washed away the day's grime with a long, hot shower, spending that time to reflect. She'd taken a minute to look at Clark Jennings's jump photos. They'd turned out better than good and she was feeling smug. The images would probably earn her some extra cash, not to mention the possibility of adding another solid client. She thought back to when she'd found herself suddenly retired and casting about for meaning in her life. The photography had started as therapy, but then became an obsession. She'd immersed herself in the craft and, once she'd become known amongst the different breed communities, the work had come in waves. It had been frightening at the time. She'd barely emerged from the horror of her scrape with death. Should she take the chance? What if the business dried up? What if she had no work during the winter months? What if, what if...

She stepped out of the shower and wrapped herself in the soft oversized towel. Right now, life was good.

Chapter 5   *New Albany, Ohio*

Though a little buzzed from the drive home, Kim still wanted to inspect the shots she'd taken. She hooked up the camera and sat back as the images started uploading. She stared at the spinning rainbow icon on her Mac screen, her thoughts turning to Albert's invitation to visit them in Egypt. Her pulse gave a little skip and she almost shivered. One of her bucket list items could be a reality. She opened her appointment calendar to December and, with a decisive click, highlighted the entire month. Returning to the upload screen, she caught a glimpse of Shareen's magnificent mare on a victory pass around the arena. *Supreme Champion Egyptian Mare.* That win had so overwhelmed Shareen that she'd reverted to her native tongue and couldn't stop babbling for at least fifteen minutes. Kim chuckled. Those horses were, indeed, Shareen's darlings, a substitute for the children she'd never borne. Kim sobered. In a society where motherhood was akin to sainthood, she herself knew only too well how hard it was to be a woman without children. But for Shareen, it had not been by choice.

The computer signaled the completion of the upload and Kim turned back to her work. First, the culling, selecting the best of the images and discarding the duds. Each photograph would then need identification and inventory assignment before she began loading proof copies into an online light-box for Shareen to view. As Kim worked through the photos, her sharp eye noted inconsistencies in backgrounds, or unnecessary people and objects that detracted from the overall image. She usually tried to compose the shots, but it wasn't always possible. Several excellent images of halter horses were marred by light poles or a banner in the background. Cropping sometimes helped, but if she had other shots, she usually just discarded the photos with distracting backgrounds.

After working her way through the arena shots, she moved on to the candid photos she'd taken around the complex, including Shareen's stall set-up. As she worked, something began to nag at her. What was her brain trying to tell her? She scanned back to the beginning of the set and clicked slowly through. Sahara Riih's stalls and displays were beautiful, but she didn't see anything unusual. Too bad she'd been unable to keep the security guards out of the pictures.

"Oh, my gosh, that's it!" She leaned closer to the screen. "They are in *every* shot!"

Had they been purposely keeping *her* in their sight? She shivered, then tried cropping or cloning the men out. It would take some time, but she could eliminate them from most of the photos. Unfortunately, she couldn't eliminate their reason for being there.

The situation with Talisman and Teri Fortune rose to the top of Kim's thoughts. She'd been so busy the past few days that she hadn't thought much about it. Maybe there were new developments. She'd give Teri a call on the pretense of checking to see if the photo CD had arrived. She scribbled a note to herself, then returned her attention to the Kentucky photographs.

As she worked through the candid shots taken around the Horse Park, her interest sharpened. In almost every barn shot, a man and woman appeared in the periphery or background. A small coil of concern moved through Kim's chest. She zoomed in on the figures in one image and examined their faces carefully, then moved to the next photo, and the next. They were the same people. Were they owners or breeders? Possibly scouting for horses to buy? Maybe something worse?

To the casual observer, this would have been a coincidence. To Kim Kovak, retired special duty police officer, there was no such thing as a coincidence.

A soft knock on the door sent a jolt through Kim's chest, then she exhaled sharply. Would she ever learn to relax?

Dixie came through the door carrying two frosty bottles of Corona and a large lime.

"Quittin' time!" She headed for the kitchen. "I thought we could celebrate my upcoming doggie training."

Kim got up to follow. "Aren't they going to give you a dog that's already trained?"

Dixie turned, her eyes sparkling. "I have *no* idea, but I can't wait! I haven't been this excited about anything since I was a kid."

Kim found a bottle opener, then cut the lime while Dixie expounded on her new career.

"I can't decide whether I want to do drug detail or search and rescue."

"Are you given a choice? I suspect the department will use you where they need you."

Dixie clinked her beer bottle against Kim's. "Doesn't matter, I'm gonna love it."

A minute later, she leaned close to Kim's laptop screen. "Pretty horses, but it looks like a lot of work to do that showing stuff."

"Yep, and expensive."

Dixie sat down. "Speaking of expensive, you ever hear anything more about that switched-out horse?"

"No, but I'm beginning to think it was more than an accidental mix-up. My trip to Lexington was a real eye-opener."

Dixie listened closely while Kim related the Van Khotens' views on the state of the horse industry. Dixie finished her beer and sat back, concern knitting her eyebrows.

"Yeah, the horror stories of desperation make you wonder if the country will ever recover." Her features hardened. "And some bastards just see it as a chance to benefit from someone else's misfortune. Makes me sick when we have to deploy officers to disaster areas to prevent looting, for Pete's sake! Like the flooding last summer. God, I just wanted to go down there and start shooting!"

Kim didn't say anything. She'd never seen Dixie so fired up.

Dixie grinned. "Sorry, I need to keep my lip zipped or I'll be in trouble with Internal Affairs." She glanced at her watch and stood up. "Speaking of which, I have to be at the training center early tomorrow. I'd better scramble."

"Good luck. Be sure to let me know how your first day goes."

As the door closed, Kim's phone rang and an unfamiliar area code appeared on the screen.

"Kim Kovak Equine Imagery."

"Hi, this is Clark Jennings in Pasadena. You took some pictures of me at the Horse Park last week."

"Hello, Clark. Nice to hear from you."

"I was wondering if you got any good shots."

"I did, and I'm in the process right now of downloading and preparing proofs. Give me about thirty minutes and you can look at them on the website."

"Great. Hey, listen, would you be interested in being the photographer for our regional qualifier show? It's next month in Burbank. I know this is short notice, but we had some internal problems in the organization and the person in charge of show photographer dropped the ball."

Kim opened her calendar screen. "What are the dates?"

"Fourth of July weekend. It's a nice show, and the facility is fabulous."

"That works for me. Send the show contract within the next three days to confirm it. You might want to check my website for my fees."

He chuckled. "Oh, I already did that. We're good."

"Thanks a lot. I'll look forward to this. I haven't been to California in years. Those proofs will be available shortly. Let me know if you like any of them."

"After looking through your website, I'm sure they'll be spectacular. Thanks again."

Kim set the phone aside and blocked out the California dates, then surveyed her upcoming photo shoots. She'd need to be careful about over-scheduling or she'd be exhausted before December.

The photos of Jennings were mostly good, needing no cropping or adjustment. She uploaded the thumbnails to her website and verified all the links. She was just composing a quick e-mail when Teri Fortune called. Kim's thoughts turned to how she would steer the conversation.

"Hi, Teri. Did you get the photo CD?"

"It came yesterday, but I haven't had time to look at it."

Something in the girl's voice told Kim that things were not going well.

"Hopefully because of lots of new business?"

"I *wish*. Actually, just the opposite. One of my oldest clients is taking her horses home. Says she can't afford me in this economy, but my paranoia is telling me it might be because of the problem with Talisman."

"How would anyone know about that so soon?"

"Hah! The horse grapevine is faster than the speed of light. And Jasper is a regular megaphone when it comes to something that involves *him*."

"Where's he from, anyway?"

"Altadena, California. I wish he'd go back there and leave me alone."

Kim chose her words carefully. "Is he still threatening you?"

"Not in person, but a private investigator for the insurance company called yesterday. He'll be out here snooping around on Wednesday. I can't believe Jasper is doing this to me."

"Wait a minute, Teri. An insurance investigator would be looking into Jasper, not *you*."

"You're probably right, but this whole thing is going to affect me in the long term."

"If you want, I can come up to lend moral support. I have some prints to drop off over your way."

Teri's voice broke. "Would you? I could sure use a friend right now."

"I'll be there."

Kim hung up and opened MapQuest.

"Well, now isn't *that* interesting. Altadena is just a few miles from Burbank."

She paced about the living room, her head whirling with the Talisman mystery. Something soft bumped against her ankle and she leaned down to stroke her roommate's silky fur.

"And where have *you* been all day, Miss Kitty? Sleeping in my clean laundry again?"

She scooped up the cream-colored cat and cuddled the animal against her chest, delighting in the soft rumble of contentment. She thought again about Teri's distress—the girl had good reason to worry about her reputation, but should certainly welcome an investigation into the problem. If she had nothing to do with the switch, she had nothing to worry about.

Kim stopped abruptly. *If* she had nothing to do with it? Why would that thought even cross her mind? Teri Fortune was the last person anyone would suspect of being involved in something shady.

But Albert Van Khoten's words rang in Kim's head. *Desperate people do desperate things.* Could Teri be in dire enough financial straits to try something so risky? And for what gain?

Kim began pacing again. No, someone else had pulled this stunt and Kim's instincts homed in on Jasper Martin.

Miss Kitty let out a plaintive meow when Kim deposited her on the couch. A minute later, Kim searched the Internet for the trainer and his fancy horse. The last mention of Martin and Talisman had been in November when the horse competed at the Washington International Horse Show. Kim had attended that event as a spectator and she remembered watching Talisman at the jump-offs. He'd seemed perfectly sound, so why would Jasper take him off the circuit for so long?

She typed in the web address for that show and looked through the links. As she'd hoped, video footage of the event was available online. A minute later she found the highlights of the jump-offs, and Talisman in all his glory, sailing over obstacles without a hitch. She sat back and nodded. Could the claimed tendon pull be a cover story? But for *what?*

She moved away from the news items and video clips, searching her portfolio for the photos that she'd taken herself during the Washington show. Two hundred and thirty images appeared. Surely, in all of these, she had pictures of Talisman. What difference it made, she didn't know, but she still wanted to check. As she scanned slowly through the photos, a cold pool of recognition flooded her gut.

Two familiar faces showed in the background of almost every candid shot. The same man and woman who'd been at the Kentucky show the previous week.

Chapter 6   *Cleveland, Ohio*

Garrett Quaid scowled at the manila folder in front of him. What the hell was going on? This would be United Equine Assurance's fourth theft claim this year that involved using a look-alike horse. Someone was being quite clever, buying time so the trail would go cold. But the emerging pattern sent a powerful message of skillful organization.

He slipped the file into a black leather portfolio, then walked down the hall, passing several cubicles where insurance adjusters worked. Stepping into a large comfortable office, he smiled at the woman behind the desk.

"I'm headed for hicksville to sort out this latest switcheroo deal."

"If anyone can figure it out, it'll be you. Bring me some money-saving news."

Quaid's reflection in the polished elevator doors made him straighten up and suck in the small gut that had appeared out of nowhere in the past year. Damned desk job didn't help his fitness routine. He frowned. What fitness routine? He'd been slipping lately, losing his drive to stay lean and mean since leaving the Army. A heavy pressure moved into his chest and he looked up at the green numbers slowly marking his descent to the lobby. Had it really been four years already? A loud ding, the doors opened, and Quaid stepped away from the memories that gunned him down in every unguarded moment.

Striding across the marble floor toward the exit, he did a mental review of the cases that bore such resemblance to each other. They had the earmarks of fraud, but so far he'd been unable to prove that. Too much coincidence for his taste and he knew, if he dug deep enough, he'd find at least one common element. Even the fact that the cases were from all over the map didn't sway his belief that they were perpetrated by the same person or group. The big question was, just how many people were involved? If horses were being taken out of the country, quarantine stations and customs and all the other red-tape would need to be compromised to swing it. Could this be something that big? But why did he even think the horses were being exported? Maybe they were simply being taken to slaughterhouses in Mexico or Canada. He shook his head. No, selling valuable horses for big prices was the answer, otherwise the operation was just too chancy for all involved. But someone was going to a great deal of trouble to find exact doubles for the theft-targeted horses.

An hour later, he pulled into the grassy parking spot next to his tiny house in Chagrin Falls. Climbing out of the car, he took a deep breath, always happy to come home. The cottage had cost him a small fortune, but had been a refuge during the hardest time of his life. A place to hide, lick his wounds, and satisfy his need for solitude. He walked toward the back door, glancing at grass that needed mowing and landscape beds that needed weeding. Spring had surged over the state early and he hadn't caught up yet.

His cell phone rang as he entered the kitchen, and his sister-in-law's number appeared on the screen. Jenna only called when there was a problem. He took a deep breath, then answered in a deep, gruff voice.

"Private Detective Garrett Quaid of the Fraud Squad. What is the nature of your business?"

Jenna's tone indicated that she was not amused. "In case you don't remember, Ricky's birthday party is on Saturday. Are you planning to be here?"

Quaid winced, acknowledging Jenna's unspoken accusation, remembering a couple of other birthdays he'd missed. Not because of time conflict, but because he'd bailed at the last minute, unable to cope with the turmoil churning through his life.

"Absolutely. I'm working on an out-of-town case right now, but I'll be back by the weekend. Does the kid still love Star Wars?"

"That was several years ago, Garrett. He's twelve now."

Quaid swallowed the uncomfortable lump rising in his throat. "I'll come up with something good, I promise."

He said goodbye, then sank into his favorite chair, blinking hard at the sting behind his eyelids. How could something that had once been so right, now be so horribly wrong?

Chapter 7

When Kim arrived at Teri's barn the next afternoon, two vehicles sat in front, a dark blue late model truck and a black Cadillac with a rental sticker in the back window.

"Oh, great, I'll bet that's Jasper."

She grabbed her camera bag and hurried toward the barn.

Teri turned as Kim walked down the aisle. "Hey, we were just talking about you."

Kim glanced at the two men standing near Talisman's stall door. Her attention moved past Jasper and came to rest on a tall, sandy-haired man who was looking at the horse. Jasper was gesturing expansively as he talked.

Kim turned to Teri. "How long have they been here?"

"About five minutes, just long enough to introduce themselves. You're timing is great."

Kim lowered her voice. "What's the atmosphere like? Jasper looks like he's being fairly cordial."

"He's a master at being everybody's best friend when he needs something. The rest of the time, he treats everyone like crap."

As though summoned, Jasper walked across the aisle and smiled at Kim. "Howdy, you must be the photographer." He stuck out his hand. "I'm Jasper Martin."

"Kim Kovak. Nice to meet you." Her gaze moved past him to the other man who was taking pictures of the horse. "What insurance company?"

"United Equine Assurance out of Cleveland. Listen, you were here last week when I discovered the theft, right?"

Kim lifted an eyebrow. "The theft? You know that for sure?"

Jasper's pleasant expression morphed immediately into that of a bully accustomed to having his own way. He took a step closer, but Kim stood her ground. Their eyes locked and she saw the hard glint of a man with little concern for anyone but himself.

"Lady—"

"My name's Kim."

"Whatever. You'll need to give this guy your statement about the situation."

Kim glanced past Jasper. "If he wants to ask me questions, I'm more than happy to answer, but I only know what I heard you say to Teri last week."

Jasper's face paled, but he didn't respond.

A deep voice broke the uncomfortable silence. "Miss Fortune, would you bring the horse out so I can get pictures from all sides?"

Teri hurried toward the stall and Kim followed. While Teri haltered the horse, the man came forward and offered his hand.

"Garrett Quaid."

His large hand was warm, but not as soft as she'd expect for a white collar worker. The skin was firm as though those hands had been working hands. Not heavily callused, but definitely capable hands. A white scar curved across the top of his left hand, intersecting with the last three fingers.

"Kim Kovak. I'm an equine photographer."

"So I hear. You do much business in these parts?"

She chuckled. "I travel all over the country. Just came back from Kentucky, headed to California next month, then Egypt in December."

As she talked, she examined his features. He was nice looking, but not handsome. He wore square wire-rimmed glasses. Freckles roamed across his tanned cheeks and, at this close proximity, she could see flecks of gray sprinkled through the short sandy hair. He looked to be about her age, maybe a little younger.

His hazel eyes held a hint of amusement. "Egypt, huh? Never wanted to go there." He glanced at Teri, standing patiently with the horse. "Excuse me, gotta get back to work."

Kim noticed Jasper rocking back and forth on the balls of his feet. Why was he so nervous? What he was hiding?

The investigator walked slowly around the big brown horse, snapping photographs from every angle. *Garrett Quaid.* She was pretty sure she'd heard the name associated with something big. She thought for a few minutes, then remembered and shuddered. A terrible barn fire a few years back had grabbed the attention of the region, and Garrett Quaid had been the lead investigator. Kim glanced at Jasper. If he thought he could put anything over on *this* guy, he was sadly mistaken.

Twenty minutes later, Quaid approached Kim. "Mr. Martin says you were here on the day he discovered that the animal in question was not his horse. Is that right?"

Kim nodded. "I was outside when he arrived. I was *not* in the barn when he talked to Teri, so I have no idea what he *did* or *did not* say."

Quaid raised an eyebrow. "It was a simple question. No need to be so bristly."

Kim resisted the urge to tell him exactly what she thought of Jasper Martin and his insurance claim, but she'd learned a while back to put the old Kim behind her.

"I'm here to support Teri. If I can answer any questions that will help her, I'll do that."

"Meaning you won't answer questions that would *not* help her?"

Kim met his gaze. She could play this game too. A hint of a smile tightened his mouth and he nodded, then wrote something in his notebook.

"Did you take any photographs of the horse in question? It would help verify that the horse in the stall now is the same one he claims was there on that day."

"I did, but only because he's a good looking horse." She smiled thinly. "That's what I do, sort of an addiction."

"I'll need to see those pictures. Would you e-mail them to me?"

Kim did *not* want to share her photos with this guy. She had no idea what she might have captured on the camera, or how it might help Jasper—or harm Teri.

"I deleted them. They weren't that great, just snapshots of a horse munching hay."

Quaid's eyes narrowed. He'd sensed her lie. Anyone good enough to rout out fraud criminals would have a good ear and an eye for body language. Just like a cop. She didn't break eye contact. That would give her away instantly.

A knowing smile spread over the investigator's face. "Well,

that's too bad. Have you ever taken photographs of the allegedly missing horse, Talisman?"

"I might have. I do visit a lot of horse shows. I can look at my archives and let you know."

He held out a crisp white business card and she pocketed it without looking at it.

He stepped back, the smile gone. "Nice meeting you, Miss Kovak."

"It's Ms."

"Oh, right...it *would* be."

Irritation prickled Kim's neck as she watched him walk toward Jasper. *What did that mean?*

Teri's soft voice was close by. "I can't tell if he believes me or not."

"That's the trademark of a good investigator. Never let anyone know anything. Keeps folks on their toes, or puts them at ease so they can screw up." She looked toward Talisman's stall. "Teri, do you happen to know how Jasper knew that horse wasn't his?"

Teri's face brightened. "Actually, I overheard the agent ask him that same question. Jasper said that this horse came right over to him."

"And that means what?"

"Apparently Talisman is one nasty animal. He's even attacked Jasper."

Kim narrowed her eyes. "You suppose he abused the horse? They never forget, you know."

Teri nodded. "That's a good possibility." She gestured toward Talisman's stall. "That horse—whoever he is—has a sweet disposition."

Kim watched the two men talking. Jasper's body language indicated that he knew he was in over his head.

"What do you think will happen next?" asked Teri.

"I suspect Inspector Quaid will start digging into Jasper's business and his past to see if there are any red flags."

Teri's tone was plaintive. "What about me?"

"If he turns up anything that looks like you were knowingly involved, he'll start snooping around your business too." She put a hand on Teri's arm. "I wouldn't worry about it. You've nothing to hide, and the truth will eventually come out."

"How do you know so much about this investigation stuff?"

A deep ache ran through Kim's thigh, a reminder of why she was standing there.

"I read a lot."

Outside in the parking lot, Kim looked at the information on Quaid's business card, then stuffed it into her pocket and climbed into her car. Why had she lied about the Talisman photos? And why was she sure Quaid knew it? Did she have any legal obligation to hand over her work in a non-criminal case? She examined her motives from a personal standpoint. What she *didn't* want to do was provide anything that would hurt Teri Fortune. Gut instinct said the girl was not involved, but experience told Kim that she could be so wrong. On the other hand, if her photographs could help snare Jasper Martin, why shouldn't she let the investigator see them?

From the corner of her eye, she watched Quaid climb into his truck. She started her engine and drove quickly down the lane, wanting to distance herself from the man who'd subtly insulted her femininity. Or maybe he was referring to her in-your-face attitude, a personality trait she could no more help than being female. At least she had the advantage of a law enforcement background. Rent-a-cop Garrett C. Quaid wouldn't be putting much over on *her*.

⁀

Quaid grinned as he watched the aged black Beemer move briskly down the farm driveway. He'd really pushed Kim Kovak's button with that last dig. He put the truck in reverse. But she'd asked for it. Nothing he hated more than aggressive women who always seemed to be out to prove something. Too bad. She was good looking.

His thoughts turned to the case. Jasper Martin was smarmy, no doubt about it. Just the type to try to ease a financial strain by pulling an insurance deal. Problem was, unless there was a way to prove that Martin himself had made the switch or gotten someone else to do it, the insurance company would pay the claim.

Quaid shook his head. "A hundred grand. What a way to make a quick buck." Then he sighed. At least the guy hadn't torched a barn to get his payoff.

He shuddered and turned off that train of thought, glancing at his watch. Too late to drive home and too early to call it a day. He cruised through the small town, but didn't see anything that made him want to stay. Maybe he could use this time to find a great gift for his nephew's birthday, maybe have a good meal somewhere in Columbus. Tomorrow he would go back to Fortune Farms to talk to the owner without Jasper Martin hanging around. Teri Fortune had seemed genuinely upset over the whole thing and Quaid's instinct told him she was the victim in this mess.

Chapter 8

Kim pulled into the parking space in front of her condo and a hollow feeling moved through her chest as she glanced over at Dixie's empty spot. Why were emotional issues such a problem? If she and Dixie were to remain friends, Kim would need to share her past, and clear the air about their personal relationship. A hard lump rose in her throat. She really liked Dixie, but not in the way Dixie seemed to want. At least Kim thought she knew what Dixie wanted. But she could be wrong. The only way to find out would be to open the discussion and see where it led, starting with an apology and a not-so-happy "Once Upon a Cop" story.

Miss Kitty met her at the door, meowing plaintively as though she hadn't eaten in days. Kim laughed and scooped her up, tossing keys and sunglasses onto the hall table. The long shadows of early evening bathed the front deck in soft peach hues, enhancing the brilliant pink begonias in the corner planter. Kim sank into one of the cushioned chairs and gazed out at the tree canopy that gave a deep, secluded feel to the area. The cat purred against her chest and Kim closed her eyes, letting the tension of the day drain away. Thoughts of Egypt drifted through her head and she dozed.

She jerked awake. Was someone knocking on the door? Her head cleared and she heard it again, realizing it was next door. She peered over the railing. A brown sedan was parked in Dixie's spot, but Kim couldn't see who was at the door. A sturdy woman came into view and climbed into the car. Kim stared at the emblem on the car door and a hard knot formed in her chest. *Ohio Senior Services.* Had something happened to Dixie's mom? Kim whipped out her phone and dialed Dixie's number. It rang three times, then an automated voice message came on. Kim hung up. She couldn't leave a cryptic message, especially since she had no idea what might be going on. Surely if this was about Dixie's mother, whoever that was in the brown car could get in touch with Dixie by phone, or through her barracks.

Kim moved slowly back into the house, feeling helpless and

isolated. She jammed her hands into her pockets and stared at the refrigerator. Her fingers touched something in her pocket and she pulled out the insurance investigator's business card. She grabbed a soda from the fridge and headed toward her office.

An Internet search for Garrett C. Quaid turned up hundreds of hits, but the one that knocked her back in her seat was a two-year-old news article about a barn fire investigation in Kentucky where seven horses had perished. The official investigation had been closed with no firm evidence of wrong-doing, but Quaid had continued his quest for the truth, working on his own time and without pay. Through his diligence, he'd discovered a factor that had gone unnoticed during the emotional frenzy of the tragedy and, as a result, a disgruntled horse owner was arrested and charged with arson. The man had eventually admitted that he was mad at the stable owner for not showing his horse in an important horse show.

Kim felt sick. What made people so crazy? Destroying property and beautiful animals over ego? She shuddered, then thought about Garrett Quaid. If there was wrongdoing in this Talisman thing, Quaid would go after it like a pit bull.

Another story farther down in the search was a brief personal profile on his business site. He'd been a private investigator for four years after leaving the Army. She sucked in her breath and leaned closer. He'd been with "The Old Guard," the Caisson Platoon tasked with escorting the flag-draped caskets to Arlington National Cemetery. What an honor to serve with that unit, care for those fabulous horses, and pay tribute to the nation's fallen heroes.

She closed the browser window and opened her photo archives. She needed to get those horse show pictures sorted out for Quaid.

First she pulled up the snapshots she'd taken of the horse in Talisman's stall. Feeling ashamed for lying about it, she examined them closely, then chose two good ones that showed the horse's body and his head up close. She saved low resolution images to a folder labeled "Quaid", then moved on to the Washington National Horse Show photos. As she looked at them, she was again disturbed by the two familiar people in most of the backgrounds. Maybe she was just being paranoid, but her instincts told her differently. Several close shots of Talisman, both jumping and in the warm-up ring, showed the horse's conformation clearly and would be good comparison images for Quaid. Then she examined the people in the background. On impulse, she blurred their faces.

She sat still for a moment, wondering why she felt so proprietary about those people in the photograph. Her instincts were telling her that the man and woman in the background were important parts of this puzzle, but she wanted to first check it out herself. Besides, if Mr. Hot Shot Private Investigator was as good as everyone said, he'd find them without her help.

Five minutes later, the pictures were on their way to Garrett Quaid.

Her e-mail alert chimed and she opened the latest issue of HorseNews. The top headline read "National Champion Show Jumper 'Talisman' Disappears."

The rumor mills were grinding away and Kim was certain that Jasper Martin had started them. The story was sketchy, only stating that Talisman had disappeared at some point on a trip from his home barn to a horse show. No mention of Teri's barn. Jasper had been quoted as saying he was "devastated" over the theft. The article ended with a contact number for anyone with information about the case.

Kim dialed the number. The phone rang several times, then a familiar voice came on the line. "You have reached Jasper Martin at Rocking J Ranch. Can't come to the phone right now, but leave a message and I'll get right back to ya."

Kim hung up and stared at the computer screen without seeing. This whole thing was beginning to get to her. On the surface, it seemed that stealing a horse would be a difficult thing to do, especially a high-profile animal such as Talisman. Just how prevalent *was* horse theft? What were the motives in most cases? Simply quick money at the killers? The thought sent horror slithering through her chest. She lurched forward and quickly typed "horse theft" into the Google search bar. Over thirty thousand hits appeared and, at the top of the list, an organization known as Stolen Horse International. She was stunned at the scope of the site. What had seemed an unlikely crime was so prevalent as to be almost epidemic. Thousands of horses were reported stolen or missing every year, and a large number of them were valuable show animals or breeding stock. The thieves took horses from pastures, or during outdoor horse shows. Some even entered barns at night and led the horses off the property. Kim scrolled through the news articles, shaking her head. The problem even existed in other countries. Four valuable horses were stolen from a movie set in Russia. Someone just walked in at the right moment and led them away. In the turmoil of movie making, no one had given it a second thought. After all, *someone* had to care for the animals while they weren't on stage. Kim read further. Apparently, the animals had been recovered, but the article offered no information about who'd done it.

She bookmarked the website and sat back. No wonder Shareen was so terrified.

Kim's cell tones drifted from the kitchen. By the time she picked it up, the caller had hung up, but the number showed on the screen. Kim immediately hit redial.

"Dixie? Sorry, I was in the other room."

"I'm at Booster's in Easton. Can you come have a beer with me?"

Kim closed her eyes. Did this have anything to do with that brown sedan?

"I'll be there in twenty minutes."

⁓

Quaid left his truck in the covered parking garage and took the elevator down to the main level of the Easton Town Center. Stepping out into the main plaza, he gaped around at the complete village of shopping and restaurants. Throngs of people milled about or filled the sidewalk seating of the many eating establishments. He walked about a half-block, then spotted a toy store across the street.

A young man smiled. "May I help you find something special?"

"Twelve-year-old boy, pretty smart for his age."

"Does he have a Wii?"

"A what?"

The young man chuckled. "Follow me. I'll show you some possibilities."

Quaid moved along the aisles filled with colorful games and

toys of every description. The sales clerk unlocked a glass case filled with electronic equipment, then pulled out a box.

"This is the latest model. Kids of all ages love this. They can play interactive games, or do exercises or dance or karaoke. The programs are limitless."

"So this is a just a computer game?"

The young man's features wrinkled with disdain. "*Far* more than a game. This is a learning experience."

Quaid pulled out his wallet. "I'll take it. What else does it need?"

Fifteen minutes later, he left the store $180 poorer, but at least he had a decent birthday present. Maybe this would lighten the tension between him and his sister-in-law.

الله

Dixie sat at the far end of the bar, her blond hair a beacon in the dim light. Kim waved and headed that way. She took the stool to Dixie's right, mildly surprised at still feeling the need to always have a clear view of the entrance.

After ordering a draft beer, she smiled. "How's the dog training going?"

"Great. Tomorrow I get to choose a dog." She giggled. "I hope he doesn't bite me when he finds out he's been teamed with a rookie."

Dixie's body language didn't seem to reflect any bad news, but Kim would need to ask about Dixie's visitor before the evening ended.

Dixie set her beer on the bar. "I wanted to talk to you about something we've never discussed." She fiddled with the cocktail napkin, folding the corners down, then took a big breath. "Your friendship is so important to me and I don't want to lose it."

Kim couldn't hide her surprise. "Why do you think that would happen?"

"Sometimes I feel like you're uncomfortable because I'm gay."

"Oh, no! You're wrong. I love you dearly, like a sister..."

"I know, and I'm okay with that. I just..." She smiled and shook her head. "Never mind."

Kim couldn't think of an appropriate response, but this seemed like an opportunity to change the subject. In this new life she'd built, Dixie would be the first person she'd ever told about her background. And, of course, the first thing Dixie would wonder was, why had it taken so long?

Kim took a sip of beer, set the mug down purposefully, and turned to her friend.

"There are a lot of things you don't know about me, and I'm not sure why I kept them secret, but I did." She took a deep breath and plunged in. "I used to be—"

A movement by the door caught her eye and she exhaled sharply.

Garrett Quaid stood just inside the entrance.

Chapter 9

Quaid shifted the bulky package to his left arm and waited for his eyes to adjust to the dim room. Booth or bar? He glanced at the bar and frowned. Was that the photographer broad from Fortune Farms? Crap, he just wanted a quiet, uncomplicated dinner.

Just then, she looked his way, and the blonde sitting next to her did the same. *Damn! Now that's a good looking woman.*

He strolled toward them, paying particular attention to the photographer's expression. She was clearly not happy to see him.

He stopped and grinned. "Fancy meeting you here. It's Tina, right?"

Her eyes narrowed and he repressed a grin.

"Kim Kovak."

"Oh, yeah—*Miz* Kovak."

The look on her face was priceless. Laughter fought to break free, but he kept it capped. He set his package on the bar stool and addressed the blonde.

"Hi, I'm Garrett Quaid."

Never in his life had he seen such a dazzling smile. And those blue eyes sent a jolt right through his chest.

She offered her hand. "Dixie Davis, nice to meet you."

Her handshake was firm, her skin soft and warm.

Her eyes sparkled. "Been shopping? Anything good?"

He laughed. "I have no idea if it's good. The sales clerk said it was perfect, so I bought it."

Dixie leaned forward, a devilish smile curving her delectable lips. "Is it lacy and black?"

Heat surged up Quaid's neck and he cursed the warmth that was fanning across his face at the thought of what *she* would look like in lacy and black.

"Uh, no, it's a Y."

Puzzlement replaced Dixie's smile. "A what?"

"That's what I said, but the clerk said all the kids were crazy about it."

Both women burst into howls of laughter, causing other customers to turn and look. Quaid suddenly felt stupid. How had he stumbled into this?

Kovak recovered first. "Sorry. It's called a Wii. You made a great choice. The lucky kid will love you forever."

Quaid met her gaze. Her good looks paled next to Dixie's.

"I hope so."

Dixie said, "Buy you a beer?"

He glanced at Kovak's frown, then grinned. "Absolutely."

ـے

Kim stared into her beer, listening to the two of them carry on like college kids. Quaid was obviously smitten with Dixie. *Some investigator he is.* And Dixie! What was she *doing?* Outright flirting, that's what.

Kim threw a sidelong glance at the two, her gaze lingering on Garrett Quaid. Outside his workplace comfort zone, he was just an ordinary guy. A nice-looking ordinary guy, but not a heartthrob. She wondered about the child who would receive the expensive gift. She glanced at his left hand. No ring, but that didn't mean a darn thing anymore. Maybe he was one of the walking wounded from the war. Maybe he'd come home an irreversibly changed person and his marriage had fallen apart. That might account for buying expensive gifts for a child, a way to atone for the sins of the parents. Maybe the child was his, but he hadn't married the mother. Maybe...

"Kim? Is anybody home?"

She blinked. "Sorry, thinking about my trip to Egypt. What did you say?"

"Let's move to a booth and order something to eat."

Kim glanced up at Quaid's face, saw the smirk in his eyes, and shook her head.

"I have an early farm call. I'll leave you two to get better acquainted."

She gave Dixie a pointed look, then laid a twenty on the bar. "Call me if your police dog bites you."

Turning to Quaid, she said, "Those photos of Talisman are in your e-mail."

As she walked out into the early evening light, a heaviness

settled into her chest. She still hadn't told Dixie her secret and she still didn't know why the state senior services agent had come by. Inspector Quaid had totally screwed her up.

The next morning, Kim fumed while she fed Miss Kitty. Dixie had come home very late.

"What do you suppose she's up to?"

Kim set the cat's dish on the woven mat in the corner, then stroked the silky fur once.

"Maybe she swings both ways. Is that possible?"

Miss Kitty did not answer, her face buried in Ocean Delight Paté.

Of course it was possible. Kim and Dixie had only been friends since Dixie's arrival at the condos less than a year ago. How could Kim know everything there was to know? Much of Dixie's personal life was a mystery.

Kim stepped onto the deck, inhaling the fresh early morning air and savoring the quiet. Last night had been interesting. She'd watched Quaid preparing himself for the biggest jolt of his life, and realized she'd actually felt sorry for him.

A blue jay landed on the deck rail and cocked his head to examine the decking for any fallen tidbits. Miss Kitty appeared in the doorway and the jay let out a loud squawk, lifting off to fly away, calling the warning to the rest of the world. Kim listened to his call fade, wondering exactly what had happened last night. It wasn't any of her business, but still... She walked back into the house, her thoughts turning to Shareen's photographs. She'd seen two e-mails from Sahara Riih Arabians last night before she'd rushed out to meet Dixie. Shareen was probably ready to order.

The first message was, indeed, about ordering prints and selecting images for the farm brochure. Kim sucked in her breath. This order alone would pay for her plane ticket to Egypt. The second e-mail was cryptic, obviously trying to convey a message without actually putting anything in writing.

Kim, have info about that subject you asked. Call me. Shareen

Only one subject could make Shareen so nervous. Horse theft.

Kim checked the time. Her ridiculous biological clock woke

her every morning at five and she was usually working by half-past. But Arizona was three hours behind and she couldn't call Shareen until later. It would be a long morning.

۔ئہ

Quaid drove up to Delaware early that morning. He hadn't called ahead, hoping that the impromptu visit would shake loose some information that might otherwise be held back. He'd had a hard time refocusing on his investigation after his evening with Dixie.

What a doll. And who'd have ever guessed she was a cop? He grinned, picturing her in uniform, her small frame trying to support all the stuff law enforcement officers had to haul around these days. More interesting was her excitement over being selected for the K-9 training. He could see that a woman police officer might have an edge with a criminal, but having a sturdy, eighty-five-pound police dog by her side wouldn't hurt.

Quaid's mood was the best it had been in months. The evening had been enjoyable, filled with laughter and stories, and no small amount of flirting on Dixie's part. But at the end of the night, she'd disengaged herself graciously, her 6 a.m. duty call a top priority. But she'd scribbled her phone number on the back of her business card. He would definitely call her. Soon.

He pulled up in front of the Fortune Farms barn.

Teri Fortune's face blanched when he came into the barn office.

"Oh! Mr. Quaid. What are you, I mean, can I help you?"

He tried to put her at ease with a friendly tone. "I hope so. I thought yesterday's interview was a little tense, what with Jasper Martin hanging around. Do you have some time to talk?"

She relaxed a bit. "Yes. Please, sit down. You're right, Jasper makes me nervous, always has. There's something about him…"

Quaid wanted to pursue that, but decided to bring it up again later.

"Can you tell me how long it was between the day Martin says he put the horse on the trailer and the day the horse arrived here? I need dates, if you have them."

Teri nodded, opening a large scheduling book and leafing back through the pages.

"Here it is. He called me right after Christmas. The transport was due to pick up Talisman on December 29. The truck arrived here on January 10th."

Quaid did some quick addition. "It took *twelve* days to travel from southern California to Ohio?"

"The trucker ran into a nasty ice storm going through Texas. He said he was held up for three days. At least, I think that's what he said. Sorry, I don't remember for sure."

"That's good to know. Did you personally take delivery of the horse when he arrived?"

Teri's gaze shifted away. "I signed the paperwork."

"But did you *physically* take possession of the horse when he came off the trailer?"

Teri's shoulders sagged. "No, my barn manager was here when the truck arrived, but I came as soon as she called. I was at the bank." She looked up, her eyes dark with fear. "Please don't tell Jasper. He's determined to make this *my* fault."

Quaid wrote down everything she'd said, then nodded. "I don't think he needs to know unless we go to court. Then, of course, everything will be out in the open. I'll need to see all the paperwork you have for the transport and delivery, as well as board bills, vet care, and so forth."

Teri rose from her chair. "It'll take me a few minutes to gather it all."

"While you do that, I'd like to talk to your barn manager."

"She no longer works here."

Quaid cocked his head and waited. Finally Teri looked away.

"I fired her after I caught her doing drugs in the hay barn."

"When was that?"

"Three months ago. She had the nerve to file for unemployment. I had to spend a whole bunch of time dodging *that* bullet. I'm barely making it month to month, I can't afford to be paying some junkie to be unemployed."

Quaid raised an eyebrow, but didn't voice the thought moving through his head. If Teri Fortune was on the brink of financial disaster, her innocence in this deal might not be as clear-cut as he'd thought.

Teri handed over a folder with Jasper Martin's name written across the tab. Quaid leafed through it, then looked up.

"You have a copier? I'll need all these, plus the contact information for your former barn manager. What was her name?"

"Roberta Dodge." As Teri took the folder, her phone rang. "Fortune Farms, Teri speaking. Hi, Amanda..."

Teri's smile faded and despair seeped into her features.

"Amanda, can we talk about this first? If there's something I can do..." Teri closed her eyes. "Okay, I'll be here."

She laid the phone on the desk and stared at the folder in her hand, then turned quickly and walked to the photocopier, her posture stiff and unnatural. Quaid recognized that she was trying hard to act normal. The copier clicked and whirred and, while she was busy, Quaid studied the wall behind the desk. Numerous framed citations and awards mingled with photographs of beautiful horses, many of them sporting blue ribbons. He'd need to do some research on Teri, see if he could get a feel for her situation.

He rose from the chair as she returned with the copies. Her features were pinched and she didn't meet his gaze directly.

"Thanks, Miss Fortune. I'd like to have another look at the horse that is *not* Talisman, then I'll get out of your hair."

"He's in his stall, help yourself."

"I'd appreciate it if you'd come along, in case I have questions."

She let out an exasperated sigh. "I can't, Mr. Quaid. One of my clients will be here in a few minutes to remove her two horses from my care. I just don't have time to screw around with Jasper Martin's drama."

Chapter 10

Shareen's rich voice answered on the second ring. "Sahara Riih Arabians. This is Shareen, may I help you?"

"Hi, it's Kim Kovak. I got your message."

"Ahh, Kim, so nice to hear from you. How are you?"

"I'm well, thank you. And you?"

"Very good. It was so nice to see you in Kentucky, and the photographs are wonderful. You received my order?"

"Yes, and thank you very much. I'll have the prints expedited and sent out as soon as possible."

Kim squirmed, wanting so much to get to the other part of the conversation.

Then Shareen's voice lowered to almost a whisper. "One of Victory Arabians' futurity yearling fillies was stolen on the last day of the show. Did you hear about it?"

"No! Do you have any details?"

"She was moved to a different stall while the groom cleaned. Then apparently, the groom got distracted and left the barn for some reason. When the owner came through and found the filly's stall empty, he panicked. They found the groom wandering around behind the barns in a daze. By the time he was able to tell them where he'd put the filly, she'd disappeared." Shareen's voice caught. "Someone just walked in and led that baby away."

"That's awful. Surely the horse was freeze-marked or something."

"I don't know. It's no longer required by the registry. This is why we have armed security. You were curious—there is your answer."

"I understand completely. Thanks for sharing this with me. You'll let me know if you hear anything more?"

"Of course. But let us talk about happier subjects. Have you chosen the dates you will join us in Cairo?"

"I've actually blocked out the whole month so I can choose exactly when I want to come. What's best for you and Albert?"

Kim smiled, listening to Shareen chatter about the things they would do, rides in the desert, food and festivals through the month and, of course, many photographs. Kim was so ready for this vacation.

Twenty minutes later, she stared at her computer screen, entrenched in the NetPosse site. In all the horses listed as missing or stolen, the filly was not among them. Why weren't the owners taking advantage of this amazing resource? The networking capabilities were mind-boggling. She switched to Google and did a keyword search for stolen horses in Kentucky. Most of the hits were old, but one looked promising. She clicked on a news article that mentioned the loss of a young gray Arabian on the Horse Park grounds. The article gave no other information except the number for the local sheriff's department.

Kim looked up Victory Arabians and found two similar farms—one in Sylmar, California and one in Morris, Minnesota. After visiting both websites, Kim's instinct pointed her to the California breeder. She made a note of both phone numbers, then called the farm in Sylmar.

A woman's voice answered, an unfriendly, chesty cigarette voice. "Victory."

"This is Kim Kovak. I'm a photographer and—"

"We're not interested in pictures, we take our own."

Irritation coursed through Kim's head. "Listen, I'm calling about your filly that was stolen in Kentucky. Are you interested or not?"

"Oh, you'll have to talk to the owner. He ain't here right now, but give me your number and I'll tell him you called."

A minute later, Kim hung up. *Barn help should not be answering the phone. Stupid bitch.*

Her irritation faded as she thought about the missing filly. A horse that young would not be stolen to sell for slaughter. No, this one would be slated for resale somewhere, especially if she had wonderful bloodlines. Kim returned to the farm's website and searched through the photo gallery. The place had over thirty head of horses, most of them show champions or highly-pedigreed breeding stock. Nowhere did she see a young gray filly.

Kim sat back. Something was telling her that maybe they were another operation in financial trouble. A quick map search gave her another interesting tidbit: Sylmar was not far from Burbank.

By mid-afternoon, Quaid had done all he could at Teri Fortune's place. He stared at Dixie's business card, wondering if he should call so soon. He laid the card aside and looked out the windshield. He'd sure like to see that beautiful smile again before he went home.

She answered on the first ring. "Inspector Quaid, how nice to hear from you."

"I hope I'm not calling at a bad time. I just, well, I..."

"No, not at all. We just finished up and I'm headed home for the weekend. We have tomorrow off."

Quaid's brain ran wild. Was that an invitation?

"Would you like to have an early dinner? I'm due back in the office tomorrow, but I have to eat."

"Garrett, I'd love to, but my mother's having some problems and I have a meeting with the state senior services. May I have a rain check?"

Disappointed didn't come close to describing Quaid's reaction, but he couldn't let her know that. "Sure, no big deal. I'll just head back now."

"Where is your office, anyway?"

"Cleveland, but I do a lot of work from my home in Chagrin Falls. If you're ever up my way, be sure to give me a call."

"You got it. Hey, talk to you later."

Quaid tossed the phone on the passenger seat and frowned. He wasn't much of a ladies' man, but he sure knew a brush-off when he got one.

He drove toward the main road, feeling more melancholy than he had in years. His mood deepened as he tried to focus on the current investigation, but memories crowded in, effectively obliterating any productive thinking. At the ramp to I-71, he suddenly had no desire to join the seventy-mile-an-hour club. Instead, he continued east on Route 30. The country scenery would do him good. Minutes later, he found himself in the town of Sunbury, moving along at a snail's pace in late afternoon traffic.

"Maybe this wasn't such a hot idea," he muttered, staring at the line of cars creeping along in both directions.

The car ahead of him stalled and another cycle of traffic lights began. Quaid sighed, then glanced out the passenger window. A sign caught his eye. "Ohio Fallen Heroes." From those words, his gaze drifted to the scene laid out over lush turf. Stark white crosses formed perfect rows, leading the eye to a monument at the back of the green.

The light changed and Quaid wheeled into the entrance of the memorial park.

Kim spent the afternoon in her studio preparing Shareen's photographs to send to the lab. While she worked, she thought about the stolen filly, Dixie's strange behavior, and her own ambivalent feelings about Garrett Quaid. Those thoughts faded when she began adjusting the candid shots in the barn. Again, the mysterious man and woman appeared in several of the photographs and Kim began to feel more than a little uneasy. Were they scoping out Shareen's horses?

Kim zoomed in on one of the pictures that had a good view of the couple. They looked familiar, but probably only because Kim had been noticing them in most of the photos. She cropped just their heads, enhancing and sharpening until she had a good image. The man had dark, deep-set eyes and heavy brows. His face was rugged, almost brutish, and his lips formed an unpleasant thin line. The woman was classic Latina, but her good looks had faded with age.

A minute later, the printer spit out the picture and Kim examined it, trying to memorize the features so she'd recognize them again. Too bad she couldn't get one of her old buddies to run the photo through the face recognition database. A hollow feeling crept into her chest. She'd purposely avoided anyone from her old division for over five years. Better to leave the memories where they lay.

She ran a hand down her thigh, gently massaging the ache, her fingertips lightly exploring the indentation in her flesh where the surgeon had removed the bullet.

A car honked outside and Kim went to the deck doors to investigate. A county patrol car sat in Dixie's driveway. The door opened and she waved. A few minutes later, she came through the door. Her cheeks were flushed and her eyes sparkled.

Kim nodded. "Dog duty seems to agree with you...or is it something else."

Dixie cocked her head and gave Kim a teasing look. "You have something to say?"

"No, of course not. You always stay out late with a hot guy."

"You think he's hot? Oh, man, I see what's going on. No wonder you took off."

Kim scowled, not even slightly amused. "Well *I* certainly don't see what's going on. You want to enlighten me?"

"I just enjoy good company. You can have him." She winked. "He's not my type."

"I'm totally confused."

Dixie started toward the kitchen. "Don't be. I am what I am and Garrett Quaid is no dummy. I think he was just trying to make you jealous."

"Garrett Quaid couldn't quit slobbering all over himself, and that had nothing to do with me. He's not as smart as you think."

Kim suddenly remembered the state car. "Did you get a message from the state senior services department?"

Dixie blinked. "Yeah, how did you know?"

"Someone was here yesterday, knocking on your door. I thought maybe something happened to your mom."

"No, but she's applied for financial assistance to pay her utilities and they want to interview me. Probably want to know why I'm not helping her." Dixie's shoulders slumped. "I give her as much as I can spare, but with the reduction in hours, it isn't much." A scowl flashed across her face. "I can't believe she did this without telling me."

"Elderly people desperately want to remain independent, Dix. It has to be a horrible feeling to become the cared-for instead of the care-giver."

"What do you mean?"

"Parents spend their lives looking after their children, making their decisions, keeping them safe, helping them grow up." Kim stopped, surprised at her clinical analysis of something she knew little about, since her own parents were long gone. "Then, at some point, the tables turn and the children must look after the parents. Not always willingly. I think elderly people can tell when a person resents doing things for them. That might explain why your mom decided to handle her own problems."

"You think she knows how much I bitch about her?"

"Maybe not directly, but I think when we're busy or stressed, we can't hide tiny reactions to things like demands to visit or call."

Dixie sat quietly for a moment. "You're right, I need to be more charitable. She won't be around forever and I sure don't want to have any regrets when the time comes." She stood up. "Thanks, I needed that. I gotta get going, I'm meeting the counselor in an hour." She headed for the door.

"Hey! Aren't you going to tell me about last night?"

Dixie's laughter drifted back into the house, then the door clicked shut.

Chapter 11

Quaid pressed the doorbell and stepped back, wishing he was twenty other places. The small nondescript house in the ordinary Cleveland neighborhood didn't help his mood. No one answered the door, so he pressed the button again. The door opened quickly and Jenna's scowl appeared.

"For Pete's sake, Garrett, give me a minute to get here." She moved aside. "Come in, everyone's out back."

Quaid recoiled at the animosity in her voice. *What the hell's the matter with her?* He took a quiet breath and moved across the threshold of his dead brother's home. The living room looked the same as it had since the day of the memorial service, crowded with comfortable mismatched furniture, exuding a somewhat chaotic, lived-in feeling. The fireplace mantel held a parade of photographs and Garrett's gaze was instantly drawn to one of the last pictures taken, an image of his older brother's smiling face beneath a rumpled desert camouflage hat. Garrett clenched his jaw and followed his sister-in-law as she led the way toward the kitchen.

"How've you been, Jen?"

"Okay. I'm doing some volunteer work. Helps fill the time."

Quaid wrinkled his brow. "What do you mean?"

Strain tightened her features. "Well, of course, you wouldn't know since we never see you…I was laid off last month."

"Aw jeez, I'm sorry. Anything I can do?"

She looked away. "Ricky could sure use some moral support. He failed sixth grade and now he's in summer school."

Quaid's chest tightened. He and his nephew didn't have the best rapport. The kid was sullen and uncommunicative, sometimes downright obnoxious. But who could blame him? One day everything is great, he has a hero for a father. The next, he has a dead hero for a father. Quaid looked down at the gift bag he carried. There wasn't a present in the world that could fill that void. For either of them.

"I'll try, Jen, but you know how he feels about me."

Jenna's eyes glistened with sudden tears and her chin quivered.

"I need to get back to the party."

Did his sister-in-law know why Ricky had withdrawn from what had once been a great uncle/nephew relationship? For the life of him, Quaid sure didn't.

She turned and strode toward the back door. Quaid took a deep breath and followed.

Jenna's sister and mother sat in lawn chairs, watching several kids play badminton. They looked up and waved, then turned back to the game.

"Ricky! Your uncle's here," Jenna called out.

Quaid's nephew looked over and waved.

Twenty minutes later, after bumbling through small talk with the women, Quaid handed the gift bag over to Ricky. The other boys crowded around to see what was in it. Ricky pulled out the box and a wide grin lit up his freckled face, the first smile Quaid had seen in a long time.

"Wow! A Wii! How did you know I wanted this?"

A wave of relief swept through Quaid's mind, then he caught sight of Jenna's grim expression. *Okay, so what's the problem?*

He tried to ignore Jenna's daggers. "I just know you like to be challenged. The store clerk said this was the latest and best."

"Thanks! Come on, you guys, let's go try this thing out!"

They disappeared through the screen door and an uncomfortable silence settled over the group.

Jenna finally spoke. "I can't believe you spent that much on a toy. Do you have any idea how many groceries that would buy? Or school clothes? Or pay a bill?"

"Wait a minute, I only just found out about your situation. Give me a break!" He stood up. "I need to get going. I'll let myself out."

He went in through the back door and into the living room where the boys were setting up the game. "Happy Birthday, Ricky. I'm glad you like the Wii. I'll come over one of these nights and you can show me how it works."

The boy looked up and, for a split second, Quaid saw the pain. Then it was gone.

"Sure thing, Uncle Garrett."

By the time Quaid reached his car, Jenna had come around the side yard.

"Wait." She came up to within a couple feet of him, not meeting his eyes, but shaking her head. "I'm sorry. I overreacted. Thank you for getting him such a nice gift."

Quaid let his irritation recede, tempering his tone. "Jenna, why do we have such a hard time?"

She took a deep breath, then met his gaze. "Because every time I look at you, I see Ben. It's almost more than I can bear, even after all this time."

⁂

Kim listened to the man's voice on the other end of the phone, a voice that should have been colored with concern, but instead sounded quite calm.

"We're not sure how it happened. The filly wasn't easy to handle. Whoever took her certainly had their hands full."

The owner of Victory Farms sounded too matter-of-fact.

Kim narrowed her eyes. "Have you questioned all your employees who were at the show? Maybe someone saw something they didn't think was important."

"Yes, yes, we did all that. Who did you say you are?"

"Listen, I was just concerned since there've been quite a number of show thefts recently. If you're not familiar with Stolen Horse International, you should go to the website and post the horse's information. You might get her back."

"Okay, well, thanks for calling."

The line went dead and Kim stared at her phone. "That was weird," she muttered.

He almost sounded like he didn't *want* to find the horse. She sat back and thought for a minute. *I wonder what insurance company they use. How could I find out?* Garrett Quaid would be able to do that, but she'd have to use some finesse. And what reason would she give for wanting to know? Idle curiosity? That would never fly. No, she'd be revealing way too much if she let Quaid know she was following leads on the Talisman case. But what did she intend to do with any information she might get? Realistically, she'd have to turn it over to Quaid. How was *that* going to work?

She picked up a stack of mail from the corner of her desk

and sorted through it. Mostly bills and advertisements, and one thick white envelope hand-addressed to her. She slit the top and pulled out a contract and retainer check for the Burbank horse show. She nodded thoughtfully as an idea formed. A couple of extra days in the area would give her a chance to snoop around Jasper's operation and maybe even look at these Victory people.

Then a yellow flyer for a Cincinnati charity horse show caught her eye and she glanced at her watch.

"Nuts, I need to get on the road."

᚜

Quaid sank into his recliner, took off his glasses, and massaged the bridge of his nose. At least now he knew why his sister-in-law had been so unpleasant for so long. He wished he'd known it sooner—that might have helped them over some rough spots together. But there wasn't much he could do about the way he looked. Though three years apart, Quaid and his brother Ben could easily have been twins. He smiled without humor. Just like Talisman and his clone.

Quaid's brain discarded the painful personal realm for the reality of his work. Teri Fortune had provided some new data and now he needed to put it all together to see what came out of it. Especially now that he wasn't quite so sure that she was blameless.

The small room Quaid used for an office was dark and cluttered. He flipped on all the lights and scooted a stack of stuff to the back of the desk, then sat down and started his computer. The first thing he needed to do was transcribe all his notes from the second visit to Fortune Farms. Following that, he would research the owner, and also see if he could locate the former barn manager.

A flagged folder caught his eye and he opened the images that the photographer had sent. He zoomed in on the photos of the horse in the stall, the ones Kovak said she'd thrown away. He then moved to the show photos of the big bay jumper. She'd marked the photos with the date and "Washington National Horse Show, Verizon Center Arena", which at least gave Quaid a timeframe from then until the date the horse had supposedly been put on a trailer in California. On close comparison, the horse at Fortune and the horse flying over the parallel oxer were identical. But Jasper Martin had been adamant that he could prove that the horse at Fortune was *not* Talisman. Why hadn't he done so during Quaid's first visit? Why had the guy been so damned nervous? That bullshit about the horse being too nice just wouldn't cut it for proof. Quaid didn't know a whole lot about performance horses, but he couldn't believe that a horse with a vicious personality could be trained to become a national champion.

He returned to Kovak's e-mail and, on impulse, clicked on her website. A minute later, he let out a slow breath. The woman had amazing talent. Her portraiture and action shots were some of the best Quaid had ever seen. Too bad she had such a hard-on. He leaned forward to take a closer look at one of the photos on her home page. It was definitely Talisman at the National, but it wasn't one she'd sent to him. Almost identical, but just a second later in the jump flight pattern. What was different? He switched back to the shots she'd sent him and located the one he was thinking about. Back and forth, examining both photos. Then he saw it.

In the image she'd sent him, the people standing at the rail had been blurred out. Not all the people, just two. Why would she do that?

He downloaded the web image and blew it up to three hundred percent to get a good look at the man and woman on the rail. After a moment, he moved the photograph to his work folder.

"Okay, sweetheart, let's just find out what you're up to."

A quick search on her name only brought up her website and various references to her work. Using the skill that had made him so successful in his work, Quaid delved deeper into the Internet, using keywords and phrases that eliminated the sources he didn't want, but focused on keywords in the content. Within a few minutes, a five-year-old newspaper article appeared and he clicked on the link.

"Police officers injured in post-game riot."
Columbus, Ohio—Three Columbus Metro police officers, including one mounted patrolman, were injured in Saturday night's post-game riot. Fueled by copious quantities of alcohol and an OSU victory over Michigan, hundreds of fans thronged the streets, setting fire to trash cans, breaking windows of homes in the area, and tipping over two parked vehicles. Police were

already on hand during the game, anticipating trouble from this historic rivalry, but well before the game ended, reinforcements were called in. The riot turned ugly and, at some point, shots were fired. Mounted police officer Kim Kovak caught a bullet in the leg and her horse was badly injured. The animal was destroyed at the scene...

Quaid's mouth went dry, his brain on fire. *It couldn't be the same person. Could it?* If it was, that might explain the attitude. Maybe she was working undercover. Nah, she was too good with that camera. Then he squinted at the screen. Once a cop, always a cop. He'd bet money that she was still working—if this was the same person. He punched her name into the image database and scanned the returned images. There she was, in full uniform, that red hair pulled back under a riding helmet, a big chestnut horse at her side.

He grinned. "Officer Kovak. You. Are. Busted."

Quaid printed the article, then turned back to the Talisman case. Jasper Martin lived in Altadena and the best way to get a handle on this guy and what he was up to would be to go out there and snoop around.

☙

Kim pulled into an empty spot at the far end of a grassy field where dozens of vehicles and horse trailers were parked in a not-so-orderly manner. She retrieved her camera bag and locked the car, then wended her way through the trailers and trucks, following the sound of the announcer. The closer she came to the arena, the more activity she encountered. Horses tacked up and tied to trailers, waiting for their turn. Owners and riders polishing tack or adjusting helmet straps. The occasional smile or nod.

Kim loved outdoor shows. They seemed more friendly and relaxed, though the jumper circuit was one of the more competitive areas of horsemanship. Still, the fresh air and sunshine seemed to energize everyone involved. She pulled off the lens cover and drifted through the area, framing candid shots that might work well for a general show article in one of the riding magazines.

The announcer called for a ten minute break and Kim headed

toward the show secretary's post.

"I'm Kim Kovak. May I have one of your schedules?"

The girl looked up, then down at Kim's camera. "Did you check in with the show steward yet?"

"Oh, I'm not here officially, just enjoying the show."

"You'll still need to leave your name with the steward." She handed over a sheet of paper with the classes, then went back to what she'd been doing.

Kim found the steward and made her presence known, then walked to the arena to begin work in earnest, capturing the beautiful athletes as they soared over the elaborate obstacles.

After two hours, Kim's feet began to ache and she headed for the wooden bleachers. A quick glance at the schedule told her that this event would go for many more hours. Each class seemed to have a lot of entrants, but the field would narrow as the afternoon progressed. She watched young girls guide their horses through the pattern, amazed at how well some of the youngsters could ride. But then, they'd probably been at it since they were little girls with pony passion. Kim remembered the feeling well. How she'd longed for that fat little Welsh Pony that had finally graced her grandfather's pasture on the day Kim turned twelve.

She let her mind wander back through those happy years with Scout. He was undoubtedly the most obnoxious horse alive, but she adored him and always forgave him for dumping her at least once on every ride. It was a good thing Grandpa saw more than one of those incidents because, otherwise, she would never have learned to ride a real horse.

A young rider came into the arena on a sturdy palomino and Kim exhaled sharply. The horse was almost identical to her first show pony. She lifted the camera and began capturing images of the dream that had carried her through those horse crazy years to adulthood.

A few minutes later, Kim's breath caught in her throat as two familiar people appeared in the viewfinder. She zoomed in and a chill ran over her shoulders. She was looking at the couple who had appeared in her other show photos. She clicked off several shots, then lowered the camera and gazed around. The riders were mostly students and amateurs. She turned her attention back to the horses in the waiting area. They were all nice, some even very good, but not spectacular. Kim looked back at the couple and watched them move casually around the rail toward the in-gate. She climbed down and headed that way herself, heart thumping. Stopping at the end of the bleachers, she focused on the woman's face and snapped off two shots, then found the man in the viewfinder. Her finger froze over the shutter button. He was looking directly at her, his eyes dark with concentration.

Kim busied herself with going through the motions of adjusting her camera settings, all the while watching the couple from the corner of her eye. She sat down, just to make it appear that she was intent on what she was doing. The man said something to the woman, then looked Kim's way again, sending a jolt through her pulse. He headed toward the show secretary's booth, but Kim stayed focused on the woman lingering by the rail. A few minutes later, the man returned and the two of them headed toward the grassy area where all the trailers were parked. Kim rose slowly and made her way to the in-gate, keeping track of the couple's location. They wandered casually through the staging area, stopping occasionally to speak to a rider or stroke a horse's neck. Kim stayed a good distance back, snapping off several shots when they stopped to talk. The man glanced back once, but Kim was well hidden behind a pickup truck, watching him through the windows. He scanned the area, then nodded to the woman and they walked briskly toward the car parking area. Kim followed as best she could without being spotted.

They climbed into a small red sedan and Kim scurried closer to get a good shot of the license plate. Just as she pressed the shutter button, a horse and rider walked in front of her.

By the time the horse moved out of the way, the car was gone.

&

Quaid knew he should give it some time, but it was worth a shot. Dixie had been on his mind nonstop. When she'd declined the first dinner invitation, she'd seemed genuinely apologetic. Maybe she really did have a previous commitment. What would it hurt if he tried again? If she shut him down this time, he'd at least know for sure.

She answered on the second ring. "Hi Garrett, I was just thinkin' about you."

He tried to sound cool. "Yeah? Well, I'm headed back your way this afternoon. Want to try for that dinner again?"

"I'd love to. What time and where?"

Seconds later, Quaid disconnected. *"Yesss!"*

He jumped up and looked at his watch. His impromptu plans didn't leave him much time for the trip back to Columbus, but he didn't care. A quick shower and he'd be on his way to see the lovely Dixie Davis. Even though he knew better than to date a girl who carried a gun.

Chapter 12

All Kim's instincts and training surfaced, convincing her she was on to something. Too far fetched for the mystery couple to be owners in so many places. The most likely scenario was that the couple who showed up in all the photographs were scouts for possible theft. Or they were scoping out look-alikes.

She sat in her car, fingers trembling as she dialed Dixie's number. She needed to bounce some of this stuff off another person.

"Hi Kim. What's up?"

"I think I've stumbled onto something. Can we get together and talk later tonight?"

"Sure, but you sound frazzled. Everything okay?"

The unmistakable sound of background laughter came through the phone. "Yeah, but where *are* you?"

Dixie chuckled and lowered her voice. "Having dinner with your new best friend."

"*Quaid?*"

"The very same. I'll come over when I get home."

Kim mumbled something and hung up. If Dixie was hooking up with Garrett Quaid, then Kim couldn't possibly talk about her suspicions. But maybe Dixie was doing the honorable thing, telling Quaid that she wasn't the girl for him. Maybe. Kim's confident thoughts faltered. Dixie had sounded a little too pleased with the date. Besides, if she was going to tell Quaid about her sexual persuasion, why do it in person?

"Dammit! Why do I care? *I'm* not the girl for him either."

꿈

Quaid watched Dixie's face as she talked on the phone. She almost looked as though she was talking to someone she cared about deeply. A boyfriend? A twinge of jealousy ran through his chest. Maybe he was assuming too much. Anyone as good-looking as Dixie would most likely have someone, right? But then, why was she sitting here with him, batting those beautiful blue eyes over the rim of her wine glass?

He grinned as she hung up. "Fan club?"

She chuckled. "No, just my neighbor."

Quaid searched his memory of the last time he'd been with her. Something about neighbors, but he couldn't remember what. Way too much beer for good detail retention.

Dixie tilted her head and a wisp of blond hair brushed her cheek. "You remember Kim? The photographer?"

Quaid's jaw dropped. *That's right, they're best friends.*

"Oh, yeah, the redhead. She's an ex-cop, right?"

Dixie's expression froze and, for a moment, she didn't even blink.

"Where did you hear that?"

Quaid's expertise in all things other than women wouldn't help him now. "Uh, I came across an article about her." He pursed his lips and blew out a soft breath. "You didn't know?"

Dixie just stared at him, then pushed her drink aside. "You must be mistaken, it's probably about someone else with the same name. I've known Kim for almost a year and I'm sure she would have said something."

No way would Quaid pursue this. Even though he'd seen the photograph of Kim in uniform, he knew better than to try to push the point.

"You're probably right. It's not an uncommon name." He found his most charming smile. "So, Miss Dixie, what would you like to have for dinner?"

Though she smiled, her manner was brittle, and Quaid knew the magic of the evening had just disappeared like a rabbit in a hat.

∗∘∗

On the drive home from the charity show, Kim wrestled with all the possible scenarios that presented themselves. If she was right—if this couple were scouts for possible look-alike horses—then the Talisman case took on a much broader scope. Was this a theft ring of national or even international scale? The man and woman were getting around to horse shows at a fairly steady rate, but maybe they weren't the only scouts involved. Especially if the situation extended to other countries. What if she could match up the places she'd seen this couple with information about stolen or missing horses in the same region? Would it prove anything? Maybe not, but at least it might solidify her suspicions.

Dixie's truck wasn't in its usual spot and Kim frowned. Had Dixie slept with Quaid that first night? Kim closed her eyes and exhaled sharply. *Why* did she keep worrying about this stuff? It wasn't like she wanted Quaid for herself. More like she wanted Dixie to herself and to keep Quaid out of it. He was already an obstacle to any conversations she and Dixie might have about the Talisman case.

Miss Kitty waited at the door, complaining loudly about being left alone all day. Kim chuckled and headed for the refrigerator.

"Hold on, girlie. You'll get it in a minute."

After feeding the cat, Kim settled onto the couch with a glass of Merlot and picked up her phone. As she dialed Dixie's number, someone knocked on the door.

She opened it and grinned. "Great minds think alike."

Dixie's expression was strained. "Yeah, must be some psychic thing we have for each other."

Kim's alarm system went off. Something was not right, and that something probably involved Quaid.

Dixie glanced at Kim's wine glass. "Got some more of that?"

Kim poured the wine, her brain trying to sort out a reason for Dixie's mood. She'd never seen her like this. What could have happened that had upset her?

"How was your dinner?"

"Fine. We went to Brio's, had the crab cakes." Dixie didn't sound enthused.

Kim took a soft breath. "I can see that something's wrong. What did Quaid do, try to put the moves on you?"

Anger flashed across Dixie's pretty face. "Dammit, Kim, just because I'm gay doesn't mean I'm a freak! Don't you think I can handle myself?"

Stunned, Kim stammered, "Of course. I just don't understand why you're fooling around with the guy."

"I happen to enjoy good company. He's interesting, he makes me laugh. I have a number of men friends." She took a lingering sip of wine, then looked directly into Kim's eyes.

"You want to tell me about your police background?"

Surprise slammed through Kim's stomach and her mouth flew open. "How did you...Oh, God, Dixie..."

Silence pressed in around them and Kim couldn't bear Dixie's hostile expression.

"That's what I've been trying to tell you," she whispered. "I'm so sorry."

Dixie rose and retrieved the wine bottle from the counter. She topped up both glasses, then sat back and gazed at Kim.

"So tell me now."

"I spent ten years with the Mounted Unit of the Columbus Division of Police." Kim's voice softened. "I loved it, had a great horse, a big chestnut named Red." Her throat ached. "Most of the time, I worked the parks and some traffic, but occasionally, we were called on for crowd control. Anyway, after one of the important university home football games, the crowd went crazy. Some asshole started firing a gun. My horse went down and shattered his leg. I caught a bullet." Tears stung her eyes. "They destroyed Red right in front of me while I was being loaded into an ambulance."

Dixie moved closer to Kim, her voice filled with compassion. "Oh, honey, I'm so sorry..."

Kim shook off the horrible images. "I spent quite a while in surgery, then months in rehab. But the real damage was done up here, in my head. I finally had to retire. I couldn't go back."

﹏

Quaid rolled into his driveway well past midnight. A long drive for such a disappointing evening. Dixie had been just fine until he'd opened his big mouth about that photographer. Why had he done that? Jeezus! Would he never learn? Without a doubt, Dixie knew nothing about Kim Kovak's police background. At least not until tonight. And that had been the end of any chance for a romantic evening. What puzzled him was, why would Kovak keep that information from her best friend? It certainly made the case for her working undercover. How could he find out what she was after?

He let himself into the house and flipped on all the lights, a habit he'd acquired since his retirement from the Army. He'd spent enough time in dark places that he didn't need to do it at home too. He flopped down in front of the television and fiddled with the remote. This wasn't how he'd planned to spend the night.

Chapter 13

First thing Monday morning, Quaid made a cup of instant coffee and headed straight for his computer. All the leads and questions in his mind needed to be answered, or at least checked, before he started poking around in Jasper Martin's life.

Opening his notebook, he looked at the list.

Point 1: Alleged secret mark on the real Talisman. Why hadn't Jasper revealed what it was at their first meeting? Fake lead? If real identification mark, it should be on the horse's records.

Point 2: The overly-long time it took the horse to travel from Altadena to Ohio. Talk to the transport company.

Point 3: Ice storm in Texas. Check weather reports for those dates. Verify with the driver.

Point 4: Background check on Teri Fortune's finances.

Point 5: Find Roberta Dodge.

Quaid started with Talisman's file. The photograph was of no help because, of course, it looked exactly like the horse standing in the stall at that moment. Quaid examined the registration paper carefully. The horse had no markings and no record of a microchip or other identifying medium. Quaid sat back and frowned. Why wouldn't a valuable horse have some way to positively identify him?

He blew out a hard breath and picked up the phone number for the transport company, only to realize he'd have to wait until midday to call a California outfit. He scowled at the screen, then opened the browser and looked for the weather history. Minutes later, he found it: the worst freak ice storm in a decade had inundated the Texas Panhandle during the timeframe that Teri had given.

Quaid did some mental gymnastics.

Suppose the driver was in on the theft. Having a weather layover would be a perfect cover for the crime. But how could he or she have anticipated such a perfect and un-forecasted opportunity? And how would one carry out an elaborate switch on short notice?

The look-alike horse would have to be in place already, or close by. Where did animal transports stop for overnights and weather-related delays? You didn't just pull over on the side of the interstate with a load of animals. No, it didn't seem reasonable that the driver was part of the plan.

But how would the criminals know the truck would have to stop because of the storm? Maybe they didn't know, but followed the truck knowing the driver would have to stop for rest and food at many places along the way. It didn't make sense that the perpetrators of the switch would purposely pick an ice storm to carry it out. Was this nothing more than a crime of opportunity?

Quaid sat back and contemplated the screen. He was giving Jasper Martin the benefit of the doubt, but his gut was telling him the guy was responsible for the whole thing. Quaid would bet his Silver Star that the horse Jasper loaded onto the trailer was not Talisman, or he'd arranged for it to happen along the way somewhere. Why else would the man avoid telling Quaid exactly what the secret identification mark was?

Quaid looked at his list again. Though Teri Fortune might be in financial distress, he doubted that she had the balls to be consciously involved in something that could ruin her life. That she'd willingly turned a blind eye to the fact the horse wasn't injured gave Quaid pause for thought, but it basically only amounted to petty thievery. And Jasper probably knew she needed money and wouldn't pursue the issue of a perfectly sound horse being sent to her for healing therapy. Again, Jasper was looking good for it.

Quaid switched from the browser to his secure access to state records. Arrests, convictions, and sentences were all available to the public, but most folks didn't have a clue how to go about getting the information, and calling city hall was a joke. The average citizen had a limited knowledge of how to use the computer to do such things, but Quaid's PI license gave him a lot of advantages.

Roberta Dodge popped up in the first search. Typical hard-luck-story girl, high school dropout, a series of short term jobs in bars and taverns, and a couple of stints as a stall cleaner. Two arrests for drug use, one for disorderly conduct. No jail time served. How the hell had someone like that become Teri Fortune's barn manager?

She must have been willing to work for practically nothing. He shook his head and jotted down her last address in a place called Valeville in southern Ohio, just about one of the poorest areas in the state. He'd have to do some legwork on this one, but he needed to hear what the woman had to say about the delivery of the fancy horse from California.

The closest police department was in Shawnee, about thirty-five miles from Valeville. According to the information, the station was staffed on a rotating basis. The phone number rang six times before a man answered.

He sounded fairly young. "Shawnee police department."

"This is private investigator Garrett Quaid. I'm trying to locate a young woman who lives in Valeville, but I don't find any law enforcement contacts there."

The officer laughed. "Valeville has a gas station. Period. We're as close as you'll get. What's her name?"

"Roberta Dodge."

"Name doesn't ring a bell, but you might call the old guy who owns the gas pumps there. He'll know who she is."

Quaid wrote down the number, said thanks, and glanced at his watch. Getting an early start sometimes worked against him. No one would be up yet in a one-horse town.

A gravely voice answered. "Barker's. He'p ya?"

"I hope so. I'm lookin' for an old friend who lived in Valeville. A guy in Shawnee said you might know her. Roberta Dodge?"

The voice became wary. "Whatcha want 'er for?"

Quaid tempered his tone, trying to sound casual. "We hooked up a few years ago, then I lost track of her. I'm back in the area, so was hoping I could find her again. Do you know her?"

The voice cackled. "Yep, I know 'er. Yer probably better off just movin' on through. She's a passel o' trouble."

Quaid chuckled. "Yeah, I remember she was a piece of work. Well, anyway, you know where she lives?"

"Out highway seventeen. When she ain't in jail."

Quaid mumbled his thanks and hung up. He checked the time, then dialed United Equine Assurance. A young woman's voice answered.

"Travel, Becky speaking."

"Hi, it's Garrett Quaid. I need a flight to Los Angeles."

"Oh, hi Mr. Quaid. When did you want to go?"

"This coming weekend."

"Oh, boy, lots of luck with that. It's the Fourth of July on Sunday. You have any idea how many people are—"

"I know, just get me something."

While he waited, Quaid's thoughts wandered to Dixie. What would she be doing for the big celebration weekend? He knew almost nothing about her. She had a mother, he knew that much. Would there be a family picnic somewhere? Would she have to work the weekend, watching for drunk drivers? Then he remembered she was training for the K-9 unit, and so thrilled about not being on regular duty any more.

"Mr. Quaid? I can get you a flight Thursday with a return on Tuesday morning."

"That's two extra days."

"I know, but there are no seats on Friday or Monday, except first class."

"So put me in first class."

"You're not cleared for that. You'd have to pay for it yourself."

Quaid thought for a minute, then decided he could certainly put the extra time to good use.

"Okay, I'll take the Thursday and Tuesday flights."

"Your tickets will be at the Delta express counter. Do you need hotels or a car?"

"Oh, yeah, get me a car reservation. I'll take care of finding a motel myself."

He said goodbye and immediately dialed the transport company in Oregon. A gruff recorded voice informed him that the office was not staffed until noon, but to leave a message and someone would call him back.

The phone rang and Jenna's number appeared. Soon he would have to try to mend fences with Ricky, but first he'd need to work through the emotional situation with Jenna.

Her panic surged through the phone. "Can you come over right away? Ricky locked himself in his room and won't answer me.

Garrett, I'm scared!"

Twenty minutes later, Jenna answered the door, her features drawn with worry.

"Thank God, you're here. I don't know what to do."

Quaid stepped into the house. "Tell me exactly what happened. Don't leave anything out, even if you think it's not important."

"Ricky played all yesterday with that thing you bought him. He really loves it. Anyway, after dinner I asked about his schoolwork and he said he didn't have any. Remember, I told you he has to go to summer school? So I asked again because we've been through this before. He gave me some lip and I demanded to see his schoolbag. He just ignored me, so I got it out of his room and brought it downstairs, told him to show me."

Quaid noticed her fidgety hands, the fingernails bitten to nubs, the torn red cuticles. The woman was a nervous wreck. Why didn't he know any of this? Had he been so wrapped up in his own private hell that he hadn't seen the signs of a family in trouble? His gaze moved from her hands to her face.

She looked beaten. "We had an argument and, sure enough, his schoolbag was filled with homework papers, some dating back at least two weeks. He hasn't been doing any of it." She exhaled sharply. "So, I took away his new toy and grounded him until he gets caught up and brings me proof."

"So he's just giving you the silent act? Sounds pretty normal to me."

"It would be, except he wouldn't answer me this morning when I went to get him up for school. And the door is locked." Her chin quivered. "He never came out—that's when I called you."

Quaid frowned. "Are you sure he's even in there? Maybe he climbed out the window to give you a scare."

"He wouldn't have to do that to frighten me. His final words last night were enough."

"What did he say?"

"He shouted, 'I just wanna go be with Dad!'"

"Oh crap, Jen! Why didn't you—"

Quaid bolted down the hall and took the stairs two at a time.

Ricky's door had a large colorful poster warning intruders they'd be vaporized by Darth Vader. Quaid pounded on the door.

"Ricky! It's Uncle Garrett. Come on out, you're scaring us!"

The silence set his neck hairs on end.

"Ricky, dammit, open the door!"

Nothing.

Quaid stepped back and threw his shoulder against the door, nearly falling down when it gave way easily. Jenna came in behind him and they both looked around the room.

Ricky was not there.

Jenna sat down on the bed. "I don't know whether to be angry or relieved."

Quaid put a hand on her shoulder. "Has he ever said anything like that before? Have you had any reason to believe he was depressed enough to do something drastic?"

She bowed her head. "We've both had a hard time accepting that Ben's gone. I might not have seen the signs." A sob broke through and she looked up at Quaid with brimming eyes. "Do you think he'd really...Oh, God."

"Jeez, Jen, I'm sure not the one to know much about him and I'm so sorry about that. But let's see if we can find him. What time did he lock himself in?"

"Last night, right after the argument. Must have been about quarter to nine."

"And you haven't seen or talked to him since?"

She shook her head from side to side, the tears returning.

"Okay, so he might have run away last night sometime. Would he go to a friend's house?"

"Maybe, only I would think the mother would call me."

Quaid took Jenna's arm and urged her to stand up. "You go downstairs right now and call the school. Find out if he came to his classes this morning."

While Jenna made the call, Quaid wandered over to the mantel. His brother's face smiled back and Quaid whispered to the image.

"I'm so sorry, Bennie. I haven't had your back, but that's going to change. I promise I'll find Ricky and take more responsibility for him."

Face to face with the image of his blood brother, Quaid's chest quaked just like the day he'd walked through Arlington Cemetery alongside the caisson bearing Ben's body. He could imagine no greater pain, unless it would be losing Ricky too.

Jenna's voice came from the kitchen. "Garrett! He's at the school!"

Quaid stepped back from the mantel and slowly saluted his brother's picture. "On duty, Sir."

For more than an hour, Quaid sat with Jenna, trying to decide how best to handle Ricky's defiance. Clearly, the boy had issues that could escalate into something no one wanted to think about.

"Have you considered taking Ricky to a child psychologist?"

"I hadn't thought of it, but it wouldn't be that easy. The nearest base with that kind of support is in Dayton." She looked down at her fingers. "But I might have to move there anyway. I'm not sure I can afford to stay here much longer."

Quaid reached out and stilled her nervous fingers. "This is serious enough I think you should get an appointment and make the trip. I'll pay for a motel and your gas."

She looked up, defeat masking what had once been a pretty face. Jenna Quaid's life had drained away like Ben's blood on the desert sand.

"Thank you," she whispered.

"In the meantime, I think you need to act as normal as possible about this incident. I suspect Ricky will come home today and be apologetic. Maybe not, but in any event, don't pick any fights with him. Not until we find out if he's on the brink of disaster."

෴

Since he was already in the area, Quaid swung by the insurance company to check in with the boss and drop off his expense sheet for the previous week. As he drove through the city streets, he thought about the emotional stability of his nephew. Kids were prone to theatrics when they were upset. Running away or locking the door were not particularly unusual, but veiled allusions to suicide were not to be taken lightly. Was that actually what Ricky meant? Quaid was taking the wording as fact, though he was hearing it second-hand from a hysterical mother. Maybe those weren't the exact words, and didn't mean what they sounded like. An idea surged into his head. Maybe Ricky just wanted to visit his father's grave. He'd never been back since the funeral.

Quaid pulled into the parking garage under the building. As soon as he could swing it, he and Ricky would take a much-needed trip to visit Ben.

Chapter 14

After a frustrating hour online, searching for a flight to Los Angeles, Kim gave up and called the airline directly. Following the many touchtone options, she finally connected with a recording.

"Thank you for calling Delta Airlines. All our representatives are helping other customers, but we value your business. Please stay on the line for the next available agent." Music replaced the voice, but soon the recorded voice came on again. "Thank you for your patience. Your approximate wait is 3 minutes." More music. Another recording of the time remaining, then, a live person came on the line.

Forty minutes later, Kim hung up. "What ever possessed me to take a job over the holiday weekend?"

She looked at her notes. The best she'd come up with was a morning flight on Wednesday, getting her into Los Angeles at 5:45, smack in the middle of rush hour. At least she'd have a chance to get settled in Burbank and have a good night's sleep. Then first thing Thursday, she'd check out Jasper's operation. Victory might have to wait, depending on how much time she had and how far she had to drive. But Jasper was the highest priority. If she had to, she'd go to Victory Farms on Sunday.

Miss Kitty appeared from nowhere and jumped lightly onto Kim's lap, purring loudly. Kim stroked the silky fur, then opened her laptop and went straight to Stolen Horse International. On a legal pad, she drew two columns, labeling one for quality horses and one for pet horses. Working methodically through the most recent additions, she listed fourteen posts that were good show horses, and eight that had been either pasture animals or pets. She printed out all the description pages, her heart aching with the scope of the theft problem.

Moving to her work table, she spread the pages out so she could see them all at a glance. The first thing that became obvious was that the show horses were almost all nondescript in color and markings. Lots of browns and chestnuts, a couple of snips or a star.

No loud pintos or distinctive face markings like blazes. Reasoning took hold. It would be far easier to switch out a horse that looked unremarkable. Talisman's double was a perfect example. Unless someone knew the horse personally, no one would ever suspect he wasn't the real Talisman.

Had someone lost the lovely gelding standing in Teri's barn? Was a young girl somewhere heartbroken over the theft of her beloved companion? This mess wasn't just about the theft of valuable horses. Ordinary folks were victims too. Kim returned to her computer and pulled up the photos she'd taken of the horse in Teri's barn, then moved to the horse theft website. For the next thirty minutes, she searched through all the listings. She'd just about given up on the idea when one photograph caught her eye. She clicked on the image to enlarge it, then held up her own photograph. A band tightened around her chest. Almost without a doubt, a horse named Bandit—listed as stolen six months ago—was the double for Talisman.

⚓

Quaid swung by his house to pick up his laptop before heading for the southern reaches of the state. Valeville was a good four-hour drive, and who knew how much farther he'd have to go when he got there. The town was so small it wasn't even on a map. He sure as hell hoped this Dodge person still lived there.

Traffic was light on the interstate and Quaid used the time to consider all the ways that Jasper himself might make the switch. To be absolutely certain he didn't get caught, he'd have to make sure no one was around his barn when he loaded the look-alike horse on the transport van. How would that be possible with a big operation? He'd probably have to arrange to have the horse picked up in the wee hours before the stall cleaners arrived for work. Okay, so would the transport people agree to a pickup at a stupid hour? Probably not.

Quaid smacked the steering wheel. "Nuts, I forgot to call them back."

At least the three-hour time difference for California would be in his favor for the rest of the day.

If Jasper had loaded the look-alike himself, where was Talisman at that time? Had Jasper already taken him to another location to be picked up by whomever was helping sell the horse? And how could Talisman's sale be kept under wraps? The buyer would have to agree to keep the whole thing a secret. So, if the buyer wanted the horse for competition, that would involve false registration papers and change of name. Plus, wherever the "secret mark" was, it would have to be removed. Well, not really, because the only person who knew about it was Jasper, and he...

This was getting way too confusing. *Stay on track that Jasper is behind the switch.*

But what if he isn't?

Quaid was so wrapped up in his thoughts that he almost missed the ramp to I-70. He focused on the scenery, his mind wandering back to his childhood and the homestead that lay only a few miles to the east. He'd spent his teen years plotting and dreaming of getting out of that dump. At the time, he'd been sure he never wanted to see another steer in his life. Cattle ranching was not where his aspirations lay. At the time, he hadn't known exactly what aspirations were, but he'd known that something better waited for him out there somewhere. Guilt crawled into those thoughts. His mother had struggled with the small ranch operation for years after his dad died in a freak farm accident. Quaid and his brother had worked their butts off, but unlike Quaid, Ben never complained. Then he'd joined the Army. Quaid was furious at being left behind to shoulder the whole thing. By that time, their mother was too old to do much more than cook and do laundry, so she finally agreed that the livestock should be sold. After that, there was nothing to keep Quaid there and, within a year, he followed his brother into the service. His mother died six months later.

He swerved into the right lane, barely making the exit into Zanesville, and leaving the memories behind.

🖉

Teri Fortune didn't answer, but why didn't the farm's answering machine pick up? Kim dialed again, worry growing in her mind. Still no answer and no way to leave a message. Grabbing the printed description sheet for Talisman's look-alike, Kim headed for her car. With all that had been going on with Teri's business, trouble might be brewing.

Forty minutes later, Kim pulled up in front of the big white barn. The parking area was empty—surprising because the lot usually held at least two or three cars at any given time. Kim pulled out her phone and tried Teri again. Still no answer. Picking up Bandit's page, she climbed out of the car. For a weekday, it was unusually quiet. A few birds twittered and a dog barked somewhere in the distance. Kim's wary instincts kicked in and she automatically patted her hip, mildly annoyed that she couldn't seem to rid herself of that ingrained response to the unknown.

The barn door was partway open and Kim stepped through. A chorus of whinnies echoed through the big building and she grinned. You couldn't slip much past a horse.

"Teri? You in here?"

Hearing no response, Kim moved farther into the aisle, looking up and down both sides. Several stalls were empty. That did not bode well in a therapeutic facility. A familiar brown head popped over the door of the last stall and Kim laughed.

"Hey, buddy, how are ya?"

She started toward the horse, then remembered that he might have a name. When she was about five feet from the door, she took a deep breath.

"Bandit?"

The horse's head came up, his ears pricked straight forward, a light coming into his large kind eyes as he chuckled softly.

م

Quaid rolled slowly into downtown Shawnee, a town that time had passed by. The buildings were the originals from the height of the mining operations in the area, and Quaid had the odd sensation of driving through a Hollywood movie set. But this was real. Tall wooden buildings with false fronts and second story balconies, just like in old western movies. Grass grew through the cracks in the sidewalks and many of the storefront windows were dark or boarded up. At one corner, a small café broke the monotony of the drab street. A brilliant mural covered two sides of the building, radiating blues and greens and yellows. Quaid eased off the gas to take a closer look. The painting depicted the town, showing several of the stores he'd just passed. The artwork was primitive, but interesting. The mural was the only bright spot in an otherwise depressing view.

The narrow, winding road continued southeast out of the village and immediately plunged into the rolling hills that were the hallmark of an area developed by mining. The feeling of isolation was strong and Quaid tried to compare it to his own childhood home in Belmont County, but this was desolate and depressing. Once the heart of coal mining, these places had been called "black diamond" towns. When the coal was exhausted, the only things left behind were those who knew no other life. Hard times fell on the area and the land sank into neglect.

In thirty minutes, a sign for Valeville appeared, a village with a population of 102. Quaid slowed to 25 mph and scrutinized the wide spot in the road that was the town. Barker's Gas Station sat on the left side of the road, a testament to history. The yellow tile walls of the early 1940's building were the same façade that had once been the sign of prosperous times for the ceramic and pottery industry that grew from the region's distinctive clay. Those yellow tiles covered floors or lined tunnels all over the country.

Several ancient cars sat next to the station, grass growing through the windows and rust obliterating whatever color the vehicles might have been at one time. The old-fashioned sign was faded, but Quaid supposed that didn't matter since anyone in the area would know the place. One ancient gas pump stood in front, and a sign in the window offered chewing tobacco, but no liquor sales.

Quaid continued on past a couple of old houses on either side of the road, then a gray barn and pasture. He watched for the turn-off to Route 17 as the highway dipped steeply into a valley. About a mile farther, a white road sign pointed to the right. Quaid turned there and drove slowly along the dirt and gravel road, heading into dense woods. *How many people could live out here?* he wondered. The old man at Barker's hadn't given Quaid a house number, but maybe the mailbox would have a name. But what if Roberta Dodge lived with someone else?

Quaid pulled over and got out his cell phone. He'd call Barker's and ask for specific directions. The screen lit up and the signal icon showed a large red X through it. Disgusted, he tossed the phone on the seat and drove on. The road wound through the trees and the gravel gave way to packed dirt.

"That's it. I'm going back to the gas station."

Finding a place to turn around proved to be a challenge. He drove another two miles before the dense forest thinned out and the road widened. Up ahead, he spotted a place he could pull into and, when he got there, it was a driveway. A battered black mailbox claimed that he had arrived at the Dodge residence.

The truck bumped along two ruts that served as access to the property, taking him back into the dim interior of the woods. Quaid suddenly wished he'd brought his gun. The track turned sharply to the left, then into a clearing. Four large dogs exploded off the porch of a rambling house, setting up a racket that would eliminate Quaid's need to announce his presence. The dogs danced around the truck as he turned off the ignition. Did he dare step out into that pack? A movement near the house caught his eye, and a man crawled out from under one of the five old cars parked there. He stood up and hollered, and the dogs turned and raced over to him.

Quaid opened the truck door and stepped down, uneasily aware that the man was just standing there, staring at him. Quaid put on his best smile.

"Howdy, this the Dodge residence?"

The man did not smile back. "Who wants to know?"

Quaid walked slowly toward him, looking at the car.

"Nice 'Cuda. 1970?"

The man's features relaxed a little and he grinned. "Seventy-one. Yeah, she's a honey. I had one when I was a kid. Never shoulda give it up."

Quaid stepped over to the faded green car. "What's under the hood?"

"Four-twenty-six Hemi."

"Holy shit, there weren't many of those even made! You musta paid a fortune for this."

"Nope, found it in a wreckin' yard in Logan. You mind tellin' me what yer doin' here?"

Quaid tried to look sheepish. "Actually, I'm lookin' for Roberta. She and I—"

"Don't gimme that shit. Bertie'd never hook the likes of you." The man's eyes narrowed. "Yer with the law, ain't ya?"

"Hell, no! But hey, is she in some kinda trouble?"

A derisive cackle broke the tension. "Man, she's *always* in trouble." He leveled Quaid with a meaningful look. "You'd be better off not findin' 'er, but if yer determined, she left awhile ago to go up to New Lex to look fer a job." He shook his head, muttering, "Not that she'd be able to keep one if she found it."

"Thanks." Quaid patted the hood. "Enjoy your classic." He headed toward his truck, then turned as though just remembering something. "Hey, you any relation to Roberta?"

"Yeah, unfortunately. She's my sister."

"Well, if you see her again today, tell her Ray was here. Ray from Buckeye Lake." Quaid winked and grinned lecherously. "She'll know who you're talkin' about."

A few minutes later, Quaid drove farther down the road, turned around, then pulled off on the side where he had a clear view of the Dodge mailbox. He didn't have to wait long.

Chapter 15

Kim stepped up to the horse and stroked his neck, whispering his name over and over. He nosed her shoulder, then backed away from the door and swung around to his feed tub. But instead of eating, he stood there and looked back at Kim. She watched him for a moment, then turned to look at the other horses. They were all hanging over stall doors, watching her expectantly.

"Uh-oh," she whispered, stepping into Bandit's stall.

The feed tub was empty, one water bucket was empty and the other had only a cup or so in the bottom. There wasn't a scrap of hay on the floor. A band tightened around Kim's chest. She left the stall and hurried across the aisle. More empty feed buckets and low water. Then another. She looked at her watch. It was ten o'clock in the morning and these horses hadn't been fed or watered.

She stood in the center of the aisle and looked around. Where were Teri's barn helpers? How could the place be completely deserted? One of Teri's comments about the economy edged into Kim's mind. Just possibly, Fortune Farms no longer had any barn help. But Kim knew Teri would never let the horses go hungry, even if she had to get up in the middle of the night to take care of everyone. Something was terribly wrong.

A bay mare in the next stall whinnied loudly and Kim strode toward the feed room. If nothing else, she could take care of the immediate problem.

Thirty minutes later, horses happily munched through fragrant hay. Kim rinsed all the water buckets and refilled them. Hay and water would suffice for now. She didn't feel comfortable doling out grain when she didn't know the horses' needs or schedules. She stood for a moment, listening to the soothing sounds of a horse barn. Familiar longing pierced her chest. A life loved, but long-gone. She dismissed the melancholy and moved toward one of the empty stalls with the door hanging open. The name plate said "Goldie". Kim glanced inside, noting the stirred-up soiled bedding and tipped-over feed tub. Perhaps this horse had a problem. As she turned to leave the stall, she spotted a small orange object in the shavings. Scooping it up, her chest tightened as she stared at a syringe cap, confirming her notion that Teri was with a sick horse.

A phone rang in the small office at the end of the aisle. Kim pocketed her find and hurried toward the sound, arriving as the ringing stopped. She checked the answering machine. It was unplugged.

"Now, that's just plain weird."

Glancing around the small room, she saw nothing out of the ordinary. She moved to the desk and noted a stack of unopened envelopes. The top one was from a mortgage company. She nudged the stack apart, reading the return addresses on most of the pieces. All of them were either the same mortgage company or one of two banks. *Could be some significant financial problems in the mix.* A dry-erase board hung near the door. She pulled out her cell and moved closer. Someone on this phone list might have some information on Teri's whereabouts. The contact choices included the veterinarian, farrier, feed store, sheriff's office, and someone named Roberta Dodge whose name had been crossed off. It looked as though Teri had eliminated the cost of employees. Things must be really bad.

She gazed at the list for a minute, then decided to call the veterinary clinic first. On a hunch, she walked to the desk and picked up the landline phone. The dial tone came on and she pressed "redial".

A woman answered, "Hanover Equine Clinic."

"Hi, is Teri Fortune there yet?"

"No, she didn't ever show up. Oh, can you hold, please?"

Kim hung up the phone. "Not good. Not good at all."

She strode out the barn door and walked around the side of the building. Sure enough, a grassy spot with wheel imprints showed where the horse trailer had been parked. Teri must have had an emergency and figured she'd feed when she got back. But if she never made it to the clinic, where was she?

Kim went back into the barn and turned off the lights. As she slid the barn door back to its original position, she tried to decide what to do next. Just for the heck of it, she dialed Teri's cell phone again. This time, Teri answered.

"Oh my God, Kim, you will not believe what happened to me this morning!"

اَلـَه

Quaid squinted as an old gray Toyota eased out of the Dodge driveway onto the main road. The female driver had long hair and wore sunglasses. Quaid waited until she rounded the curve, then pulled out to follow. He hadn't made his reputation as a PI by being stupid. Brother Dodge had tried to say one thing while his body language said something else. The driver of that car was either Roberta herself, or someone else headed out to warn her. Either way, Quaid would find her.

He stayed well back, but kept the car in his sight. On the outskirts of Shawnee, he slowed way down in case she parked somewhere. The Toyota turned south, then picked up Route 93. She was headed in the opposite direction of New Lexington. He continued to stay well back, since whoever had been at the house during his visit would have seen his truck. Maybe that person was deliberately leading him on a goose chase, but he was certain that he'd parked well out of sight of the driveway.

Signs for New Straitsville appeared and, in minutes, Quaid pulled over when the Toyota parked at the curb down the street. The woman climbed out and disappeared through the door of a place called the Empire Bar & Grill. Quaid turned off the ignition and waited about five minutes, then got out and strolled down the sidewalk. Stepping through the door to the bar, he almost reeled back from the strong odor of stale liquor and cigarette smoke. *So much for no smoking in public places.* He entered and waited for his eyes to adjust from the bright sun to the dim light. The woman was sitting at the far end of the bar and the bartender was leaning close as they talked.

Quaid took a seat next to the woman. "Hello, Roberta."

"I don't know you. Get lost." Her voice was thick with a longtime cigarette habit.

Quaid looked at the bartender. "I'll have a draft, and the lady will have another of whatever she's drinking."

Up close, she looked to be in her mid-thirties, but it had been a tough thirty years. Her blonde hair was dull and stringy with dry, twisty tendrils of an old bleach job and permanent wave. Her skin was sallow and rough, and her eyes were dull with the bleak look of someone who's given up.

Quaid pulled out his business card and laid it on the bar. "I need to talk to you about Teri Fortune's barn."

"That bitch. Why would I help *her?*"

"I'm not asking you to help her," said Quaid, formulating an idea to drive the conversation. "I'm actually trying to prove she did something wrong."

The dull blue eyes lit up. "Yeah? Well, I can sure help with that!"

⁓⁂⁓

"Calm down, Teri. Tell me what happened. Where are you?"

"I'm at the sheriff's office."

Stunned disbelief filled Kim's head as Teri's story unfolded.

"I had to take that pretty palomino mare to the vet this morning. They couldn't get out to the farm until afternoon, and I couldn't afford to lose a client's horse to colic. At least I thought it might be colic. She was acting bizarre and I couldn't think of anything else it could be. God, I can't believe this is happening! I've physically lost a customer's horse!"

"Go on, Teri, I'm listening. Take your time."

"I was headed down Horseshoe Road when a small red car raced up and sped past me. About a half mile farther, I saw the same red car down in the ditch, so I pulled over and ran down to see if the driver was okay. She was slumped over the wheel. God, it scared me, I thought she was dead.

"Anyway, I tried to revive her, kept shaking her, and she finally roused and looked at me like she was confused. I started to dial for help, but she stopped me. Said she was okay and she'd call her husband. She didn't want the police involved 'cause she'd lose her license. She didn't speak good English and I had some trouble understanding her. I offered to call a tow truck and she said not to, that she'd be fine."

Teri fell silent and Kim waited a few seconds before urging her to continue.

"I returned to my truck and went to the back of the trailer to check on the mare. Kim, she was gone!"

"The doors must not have been latched."

"No. The doors were closed and latched. I have no idea how this happened. The deputies scoured the woods looking for her. There were hoof prints in the dirt beside the road, so we know she was out of the trailer. But she couldn't have closed the doors herself, so someone came along and let her loose."

Kim knew better than to ask Teri if she'd noticed anyone around during the incident. Obviously, she'd been focused on the driver of the red car. For Kim's analytical mind, this was no random act—this was a carefully planned theft.

"Did you get the woman's name or her license number?"

Teri's voice caught. "She drove off while I was checking on the mare ."

Kim's instincts were correct.

"Teri, I'm at your barn right now. I gave the horses some hay and water. Is there anything else you want me to do?"

"Thank you so much. I never dreamed I wouldn't be back by now. I'll grain them later...why did you go to my place?"

"I wanted to show you something amazing, then I realized you had a problem. I'll tell you all about it later after you get this mess sorted out."

Kim drove home slowly, using the time to consider all the aspects of Teri's story. Though the poor girl obviously hadn't made the connection, it was clear to Kim that the red car had been a deliberate diversion. In her mind, she could picture Teri down in the gully tending to an "injured" driver while a horse trailer backed up to the Fortune rig and transferred the mare. They only made one mistake—closing and latching the doors. Had they left them open, valuable time would be lost in fruitless search for a horse loose in the woods. But the perps probably never dreamed Teri would check the trailer before she continued on to her final destination.

The worst part of the whole thing was the impact on Teri. She'd now had a problem with two horses under her care. News travels fast and it wouldn't be any time at all before her customers made a mass exodus.

Kim glanced over at the page with Bandit's description. She

was dying to show Teri and start the process of getting that lovely horse back to his rightful owner. But Kim's pleasure was short-lived. Bandit was part of an active case. Jasper Martin would have a fit. But actually, he had no right to the horse. And, of course, Garrett Quaid would have a few choice things to say about her plans. *A pain-in-the-butt, but excellent at what he does.*

اهی

After a brief love-fest with Miss Kitty, Kim sat down at her computer to finish the research she'd started earlier. She read through the list of stolen horses, using a yellow marker to highlight each horse's home town and state. Of the fourteen show horses, nine were from California, not including Talisman and the Victory Farms allegedly stolen filly. The remaining five horses on the stolen list were from different states: Washington, Arizona, Michigan, New Jersey, and Vermont—all states with heavy horse populations. The wide distribution almost confirmed her idea that the theft ring was big.

She looked at the list of eight pet or pasture horses, again highlighting the locations. Three from California, two from New York, and one each from Ohio, Missouri, and Oregon. There didn't seem to be any pattern on this list, except the California horses. Maybe the information would make more sense after she compared it to horse events.

She started a new list, one that documented the horse shows where she'd seen the mystery couple. If what Kim suspected was true, she'd find the answers online in show photographs.

At the top of the list, she placed her own documentation from the Washington National Show, the Egyptian Event in Lexington, and the charity show in Cincinnati. An involuntary shudder passed over her shoulders at the recollection of the man with the hard, dark eyes. He'd seen her, knew she was watching him. If she ran into him again, he might go underground and no one would ever find out what was really going on.

She continued searching her own show photos, soon coming across the images she'd taken the previous September at Delaware's famous Little Brown Jug harness racing event. Instead of examining the speed-demon Standardbreds flashing before the camera, she concentrated on the spectators. Thousands of them, from all over the country, there to watch the second leg of the prestigious Pacing Triple Crown. In moments, Kim was staring at the dark-eyed mystery man. Throughout the series of images, he appeared at the rail, in the grandstands, and at the betting windows. Two photos showed him deep in conversation with other spectators. Kim shuddered and added the information to her list. With purses upwards of $600,000, the Little Brown Jug would be an attractive arena for connecting with moneyed folk.

Continuing on with important horse shows in California, Kim pulled up website after website, scanning the photographs for the familiar faces in the crowd. After six or seven deadends, she was ready to abandon her theory. Checking just one more, a regional Quarter Horse show in Sacramento, she saw the couple again, standing at the rail of a final performance class, watching a big, muscular roan winning the regional grand championship trophy. She read the caption to find names. "Joe Cody's Buddy" was on Kim's list of stolen show horses, an animal with a string of national titles and worth over $100,000. He'd been reported stolen from his own stall six months ago after the owner realized that the horse at the training barn was a look-alike. Kim shook her head. Another case of an absentee owner. Would that be a factor in some of the other thefts?

Chapter 16

Quaid took a sip of beer, then opened a small notebook. "Roberta, how long did you work for Teri Fortune?"

"Over a year. I took care of everything at that place, the stalls, the feeding, the trips to town to pick up stuff. All she did was bitch. Nothing suited her, but she was desperate for the help. You'd think she'd be appreciative, but nooo." Roberta finished the last of her first drink and reached for the fresh one. "I showed up on time every goddamned day, sometimes worked later than usual. An' she fires me for lighting up a joint. Hell, I wasn't even anywhere near the hay barn. An' why did she care? I was on break."

Quaid noted the discrepancy between Teri's story and this one. True, marijuana was considered a drug, but Teri had led him to believe the girl was shooting up or snorting. Another thing that popped into his mind was that the dismissal might have had more to do with wanting Dodge out of the picture because she knew something that Teri didn't want discovered.

"Roberta, think back to January if you can, when a horse from California was delivered. His name was Talisman."

She smiled for the first time. "Yeah, big bay. Nice horse."

The smile changed her face completely.

"Ms. Fortune says you took delivery of Talisman. Is that right?"

She nodded. "Teri was always running into town for something. I ended up managing the place most of the time. I personally think she had a boyfriend—probably married—which would explain the sudden trips in the middle of the day."

"Tell me everything you remember about the day the horse was delivered."

"Not much to tell. The transport arrived around eleven in the morning. I went into the trailer and led the horse out. The driver handed me the paperwork, which I signed, and he was on his way. I put the horse in the stall and left the papers on Teri's desk."

"Did the driver act nervous or anything like that?"

She thought for a moment. "No, he was pretty much just doing his job. He did take a couple minutes to sweep out the trailer before he left."

"Do you remember anything about the horse that day?"

Roberta cocked her head, her dark eyebrows knitting together. "Yeah, the poor thing was a nervous wreck. Jumpy as hell, flinching at every touch. And oh-my-God, he hollered for the rest of the day. Like he was lost or something."

Quaid blew out a long breath. "He was. Someone stole him and switched him for the real Talisman."

"You are *shittin'* me!"

"Nope, and I'm hoping you can help me find out if Teri Fortune had anything to do with that."

"I've already told you what I know, which ain't much." She pursed her lips and looked away. "I do need to find a job, so if you have any suggestions on that, I'd appreciate it."

Quaid laid his business card on the bar and nodded. "I'll see what I can do. Meanwhile, if you think of anything else, give me a call." He hesitated. "I'll need your number in case I hear of work."

She looked at him long and hard, as though weighing the disadvantage of being easily found and the advantage of finding work. Finally, she jotted her number on a napkin.

Quaid scooped it up and laid a twenty on the bar. "I'll be in touch. Thanks again for your help."

"Don't mention it. A chance to screw Teri Fortune would be a good thing."

Quaid pondered that comment as he drove back toward civilization. Would Roberta Dodge fabricate information just to get back at the woman who'd fired her? He didn't know, but it was a chance he had to take. At this point, the horse healer was looking better and better for deliberate involvement in this case.

Heading north again, Quaid remembered the transport company. He pulled over and situated his Bluetooth, then dialed.

"This is Garrett Quaid with United Equine Assurance. I need to talk to someone about a delivery job back in January."

The woman who answered took the information, then put him on hold. A radio talk show droned into Quaid's head, chatter about some politician. A minute or so later, a man's voice came on the line.

"This is dispatch. You're asking about a single horse transport from California to Delaware, Ohio in January? I have one job matching that description, but it was a December pick-up."

"Yes, but the delivery was January 10th. Owner's name is Jasper Martin."

"Okay...here, I got it. That job was done by one of our oldest and best drivers."

"I'd like to talk to him personally. Could you give me his number?"

The dispatcher cleared his throat. "I'm not supposed to give out personal information about our drivers."

"I'm looking into a theft case. You can let *me* talk to him, or you can deal with the flack after the police get involved."

"Gimme a minute."

Quaid tried to tune out the talking heads. They hadn't moved off politics.

The dispatcher came back on the line. "Talked to my supervisor. He gave me the go-ahead, but I can tell you, ol' Butch never did a dishonest thing in his life. He's been with us—"

"Sir, the driver is not being investigated. I just need verification of some dates and times."

"Oh, well, okay then. He's on the road right now, but he has a cell phone."

Quaid took the number, thanked the man, and disconnected. He was just outside New Lexington as he dialed the driver. A man answered almost immediately. The dispatcher had probably called to give him a heads up.

"Is this Butch Hunt?"

"Yeah, who's this?"

Quaid identified himself and made some small talk before getting to the point of the call. The driver seemed agreeable to answer some questions.

"I can't talk long, cuz I'm gettin' close to my next delivery in Newark."

"Huh, you're clear out in New Jersey? That's a long haul."

"Newark, Ohio. I don't do the East Coast anymore."

"Butch, I'm not far from Newark right now. Could we meet? I'd rather talk to you in person."

"Sure. I'll be there in about an hour."

Quaid took the address of the ranch were Butch would deliver his cargo.

"Okay, I'll see you there."

"Wait, that's probably not a great idea. I'll meet you at that truck stop just off Route 16 at the Granville exit."

Quaid entered the ranch address into his GPS anyway. This was working out better than he'd expected. Reading body language was one of his best skills and he'd be able to witness the driver's reactions to the questions.

Kim's tenacity drove her research. After finding one connection, she eagerly visited dozens of show results, adding several more matches of lost or stolen horses to shows where the mystery couple appeared in photographs. This could be no coincidence. If all the events were in a single location, then it would not be unusual to see the same people over and over, but with shows spread across the country, no way.

She sat back and rubbed her neck. She'd found four "for-sure" stolen valuable horses. Now, if she could match up possible doubles from the list of non-show animals, she'd have something concrete.

"And just what am I going to do with this?"

If her suspicions were correct, then she had a responsibility to give the information to the authorities. Or to Quaid? No, he was working on a single case, not a possible theft ring. She wandered into the living room and looked through the doors onto the deck. The sun was almost down, casting a soft glow into her living room.

What would Quaid think of her theory? Remembering the smirk in his eyes the last time she'd seen him, she frowned. His arrogance annoyed her beyond reason, yet she couldn't dismiss his reputation or his skill as an investigator that she'd seen firsthand. What did he think of her now that he knew of her police background? He'd screwed her up by telling Dixie about his discovery. What had possessed him to check up on her? A little self-satisfaction sneaked into her brain. Could it be that he was interested in her? *Hardly.* More like he was checking her out as a threat to his investigation. Would he slough off her idea as ludicrous?

More important…could she, in good conscience, let this go?

This theory involved horses and owners who'd been separated and put through hell for the sake of someone's wallet. If nothing else, Kim could at least alert someone to what might be going on. But it wouldn't be Garrett Quaid.

Quaid arrived in the Granville area about forty minutes later. With time to kill, he decided to go have a look at the ranch address that Butch had given him. Pulling off the road next to a pristine farm with white board fences, he gazed at several nice pintos grazing in the pasture on the right side of the driveway. On the left, two big brown llamas watched him with large, suspicious eyes. The house and barn were set at the back of the property, and some expensive cars sat next to the house.

The horse transport truck was already there and two men stood talking at the rear of the trailer. Quaid watched for a minute, then drove on past and headed back to the truck stop. He'd look up the ranch owner later. Probably unrelated, but it never hurt to have too much information.

Twenty minutes later, Quaid watched the black truck and sleek horse trailer with "Cross Country Equine Transport" emblazoned across the side. The driver expertly maneuvered the long rig into a spot that wouldn't block anyone's access to the road. The door opened and he climbed down, then looked around. Quaid honked and got out of the car.

"Butch? I'm Garrett Quaid."

The man was older than Quaid had expected, sporting a couple days' beard stubble and wispy gray hair poking out from under a faded blue ball cap embroidered with "Quarter Horse Congress".

His handshake was firm. "Good to meet ya. Let's get a cuppa. I need to get the rubber outta my legs."

Quaid glanced at the trailer. "You need to check on horses first?"

"Nah, I'm empty. Time for a shower and a good night's sleep, then over to Pennsylvania to pick up a load."

Quaid felt almost disappointed. Nothing about this man indicated that he might be mixed up in something illegal. The guy was just a regular working man, probably glad to be still employed, though he looked as though he could have retired a few years back.

They slid into a booth in the restaurant and the inviting aromas coming from the kitchen reminded Quaid he hadn't eaten anything all day.

He grabbed a menu. "You gonna eat?"

"Just coffee. I had a sandwich on the way here. So, what do you want to know?"

Quaid set the menu aside and took out his notebook. "You picked up a horse in Altadena, California last December 29th from a man named Jasper Martin. The horse was going to Delaware, Ohio. Can you tell me anything about that trip? The pickup? The delivery?"

Butch screwed his eyebrows together, then nodded. "That fancy show horse. Yeah, *that* was the trip from hell."

"Meaning?"

The waitress brought coffee and asked about food. Quaid shook his head. "We're good." His stomach growled.

Butch stirred three sugars into his coffee and took a sip before answering.

"Well, the guy was a real jerk. Insisted that I pick the horse up at three a.m., said he'd pay extra for that service. Cash." Butch grinned. "Can't pass up a three-hundred-dollar tip. Anyways, he had a helluva time gettin' that horse on the trailer. What a sucker! Kicked and reared and damned near knocked the guy down. I told him I wasn't takin' that horse off the trailer, not with a bad attitude like that."

Quaid made a note, remembering Jasper's comment about the friendly horse at Teri Fortune's place.

"How'd he react to that?"

"Never batted an eye. Said he had some calming pills I could put in the horse's water so he could be handled."

"Do you remember what the pills were called?"

Butch shrugged. "I'm just the driver, I do what I'm paid for."

"So after he loaded the horse and gave you the pills, what happened next?"

"I picked up another horse just outside San Bernardino and got on Route 40."

"Wait, you picked up another horse? What did it look like?"

Butch gave him a quizzical look. "Hell, I don't remember. Just a horse from some people who were dispersing their herd. There's a lot of that going on right now, cost of feed 'n' gas."

"I need the address where you picked up the second horse and where you delivered it."

"I'll have to get my logbook for that. You know, you're makin' me kinda nervous. Am I in any trouble?"

"No, not at all. I'm just trying to gather all the details about the transfer of Jasper Martin's horse."

"Mind if I ask why?"

"The horse you picked up from Martin was not the same horse that you delivered to Ohio."

All the color drained from Butch's face and he let out a low whistle, confirming in Quaid's mind that the driver had not been involved in the switch.

⚓

Quaid sat in his truck and watched the horse transport ease slowly out onto the highway. Once Butch had recovered from his shock, he'd been quite helpful. Quaid looked at his notes. Butch's trip had been uneventful until he reached the Texas Panhandle, then it had gone all to hell. He said the calming pills had worked pretty good on Jasper's horse, but he thought it had more to do with having a companion for the ride. *Damn! It would sure be nice to know what that other horse looked like. Wouldn't it be something if Talisman's twin had been right there on the trailer with him?*

One thing that really bothered Quaid was the issue of paperwork. Talisman's Coggins and shot record would be mandatory for interstate transport and, more than likely, his registration papers and photo would have been part of the package. Either Jasper had paperwork that matched the switched-out horse, or someone had gotten into Butch's truck and made the change. The only time the rig was left unattended, according to Butch, was during the ice storm in Texas.

He'd located a layover ranch not far from the interstate and, rather than upset the horses, he'd left them on the trailer for the night. The next day, the roads had not improved enough to continue the trip, so he'd unloaded them and paid for stalls. He'd been adamant that nothing was amiss.

"One of the barn hands helped me get that sucker off the truck, but it was a struggle. I guess the pills had worn off. I made sure to put an extra one in his water bucket that night."

The storm had passed by around noon the next day and Butch retrieved his cargo and headed east, unloading the second horse in Tulsa. Quaid looked at the name and address of the layover in Texas. This was a perfect place to make a switch.

He closed the notebook and listened to his stomach growl. Dixie's face swam before him, an unexpected mental detour. He toyed with his phone. *Should he?* His stomach growled again and he put the phone down.

Stick to the original plan. Not ready to be shot down again.

꙳

Teri Fortune called later that evening and Kim listened to the girl's ordeal. True to Kim's suspicions, the police had found tire tracks in the dirt near the hoof prints. Teri was incredulous that someone could pull off such a bold stunt.

"I was only down in the ditch maybe twenty minutes."

"That's plenty of time to unload a horse." Kim remembered the syringe cap. "Had you given the mare anything?"

"No, I wasn't sure what was wrong with her."

Kim bit her lip. It looked as though someone else had been in that mare's stall—someone who knew their way around Teri's barn.

Defeat colored Teri's voice. "We're putting out an announcement to ask if anyone saw two trailers on that road at the same time." Her voice caught. "I just can't believe all this crap is happening to me. You can't imagine the conversation I just had with the mare's owner."

"I think I can. And I'm sure sorry, but maybe everything will turn out okay."

As she said it, Kim knew it was a lie. Teri Fortune's *mis*-fortune would be her undoing.

"Maybe. But tell me more about the information you got on the Talisman twin."

"How 'bout I come by in the morning and show you? We can figure out what to do then."

"Hope I'm still standing."

Kim chuckled. "You will be."

⁂

Feeling like she'd been up all night, Kim stumbled into the kitchen the next morning. She hadn't slept well. Too many thoughts racing through her brain. Miss Kitty was rested and ready for breakfast and love. But not in that order. She meowed over and over while Kim made coffee, then the minute Kim sat down, the cat leaped onto her lap.

"You love me more than food?"

The cat rewarded her with a wet nose-tap and a kiss on the chin. Warmth spread through Kim's heart. Some things were simply priceless. Unconditional love was one of them. It didn't seem to matter whether they were cats or dogs or horses, if you treated them right, they'd be loyal forever. *Unlike some humans.* Sadness edged into her mind.

Bandit had obviously had a loving home and doting owners. Though displaced, he had a trusting personality and kind eyes. Kim thought about Jasper's description of Talisman. A horse with those temperament problems was usually the victim of abuse. Was Jasper a heavy-handed trainer, using force and fear to get the required results? How could people conceive such cruelty? A sudden image smashed into her brain. Her wonderful police horse, Red, had been a gentle giant, strong and solid, afraid of nothing. Trusting her to keep him safe. And she hadn't lived up to that trust.

The images haunted her life. Why such a senseless act to an innocent animal? The one wielding the gun was the real animal. And where was he now?

She exhaled sharply and stood up, depositing Miss Kitty on the couch. She had work to do before her trip to California, not the least of which was figuring out how to get Bandit back to his rightful owners.

⁂

Kim entered Teri's barn and stopped for a moment to listen to the pleasant sound of horses munching. The air was still cool inside, and no one seemed to be around.

"Teri? Hello?"

She glanced at the stalls. Only six horses in twelve stalls. Had Teri lost that many customers? Moving down the aisle, she headed toward the back door of the barn. Teri might be turning a horse out. Only one horse grazed in the morning sun. Teri was not to be seen. Kim headed toward the hay barn. The doors were ajar.

Not wanting to startle the girl, Kim called out. "Teri? Hey, you in there?"

She stepped through the doors and squinted into the dim interior. As her eyes adjusted, her heart stopped and she couldn't get a breath.

Teri Fortune hung motionless from the rafters.

Chapter 17

"Dixie, oh my God, Teri Fortune committed suicide!"

"The woman in Delaware, the one with the switched horses?"

Kim closed her eyes, still reeling from the events of the past two hours.

"Yes. She was in a lot more trouble than that...are you busy right now?"

"For you? Never."

"I'm just leaving the farm. The police are here and the coroner is working on her." A band tightened around Kim's chest. "I've given my statement, but I need to be with someone sane right now."

"Meet me at the coffee shop in Centerville. I'm just leaving my mom's."

Kim closed the phone, then sat quietly in her car, willing the trembling to stop. She watched the people who were tasked with inspecting a possible crime scene. They came and went in a matter-of-fact manner, unaware of the turmoil that might lay behind Teri's death. At least, not right now. Kim closed her eyes, trying to shut out the vision of a small body dangling from a rope. In all her years of police work, she'd never become immune to the impact of death. Shaking off the bad feelings, she started the car and drove down the lane. Right now, she wanted nothing more than to bask in the comfort of Dixie's love.

Dixie was waiting in the parking lot outside the coffee shop. As soon as Kim pulled in, Dixie hurried over and hugged her tightly.

"Are you okay?"

Kim leaned against her friend, grateful for the chance to simply be needy. "I will be. It was just such a shock...I'm glad you had time to meet me."

They entered the coffee shop and took a booth.

"Tell me what's going on. Everything," said Dixie.

Kim explained her research into the missing horses and about finding Bandit. Dixie nodded, but didn't interrupt. Then Kim related the stunning story of the theft of Teri's mare on the way to the vet.

Dixie nodded. "Remember I told you horse theft was big right now. The bastards are getting more cunning by the month."

Kim nodded, thinking about the few minutes she'd had to herself after finding Teri. She'd called 911, then left the hay barn and sought the comfort of the warm bodies in the main barn. While she waited for the police to arrive, she'd returned to Teri's office and examined the photographs on the walls. Had she expected to see the mystery couple somewhere in that collection? Possibly, but mostly she'd wanted to confirm to herself that Teri was a good person, a skillful horsewoman, that she'd had nothing to do with the chilling strategy of an organized theft ring.

Dixie spoke softly. "Anything else you want to share?"

"I was just thinking about Teri, and my determination that she not be involved in any of the bad stuff, but I'm not sure..."

"You can't ever know the extent of someone's private hell. She would certainly be a person of interest in these thefts."

"Earlier this morning, I leafed through her mail. There were at least a dozen pieces from a mortgage company and the local bank. I know she'd lost customers lately and was frantic about that."

Dixie stirred her coffee. "If she was about to lose her barn and had no way to pay her bills, she might have seriously considered something illegal, or at least unscrupulous."

"But if she was in such desperate straits, maybe she just gave up. Ended it."

"Or someone ended it for her."

⁓

Quaid listened to his sister-in-law's voice, heard the worry that edged the words.

"Ricky's not talking much today. You thought he'd be sorry when he got home yesterday, but he was pretty obnoxious. I did what you said, didn't press him. Garrett, I'm scared. I think he might be deeply depressed."

"Call the base and make that appointment. I'll come by this morning and talk to him, if you'd like. I think he needs some help, both from professionals and us."

Quaid hung up and flicked on the television to listen to the early morning news while he made oatmeal. The girl reporting the news gave an update on a neighborhood dispute, then she moved on to a breaking story. Quaid glanced at the screen and stopped stirring the pot. The big news of the morning was an apparent suicide at a horse barn in Delaware. The cameras zoomed in on the distinctive white barn at Fortune Farms and Quaid moved closer to the set to listen.

"You have to be kidding me!"

But no one was kidding. The woman at the center of Quaid's investigation was dead.

A strong odor drifted on the air and he ran back into the kitchen to snatch the smoking pan off the burner and throw it into the sink. He didn't have time to eat anyway.

Ten minutes later, he called Jenna. "Hey, listen, I can't come by until later. I have an emergency with a case."

"I already told Ricky you were coming. Do I really have to tell him you're blowing him off?"

"Jenna, I have to handle this situation right now. I'll come as soon as I can. Tell him I'm sorry."

Guilt surged through Quaid's chest as he hung up. One of the problems he'd always had with the family was his dedication to work before everything else. Probably not a great lifestyle, but it kept the demons at bay. Mostly.

He did a quick calculation. It was two and a half hours to Fortune Farms. By the time he got there, they'd have it buttoned up and no one would be around to answer questions. The local police probably wouldn't give him the time of day. Would they leave someone to watch over the place? And what about all those horses? Who would take care of them? He hadn't yet delved into Teri Fortune's personal life, so he had no idea if she had family or anyone to step in. Roberta Dodge had mentioned a theory about Teri's married lover, which might preclude a Mister Fortune. Or not.

Quaid's phone rang and he stared at Kim Kovak's number.

Her voice was softer than he remembered. "Mr. Quaid? This is Kim Kovak. I have really bad news."

"I heard it on television. You know anything about it?"

Kim hesitated. "I was there. I have some theories."

"You willing to share?"

"Yes, but not on the phone. Can we meet somewhere?"

"I can be in New Albany in a couple of hours. Give me an address."

Quaid hung up and exhaled sharply. Why had Kim Kovak been at Teri's barn so early in the morning? And why wouldn't she talk about it on the phone? Possibly, her undercover case had something to do with his own investigation. Just what he needed.

اللہ

Kim drove along the winding road through the condo complex, slowing down to ease over several speed bumps aptly named "Velocity Moderators." The closer she got to her apartment, the more she wished she'd arranged to meet Garrett Quaid in some public place. But her physical and mental resources had been at an all-time low and she'd simply wanted to go home.

Besides, she still had to pack for her trip. Her shoulders sagged. All her enthusiasm for attending the California show had waned, and the excitement of continuing her investigation of the thefts now seemed like a foolish waste of time. It wasn't her job. The best of the best was on the case and she had no doubt that he'd already figured out all the same things she had.

She let herself into the house and kicked off her shoes. She would give all her information and theories to Quaid and just go back to being a camera geek. She was still a little amazed at how easily Dixie had convinced her to call Quaid about the suicide. Kim was well aware of her own tendency to be a loner and hold things close, but Dixie's view of the matter made so much sense. She'd known that Kim was in no mental condition to deal with the situation alone.

Outside, a car door slammed and Kim moved to the deck slider. Quaid's blue truck sat next to her own car and, a minute later, the doorbell rang. She moved down the hall, stopping briefly to check her reflection in the round mirror next to the coat closet.

Quaid's nice, lopsided smile sent creases rippling across his cheeks. "Hi."

He came through the door and stopped. "Thanks for calling me. It was quite a jolt to see the news this morning."

"I was the one who found her."

"Oh, Jeez. Really?" His face reflected sincere empathy.

Kim closed the door and gestured toward the living room. "Come on in. I just made some coffee."

He sat down on the couch and took out his notebook and pen. "You mentioned some theories."

"Yes, but first I'd like to know where you are in the Talisman investigation."

He gave her a quizzical look. "Why does that matter? Will it interfere with your undercover work?"

For a moment, Kim was speechless. He actually thought she was still working as a cop. Could she play that to her advantage?

She picked up her coffee mug and composed her features. "Whatever do you mean?"

"Don't give me that. I know about you. And I know that police work runs in the blood, even after retirement. But you never actually retired, did you?"

"Mr. Quaid, do you want to hear what I have to say, or are you just interested in things that are none of your business?"

The friendliness left his face. "There's a good chance that Teri Fortune was mixed up in the show horse switch. Do *you* know anything about it?"

Kim decided to play nice. "I wondered the same thing for awhile, but I had spent quite a bit of time with her and my instincts say she was a victim." A hard knot formed in Kim's throat. "Now that she's dead, I'm not so sure."

"Tell me about this morning. Everything."

Like a documentary, Kim outlined every step she'd taken leading up to finding Teri in the hay barn. Quaid wrote it down as fast as she talked. When she got to the part about calling 911, she stopped and he looked up.

"What did you do while you waited for the police to show up?"

"I looked around her office. I didn't open anything or go through any files, but I'm almost positive she was in deep financial trouble. Clients were pulling horses out of her barn almost daily, and she had let all the barn help go. The poor girl was doing all the work by herself. She must have been exhausted."

Quaid nodded, continuing to write.

Kim leaned forward. "Tell me what you've found out about her."

"I spoke to the woman who used to manage the barn. She'd been fired for some small infraction, and had no good feelings for Teri. I'm considering her as a possible accomplice in the switch, although her description of the horse's personality doesn't match the one Jasper gave us."

"I know! And I found out who that horse belongs to. That's why I went to Teri's so early this morning."

"Hold on a minute, what do you mean?"

"I found a record of a stolen horse matching the description of Talisman. His name is Bandit and he was stolen six months ago. He is an absolute twin to Jasper's horse."

"Can you be sure it's the same horse?"

"I think so. I didn't have a chance this morning because, well, you know. But the horse responded to his name. Even without positive identification, I *know* this is the same horse."

She rose and retrieved the flyer from her shoulder bag and handed it to Quaid.

He whistled. "Amazing. But we need to verify his identity." He looked up. "Any chance you'd like to take a ride back up to Delaware?" He looked at the flyer again. "Stolen in Texas. Now isn't that just handy."

Kim tilted her head. "How so?"

He grinned. "I'll tell you after we visit Bandit."

A few minutes later, they stood in Kim's driveway after agreeing to take both vehicles. Kim stowed her camera bag on the passenger side of her car. Quaid opened the door to his truck, then glanced over at Dixie's door.

"So this is where your friend lives, huh?"

Kim straightened up and looked at him. He had a goofy expression, and that crooked smile outed his thoughts. She closed the car door and walked over to stand beside him.

"You *do* know she's gay?"

He blinked, then snorted. "Oh, yeah, *right*."

꙰

Quaid glanced in the rearview mirror. His experience with

women wasn't all that broad, but he hadn't expected Kovak to come up with such an outright lie about her friend. Did she really think he'd believe her? Was it a ploy to destroy his attention on Dixie so that Kovak herself could have a go? The thought was intriguing.

In all fairness, he'd seen a side of her that surprised him. She'd been genuinely stunned by the death of the horse healer. Now that he thought about it, she hadn't directly answered his question about her police work. He slammed his hand on the steering wheel. She said she had some theories to share. About what? If she wasn't undercover, why would she have theories?

He watched the black Beemer in the rearview mirror. With her solid law enforcement background, he'd have to be a lot cagier in his approach if he wanted genuine answers.

Chapter 18

Kim stared at the truck taillights and scowled. The man was a real boob. So arrogant, like he was the only one in the world who could figure stuff out. Well, let him. As of now, she had no intention of sharing her ideas. The two of them had absolutely nothing in common and a personality conflict on top of that. As far as she was concerned, this trip to Fortune Farms was simply a way to get Bandit identified and back to his rightful owner.

By the time they arrived, the parking area was deserted and the police long-gone, but yellow crime-scene tape cordoned off the barn doors. Kim got out of her car and glanced around. The police hadn't even left an officer to stand guard.

Quaid waited by the truck. "Hope they don't come back while we're here."

"Not a problem, I'll just tell them I'm here to feed the horses." She stopped short. "Speaking of which, someone will need to take care of them until…well, I'm not sure what. I don't think Teri has any family."

"I'm sure the county will handle it."

Kim pulled out the rumpled flyer. "Let's go see Mr. Bandit."

Horses whinnied as they entered the barn. They walked toward the end stall and the handsome brown head popped over the door.

"Hey, Bandit!"

He let loose with a long, loud whinny and bobbed his head.

Quaid laughed. "Well, that's a start. Now, what is the positive identification mark?"

"He supposedly has a mark on the inside of his right hind hoof. An indented white cross."

Quaid stepped aside. "You go ahead. I have some unhappy experiences with the hind end of a horse."

Kim entered the stall and stroked Bandit's neck. "Hey, big boy, we're gonna get you home real soon."

She ran her hand along his back, talking softly as she moved to his hindquarters. Running her hand down his hock, she pressed gently on the fetlock and Bandit lifted his foot off the ground.

"It's here. Exactly like the drawing." She ran her thumb over the deeply-indented mark in the hoof wall, noting that the top of the cross disappeared into the coronary band. "Come take a picture."

Quaid entered the stall and squatted down. The camera lens hummed as he zoomed in on the disfigured hoof.

"How did he get that?"

"The description doesn't say, but a bad injury to the coronary band would cause the hoof to grow out this way. Kind of like our fingernails when we damage the quick."

Quaid stood up. "Well, as far as I'm concerned, this is the horse on the flyer."

"Fabulous! I'll call the owners right away."

"Not so fast. This horse is part of an ongoing investigation, which I might add, now involves a possible homicide."

Kim's skin chilled as the blood drained from her face. "Why would you say that? Teri committed suicide."

"I listened to the police band this morning. They're not ruling out foul play." His features softened a bit. "Would you see if you can find out if Teri has any relatives?"

Kim nodded, suddenly hating this man who'd taken over.

ﺔﻟ

At six o'clock, Quaid pulled up next to Jenna's car in the driveway. She answered the door and gave him a disgusted look.

"Well, nice of you to show up."

"Knock it off, Jenna. I told you I had an emergency." He brushed past her. "Where's Ricky?"

"Out back with a friend. But since when is a work-related emergency more important than a child-related emergency?"

His shoulders dropped. "It's not, and I was wrong. I'm sorry."

Quaid walked through the kitchen and stepped out the back door. His nephew was tossing a football to another boy.

"Hey, Rick, nice throw!"

The boy looked up and, again, a brief flash of pleasure, then the curtain came down. Quaid took a deep breath and headed across the lawn.

"Toss it here."

He caught the ball, then sent a spiraling pass to the other boy.
"Man, you're good!" said Ricky.

"Lots of practice."

He jumped to catch a wide pass, lost his balance and crashed into the ground. The boys howled with laughter as Quaid got up and brushed himself off. At least he'd broken the tension.

Jenna stuck her head out the door. "Tommy, your mom says come home for dinner."

Quaid sat down on the picnic bench and watched Ricky roll the football around with his foot.

"How's the Wii? Still like it?"

"Yeah, wanna come see how it works?"

They walked into the kitchen as Jenna was pulling a pizza out of the oven. Quaid's stomach growled.

Ricky said, "Can Uncle Garrett stay for dinner?"

"Of course, go get washed." She looked at Quaid's grass-stained jeans. "Both of you."

A few minutes later, Quaid took a bite of pizza, struggling with the strings of mozzarella that threatened to hang off his chin. Ricky laughed and Quaid made a goofy face. It was good to see the boy smiling.

Jenna passed the pizza plate and gave him a pointed look. "We're going to take a little ride over to Dayton this weekend. Want to come?"

Ricky's face lit up. "Mom's taking me to see the big air museum. They have a Stealth bomber!"

"Gosh, I'd love to, but I'm going to California on Thursday. But darn, that sounds like fun."

Ricky's face fell and he set his pizza down. Quaid threw a glance at Jenna and she shook her head. Ricky asked to be excused and left the table.

Why does my work always seem to screw things up?

Jenna pushed her plate away. "Don't worry about it. He's just so emotional these days. I know it was short notice for you. I got the appointment for Friday and thought we could drift around and see what Dayton is like. I might be able to get base housing, but I need to fill out an application in person."

"Listen, when I get back from this trip, I'll take Ricky and we'll go someplace special. I promise."

"Oh, Quaid, don't make promises. They have a way of disintegrating and then you feel bad."

He looked her in the eye. "This promise will prevail."

After helping Jenna with the dishes, Quaid climbed the stairs to Ricky's room. Had it only been yesterday that he'd stood outside this door, terrified that something awful had happened to the boy? He knocked and pushed the door open.

Ricky sat at his computer, but didn't look up.

"Rick, I'm really sorry about this weekend, but when I get back, would you like to go on a little trip with me?"

"Like where?"

"How about Washington, DC? We can go to the Smithsonian and see all the nation's important buildings."

Ricky's face brightened. "That would be cool!"

Quaid took a deep breath. "And I thought we might go down to Arlington and visit your dad."

ـۂـ

Kim blocked out the noise of the passengers in the Delta terminal waiting area, reading through all the notes she'd made regarding the Talisman situation. She checked to be sure she'd picked up the maps to both Jasper's and Victory Farms, then stuffed everything back into her shoulder bag. Rather than chasing this elusive mystery, she should be concentrating on earning a living. But Teri's death had changed everything and now Kim's involvement had become serious.

She reached into her bag and pulled out Teri's client list. Unfolding it, she read the names and phone numbers. She felt a twinge of guilt, then shrugged it off. Quaid didn't need to know *everything*. Besides, he was probably withholding information from her, too, as in his discovery of the barn manager. Why wouldn't that person be a prime suspect in Teri's death? Disgruntled employees often took drastic measures for revenge. Kim glanced up at the line of passengers forming at the gate, then stuffed the list back into her bag. She'd make those calls during her layover in Denver. *Someone* must know about Teri's private life.

Finally settled in the narrow seat jammed against the window, Kim thought about her own personal life. For so long, she'd been smug about being independent, not having all the turmoil and drama that seemed to surround most women. She'd often thought she had the best of the best. Heaviness seeped into her chest as she realized that being alone and isolated hadn't been her best choice. At fifty, did she have any chance of changing that? Did she want to? Could she deal with it?

The plane leveled off, cruising above white billowy clouds. Kim gazed over the vast whiteness and made a quiet vow to change her life.

⸎

Quaid took the elevator up to the seventh floor of United Equine's building and stepped out into the reception area of the insurance company. At that early hour, most of the employees weren't at work yet. He moved down the hall toward the small office where he usually handled in-house business. A phone rang somewhere, then stopped. He set his briefcase on the desk and moved to the window to drink in the magnificent view of Lake Erie. He never tired of watching the ships and boats working along the docks or motoring through the channel. To his left, the Cleveland Browns Stadium commanded the view, and off to the right in the distance, planes landed and took off from the Burke Lakefront Airport. The scene was so dramatically different from the landscapes of his youth. Exactly what he'd wanted—to disengage himself from the rural blahs.

Someone knocked on the door behind him and he turned away from the window. The young man who assisted him grinned.

"You're certainly an early bird."

"Gotta get those worms. Is the travel girl in yet?"

"I think she has the day off. You can look at the schedule in the break room."

"Damn, I need to adjust the trip I'm taking tomorrow."

"You can just do it yourself, then turn in whatever receipts you get, as long as the trip was originated by the travel department."

"Okay, thanks. I have a bunch of calls to make this morning, so I'll do that too."

The young man nodded, then walked away.

115

Quaid dialed Roberta Dodge.

She answered almost immediately, suspicion coloring her voice. "H'lo?"

"Good morning, Roberta, it's Garrett Quaid."

Her tone brightened. "You find me a job?"

He hesitated. Surely she knew about Teri Fortune's death, but he'd better start at the beginning.

"You heard about Teri Fortune, right?"

"What'd she do now, kill a horse?"

"She's dead, Roberta."

"No fuckin' way! When? Hey, wait a minute! You think I had something to do with it?"

Was her reaction *too* strong? Hard to tell, over the phone. Quaid tried to temper his next comment.

"You would certainly be on a suspect list, given your unpleasant history with her."

"Listen, Buster, you think I don't have enough trouble in my life without making it worse? Why the hell would I do that to myself? Jee-zus Christ!"

"I'm actually calling to see if you know any of her relatives or friends."

"Oh, yeah, we were bosom buddies. You must think I'm pretty stupid. Fuck off."

The line went dead and Quaid tossed the phone on the desk. How had that conversation gone sour so quickly? Was he losing his touch?

He picked up the phone again and dialed Kovak. She answered on the second ring, her voice lost against the noise of some public place.

"Hey, it's Garrett Quaid. I just spoke to the Dodge woman and she wasn't exactly helpful. Where *are* you, anyway?"

"I'm on my way to a horse show. I haven't done anything yet about locating any of Teri's family, but I will later this morning. I'll call you when I have something."

"Okay. Hey, I never thanked you for sending the photographs. They're a big help, but I do have one question. One of the show photos looks like people are blurred out in the background, but the same picture on your website shows them plain as day. Any comments?"

The noise in the background on Kovak's phone got louder, then suddenly disappeared. Quaid looked at the screen. *Dropped call.*

For real? Or intentional. He pressed "redial" and was taken immediately to Kim's voice mail.

"*Miz* Kovak, if you're holding back information that pertains to this case, you'll regret it. I suggest you call me back."

Quaid sat back and stared out the window with absolutely no doubt in his mind now that Kim Kovak was working undercover on *his* case.

Chapter 19

Kim laid the phone in her lap and groaned. *Of all the stupid mistakes. I never even thought about the pictures on my website.* How would she explain the discrepancy to Quaid without admitting that she was doing a little sleuthing on the side, and that she *had* kept information from him? Though she'd already considered giving him everything, she still felt proprietary about what she'd discovered. Funny—he'd never asked her how or why she'd found the information on Bandit.

She glanced at the clock on the wall at the gate. Denver time was different from Ohio time and it took her a minute to figure out that it wasn't too early to call Teri's client list. She smiled wryly. Another piece of information she'd withheld from Mister Private Investigator.

The list was arranged by client name, followed by the horse's name, followed by a phone number and town. Of the eight names on the list, only two were in Ohio. The remaining customers lived all over the country. *What a shame. Teri had such a good business, a much-needed service for horse owners who wanted a more holistic approach to horse care.*

She started with a contact in Iowa. Dialing the number, Kim composed her opening comments. If not handled carefully, the calls would be useless.

"This is Kim Kovak, a friend of Teri Fortune's. I don't know if you heard yet, but Teri died yesterday."

The man's voice registered shock. "Oh my gosh! How awful! What happened? No, wait, what about my horse?"

"Your horse is just fine, being cared for as usual. I believe you'll need to arrange to pick up the animal fairly soon. The county is watching over the barn until all the owners have taken responsibility for their horses."

"I can get out there by tomorrow afternoon. Jeez, what happened to Teri?"

"Ah, it looks like suicide. But I don't know all the details…Did you know her well?"

"Not really. One of her other clients recommended I send the horse for treatment. Gosh, suicide. That's awful."

"Yes, it is. Could you tell me the name of the person who referred you?"

"Bob Fisher. He's retired now, but he used to have lots of show horses."

Kim wrote the name and phone number on the list and thanked the man for his help.

She immediately called Bob Fisher. The call went directly to voice mail. She left her name and number, plus a vague message about show horses. She looked up at the clock, then dialed the next client on Teri's list. A farm in New Dover, Ohio, not far from Marysville.

A woman's voice answered, a throaty voice with a heavy Spanish accent.

Kim went through the same opening routine, only this time the reaction was lukewarm.

"How'd it happen? Accident? Was she sick?"

"I'm surprised you haven't seen it on the news. The police believe it was suicide."

"Can I come get my horses?"

Kim tried to keep astonishment from coloring her voice. "Yes, the sooner the better, I would think...How well did you know Teri?"

The woman barked a nasty laugh. "My husband could give you a better answer."

"Oh, is he the horseman in the family?"

Venom seeped through the phone. "No, he's the stud in the family and he couldn't keep it out of that little slut."

Kim couldn't speak. In the space of one second, another possible suspect had surfaced.

∽

Quaid spent the next hour reorganizing his flights so he'd have time to drive to San Bernardino, then catch a flight to Amarillo where Butch Hunt had waited out the ice storm. Again, he pondered the logistics that would have been required to track the horse trailer for over a thousand miles, waiting for the right opportunity. That still didn't make any sense. The most plausible scenario was corroboration with the layover ranch.

He sat back in the chair and thought about Kim Kovak. She was definitely playing games and he didn't like that one bit. Giving him that shit about Dixie being gay was just confirmation that the photographer would stoop to just about anything to be in control.

Thinking of Dixie made him smile. No way was she gay.

By mid-afternoon, Quaid had amassed a large volume of notes on the various aspects of both the theft-ring idea and Teri Fortune's possible involvement. As he sketched out a flow chart using each factor, he became more puzzled. The dots didn't connect in the right places. Somewhere in the middle of all this lay a missing piece, a common denominator in the equation. Or possibly he was chasing an imaginary plot and none of the events were related.

Teri Fortune, for example. It was hard to believe that she'd had the bad luck to be involved in the loss of two horses within a short period of time. *That* piece of information had come to him quite unexpectedly when he'd called Teri's veterinarian. The girl answering the phone had refused to give him any information about Teri's vet bills, other than the fact she was a regular customer. But sometimes a little charm went a long way and, though he didn't obtain any financial information, the girl had been eager to share the case of the burgled mare. Quaid had carefully orchestrated his responses so that the girl on the phone continued to babble, offering more and more information about the incident.

Now if he could just figure out what horse it was and who owned her, he might have another piece of the puzzle.

Realizing that phone calls weren't the best way to gain information, he tapped into his network of resources to find out exactly into what kind of financial mire Fortune Farms had sunk. By late afternoon, he had all the information he needed. Teri Fortune was double-mortgaged, three months behind in the payments, on a short list for foreclosure, and thousands of dollars in debt to veterinarians, farriers, and feed stores. With the loss of revenues from the business, there was no way she could catch up. Plenty of reasons to end her life.

But why were the police considering her death a homicide? He reached for the phone.

"Delaware County Sheriff's Office, how may I direct your call?"

"This is Private Investigator Garrett Quaid with United Equine Assurance in Cleveland. I'd like to talk to the officer who handled the death at Fortune Farms yesterday."

"Please hold."

A woman's velvety voice came on the line. "Deputy Sheriff Dexton, may I help you?"

"I hope so. I'm investigating a theft claim at Fortune Farms and I understand that your department is treating Teri Fortune's apparent suicide as a homicide. Can you tell me why?"

"I can't give out information about an ongoing case. You should know that."

"It might be relevant to the case I'm working on, so anything you can—"

"I'm sorry, sir. I can't help you."

Quaid thanked her and hung up. He thought for a minute, then called in a favor.

من

Kim stared at the sea of taillights stretching ahead of her as she left the Los Angeles airport.

"Oh. My. God. I can't believe people do this every day."

A dull throb had formed at the base of her skull and her eyes were beginning to burn. While the Los Angeles commuters were rushing in slow motion toward home and dinner, Kim's body was aching for her bed. It was nine o'clock at home.

The saving grace was that she'd have a full day to recover before the horse show, a day in which she intended to find out exactly what Jasper Martin was up to. She'd also figure out how to field Quaid's questions about the photograph. When she could think straight, something would surely come to her.

As the three-hour time difference had exhausted her the night before, it kicked her butt in the wee hours and Kim found herself wide awake at three o'clock. She climbed out of bed and made coffee in the tiny coffeemaker on the desk. While the brew dripped, she jumped in the shower, filled with enthusiasm for the day. The hot water felt good and she thought about how she had always looked forward to each day when she was on the force. Getting to the stables early and grooming Red for the day. A soft twinge moved through her heart, but after so many years, the pain was finally beginning to ebb—as long as she didn't allow the visuals of that day to enter her mind.

The coffee was awful, but it would do until the motel office opened at six. She sat down and started her laptop to reacquaint herself with the important points of the case. She did a detailed search on Jasper Martin. The top hits were all about his horses and his business and his show wins and so on. But the deeper she dug, the fewer stories came up about the business side of him. Then, several levels into the search, a short headline caught her eye. A news story in the local paper eight months ago mentioned tax evasion and she went for it.

__Altadena horse farm owner pleads guilty to tax evasion__
-- Jasper Martin, owner of Rocking J Ranch, pleaded guilty Friday to underreporting taxes by $1.1 million and not paying the farm employees' income and Social Security taxes for two years. According to the guilty plea, Martin reported earnings of about $1.65 million between 2005 and 2008. In fact, Martin's earnings were $3.75 million. Failure to pay employee income tax and Social Security resulted in another nonpayment of over $350,000.

"Oh wow! Jasper, you are in deep doo."

She did a mental review of the past six months, which included Talisman's exhibition at the Washington National Show, the same event where he showed no evidence of injury, as noted on the videos. If Jasper had just gotten snagged for tax evasion, he'd have been looking for ways to make money to get out of trouble. Kim didn't know much about tax law, but she knew for sure that there was no statute of limitations on defrauding the government of its due. Jasper would owe the money and the huge interest for as long as it took him to pay it off. Had Talisman been a casualty of the man's foolhardiness? Would an insurance payment of $100,000 even make a dent in that tax debt?

Kim skimmed down the paragraphs to see if and what sentence was passed.

Martin's assets were seized, including over $1,000,000 in cash found in a safe deposit box under Martin's sister's name. Additional funds were deposited in the sister's bank account in Pasadena, and $500,000 in cash was found in a safe at the farm. Martin was prohibited from selling any horses or property until further notice.

Kim sat back, stunned. This was critical enough that Quaid should be alerted. Why he wouldn't already know it, she couldn't fathom, but as a responsible ex-cop, she felt obligated to share.

Once she figured out how to answer his questions about the blurred photograph.

⁓

Jasper Martin's spread was not far from the foothills of the Angeles National Forest and as Kim drove, she gaped at the barren hills that had once been lush with vegetation. Forest fires had all but decimated the terrain and, though it had been a couple of years, nothing seemed to be growing yet. She shivered. As beautiful as California was, the residents who chose to live in this part of the state existed with a cloud of imminent disaster, either from wildfires or earthquakes. But all the television footage she'd seen showed resilient people who preferred to live where they chose and take their chances with Mother Nature.

A few yards from the entrance to Jasper's driveway, Kim pulled over to the side of the road. A classic western-style wooden sign with a brand on either side was posted over the drive: "Rocking J Ranch". She looked at the several corrals at the front of the property. No grass, just tan dirt surrounded by boxwire. A few horses stood near the fence, mildly interested in her presence. The animals did not look like top show animals, but she suspected that the good horses were kept in the barn. She eased the car forward a bit to get a look at the outbuildings. A large, expensive eight-horse trailer was parked by the main barn and a shiny silver dually sat in front of the ridiculously small house. The entire property was a little on the shabby side, not what she'd expect from such a stellar trainer. Whatever he'd been

123

doing with his money, it hadn't been spent on paint and upkeep.

Kim lifted her camera and clicked off several shots of the place, along with a photo of the sign and mailbox. She wasn't sure why she wanted those pictures, but the moment was there so she used the opportunity.

A few miles down the same road, she saw a sign for riding lessons and, on impulse, turned in. The place was in no better shape than Jasper's and Kim wondered briefly if the horse industry was in worse shape than anyone knew. Compared to some of the stables in Ohio, these were pretty sorry.

She parked the car and climbed out. A middle-aged woman came out of the barn, wiping her hands on her jeans, a smile crinkling her cheeks.

"Howdy. Welcome to the Riders Ring."

"Hi, I'm Kim Kovak. I'm a photographer and I'm drifting around the area taking candid shots of the horse farms."

"Well, ain't that nice. You just make yourself at home. I got a lesson starting in a couple minutes. You're welcome to take pictures. I'm sure she won't mind."

"Thanks, that would be super." Kim fell into step alongside the woman. "Say, I stopped down the road at Rocking J Ranch and the place looks deserted."

The woman clucked her tongue. "That man is in so much trouble. An' I worry about those horses."

"Oh? The ones in the corral looked fine to me."

"Oh, I don't mean they're abused or anything. It's just that Jasper has had several animals stolen right out from under his nose. Can't figure out why the thieves keep targeting his place, but maybe because he ain't there a lot." She threw a knowing glance toward Kim. "He's in trouble with the tax people. Probably trying to stay under their radar."

Kim had to swallow hard to keep from blurting out a bunch of questions.

"That's too bad. Stolen horses, huh? I think I'd keep them under lock and key if it were happening to me."

The woman shrugged. "I think he gets paid from the insurance company. Boy, I'd be devastated if anyone stole any of *my* babies. I don't have kids, so my horses are my family."

Kim followed the woman into the small barn. It was compact with no frills, but it was clean and in good repair. Six stall doors stood open and a young girl tossed soiled bedding into a wheelbarrow in the aisle.

Kim watched a thirty-something woman hoist her ample body onto the back of a roan Quarter Horse.

"I'd like to take some photographs of you during your lesson. Is that okay?"

The woman beamed. "Sure."

Kim pulled out a model release and handed it up, along with a pen. "If you'd just sign this, it gives me your permission to use the photos as I see fit."

"Will I be in a magazine?"

"You never know."

Kim followed the two out into the paddock, her thoughts on the interesting tidbits about Jasper. She was dying to get back to her car so she could write everything down. But for now, she'd have to carry on with her charade.

For the next twenty minutes, she snapped off photos, barely bothering to compose them. Her mind was ablaze with the thought of Jasper being the "victim" of theft so many times. Add Teri's curious instances of disappearing horses, and the connection between the two began to look very suspicious. A sharp pain lurched through Kim's chest. Teri was dead, so they'd never know if she was intentionally involved.

Unless Kim could connect *everyone* to the mystery couple.

⚜

Quaid stepped out of the L.A. airport into the late afternoon heat. Several shuttle buses sat at the curb and he found the right one to take him to the car rental lot. Mentally, he went over his proposed itinerary for the next couple of days. First would be a visit to Jasper Martin's place. The guy would be caught off guard and that might give Quaid the upper hand.

He pulled out his cell phone and scanned through the numbers until he found Kim Kovak.

She answered on the third ring. "Mr. Quaid."

"Hi, we had a bad connection yesterday, so I wanted to get back with you about that photograph."

"Can you describe the one you're talking about? I have thousands of pictures."

"Jasper Martin's horse jumping at the Washington National Horse Show."

"Oh, right. And what was your question?"

Quaid scowled. He hated playing games. "Some people standing at the rail are blurred out. Why is that?"

"Oh, that's easy. If I don't have a model release for people who appear in my photographs, I have to fix it so they can't be recognized."

"I see. So what about the same photograph on your website?"

She hesitated only briefly, then, "Must be an oversight. Thanks for pointing that out. I'll get it fixed when I get back to...when I get home."

Quaid wasn't sure he believed her, but what could he do? He didn't even know what significance the blurred faces might have.

Kovak's tone changed. "Hey, listen, did you know that Jasper was in trouble with the IRS?"

Quaid sat up straight. "He is? How did you find that out?"

"I came across it on Google one day when I was searching for something for Teri. The information might be important to your investigation."

Quaid's brain tried to juggle the new information and put it into perspective. Why had Kovak been searching for Jasper? And what did it have to do with Teri Fortune? If his suspicions were correct, Kovak's undercover investigation was running parallel to his. He smiled wickedly. With any luck, he could nail this one without her knowing she'd helped.

"Thanks, I appreciate the tip. I'm out of town right now, but I'll be in touch when I get back next week."

"I'll be around."

⸎

Kim closed her phone with a decisive snap. She'd done her good deed for the day, no, for the week. Quaid had information that would help him, and she'd managed to extricate herself from the blurred photograph predicament.

An hour later, she pulled into the parking area of the show facility where she'd be taking pictures the next day. Horse trailers and trucks were already in place and, in the outdoor corrals, riders worked their horses. She headed for the building that housed the show office.

To her surprise, Clark Jennings was at the desk. He jumped up, smiling.

"Hey, good to see you." He shook her hand, then turned to another man standing by a file cabinet. "Meet George, he's the ring steward for the show. You'll be able to count on him to help you out or answer questions. Boy, I can't tell you how glad I am that you were able to do this for us. I was in deep stuff."

Kim filled out the paperwork and gathered up her passes and name tag. "I'll just go wander around, get a feel for lighting and background."

She walked through the grounds, then entered the main stabling barn. Every stall was occupied and owners were busy with final preparations for three days of hard work. She walked up and down the aisles, looking at the horses and reading the names on the doors. She did the same in the next two barns. Just before the end of the last aisle, she stopped short.

Three empty stalls were marked "Rocking J Ranch."

Chapter 20

Quaid checked into a motel not far from downtown Pasadena. After setting the air conditioning to a less than Arctic level, he examined a map of the area. Martin's ranch was in Altadena, an easy 10 minute drive due north. Quaid glanced at his watch. Almost seven-thirty, a good time to pay a surprise visit. But he first wanted to check out the information Kovak had given him.

Jasper's name was all over the place with regard to his training and his winning horses, so Quaid fine-tuned the search to include "IRS." The first article that came up looked promising. As Quaid read through the lengthy piece, he saw a couple of factors that could figure into the man's involvement in a theft ring. A face-to-face meeting with the trainer would give Quaid a better feel for the idea.

He looked at the' map again. When his investigation here was finished, he could jump on the 210 and drive right into San Bernardino, the same route the horse hauler had taken. Quaid folded the map, collected his room key, and headed for the car. Easing into the traffic, he thought again about Kovak's glib answer regarding the blurred photograph. Why hadn't she just told him that the first time he'd asked? Because she'd needed time to think about it, that's why. Which probably meant it wasn't the real reason, and possibly not even a valid answer.

He put his phone on speaker and dialed.

"Hey, it's me, Garrett Quaid. What's the newspaper's policy on photographs of people? Do you need to get a release from anyone whose picture you take?"

"That depends on the situation. For interviews and stuff, yeah, we get a release."

"What about a public event?"

"Nah, anyone who attends something like that is considered fair game. We only get releases from people we name in a photograph."

"So someone in the crowd wouldn't have any right to complain if you published a photo with them in it?"

"Pretty much, unless the photo incriminated them in some

way. You know, like catching a guy kissing someone other than his wife, or a person in a place they're not supposed to be. Then they might come after us for invasion of privacy, but it would be a tough claim to win."

"Thanks, you've been a big help. Sorry to call so late."

"No problem. Let's get together for a beer one of these days."

"You got it."

Quaid disconnected and glowered out the windshield. This was beginning to read like a bad novel.

Fifteen minutes later, he drove slowly along the dirt driveway leading to Jasper Martin's barn. A small black car was parked by the door and lights were on inside the building.

He stepped through the entrance and called out, "Jasper? You here?"

A woman appeared from a room at the back. "He already left. You just missed him."

Quaid looked around. Most of the stalls were empty and the place had a faint odor of urine.

"Will he back soon?"

She cocked her head. "Not until he's done showing horses on Saturday. Is there something I can help you with?"

Quaid's brain throttled into high gear. Here was a chance to get some information that Jasper might not offer up. Should he tell her who he really was? Or just play dumb.

He went for dumb.

"Well, maybe. Jasper told me about a horse he had for sale out in Ohio, an' I just wanted a little more information about the animal." Quaid looked around the aisle. "Thought I'd take a look at some of the other stock he has too."

The woman's forehead wrinkled. "Ohio? You must have misunderstood him. The only horse he has out there is his champion show jumper. He wouldn't be selling him."

Quaid pretended to be perplexed. "Jeez, I'm pretty sure he said the horse was in Ohio. Hmm, maybe Iowa? They sound sorta the same."

"The only sale horses I know about are right here. You want to have a look?"

"Yeah, sure." He chuckled. "Why not? It might save me a trip to Ohio. Or Iowa. Whatever."

"All the animals in the front pasture are for sale, and two of the show horses. I was just about to bring them in."

"How many does Jasper have?"

She snorted. "More than I can handle alone, that's for sure."

"Gosh, you do *all* the work?"

"Yeah. Barn help is hard to keep. They're a transient bunch." She grabbed a halter from a hook by the door. "I'm pretty much stuck with the obligation, since I'm his sister."

Quaid followed her out the back door, sorting out all the new information to see where it fit. Five horses in the front pasture and two show horses, all for sale. Smacked of financial trouble. No employees. Smacked of even more trouble. One last question and a quick look at the sale horses, then he'd get back on the road.

The woman slipped a halter over the ears of a nice-looking palomino mare, then led her through the gate.

"If you're looking for a show horse, this mare would be perfect. She has some wins under her belt and she's got a pedigree like nobody's business, in case you wanted to breed her."

Quaid stroked the horse's neck, mildly surprised at how the touch brought a tightness into his chest. "She's real nice. Is she a jumper?"

"No, Western Pleasure. You want to try her?"

"Well, I'm actually looking for a jumper. Say, why is Jasper selling all these horses? He getting out of the business?"

The woman's pleasant expression disappeared and she pinned him with a hard look. "Who *are* you? If you're with the IRS, you can just pound sand. I'm not tellin' you anything."

Quaid was genuinely surprised by the attack. "Whoa! Hey, I'm just horse shopping. If you can't be civil, I'll just be on my way." He turned back toward the barn, struggling to keep a smile from giving him up.

Her voice followed him. "If you really *are* interested in buying something, you can go talk to my brother at the horse show."

Driving back toward Pasadena, Quaid tallied the information he'd gathered from the sister.

Either she didn't know about the Talisman switch, or she was quite the actress.

Jasper no longer had employees, probably with good reason. If he hadn't paid Social Security and income tax, they'd be pretty pissed.

Jasper was actively trying to sell off horses, even though he'd been prohibited from doing so by the government. How would he get away with *that?*

Was the woman in the barn the same sister mentioned in the news article? The one whose name was on the bank accounts?

The feeling that he was missing something still bothered him. He needed to find out where the horse show was being held. Opening the slider on his phone, he hooked into the Internet to do a search. The show was in Burbank, about twenty minutes away. Was there much point in going there at night? It was after eight. No, his body was saying it was actually after eleven. Jet lag suddenly caught up with him and he decided to put everything on hold until he'd had some sleep. Jasper wasn't going anywhere.

꧁

Kim arrived at the Burbank show grounds about six the next morning. As she walked to the show office, she thought about Jasper Martin. His stalls had remained empty all afternoon. If he planned to show any horses, wouldn't he want them settled in to rest through the night? She shrugged. They'd probably be there this morning.

At the show secretary's desk, she picked up the current version of the class list, scanned it for changes, then headed for the stabling area to check Jasper's stalls. Miss Kitty would be proud of her. Insatiable curiosity had been Kim's biggest ally—and downfall—all her life. No way could she start the grueling day without knowing Jasper's whereabouts.

Inside the main barn, the air fairly crackled with anticipation. Kim walked through and continued on to the last barn. Her step slowed, then she stopped. Jasper's stalls were still empty.

A man came around the corner leading a horse. "Heads up!"

She moved out of the way and said, "Do you know if this exhibitor is here yet?"

The man glanced at the name on the stalls, then shook his

131

head. "Nope. Been nobody at this end since yesterday morning."

Kim looked at her watch. Did she have time to go back to the show office to see if Jasper had scratched? The speakers overhead hummed. "First call for class 101, youth hunter."

Perplexed, Kim hurried from the barn. Jasper obviously didn't bother to bring horses until closer to the time of his class. If she knew anything about showing horses, that meant he didn't care whether he placed or not. So, why bother?

She moved into the arena and found the best vantage point. Lens cover came off as the in-gate opened to a string of young riders on beautifully groomed show ponies. Kim lost herself in the moment and entered the world of competition.

Twenty minutes later, she positioned herself and focused on the eight-year-old girl grinning broadly from the back of a shiny chestnut gelding sporting a large blue ribbon.

"Okay, honey, smile real big. You did good."

By midmorning, the temperature had risen considerably and Kim had consumed three bottles of water. The announcer called a fifteen minute break and Kim headed for the restrooms. Such would be the rest of her day, but maybe she could grab a quick nap during the lunch break. As she blotted her forehead with a wet paper towel, she overheard two women talking between bathroom stalls. Kim didn't pay much attention until she heard one woman mention Jasper's name.

The other voice sounded disgusted. "He doesn't deserve to even have those horses. I hope the Feds take them away from him."

"I heard they were all registered in the sister's name."

Kim held her breath, but no more information was forthcoming other than catty remarks.

Stunned, she left the restroom and walked slowly toward the arena. The IRS had found money in the sister's bank account, but no mention had been made of the horses being hers. If they were, Jasper wouldn't be able to sell them without her signature. Another piece of the puzzle?

~♘~

Quaid made short work of scrambled eggs, bacon, hash browns, biscuits, and the strongest coffee he'd ever tasted. The waitress came by to top off his cup.

"Say, do you know the best way to get to Burbank?"

She grinned. "You goin' to that big horse show today?"

"How'd you know?"

She winked. "You look like a cowboy."

Heat spread across Quaid's cheeks.

The waitress gave him simple instructions to avoid the most traffic, then topped off his coffee and walked away. Quaid stared at the steaming brew, thinking about how best to approach Jasper today. Maybe being away from his own turf would put him off guard a little. Or maybe he'd be so busy that Quaid would simply be wasting time *and* removing the element of surprise. Whatever. He'd at least go have a look, decide after he got there.

The equestrian park was huge, nothing like he'd expected. His mental picture had been a dirt rodeo arena with portable bleachers. This place was more like a movie set. He parked the car and headed toward the building with a "Show Office" sign.

A man leaned over the desk, marking something off on a large chart. He looked up when Quaid entered.

"Hi, can I help you?"

"Yes, can you tell me where Jasper Martin is stabled?"

The man came to the counter and ran his finger down a long list, then turned the page and did the same.

"He's not listed as an exhibitor. Are you sure you have the right show?"

Quaid kept his expression neutral. "Is this the regional qualifier show?"

The man nodded and Quaid shook his head.

"Maybe I have the wrong dates. Well, sorry to bother you."

"The only other possibility would be that he's helping a client show, in which case the horse owner would be listed, but not the trainer."

"Thanks, I'll ask around."

He headed for the door, anger pounding through his chest. The sister had screwed him.

An announcer's voice drifted on the air, and Quaid thought for a minute. Was it worth asking around the grounds to see if Jasper had actually come here? It looked like there were at least eight barns on one side of the show rings and four large ones on the other. Where the hell would he start? The announcer's voice rang out again and Quaid headed toward the arena. At least he could take a look. Truth be known, he missed being around horses more than he'd realized.

He found a spot on the rail near a group of people watching the riders sail effortlessly over the obstacles.

"Boy, they sure make it look easy," he said

The man next to him nodded. "Yeah, makes me wish I'd learned to ride when I was a kid."

Quaid glanced at the guy and an uneasy feeling passed through his head. The man looked a little familiar, but Quaid knew he'd never met him before. Probably just one of those faces that seemed common. The man turned and said something to a dusky-skinned woman next to him, then they moved off toward the parking lot. Quaid watched them, then turned back to the arena. The only people left were the ring steward, a judge, and the show photographer. The announcer called for the lunch break and the arena crew came in and began rearranging the jumps. Quaid watched the photographer leaving the arena. There was something familiar about her walk and the set of her shoulders. He left the rail and headed in the same direction. A few minutes later, he lost sight of her, but he had the weird feeling that he'd just seen Kim Kovak. Seemed impossible, but she *had* said she was on her way to a show.

᠅

Kim climbed into her car and turned on the AC, then sank back in the seat and set the phone to wake her in thirty minutes. In seconds, she was sound asleep.

Chapter 21

The woman had disappeared, but Quaid was near the horse barns. He entered one of the buildings and was immediately taken back to happier times, a period when he'd lived and breathed the atmosphere of stalls and fragrant hay and the warm scent of horseflesh. His gut tightened and he took a deep breath, shrugging away the sadder memories. He walked slowly down one of the aisles, stopping occasionally to inspect a bright-eyed horse peering out between the bars of a stall door. He touched a whiskery chin, let soft lips nibble his fingers, then moved on.

A woman sitting on a wooden crate rubbed a soft cloth over a shiny bit. Quaid stopped.

"Do you know if Jasper Martin is in this barn?"

She glanced up. "Haven't seen him, but that don't mean much. It's been a zoo here all morning."

"Thanks." Quaid walked on.

A man at the corner stall was just sliding the door shut. Quaid tried again.

The man thought for a moment. "I heard he was going to be here, but I haven't seen him yet. I don't think he's in this barn, but you can check with the show office. They'll tell you exactly where he's stalled."

"Thanks, appreciate it," said Quaid, moving toward the exit.

So Jasper had made it known that he would be at this show, but he'd not registered. Why would he do that? To give him time to be somewhere else? Quaid's step picked up as he headed toward the parking lot.

"I'll bet the son-of-a-bitch is planning a disappearing act!"

♃

Kim awakened suddenly, hot and sweaty, her hair plastered against her sticky cheek, and cotton clogging her thoughts. Her phone vibrated softly in her lap and she blinked the sleep away. Grabbing her camera bag, she climbed out of the car and inhaled deeply, still fighting the cobwebs. Locking the car, she headed toward the arena, then collided with someone walking past.

"Oh, sorr—. What are *you* doing here?"

Quaid cocked his head, narrowing his eyes. "I *thought* that was you." A slow grin spread over his face. "I'm working, same as you."

Kim stepped back and scowled. "Well, I'm late, so excuse me."

"See you around."

Kim strode away, stunned by Quaid's presence and more than a little annoyed that he was infringing on her investigation. *Her* investigation? She chanced a quick look back and her face flamed. He was still standing there, watching her. Grinning. How long had he been here? What had he learned? Did he know anything about Jasper's whereabouts?

The announcer made the first call as she scurried toward the gate.

Damn it, I want to know what he's up to.

⚓

Quaid worked hard to keep from laughing out loud. Rather than being pissed because she was there, he was surprised to realize that he was glad to see her. Even though she was officially working the show, he was positive she was also up to something else. Her reaction to his presence was proof. And that "something else" most assuredly had to do with Jasper Martin.

He suddenly remembered what he'd been doing before he ran into Kovak. He hurried to his car, dialing Jasper's farm as he walked. After four rings, the answering machine picked up, but he didn't leave a message. He'd be willing to bet money that Jasper had been at the ranch the whole time Quaid was there, and the horse show was simply a way to be officially "gone." Though he hadn't seen any other vehicles or trucks, or even a horse trailer, that didn't mean anything because he hadn't seen the back of the barn, an easy place to hide that stuff.

He made the drive back to Jasper's in record time. As he approached the driveway, he scanned what property could be seen from the road. Still no sign of a horse trailer or truck, and the black car wasn't there either. The front pasture was empty and the barn doors were closed. A coil of excitement ran through his gut as he turned into the drive.

He parked near the front of the barn and got out, standing by his car long enough that anyone nearby would have the chance to approach him. After about five minutes, he slowly walked past the front of the barn and peered around the corner to an area used for storing farm equipment. A tractor, hay wagon, and old pickup truck sat near the back end of the barn, but a large spot was empty, just about the size of a large rig. The grass was recently flattened by tires. He walked back toward his car, wondering if he dared go inside the barn.

Why not?

He slid the door back and looked inside. A couple of horses poked their heads over stall doors and watched him. One of them was the palomino mare he'd seen yesterday. The other was a loud pinto with blue eyes. The rest of the stalls were empty.

He walked to the back barn door and peered out. Two chestnut horses nosed through the dust in a small paddock, but he didn't see any others. *Interesting. There were seven last night. Maybe the other three are at the show.*

ↄℰↄ

Kim's feet burned and her back ached. The camera bag seemed to weigh fifty pounds, and she tried not to think about spending another day doing this. But more than the rigors of the show, the shock of seeing Quaid was giving her the biggest fits. She was dying to know what he'd learned. By now, he'd probably found Jasper and was one step ahead of her.

She focused her lens on the line-up of riders waiting for class results. She framed and captured each one, then her finger froze on the shutter button and she stopped breathing for a second. In the viewfinder, in perfect focus, the mystery man and woman leaned on the rail. Kim zoomed in and clicked off several shots, then watched them through her pseudo-binoculars. The couple seemed to be watching one horse in particular, a good-looking dark Thoroughbred with no white markings. The couple leaned together, talking and occasionally gesturing toward the animal. Kim shivered. Were they choosing their next target?

The announcer began calling out the results and a moment later, the Thoroughbred moved to the ring steward to accept the blue ribbon for the class. Kim kept her camera trained on the man and woman at the rail, seeing the satisfaction on their faces. If she didn't know better, she'd think they were the owners. That would make their presence at these events seem natural to anyone else.

The announcer called a ten-minute break and Kim hurried toward the barn to check Jasper's stalls again.

꙳

As he sped back toward Burbank, Quaid worked out the logistics that made sense for Jasper's disappearance. Tell everyone he'd be at a big show for four days, load some horses and take off. No one would even know he'd skipped town until he didn't return from the show. Maybe someone at the event would wonder why he didn't appear in classes, but with the chaos at the show grounds, anyone would think it possible that he'd scratched. With a four-day lead, Jasper could put a lot of miles between himself and the law. Quaid frowned. He hadn't seen anything in the article about criminal proceedings, but the charges against Jasper certainly warranted some jail time. So, why hadn't that happened?

Quaid headed for the arena. Time to confront Kovak about her involvement in this case. Whatever she knew, he had to find out. Time was now critical.

He arrived at the arena just as a new class began. Kovak stood in the center of the ring, panning shots of horses as they trotted past. Quaid walked around to the long side of the arena, hoping to catch her eye. He glanced at his watch. Three o'clock. How long would this thing go? Surely they'd break for dinner. He turned and headed for the show office to pick up a program, deciding to question the show secretary a little more about Jasper's non-registration.

He gave the guy his friendliest smile.

"Say, I was in here this morning looking for Jasper Martin, Rocking J Ranch. You said he wasn't registered, per se, but would his name be listed if he was showing a client's horse?"

"Usually, provided the information was sent by the deadline. Lots of folks decide to show at the last minute, so they aren't included the program." He opened the booklet to the back pages. "You see how the entries are listed? Just find the 'shown by' column to see if he's here. But like I said, there's no guarantee."

Quaid scanned the list over four pages, but Jasper's name was not there.

"What about late entries?"

"We don't allow them."

Quaid closed the program. The entire thing had been a ruse so everyone would think Jasper was at the show. Did that charade include the sister?

Quaid headed back toward the arena. He'd just have to wait until he could talk to Kovak to find out what she knew.

Two hours later, he exhaled in relief as the announcer called the show for the day. Kovak remained in the arena, writing something in a notebook, then she put her camera into a big black bag and hoisted it onto her shoulder. Quaid quickly moved down the steps of the grandstand, keeping her in sight the whole time. He had no idea if she knew he was still around or not, but he didn't want her to ditch him.

When he reached the ground, he hesitated. She wasn't headed toward the parking lot, but rather toward one of the horse barns. He followed, staying back just enough that he wouldn't show in her peripheral vision. Suddenly, she wheeled around and glowered at him.

"You want to tell me exactly what you're doing?"

He chuckled. "Sorry, just habit." He walked up to stand in front of her. "You done for the day?"

Her brown eyes had flecks of gold in them. Why hadn't he noticed that before?

She gave him a weak smile. "Yeah, thank God. I just might be getting too old for this kinda thing." Then she frowned. "You still haven't said why you're following me."

Quaid contemplated her for a moment, then decided to just play it straight.

"I was sent out here on a wild goose chase, thinking I'd be able to talk to Jasper Martin. Hah! I think he's long gone from these parts."

Kim's jaw dropped. "What do you mean? He's *here*. Or at least he has stalls here."

"You're kidding! The show secretary said he wasn't registered for the show. How could he have stalls?"

Kim didn't hesitate. "Come on, I'll show you."

Quaid followed her into one of the last barns, down two aisles, and around a corner. She stopped and gestured at three empty stalls. Each stall had a handwritten index card with Jasper's ranch name.

"I don't understand why he's so late bringing horses," she said. "He's missed the first day of qualifiers, so I'm guessing he doesn't care about winning anything."

"Or he just needed a way to be in two places at the same time."

Kim narrowed her eyes. "Not registered, huh?" She moved toward the doors at the side of the building. "There are eight barns on this side of the facility. No way would a show this small fill them all." She turned and looked at Quaid. "I'll bet he just came in here and put his name on these stalls with no intention of ever bringing horses. But why?"

"That would fit perfectly with my assumption that he's leaving town. This gives him a big head start."

"Too bad we can't put a trace on that big horse trailer he pulls. Wouldn't be hard to catch up to him."

Quaid scowled and stepped up close. Real close. "How do *you* know what kind of rig he has?"

Kovak didn't step back, but lifted her chin defiantly. "I drove by his place. So shoot me." She turned and started to walk away.

"Hold on, I think we need to talk. No point in getting huffy."

She stopped and stared at him for a moment. "Okay, but I'm starving, so whatever you have to say, it'll need to be over dinner."

Quaid turned on the charm. "Let's go."

Chapter 22

Kim slid into the passenger seat of Quaid's rental car and glanced over at him. Her initial annoyance had faded and she was more than a little surprised to realize that she was pleased to see him. Nothing romantic, just nice to see a familiar face in a strange place. And actually, she was glad to have a chance to hash out the Jasper thing. Maybe between the two of them, they could come up with some kind of answer.

Quaid started the car. "You up for Mexican? There's a place just across the road."

"Anything sounds good right now. I had one of those awful hotdogs for lunch."

"You know, they make those things outta horsemeat."

"That's not funny!"

In spite of herself, Kim laughed.

Then, she sobered. "Do you think that's what's going on with these stolen horses? Slaughter?"

He glanced over, his expression tight. "I think the only criminals who steal horses to sell them by the pound are the desperate ones. I believe we're dealing with a motivated person or group with a loftier plan. Horses like Talisman are worth a lot more than their weight. Especially to foreign buyers."

"I have a friend in Arizona...actually, she's Egyptian, but spends part of the year here. Anyway, she and her husband also mentioned the international market for good performance and breeding horses. Could be our answer."

Kim heard her use of the word "our" and Quaid's reference to "their" case. Satisfaction seeped into her head. She was back at the work she loved most, and with a good-looking partner to boot.

The restaurant parking lot was almost full. Kim fell into step beside Quaid and inhaled the fabulous southwestern aromas drifting on the air.

Quaid held the door for her. "Your Egyptian friend might be able to give us some foreign contacts."

Kim rolled her eyes. "She's terrified that she'll be targeted by whoever is stealing these animals. She even has armed guards posted at her stalls during horse shows."

"Can't blame her. Once horses are stolen, it's pretty close to impossible to get them back."

Kim's chest caved and she shuddered. "I can't even imagine how owners must feel when that happens."

A pretty, plump Mexican girl led them into the dim interior of the noisy restaurant. The walls were polished wood, and stained glass lamps hung on the walls above each booth, the light glowing through the red, yellow, and purple panes. Kim slid into one of the thick padded seats and watched Quaid remove his phone from his jeans pocket. This was Kim's first chance to look him over. He definitely looked ex-military. Not a hard-nosed veteran with a chip on his shoulder, but rather an almost executive, possibly retired-officer look. She estimated he was well over six feet tall and had clearly maintained a fit and trim body.

She suddenly realized he'd caught her staring and her face flamed.

"Something on your mind?" he said, sitting down.

"Just wondering where you got the scar on your hand."

Quaid looked down and flexed his fingers.

"Horse stepped on it."

Kim chuckled. "Funny. No, what really happened?"

"A horse stepped on it. Really."

"Jeez, I'm sorry. I thought you were kidding. It brings an interesting image to mind, you have to admit."

He gazed at her a moment. "Yeah, I can see where it would. Actually, it was more of a kick than a stomp."

A server appeared and took their drink orders, then left.

Kim sat back. "You were saying?"

"Horse was down, we were trying to help. My hand got in the way as he struggled. Clipped me with the edge of a horseshoe."

Kim watched him as he talked. She wanted to ask more questions, but didn't want him to know she'd checked up on him. Had this horse incident happened in the Army? Or perhaps Mr. Quaid was also involved with horses in some other part of his life.

Quaid drummed his fingers on the table. "What I can't figure out is why these thieves are bothering to find doubles for the stolen horses."

Kim leaned forward quickly, feigning amazement. "There's more than *one?*"

He nodded. "At least three other similar cases that I know of for my company alone. They've never bothered to follow up on the switches, just paid the theft claim and closed the files."

"Someone must have known they would do just that."

Quaid contemplated her for a long moment before speaking. "It's not a new concept, by any means, but to pull it off requires a network of people. In this case, across the entire country and maybe even beyond our shores."

Kim's brain was on fire. Her list of stolen horses, the matchup with horse shows, insurance claims, and a strong foreign market for quality horses. It was beginning to make sense. But how to get to the origination of the scheme? Who were the victims and who were the villains?

✿

Quaid watched Kovak's face, seeing the wheels turning in her brain. Her law enforcement background would make it almost impossible for her to know the details of the situation without trying to figure out the motives and principals involved. As she listened to him talk, her eyes glowed with the familiar excitement of the chase. He found himself noticing things like the roundness of her lower lip and the glint of lights in her dark red hair. He didn't see any emotional scars from her riot ordeal, but maybe she'd moved past that time of her life. But it puzzled him that she would leave the force when she so obviously loved police work.

Beers arrived and they held up their glasses.

"To Talisman, wherever he may be," said Kovak.

"Let's hope he's not in a hotdog somewhere."

"Dammit, quit saying that!"

This time, she didn't laugh.

"Sorry, I couldn't resist. Seriously though, I suspect he's stabled in some rich European's barn."

"What I don't understand is how someone could transport a

high profile performance horse without all the official paperwork, registration papers, and so on."

"You think those things can't be forged? Come on, you know better. The biggest problem in this scheme would be getting the horse through quarantine and customs here in this country. A lot of people would be involved, so there'd have to be a network of shady characters in place for those situations."

Kovak nodded. "Yeah, and it's probably not too impossible to do. I suspect a second-rate veterinarian would be able to make a good living on the shady side."

"Exactly. Just like that famous Belmont sting scandal."

Her face brightened. "Tell me. I'm not familiar with it."

"In the late seventies, a racetrack veterinarian in upstate New York bought three Thoroughbreds from South America. He sold two of the horses to wealthy men, one of whom immediately insured his horse for hundreds of thousands of dollars. Not long after the sale, the vet called that owner to tell him that the horse had fallen and fractured its skull. The owner made a claim and the insurance company paid without a hitch."

The food server appeared again to take orders. As soon as he was gone, Kovak leaned forward.

"Go on, this is fascinating."

"In the fall of that year, the vet entered one of the South American horses in the Belmont. The horse was a long-shot with terrible odds, but the vet bet heavily on him to win. He did, and the vet walked away eighty-thousand dollars richer. Unfortunately for him, a journalist in South America saw a photo of the Belmont winner and started investigating. Sure enough, the New York vet's horse was actually Uruguay's Horse of the Year, an almost identical twin to the horse that had died. The journalist reported his findings to someone in the U.S. and when the vet was questioned, he said it must have been a mix-up when the one horse died. Of course, the carcass had been rendered and there was no proof of wrongdoing, but the vet was convicted of entering a horse in a race using a false name. He paid a small fine."

"That's just bizarre."

"The hell of it is, that guy did the same thing a few years later.

He was never convicted, but he had a cloud of suspicion over him from then on."

Kovak's eyes gleamed. "Maybe that's what's going on here in reverse. Someone in another country is playing the same game."

"Could be."

"So, there has to be a common denominator in Talisman's case. Someone or something that applies to every aspect of the switch. What would be required every step of the way for this to succeed?"

He nodded thoughtfully, impressed by her logic. "A veterinarian."

꙰

Quaid's expression changed and Kim knew she'd have to either get in the game or play dodge ball. He put down his burrito and wiped his mouth with a napkin.

"Let's talk about your visit to Jasper's place."

"I only drove by to get a feel for the way he lives. I didn't go in, but I did see his truck and trailer sitting outside the barn, so I know that much."

"When was this? Before or after you came to the show grounds and discovered his stalls?"

"Before. That's why I kept expecting him to show up with horses. If he's on the run, then that might be a good indication he's directly involved in the Talisman switch."

"Or he's trying to ditch the IRS."

She leveled Quaid with a solemn look. "With them, you can run, but you can't hide. My money is on the insurance scam." She leaned forward. "So, you've been here at least twenty-four hours. What have *you* found out?"

His eyebrows came together. "*I'm* the one running this investigation, in case you've forgotten. I can't share information."

Kim slid out of the booth and tossed a twenty on the table. "Knock yourself out."

She strode toward the door, her chest aching with anger. *What a pompous ass. And I almost told him everything I know!*

When she reached the parking lot, she remembered that her own car was back at the equestrian center. She could see the entrance from where she stood, so she started walking in that direction.

"Kovak! Wait!"

She kept walking. Heavy footfalls sounded behind her and, though she knew it was Quaid, she still had the instinctive reflex to defend herself. She reached for her hip.

"Wait up. Hey, I'm sorry. That was stupid of me."

She turned to face him. "Yes, it was."

His eyes reflected true apology. "I'm just so used to working alone..."

Kim made a point of not responding, just gazing at him as though she were contemplating whether to stay or walk away.

He ducked his head. "Let's find a quiet bar somewhere and I'll tell you what I know."

She blew out a long breath. "Okay, but I need to turn in at a decent hour. First class tomorrow is at 7:30."

They walked in silence to Quaid's car, Kim wondering if they'd be able to retrieve the comfort zone they'd had before she got pissy.

Quaid pulled out of the parking lot and followed the signs to downtown Burbank. Kim gazed at the bright lights and heavy traffic.

"I can't believe how busy this place is. Makes Columbus look tame."

Quaid chuckled. "Yeah, I don't think anyone sleeps here. When I was a kid, I couldn't wait to leave the quiet hills of Ohio and see the world." He shook his head. "Some days, those quiet hills sound awfully good."

"Where is that?"

"Little town in Belmont County."

Kim waited, but he didn't elaborate.

He glanced over at her. "You?"

"Marietta. And you're right, those were peaceful times."

He pulled up to a stoplight and gestured up ahead. "I think there's a nice place on that corner. Elephant something." He glanced in the rearview mirror. "If I can just get over into the right lane."

A bit of quick maneuvering, then they turned the corner and found a parking space on the street. Kim glanced around. There were a lot of people on the sidewalks, but that wasn't surprising. It was Friday night on the Fourth of July weekend in the heart of

California. If anything, there'd be more people later on.

Quaid held the door for her and they entered the lounge. No loud music and only a few customers. They found a booth toward the back and ordered beer.

Kim sat back and crossed her arms. "I'm listening."

Quaid gave her a long look, then nodded. "I told you I found the barn manager, Roberta Dodge. Teri had fired her for supposedly doing serious drugs in the hay barn, but the woman says no. She thinks Teri was just being a bitch."

"Teri was anything but a bitch," said Kim. "I've known her quite awhile. Anyone who works with traumatized animals owns a great deal of compassion and forgiveness."

"I'm inclined to agree with you. I think there might have been something else going on at the Fortune barn."

Kim's radar came on. "Like what?"

"I'm not sure yet, but there might have been an affair with a married man. I think Dodge knew something about that."

Kim kept her face completely expressionless. Sure, she'd agreed to share her information, but somehow she couldn't let go of this tidbit. She hadn't had time to follow up on the rest of Teri's clients and, until she did, she was reserving judgment on Teri's moral integrity.

Quaid continued. "I think she was involved in the scam."

Kim shook her head vigorously. "No, I don't believe that. She was..."

"She was *what?*"

"Okay, she *was* having an affair with a married man. Hard to believe someone would kill her over that, but I guess it would depend on *who* the man was."

Quaid pushed his beer away and scowled. "And how do you know all this?"

"You asked me to track down Teri's relatives and, in the course of that task, I talked to a client who had firsthand knowledge of the affair."

"And why didn't you tell me this?"

"Oh, you mean during all of our mega-sharing?" Kim snorted. "Besides, it's *your* investigation, not mine. Remember?"

"Then why are you meddling? Who are *you* working for?"

Kim smiled wickedly. "I'm not at liberty to say."

Quaid's face darkened, but he didn't respond. Kim pulled some money out of her pocket and laid it on the table.

"I need to get going. But first, I'm curious as to why *you* are acting like a cop. Aren't you simply tasked with verifying that Jasper's insurance claim is legitimate?"

If she'd hit him alongside the head, Quaid couldn't have looked more surprised.

As they walked out of the bar, Kim grinned. *Score one for Kovak.*

The night air was warm and Kim took a minute to adjust to the transition from heavy air-conditioning. Quaid mumbled something about the crowds and Kim looked around, at once surprised by the hundreds of people moving along the sidewalks and into the street.

"What's going on? Is there a parade or something?"

"Uh-oh, I see a banner." Quaid's tone wasn't comforting.

Kim looked in the direction he pointed and saw it too. A sea of people surged toward them, waving banners and placards saying "Occupy Burbank." The noise level grew and Kim's heartbeat began to hammer in her ears.

Quaid took her elbow and started to guide her through the crowd that had formed between them and the car. Bumping each other and shouting, people flowed around them like flood waters. Quaid lost his grasp and the throng swallowed up Kim. Panic crashed through her chest and she looked around, trying to see Quaid, but she'd been carried too far into the crowd. She struggled against the forward movement, making no headway, all the while fighting the terror that threatened to knock her to the ground to be trampled. Or shot.

Someone grabbed her and she began to fight with everything she had.

"Kovak! Stop! It's me!"

Quaid grabbed both her arms and propelled her toward the edge of the crowd. He pushed her up next to a building and she blindly let him guide her to the corner. They hurried down the side street and the undulating swarm of people moved on down the main street.

Kim's body was shaking so hard her teeth chattered, then suddenly she was up against Quaid's chest, gasping for air and letting the sobs rise in her throat. He held her tightly, his voice rumbling through his chest.

"It's okay, you're safe now. Just breathe."

Chapter 23

Kovak was silent on the way back to the equestrian center, and Quaid didn't push it. He'd seen the terror on her face when she'd been swallowed up by the demonstrators. A chill ran over his shoulders. She must have been reliving her tragedy in Columbus. The stimulus of a crowd out of control, her helplessness to do anything about it. He glanced at her profile. She stared straight forward and he could see a glisten at the corner of her eye. She wouldn't sleep well tonight.

Tough ex-cop, independent woman, but she'd been soft and vulnerable in her fear. He was glad he'd been there for her. And for him. It had been a long time since he'd held a woman in his arms.

Quaid pulled up beside her car and turned off the ignition. "You okay now?"

She nodded, but didn't look at him. "Thanks for getting me out of that." Strain showed on her features, but she squared her shoulders. "What's your plan of attack for tomorrow?"

"I'm going back out to Jasper's to see if I can learn anything. Do you think we could talk some more after you're finished with the show tomorrow?"

She leveled a stern look at him. "As long as we're on the same playing field. No more games."

"You got it. I'll call you in the afternoon."

She nodded and climbed out of the car. Quaid waited until she was safely inside her own vehicle, then headed toward Pasadena to get some sleep.

๛

Kim sat in the car, trying not to think about what she'd just been through. Even with the years that had passed since Columbus, it only took one trigger incident to send her reeling into the depths of fear. Would she ever move past it?

She started the car and drove slowly around the access road surrounding the facility. Mr. Tough Guy had certainly shown a surprising side to his personality. Thinking about his comforting arms, warmth moved over her skin. In the moment, she'd only cared about being safe, but in retrospect, the sensation of being held was more than pleasant.

They'd sparred all evening, neither one wanting to give an inch to the other, playing cat and mouse with ideas and information. Her smile faded. Playing games with someone else's future. Teri murdered—it seemed incomprehensible, but Quaid certainly had the resources to get solid information. Could it possibly be the wife of the errant husband? Murder seemed a little extreme for a domestic issue, but passion could be a powerful force.

Kim's car moved slowly past the practice rings and the outbuildings, down the road between the many barns, and on through the exhibitor parking lots. She glanced around as she drove, then hit the brakes.

Jasper's rig was parked by the fence near the last barn.

꒰ઘ꒱

Quaid's phone rang just as he let himself into the motel room.

"It's Kim. I just found Jasper's truck and horse trailer parked in the lot. You might want to come back and surprise him."

"I'm on my way. Don't leave and *don't* go anywhere near him."

The line went dead and he scowled at the screen. *I see Miz Kovak is back to normal.*

Twenty-five minutes later, he strode across the parking lot toward the horse trailers. A car flashed its lights and he headed that way. Kovak popped her door lock and he climbed in.

"You think he'll be in the barn with his horses?"

She pursed her lips. "Hard to tell. We don't know when he got here, but it was obviously after the show closed."

Quaid looked out the window at Jasper's rig. "He must be here, 'cause the truck is still hooked up."

"Sometimes trainers sleep in the tack stall to be near the horses during the night. This place has good security, so I can't imagine he would need to."

Quaid opened the door. "I'm gonna go find him. You stay here."

"Hey, wait just a minute! You need to stop treating me like a subordinate. I gave you the courtesy of the phone call, and I didn't go over there, like you asked. Now, I want to see what's going on just as much as you do."

Quaid hesitated. "Okay, but let me do the talking."

She climbed out of the car and, without further conversation, they walked toward the barn with Jasper's stalls. At the end of the row, they peered into each stall, then looked at each other in surprise.

The stalls were still empty.

Quaid headed for the door, Kovak right behind him.

"He might have just gotten here and the horses are still on the trailer," she said.

"We'll know in a minute."

The trailer was empty.

"Maybe he put them in a different barn."

Kovak moved to the front of the truck and laid her hand on the hood. "It's stone cold. Been sitting here for hours. I think you might be right—Jasper has pulled off a vanishing act."

"None of this makes sense. The first time I went to his place, there were seven horses. When I went back out this afternoon, there were only four."

"Did you talk to anyone there?"

"Yeah, his obnoxious sister. She gave me jack-shit. Sent me here to supposedly talk to Jasper in person. She was gone when I went back today."

"Rumor has it that the sister owns all the horses. She could be the key to the whole thing."

Quaid exhaled sharply. "There are too many pieces to this puzzle, so I'm beginning to think we're working on *two* puzzles."

After Kovak drove away, Quaid moved the driver's seat back and stretched his legs. From where he'd parked, he had a good view of both the doors to the barn and Jasper's rig. If the guy was still on the premises, or tried to move the truck, Quaid would know it. He wrote down the license numbers, then began organizing his thoughts about what he knew. The horse show seemed a perfect cover if Jasper planned to skip town, but something didn't quite mesh.

Okay. Put his name on the show stalls so people would think he's here. Bring the rig and leave it to reinforce that supposition. Have another vehicle in place to use later? Have the sister pick him up? Is he already long gone?

A movement by one of the barns caught Quaid's eye and he

sat up straight. Someone was leading a horse between the buildings, headed for the barn with Jasper's stalls. Quaid jumped out of the car and moved quickly between the parked vehicles, keeping the shadowy figures in sight. He broke into a trot as the person and horse disappeared into the barn.

Slipping through the door, he spotted a man leading a brown horse straight toward the end stalls.

Quaid caught up to him, then realized it wasn't Jasper.

"Excuse me, do you have horses in this barn?"

The man gave him a curious look. "Yeah, why?"

"Have you seen the owner of those stalls at the end?"

The guy looked where Quaid pointed, then nodded. "Yeah, he was here earlier, but I haven't seen him since."

Quaid glanced at the animal. "Nice horse. What breed?"

"She's a Holsteiner. You own horses?"

"Not any more. Sure wish I did, though."

The man whipped out a business card and smiled like a used car salesman. "You just give me a call when you get ready. We breed top show horses from some of the best bloodlines."

"Gee, thanks. I'll do that."

The man nodded. "Well, nice talkin' to you. I need to get this lady to her bed. She has a big day tomorrow."

"Good luck."

Quaid pocketed the card and waited until the man was out of sight, then he moved down the aisle toward Jasper's stalls.

Still empty.

Chapter 24

The telephone on the nightstand shrilled and Kim came awake with a start, groping to silence the damned thing and knocking over her glass of water in the process. An automated voice announced her wake-up time of five-thirty.

She struggled to sit up and clear her head. Exhausted as she'd been when she went to bed, the crowd scene in town had dominated her brain all night. Today would be horrible, but she didn't have much choice. Lots of coffee and some energy bars would be her only hope.

An hour later, somewhat refreshed by a shower and beginning to feel the effects of the caffeine, Kim headed for the equestrian park. Thinking about how little information she and Quaid had shared, she wondered if they'd ever land on the same page and solve the mystery. Or, as Quaid had said, two mysteries. Kim glanced at the dashboard clock and calculated time differences. She could make a couple more calls to the Midwest and East before she started work. Late last night, she'd checked her voice mail and found a return call from Bob Fisher. If he knew Teri well, he might also know a relative or close friend. Someone needed to step forward and be there for that poor girl. Had her body even been released for burial? Who would bury her? Kim counted the days since Teri's death. If she'd been claimed, the funeral would probably be the coming week. If there was no family, then Teri would rest in the morgue until someone took responsibility for her remains.

Kim parked near the show office and pulled out her phone. She had forty-five minutes before she had to be in the arena. She was going to get some answers.

"Mr. Fisher? Kim Kovak. I called you yesterday, sorry I missed your return call."

The man's voice wavered with age. "Not a problem. You said you were looking for show horses? I have a few left to sell."

"Actually, no. I'm calling about Teri Fortune."

"Oh my, yes, what a shock. She was a wonderful girl."

"One of her clients said you knew her quite well...do you happen to know if she has any relatives or a husband or children, or anyone who would be responsible for her, uh, business?"

"Yes, I knew her very well for many years. She took such good care of my horses when they were stressed. One time—"

Kim tried to be gentle. "Excuse me, but you were going to tell me about Teri's family?"

"Oh, yes, of course. She never married, always said the horses were all the family she needed." He chuckled. "Said they were more dependable than husbands or lovers."

He fell silent for a moment, then continued.

"You know, I think there was a brother somewhere. She never talked about him. I think they had a big falling out when they were younger. It's too bad, isn't it, the way families fall apart over insignificant stuff? You know what I mean?"

"I do. You know where the brother might be? Or his name?"

"No idea on either count, but I do know he was in the investment business of some kind. Hah, what a bunch of crooks *those* guys turned out to be! Makin' a fortune off the backs of us ordinary people. You hear about those demonstrations in the cities? I'd be there if I was younger."

Kim shuddered and gripped the phone harder, trying to modulate her tone. "Thanks so much for calling me back. If you think of anything else, please get in touch with me."

She disconnected and exhaled slowly. The name Fortune couldn't be too common. Narrow it down to men in the financial sector and she'd probably only have a couple hundred to search through. She ran her finger along the rim of the steering wheel. She didn't have the resources to look for the guy, but she knew someone who did. If she could make even one aspect of Teri's death understandable, it would be worth it.

✥

Quaid started making calls early. He checked in with United Equine, then called Jenna at the house. Her recorder picked up immediately and he remembered they'd gone to Dayton for the weekend. He hung up without leaving a message, then dialed her cell phone.

"Hey, Jenna, how's the trip so far?"

Her voice sounded more relaxed than it had in years.

"Really good, Garrett. I'm so glad you insisted I do this." She lowered her voice. "Ricky's in the bathroom, so I'll have to make this quick. We met with the psychologist yesterday and he's given Ricky a clean mental health bill. He doesn't feel there's a risk of self-destruction, just the expected post trauma depression, which he'll treat with mild anti-anxiety medication."

"That's great news. Are you going to the museum today?"

"Yes, we'll get some breakfast in a few minutes, then spend the day just relaxing. I met with base housing yesterday and we do qualify." Her tone saddened. "I hate to move away from everything that's so familiar, but I don't have a choice. And there's plenty of work in the area, so getting a job shouldn't be too hard."

A hard knot formed in Quaid's chest. He couldn't imagine having what was left of his family living so far away. Guilt pushed at the knot. He'd been right there the whole time and had squandered many opportunities to be part of that family. He had no right to feel anything but happiness that Jenna and Ricky could get their lives back together. Now if only he could do the same.

"I'm still in California, but I'll be home Tuesday night. I told Ricky we'd take a road trip next week, so if that's okay with you, I'd like to plan on it."

"Absolutely. He's talked about nothing else. Thank you for doing this for him."

"I'm doing it for me, too, Jenna."

The phone beeped and Quaid said goodbye, but Kovak had already hung up. He dialed her back and she answered, sounding out of breath.

He chuckled. "You running with the horses?"

"No, I just let the time get away from me and had to sprint to the arena for the first class. Now they've taken a time out, so I have a minute. I have a lead on Teri's brother, no first name, but he's in the financial sector, maybe investment, maybe banking. I don't know, but I don't have any way to track him down. I thought you'd probably have better luck."

"Good work. I'll get on it right away. I was about to call the sheriff's office to see where they stand with the investigation and who's caring for the horses. I'll call you when I have something."

"Great. Gotta go."

She hung up and Quaid pursed his lips. The two of them actually worked pretty well together, except when they were competing. He wasn't used to working with anyone, especially a woman, but she might turn out to be okay.

"Delaware County Sheriff's Office, how may I direct your call?"

"This is Garrett Quaid, United Equine Assurance. I need to speak to Deputy Dexton."

"I'll transfer you."

Quaid drummed his fingers on the table while he waited. He'd better not get the runaround again.

"Dexton, homicide."

"Yeah, we talked a couple of days ago about the Fortune Farms case. I'm just following up on a couple of things."

"We didn't discuss the case, Mr. Quaid, and it's still an open investigation. So why are you bothering me?"

Quaid closed his eyes and tried to picture the woman on the other end of the line. She had a clipped way of speaking, and the image that came to mind was a tight-lipped, pasty-skinned blonde with no boobs and a flat ass. That helped.

"Actually, I need to know the disposition of the facility and those animals. Are they being cared for?"

"Yes, Animal Control sent someone out there until we find a relative or friend to take responsibility. Do you know anyone connected with the deceased?"

Quaid scowled. No help from her, but *he* was supposed to spew information.

"No, I don't, but I do know that some of those horses belong to other people and I think they need to be notified to collect their animals."

"We didn't find a client list."

"You can probably figure it out by looking through the accounting ledgers. But I'm *sure* you've already done that, right?"

Dexton hesitated just a second before answering. "Of course.

But if you have any information, you're required to give it to us."

"Hey, I want this solved as much as you do. If I find out anything, I'll let you know. Have a nice day."

He disconnected and kicked the chair. "I hate working with hormones!"

After the lunch break, Kim returned to the center of the arena to photograph each jumper as they completed the pattern. All morning she'd watched classes and, amongst the spectators, she'd frequently seen the man and woman who now seemed to play some important role in the mystery. They either stood at the rail or sat in the grandstand, always watching closely, talking, and writing things down. To outward appearances, they were simply interested and involved in what was going on, but Kim was sure that something ominous lay behind their presence.

She glanced toward the other side of the ring, wondering when Quaid would show up. Had he started looking for Teri's brother? If anyone could find the guy, it would be Quaid.

The last round of jumps finished, the announcer called for a break and the ground crew entered the arena to start rearranging the obstacles. Kim sucked up half a bottle of water, then walked toward the barn where Jasper wasn't. Many stalls were now empty, their residents on the road home after a busy weekend. Some would be going home to celebrate and others would be dejected at having spent the time and money to get to the qualifying show only to go home without enough points for the championships. Kim's memories flew back to her own brief showing career. The little girl who would rather jump fences than jump rope. She'd done okay, but hadn't had the ambition to become a world-class equestrienne. She'd only wanted to have fun with her horse. Thank God, Grandpa had recognized that. Kim remembered the horseshow moms who'd made everyone's life miserable, including those of their horse-crazy daughters.

Kim passed a woman stuffing blankets and supplies into a large tack trunk. She looked tired. A roan pony gazed listlessly through the bars of the stall. Kim continued to the end of the aisle and around the corner to Jasper's area. Peering into the empty stalls, she blinked in disbelief. Fresh bedding, and water buckets full to the brim. Someone had expected horses to fill these stalls. Was it Jasper? And why now, when the show was all but over?

She headed back toward the arena to finish the last leg of the show. She was so glad to have the work, but happy that it was almost over. Her thigh ached as it always did when she was stressed, and she wondered if the mob incident had triggered the pain.

A woman leading two horses appeared and Kim moved aside to let them pass. They were beautiful animals and, for one moment, Kim wondered if maybe it was time to own a horse again. She at least had the flexibility of schedule and leisure time to enjoy riding. She gazed down the aisle at the shiny rumps undulating rhythmically with the even cadence of the walk. Her knees wobbled and a murmur ran through her chest. Would she ever be able to do that again? The horses rounded the corner out of sight and Kim took a deep breath, then continued toward the exit.

At the door, she came face to face with the man she'd been watching for days. Her breath caught in her throat, but she nodded and started to pass by.

His deep voice formed words rounded with what sounded like a British accent. "You're the show photographer, right?" His dark eyes seemed to belie his attempt at a smile. "What's your name? We were thinking of having our stallion photographed."

"Kim Kovak. I'm from Ohio, but I could give you a referral to someone from around here."

"Ohio! Oh my, so are we. What a coincidence. Do you have a business card?"

Kim handed one over, completely baffled by his manner. Could she have lost her knack for recognizing someone who wasn't on the up and up?

He read it and smiled. "Thanks. We'll ring you up next week."

"Are you showing here? I've seen you at almost every class." The words were out before she'd had time to think.

A shadow passed over his face, then he nodded. "Yes, but mostly we're watching horses we bred. And they are doing well." He bobbed his head and took a step back. "We'll talk to you soon."

Kim was back in the center of the arena before she realized she hadn't gotten his name.

Chapter 25

Quaid stared at the list. Fortune wasn't as unusual a name as
he'd originally thought. Even refining the list to include only men's
first names, the pages listed over 150 people spread all across the
country. One in particular—a Reginald Fortune, age 49—lived
in fourteen states, but the two Ohio addresses made him a good
beginning prospect. Just for the heck of it, Quaid also entered
"Reggie" in the search field. Another thirty men of the same age
popped up and, interestingly, two more addresses in Ohio, although
not in the same towns as the "Reginald".

Quaid sat back and thought for a moment. How to narrow
the search to a reasonable number? Kovak had said the brother
might be in banking or something similar. If Reginald Fortune was,
indeed, the brother, then he wouldn't be in banking—not with that
many different addresses. Banks tended to keep people in place for
extended periods of time, maybe a move to a nearby branch, but not
all over the country. No, if the guy was involved in something about
money, it was probably for mortgages or high interest personal loans.
Or maybe one of those payroll advance places.

An idea began to grow in Quaid's head. Teri Fortune was in
deep financial trouble. How could that be if she had a family member
who was in the money business? Maybe she never told the brother she
was in trouble. Maybe she did and he refused to help her. That would
be a big blow to someone, to be on the edge of disaster and have
your own blood refuse to help. It would certainly push a vulnerable
person over the edge. Enough to commit suicide?

Quaid exhaled slowly. But that's not what happened, much
as someone wanted it to seem that way. How could this fraud
investigation have turned into such a complicated mess?

He picked up the phone and dialed the first name on the list.

Kim scanned the stands for the man she'd spoken to earlier.
Neither he nor the woman were anywhere to be seen. Kim pulled out
the class schedule and marked off the one she'd just photographed.

Only five more to go. Thinking about the bedded stalls she'd seen earlier, she wondered why Jasper would go to so much trouble just to cast attention away from the fact that he wasn't actually on the grounds.

The final rounds for the jumpers had a smaller number of exhibitors. As the first horse entered the ring, Kim nodded her approval. The beautiful Thoroughbred she'd admired the day before was, in her opinion, the best prospect for champion. He was fluid and graceful, athletic and strong, and eager. His beautiful eyes and alert ears told the story. He loved his work.

Kim followed him over every jump, using her skill at capturing the animal at just the right moment. Then, as her brain registered a familiar face at the rail, she punched the shutter button at the wrong time. She refocused, trying to ignore the dark-eyed man watching the performance.

A thread of nerves moved through her gut. This horse was a prime target for the black market in valuable horses. She leafed quickly through her program, looking for the horse's name and owner. They were stalled in the same barn as Jasper. How could she alert the owner to the danger without looking like a lunatic? The horse left the ring and Kim felt helpless. She had to stay where she was until the show was over. By that time, it could be too late.

The man at the rail had disappeared.

If Quaid were there, she could tell him of her suspicions and he could follow up. The announcer called a gate hold and Kim signaled the ring steward, pointing toward the building with the restrooms. She took off at a dead run, pulling her phone out of her pocket as she went. Quaid's phone went straight to voice mail.

Kim skidded to a stop, then waited for the tone. "Quaid, you need to get over here as soon as possible. I think there's another theft in the works."

ﭏ

Quaid crossed the tenth Reginald Fortune off the list. There had to be a better way to do this, but there wasn't. This was what private investigators did. Investigate. Track. Wait. Watch.

He started to dial the next number, then noticed an alert for voice mail. A minute later, he charged out the door to the parking lot. With Kovak's background, he wasn't about to shrug off her concern. He sped down the highway on autopilot, his brain working on what she'd said. How would she know something was happening that related to the theft investigation? The only way would be if she had some information that he didn't. Which meant she *was* working undercover and she'd been playing him all along.

Ten minutes later, he wheeled into the parking lot and took a deep breath. He'd already learned that handling Miz Kovak took some restraint, but one way or the other, he would find out exactly what she was up to.

She stood in the center of the arena and he walked to the side rail where he might catch her eye. She looked up, saw him, and nodded. A minute later, the horse in the ring left through the out-gate and there was a brief pause in the activities. She hurried over to the railing and handed him her program.

"Go to this barn, to the stalls I marked. This horse has won everything here and he's had a lot of attention by a man that sets off my radar."

Quaid looked at her, astonished. "You *have* to be kidding! You dragged me down here because you don't like the way some guy *looks?*"

Kovak's eyes narrowed and her jaw line hardened. "I don't have time right now to explain the whole thing. You'll have to trust me."

The loudspeaker hummed, then the announcer came on. "The last class of the day is scratched. Exhibitors are asked to check out with..."

She cocked her head. "Are you with me or not?"

"Lead the way. This I gotta see."

Minutes later, they entered the barn. Kovak checked the program for the stall numbers, then headed down an aisle. Her step quickened and Quaid hurried to keep up.

Her voice rang out. "Excuse me? Mister?"

A man standing in front of a stall turned toward her. "Oh, hello. Did you get pictures of Robidoux? Wasn't that fabulous?"

He turned back to the stall and stroked the nose of a large dark horse chewing a mouthful of hay.

Kovak looked confused and Quaid suppressed a smile. She'd

almost stepped in it.

"Yes, it was. You must be thrilled," she said.

The man glanced at his watch. "Yes, we are, but you'll have to excuse me right now. I'm meeting my wife and some prospective buyers."

"What's your name so I can mark the photos accordingly?"

"Bill Smith. I'll be sure to look at those pictures when you put them up."

He nodded to Quaid, then moved quickly down the aisle toward the door. When he was out of earshot, Quaid chuckled.

"That was close."

Kovak didn't smile. "This is not what it seems, no matter what you think."

"What I think isn't important. I want to know why you thought this was something other than an owner and his horse."

"Because that man—"

"Hello!" said a voice behind them. "Are you interested in buying him?" A young man smiled broadly. "If you watched the show, you know he's a contender for some national trophies."

Kovak's jaw dropped, but she recovered quickly. "You're the one who rode him?"

"Yes, I trained him from a colt." The man held out his business card. "David Craig."

Kovak took the card, then looked up. "I'm Kim Kovak. I was the show photographer this weekend. Congratulations on your wins. Your photos will be on the website early next week. The address is in the show program."

"Great, I'll look forward to seeing them."

The trainer slid open the stall door and stepped inside. Kovak turned on her heel and started down the aisle, her shoulders rigid and her stride determined. She wouldn't be easy to talk to now.

Outside the barn, she stopped and turned to face him. "You still have trouble believing my gut feelings? The first guy is the one who's been watching horses all weekend and now I'm convinced he's up to something neither of us wants to think about."

Quaid nodded. "It does seem a little strange that he acted like he owns the horse. And how does he know *you?*"

"He stopped me earlier, said he and his wife wanted photographs of their stallion. I almost bought into this last charade. If that trainer hadn't come along, it would have worked."

Quaid moved closer. "Is there something else you aren't telling me?"

Kovak's eyes flashed. "I've seen the guy before. At other horse shows."

"That's not so unusual...wait a minute! The faces blurred out of that Talisman photograph. That's who it was, isn't it? You knew all along he might have something to do with this case."

"I couldn't be sure, but now I'm convinced he's a scout looking for horses to steal."

"Based on just seeing him at a horse show?"

She met him eye to eye. "He's shown up in the background of every major horse show photo I found in areas where horses were stolen. From Ohio to Washington, DC, to right here. It's no coincidence."

"And you were going to tell me this *when?*"

"About the same time you start sharing what *you* know."

Quaid stared stonily at her for a moment, then nodded in the direction of the covered arena.

"Let's find a place to talk."

۔ۏ۔

Kim's confidence had wavered briefly during the exchange with the mystery man, but she'd seen something in his eyes that contradicted his "happy horse owner" pretext. Quaid's presence hadn't helped much either. He was too eager to discount her theory, watch her crash and burn. But personality conflicts aside, they were the only people who might figure this thing out and, if for no other reason than saving future horses from theft, Kim wanted that.

They walked in silence toward the covered arena that was the jewel of Southern California equestrian facilities. Kim was momentarily stunned by the sheer size of the place. The arena was almost the length of a football field with tiered rows of seats surrounding the performance area. The soft brown earth floor was perfectly level and showed the faint striping left behind by the arena drag. The air was cool and still, and the strain of the day began to fade. She settled into one of the seats and Quaid sat down beside her.

There in the huge building, facing an empty and quiet arena, the atmosphere seemed to encourage honest conversation. Reminding herself that this wasn't about gamesmanship, Kim took the lead.

"That dark-eyed man first caught my eye in some pictures I took in Kentucky. I was concentrating on my client's security guards who seemed to appear in every photo, and I was wondering how I could crop them out. That's when I noticed this guy and woman standing on the rail in many of the shots. They were there for the entire show, but I didn't think too much about it at the time."

Quaid nodded. "I was standing next to him yesterday."

"When I checked on those Talisman photographs for you, I saw the couple again and it was so bizarre that my mind started working on an idea. And when I finally started trying to connect the various horse thefts to shows in particular regions, the couple appeared in almost every shot."

She glanced at him. "And here they are again."

Quaid's brow furrowed. "Under the circumstances, why wouldn't you tell me this? And why go the extra step and remove them from the photo you sent me?"

Kim felt a little foolish, but she didn't let it show. "You just came on a little too bullish and it pissed me off." She grinned. "Sorry. Once a cop, always a cop."

"Yeah, about that..."

"Don't even go there. My interest and concern here is to see that whoever is stealing these horses is caught and put out of commission."

Quaid gazed at her a moment. "So this Bill Smith now has your business card and probably knows you've been snooping. Doesn't that worry you?"

"Not even a little. In the big picture, this guy is a grunt. I want the bastard who's making all the money."

"Do you think Jasper is that person?"

"No, he's involved somehow, but I think he's actually more of a victim, maybe even a pawn."

Quaid nodded. "I tend to agree with you. Here's what I know so far."

Kim listened closely as he described his talks with the horse hauler and the sheriff's deputy in Delaware. His frustration with bureaucracy was deep.

He shook his head. "I have some pretty good contacts in the metro police departments, but damn, these small town forces keep things close."

Kim grinned. "I hear you. It's always been that way." She stopped smiling. "So you don't know anything further about Teri? What about the horses, who's taking care of them?"

"Animal control. I suggested they contact the horse owners and have them picked up, since they aren't material evidence. They gave me some song and dance about not finding a client list."

Uh-oh.

His eyes narrowed and his jaw tightened. "You know anything about that?"

"I have it. I used it to track down any possible friends or relatives. That's how I learned about the brother." Kim used that forward momentum to derail the subject. "You have any luck with that?"

Quaid didn't answer right away and she could see that he was weighing out whether to light into her about stealing the client list or stay on track with the conversation. This was starting to feel like a contest again.

Finally, he told her what he'd found so far on possible matches for Teri's brother. As he talked, Kim realized that if she and Quaid were going to get to the bottom of these mysteries, they'd simply have to work together.

Quaid used every ounce of self-control to keep from steamrolling over Kovak. She'd been working on her own and finding out stuff he needed, information that could have saved him a lot of legwork and frustration. Why the hell was she so intent on solving this case herself? Sure, she had cop instincts, but if she was so crazy to do the job, why had she left it?

She sat quietly for a few moments, then cleared her throat. "Do you know if the coroner has finished with Teri yet?"

Quaid's gut clenched. He did *not* want to go there. But she'd asked and he'd have to tell her sooner or later, but for sure before she found out from someone else.

"Yes, but the news isn't good." He hesitated, seeing the concern in her eyes. "Teri was dead before she was strung up."

Chapter 26

Kim had struggled to keep from losing it when Quaid told her about Teri. Even now, two hours later, far from the show site, locked safely inside her motel room, she grappled with the grief that threatened to overwhelm her. True, she'd only known Teri as a client and casual friend for a couple of years, but being murdered made the relationship so much more painful. Was Teri's death tied to the horse thefts? Or did the murder have nothing to do with the horses and everything to do with illicit sex?

Kim paced the room, shivering in the extreme AC. She'd had every intention of telling Quaid the name of Teri's lover, but his news had paralyzed her to the point she'd forgotten all about it. Until now. Would it play any part in his investigation of Talisman? She didn't think so. What she needed to do was give the information to the Delaware County Sheriff's Department first thing in the morning. But right now, she just wanted to get warm.

Her phone rang as she headed for the bed. "Dixie, you are just the person I want to talk to."

Kim climbed into the bed and pulled the covers up close, snuggling down in the pillow and absorbing the comforting sound of Dixie's voice. It didn't matter that the conversation would soon turn serious. For now, all Kim wanted was to be connected to someone who cared.

"I'm cold and tired and wishing I hadn't taken this job. But it's over now and I can come home on Monday."

"Why not tomorrow?"

"No flights available."

"Go to the airport and sign up for standby. It's worked for me several times."

"I could try that, I guess. What have you been up to?"

"I have to move my mother into a place where she'll have some supervision."

"A *nursing home?*"

"No, thank God. It's an assisted living facility. She'll have her own room and bathroom, with access to the dining room and library and recreation room. Plus, the nursing staff is available twenty-four hours a day."

"Is she sick?"

Dixie sighed. "Not physically, but her mind is going and she is becoming a danger to herself. With my job, I can't have her here, so this is the best I can do."

Dixie sounded so dejected that Kim wanted to reach through the phone and hold her. Hug her close the way Dixie had done for her only a few days ago. This was not the time to talk about Teri Fortune.

"I'm so sorry. Is there anything I can do?"

Dixie's tone was soft. "No, this is something I have to do on my own. But thank you for caring. See you when you get home."

Throwing the covers back, Kim sat up. Her stomach growled, reminding her she hadn't eaten anything since midday. She'd treat herself to a nice pasta dinner and call it an early night. With any luck, in the morning she'd go to Victory Farms, and still have time to check in for standby flights.

As she reached for the doorknob, her phone rang. It was Quaid.

"You'd better get back here to the show grounds. There are horses in Jasper's stalls."

آيت

Quaid moved along the almost empty aisles of the big barn, listening to the sounds of exhibitors packing up and moving out. He still couldn't believe what he'd seen. It was just a fluke that he'd decided to come back and check one more time, even though the show was over. Were those Jasper's horses? In place and waiting for transport to who-knew-where, playing a part in his scheme? Quaid's original theory about Jasper using the stalls simply as a distraction had been the most logical, but now it wasn't so clear.

He glanced at his watch. Where the hell was Kovak? He'd called her twenty minutes ago and she was staying right downtown.

"Quaid! Over here."

He met her in the middle of the aisle and told her the situation, including that Jasper's rig was still parked in the same spot.

169

She nodded. "Let's have a look at the horses. I suspect some-one's just using the stalls as holding pens while they pack their trailer. But it could be something different altogether. And I think our original assumption is correct about the rig being a ploy to keep everyone guessing."

They walked toward the corner of the barn, passing the open doors. Horse trailers were cozied up to the building for easier loading, and the shrill whinnies of horses on the move filled the air.

They rounded the corner and Quaid stopped.

"Nuts. They've already moved a couple of them."

"Do you remember what they looked like?"

He rolled his eyes. "Oh yeah—brown, four legs. What do *you* think?"

She touched his sleeve. "Let's move on down the aisle and see who comes for the last one. Then we'll know."

As she started past the stall, she glanced inside. "Quaid, I think that's Robidoux!"

"Who-bidoo?

"The Thoroughbred we saw today with mystery man."

"You go see if that trainer is still around. He'll remember you. I'll stay here and keep an eye on this situation."

Kovak walked up the aisle and out of sight. Quaid moved farther away so he wasn't standing right in front of Jasper's stalls. A minute later, a short, dark-skinned man with a heavy mustache walked up to the stall and slid the door open. He stepped inside and Quaid heard a grunt. He moved forward quickly, arriving at the stall just as the man came out leading the large dark horse.

"Excuse me, Mister? Do you know where I can find a trainer named David Craig?"

The man's brows came together and he shook his head. "He go home now."

"Is he still here, is he going home soon?"

"Gone. I take the horse."

Quaid glanced at the animal. He stood quietly, his ears slightly lopped. His eyes didn't have the bright sparkle they'd shown earlier in the day. *He's been drugged.*

The groom turned and led the horse away, and Quaid charged

off to find Kovak.

She was just coming around the corner, shaking her head. "The stalls are empty, but someone in the same aisle told me David Craig and his horses left the grounds this afternoon, probably right after we talked to him."

Quaid turned and gazed back toward Jasper's stalls. "Then whose horse was that?"

Concern knitted her eyebrows. "I don't know, but we should do something."

She headed toward the doors.

"Like what?"

She didn't answer and Quaid hurried to catch up. Outside, Kovak stood still, gazing at a shiny blue horse trailer with the words "David Craig Stables" in gold along the side.

She turned and shrugged. "False alarm."

⚜

Kim watched Quaid take a huge bite of his hamburger. *So much for a nice pasta dinner.* They'd stopped at a neighborhood diner with so-so food and a lot of noise. She picked through her salad, trying to decide whether to tell Quaid everything she knew about Teri's affair. Kim had been the one who objected to the cat-and-mouse games they'd been playing, so why was she considering keeping to the same path?

Quaid wiped his mouth. "I did a license search on Jasper's rig. It's registered in his sister's name."

"Huh, just like the horses. Of course, I have no proof of that, but with the tax thing, I'm sure it was done on purpose for just such an occasion. What I don't understand is why the sister wouldn't also be implicated and charged as an accessory."

He shook his head. "I'm pretty sure the IRS cannot seize property that belongs to a family member unless they can prove that the property was intentionally transferred to engage in tax fraud. There's a timeline of some sort, but if those guys get it in their head to find something, they have the means to do it and they never give up."

"You speak as though you have firsthand experience."

"Not me personally, but I've been brought in on tax cases

before. It ain't pretty."

Kim sat back. "Listen, I have to tell you something and I don't want you getting all pissed off. I just haven't had the opportunity before now."

Quaid's features smoothed into an unreadable mask. "I'm listening, but no promises."

"We already guessed that Teri was having an affair, but I accidently learned the man's name while I was making phone calls to find Teri's relatives. He's a client's husband who lives outside Cincinnati. Teri was meeting him on a regular basis. The wife knew about it and was angry, rightfully so, but she also seemed to accept it. I thought that was strange." Kim pursed her lips. "I don't see where it has anything to do with the Talisman switch, but now I'm wondering if the wife might have something to do with Teri's death."

"Have you reported this to the police?"

"I was too upset after you told me the circumstances of the murder. It's probably too late tonight, what with the three hour difference."

"I can call the officer in charge in the morning, if you like." Quaid smiled sheepishly. "I'm a real pain in her butt, so this might warm her up a little."

"I'd appreciate that. I have things to do in the morning before I leave. Are you leaving tomorrow too?"

Quaid nodded. "What's the lover's name?"

"Wade Warren." Kim pushed her plate aside. "Maybe we'll be on the same flight."

"No, I'm driving up to San Bernardino to check on something. I'll be leaving later."

Kim restrained herself. Quaid had more information he hadn't shared, but she was really tired of the game-playing.

∽

Early the following morning, Quaid packed and checked out of the motel. San Bernardino was about an hour away, probably less on a Sunday morning. With any luck, after he met the people who'd sent their horse with Talisman, he'd have plenty of time to catch his flight to Texas. The more Quaid thought about the news of Teri Fortune's lover, the less he considered giving the information to

Deputy Dexton. She'd been obstructive and rude. Why would he help her? They had resources—he might even be telling them something they already knew. Now, if the lover had something to do with the horse switch, that would be Quaid's territory. Once he had this trip behind him, he'd look into Mr. Wade Warren.

Heading due east, Quaid allowed his mind to relax for awhile and enjoy the early morning views on a quiet day. The area was like a postcard, the town spreading over the valley, the craggy San Bernardino Mountains as a backdrop. He checked his map again and headed east, passing the airport and arriving at the address the horse hauler had given him. The ranch was small, but well-kept. A woman came out of the barn and waited for him to park.

He held out his card. "Ma'am? I'm with United Equine Assurance."

She frowned. "We don't have money for insurance." She turned to walk away.

"Wait, I'm here about something else. I'm not trying to sell you anything."

She turned back and tilted her head. "I'm listenin'."

"You shipped a horse with Cross Country Equine Transport last December, is that right?"

"Yeah, we sent Scooter to his new home. Why?"

"Do you have a picture of him?"

"Sure, come on into the barn. My daughter's whole show career is on the bulletin board." The smile faded. "She don't show no more, an' we just can't afford to keep many horses, what with the price of hay 'n' all."

Quaid followed her into a small tack room. One wall was filled with the memorabilia of a young girl's love affair with horses.

The woman pointed to one larger photograph. "This is him and her, just won the local western pleasure championship. She was sure proud that day."

The horse in the photograph was a good-looking chestnut with a cream-colored mane and tail. Certainly not a ringer for Talisman. Quaid was disappointed at reaching another dead end, but maybe he'd find some answers in Texas.

Chapter 27

Kim rose early the next morning, her head swimming with ideas about the strange happenings at the barn the night before. She was almost positive that the horse she'd seen in one of Jasper's stalls was the Thoroughbred, Robidoux. But if David Craig had left early in the afternoon, wouldn't he have had the horse with him? As well as the trainer knew the horse, a switch seemed improbable. Craig would know everything about Robidoux—markings, quirks, personality. But Jasper had also known his horse well and, yet, a double had taken Talisman's place for over five months. Could the same thing have just happened to David Craig? Had she actually watched a ringer load onto that trailer?

She opened her laptop and examined all the photographs she'd taken over the past two days. She'd liked Robidoux so much that she'd taken dozens of pictures of him. If she'd thought to take a picture of the horse in Jasper's stall, she'd have something to compare. Or maybe her imagination was simply working overtime. After all, Thoroughbreds were classically look-alikes, especially certain bloodlines. There could be dozens of horses that looked exactly like Robidoux, distinguished only by some marking or feature. The proof would be in performance. She bit her lip. David Craig's champion would be a valuable prize for someone with no scruples and lots of money.

She dug through her shoulder bag and found his business card. The training facility was located in Oregon. If she called him, what would she say? Urge him to verify that he'd taken his own horse home? What if her worst fears were realized? She'd have a lot of explaining to do, none of it making much sense, even to her. She just didn't have any proof to back up her theory.

She tucked the business card back into her bag and walked over to the window. The motel parking lot was full, and traffic moved steadily along the access road. If she was going to visit Victory Farms, she'd better get going. As she packed her suitcase and gathered her gear, she thought about the stolen Arabian filly. It had happened at a show. It had involved "musical stalls." The confusion and sheer numbers of people and horses would be a perfect camouflage for theft. Moving horses around and making the switches could be done in a matter of minutes. She snapped the latches on her suitcase. She'd be willing to bet money that Robidoux was on his way to who-knew-where. Quaid had mentioned that the horse in Jasper's stall seemed dopey when the groom led him away. If Craig had lots of help at the show, whoever loaded his horses on the trailer might not have recognized that they didn't have the same horse. Or if the price was right, they might have been complicit.

Kim pulled out of the parking lot and stopped at the street, taking a minute to look toward the equestrian center. *What the heck, it'll only take a few minutes.* When she entered the grounds, it looked different with no one around. She headed for the exhibitor parking lot and, a moment later, pulled up beside Jasper's rig sitting exactly where it had been the whole time. Only now it was flagged with bright orange tow tickets. Jasper Martin was in the wind.

᪣

The entrance to Victory Farms lay just off a scenic highway that had taken her through the foothills of the breathtaking San Gabriel Mountains. For an Ohio flatlander like her, the majesty of the topography made her think about just how small and insignificant her life and problems were. Nothing in her life couldn't change, if she wanted it to.

The farm rambled over many acres, the pastures filled with straw-colored scrubby grass. The years of drought had taken their toll on California, leaving ranchers and farmers with few options other than herd reduction or dispersal. Mother Nature and the economy seemed to be in bed together, forcing ordinary folks to do extraordinary things.

She parked and sat for a moment, remembering her phone conversation with these people and trying to decide just how to approach them about their stolen horse. The door to the house opened and a man headed toward her car.

"Good morning, are you here about the gelding?"

She closed the car door. "Uh, no, actually I'm looking for a mare. Or a young one to train."

He looked confused for a minute, then glanced toward the road. "Okay, we can probably help you out with that." He started to walk toward the barn. "You looking for Western or English?"

"I was thinking of trying my hand at halter."

He grabbed a lead rope off a hook on the wall. "I might have just the horse for you."

He entered a stall, then brought out a beautiful gray mare with dappling over her rump and shoulders. Kim's breath caught in her chest.

"She's gorgeous! Without even knowing, I can see she's got fabulous bloodlines."

He grinned proudly. "Yessiree. She's a full sister to another filly we, ah, just sold earlier this month. This gal's almost three and ready for the perfect owner. She's already started a little halter training, and she's a quick learner."

Kim composed her expression. She'd caught his stumble when he'd mentioned the other filly. Perfect opportunity to get into a conversation without him knowing what she was really after.

She followed the man down the aisle and out into the morning sun. He entered a small paddock and began showing off the mare, coaxing her into the halter pose and asking her to give her neck. She was clumsy and obviously green, but so gorgeous that, for a moment, Kim wanted to buy her. She almost laughed out loud at how close she'd come to believing her own charade.

The man smiled. "What do you think? Shall we write something up?"

Kim pretended to consider the idea, then put on an apologetic face. "Actually, I wanted a younger horse. You said you had a yearling that you just sold. Maybe something like that." She brightened her expression. "Maybe whoever bought her would sell her to *me*."

His eyebrows came together. "I doubt that, but come on back to the office and I'll see what youngsters are available."

Kim followed him into the barn and waited while he put the mare away. She might have made a mistake with that last comment, but it was worth a shot. The man took her to a large room at the front of the barn, a space filled with dozens of show photographs and ribbons and trophies.

Kim looked around. "Wow, you guys do good at the shows!"
"Yeah, we don't keep any horses that don't prove themselves immediately. Our reputation depends on perfection."

He handed her a flyer. "Here are the sale horses. I only see one youngster on there, but I don't think he's what you're after."

Kim glanced through the list, then stepped over to the wall to look at the pictures. Sure enough, a framed photo of a gray filly foal was displayed prominently. The horse had a ribbon sash around her neck and wide, frightened eyes. Kim moved closer, her pulse quickening. At the edge of the photograph, almost out of the lens view, the familiar dark-eyed man watched from the rail.

Kim tapped on the picture. "This one's gorgeous. Is she the one you sold?"

The man didn't answer and Kim's neck hairs stood up.

She turned and met his hostile gaze.

His tone was equally unfriendly. "Why are you so interested in that particular horse? A horse that's not even here."

Before she could respond, he gestured toward the door. "I think you'd better leave."

At that moment, Kim would have given anything to have a badge to flash. Instead, she drew herself up to full height and stared at him.

"I don't know what your problem is, but you obviously aren't interested in making a sale."

She headed for the entrance, glancing back once. The man was talking on a cell phone and the expression on his face said it all. She'd pushed a button.

ﮩ

Kim settled into a hard plastic seat at the departure gate for a flight to Columbus. If she got on this one, she'd have to fly to Atlanta and wait for two hours before heading back to the Midwest. The schedules and routes were a mystery, but at least she would get home a day earlier. And she was *so* ready to be home. She gazed out the huge windows. Planes taxied to and from the gates, baggage trucks zoomed around with their precarious loads, and tarmac personnel worked at breakneck speed to keep the flow of plane traffic moving.

The scene blurred as her thoughts moved to the hectic pace

she'd kept the past few weeks. She was exhausted, and weary of the intrigue surrounding Talisman. She wanted to know what had happened and how and where, but the time had come to step aside for awhile and clear her brain. She picked up her phone and called Dixie.

"Would you like to take a little trip with me this week? Can you get a couple days off?"

"You must be a mind-reader. I finish field work on Monday and don't have to be back until Friday."

"I've been wanting to go down to Marietta and visit my grandfather's old farm, kind of a trip down memory lane. It's a pretty area and there are some good places to eat in the town. I just need some company right now."

"I'd love to. Give me a call when you get back and we'll scheme something up...hey, is everything okay?"

"Yeah, but this whole Talisman theft thing is getting me down. I need to step back from it for awhile. I'll tell you all about it when I get home." She chuckled. "Sometime in the middle of the night, if I get this standby flight."

"Then I'll see you tomorrow. Take care."

Kim closed the phone and looked out the window again. The scene hadn't changed, but her spirits had. A few days of nothing but free time would be good for her head. And if she knew anything about herself, her brain would offer some revelations at the end of her time off.

Chapter 28   *Texas*

Quaid's flight to Amarillo took almost two hours, during which time he tried to figure out what might have been going on at the equestrian center. Kovak thought the dark horse in Jasper's stalls might be that trainer's horse, but they had no way to prove it. Most of these horses looked alike to Quaid. Big, brown or bay. Put them all together in a show setting and he'd be hard pressed to identify one from the other. Not like the horses *he'd* become used to.

The memories flooded in and his chest tightened. Memories of gentle black giants with hearts of gold. God help anyone who so much as said a sharp word to one of them, let alone abuse them the way he'd seen some performance horses treated.

He leaned his head back and closed his eyes. He'd had enough of this case, though it was far from solved. In just a few days, he'd leave it all and take Ricky to visit a world left behind, a world filled with pain, but also with honor.

A blast of brutally hot air hit Quaid as he left the Amarillo terminal and, by the time he reached the rental vehicle, his shirt was stuck to his armpits. He tossed his bags into the back seat and started the AC, turning it up as high as it would go. Ohio was hot in the summer, but *this* was ridiculous. A few minutes later, he relaxed back in the seat, cooler and less cranky. As he drove away from the airport, he scanned the surrounding area. The brilliant blue sky stretched as far as he could see. Flatter than flat in every direction, yet Amarillo was well over 3,000 feet above sea level. If he had time, he'd visit the Palo Duro Canyon. He'd read that it was the second largest canyon in the United States, but he'd never even heard of it.

Horse Heaven Ranch was nothing much to look at, but it had a huge parking area and two long barns with outside doors and individual turnouts. Quaid pulled up next to the door marked "office" and climbed out of the car. Horses occupied some of the turnout pens, but most were empty. He saw no houses or buildings anywhere nearby, and the road he'd just driven stretched in a straight line both directions. The isolation made his skin crawl.

A skinny guy wearing a stained cowboy hat looked up. "Ken I he'p ya?"

"I hope so. I'm doing some research on equine travel facilities in the U.S. and thought I'd stop by and see yours, since it's listed so prominently in the directories."

The man grinned, revealing a missing tooth. "Yep, we do a big business. Folks gotta have a break on a long haul, and the horses do too."

Quaid pulled out his notebook, pretending great interest. "So, how many customers do you get in a week?"

"Oh, 'bout thirty to thirty-five. Mostly folks hauling to big shows in Tulsa or Houston."

Quaid wrote and nodded. "What about professional horse haulers? Many of those?"

"Not too many. They usually plan their trips to avoid any delays." He chuckled. "'Course if'n they get tangled up in one of our famous surprise storms, they got no choice. C'mon, I'll show you the layout."

Quaid followed him out the door and around the corner of the building to large double sliding doors that opened onto a long packed clay aisle. Stalls lined both sides. The place was clean and bright, illuminated by a row of narrow windows just below the roof line.

Quaid gestured toward the door they'd just entered. "Is that where horses are unloaded?"

"Yep, there's another entrance at the back, but the big rigs can't get in there, so we just use it for the small trailers."

"You have many helpers here?"

"About five full-time people, and a couple on-call stall cleaners so we can have a break once in awhile."

"Do you man the place at night?"

"Nah, I'm too old for that anymore. I got young bucks to do it."

Quaid wrote it all down, even though he was forming a picture in his mind of what might have happened when Butch arrived.

"You know, it would give my article some special interest if I could interview one or two of your staff. Is that possible?"

The guy shook his head. "I gave everyone the day off to go to Fourth of July stuff, but a couple of my regulars will be back this evening. You wanna come then?"

Quaid nodded. "I can do that."

He tried to imagine the scenario of Butch wrestling a temperamental horse into the barn, and needing some help. With an overnight stay and a sedated horse, the switch would have been easy. But *then* what? Where had Talisman gone from there?

An idea popped into his head. "Say, you happen to know if there are any horse auctions around here?"

"Closest one is Stephenville, but most of 'em are farther south, closer to the border."

Quaid cocked his head. "Why's that?"

The man's expression darkened. "The slaughterhouses are in Mexico." He pushed his hat back. "You want me to tell my people you'll be here?"

Quaid nodded enthusiastically. "Yes, please. I'll see you around six."

He hurried to his car, his brain spinning. If the layover ranch was used for switching horses, then it was possible that the valuable horses were being transported into Mexico as "auction horses" to meet up with buyers. Could horses be trucked across the border without any need for veterinarian reports, quarantine, shot records, or registration papers? Another piece of information he'd need to dig up.

After checking his flight time for the next day, Quaid found a motel, then headed south to see the canyon. A little R&R would be a good thing right now. This case was really beginning to get to him.

&

Kim woke up slowly. A rough tongue rasped across her chin and she giggled, pulling Miss Kitty close and pressing her cheek against the soft fur. An enticing aroma caught her attention and she blinked. *Coffee?* Throwing the covers aside, she slipped out of bed and padded down the hall toward the kitchen. The coffee maker hissed and blew out a final puff of steam, then gurgled as the brew finished filling the carafe. A white bakery bag sat on the counter with an orange sticky note attached.

Welcome home. Call me when you're conscious. Love, Dixie.

Kim smiled. How could anyone have a better friend?

She peeked inside the bag and inhaled the scent of fresh banana nut muffins.

Settling into her favorite chair on the deck, she sighed. The parking areas were mostly empty, as they always were on a holiday. In the distance, fireworks popped and crackled, reminding her of the celebrations she'd enjoyed as a child in Marietta. Not just Independence Day, but others, including the fabulous Sternwheeler Festival in the fall. She hadn't been back for that event in over twenty years. It was definitely time to return to her roots. How did time just disappear, leaving gaps that seemed insurmountable? Why did we always think things would remain the same forever? Was she in for a sad disappointment on this upcoming visit to Grandpa's farm? She swallowed a lump forming in her throat. She simply couldn't stand it if the place was gone, or abandoned to time, or worse. The only way to avoid that would be not to go, but that was ridiculous. If she was going to change her life, as she'd promised herself on the trip to California, she'd need to face some demons and put them in jail forever.

Peter's face popped into her mind and she sucked in a breath. Was the history with him part of the new purge too? She'd vowed she would never let anyone hurt her that way again and, so far, she'd been able to stay disentangled. There'd been a few casual relationships along the way and a couple of outright rolls in the hay just for fun, but always that wariness that kept Kim in control. Men seemed attracted to her, but usually put off by her independent attitude. Most of them didn't even know she was an ex-cop, they just sensed that she wasn't someone to screw around with.

The sound of her cell phone drifted through the screen door and, leaving the worries and what-if's behind, Kim hurried inside to get on with the day.

⚵

Quaid swung by Jenna's house on the way home from the airport. Her car was in the driveway and Ricky's bike lay on its side by the front door. Quaid grinned, remembering how much he'd wanted a bicycle as a boy. Rancher's kids had horses instead of bikes and, even if he'd owned one, there were few places to ride it. The dusty road that ran alongside the property was riddled with potholes and bumps, obstacles easily maneuvered on horseback, but they'd have been a bitch to dodge on a bike.

He gazed at the house, remembering that Jenna would move and he'd no longer have the luxury of dropping by. A privilege he'd already squandered for years.

Ricky appeared at the door and waved, a wide smile brightening his round face. Quaid's chest tightened. Jenna might not realize it, but her brother-in-law wasn't the only one who looked like Ben.

"Uncle Garrett! I bought you a present!"

"Well, aren't you good. I bought you something too." He held out a package wrapped in brown paper and tied with twine. "I wish you'd been with me. I visited the second largest canyon in the United States. It was awesome."

Ricky grinned. "Well, guess what *I* got to do? They let me sit in the pilot's seat of a Nighthawk stealth fighter!"

"Whoa, that's pretty neat. Do you know how important those planes were in the Desert Storm operation?"

Ricky nodded vigorously. "They were able to fly over Iraq and not be seen. There was a video about them. I watched it twice."

Quaid gazed at his nephew, seeing the future. With a hero father, the boy would be driven to follow in those honored footsteps. Quaid's chest burned with both pain and pride.

"Well, open your present, for Pete's sake!"

Ricky tore off the wrappings and crowed with glee. "Wow! A geode!"

The craggy quartz crystals in the hollow center of the rock glittered like diamonds, and Ricky's eyes sparkled almost as much.

Jenna appeared and Quaid noticed immediately that her features seemed more relaxed than he'd seen in a long time.

She patted Ricky's shoulder. "We had a great time. Looks like you did some sight-seeing too."

"Yeah, time to kill, but it turned out to be a welcome respite."

Ricky set the geode down and headed for the hall. "Wait here, I'll be right back."

Quaid shifted his weight, not wanting to ask the question, but needing to know the answer. "Are you definitely going to move to Dayton?"

Jenna looked briefly sad, but nodded. "Yes, I don't see any other way. I already have a lead on a job and some housing is opening up next month." She touched his arm. "It's only a couple hours' drive. We'll still see you, at least as much as we always have."

"Aw, Jenna, that's mean. I know I've been missing in action a lot, but that's going to change. I owe it to you and Ricky *and* my brother."

Ricky bounded back into the room and held out a small paper bag. Quaid carefully unrolled the top and reached into the depths, his fingers closing around a flat, square object. A hand-painted wooden plaque showed a soldier on a horse in front of an American flag. The words "Warhorse Soldiers, 1st Cavalry Division" were printed below the image.

Quaid's voice cracked. "Rick, it's beautiful. I'll keep this right on my desk where I can look at it every day."

The boy's voice was soft, almost a whisper. "Yeah, we can't ever forget Dad."

On his way home later, Quaid reflected on the time he'd just spent with what was left of his family. Jenna would be moving on, getting her life back together, maybe finding love again. Ricky, on the other hand, was clearly having trouble with leaving the past behind. *He's afraid he will forget Ben, afraid of losing that connection.*

Could Quaid replace that male presence in the boy's life? Gripping the steering wheel, he clenched his jaw. Not from Cleveland, he couldn't.

Chapter 29

After a much-needed shower, Quaid grabbed a soda from the fridge and headed for his small office. He connected his laptop to his main computer and began backing up files. As the transfer progressed, he thought about his meeting with the barn staff at Horse Heaven. The two women who worked at the place full time had been less than helpful, almost to the point of being rude. They'd acted like he was imposing on their time with his questions. One of them had seemed quite nervous about the interview, and he wondered if she might be mixed up in what he suspected was happening to horses in that part of the state. It would only take one cooperative insider at the layover ranch to make the auction-house-to-Mexico theory viable.

The computer signaled the completed file transfer, and he opened the search database he'd been using to locate Teri Fortune's brother. Quaid's brain was stuck on the where, how, and when of Talisman's situation. How could someone have planned to switch those horses out there in the middle of nowhere, without even knowing for sure that the trucker would stop at the layover ranch? Quaid was positive that Butch had no hand in the plot, but in order for the switch to work, whoever it was would have to know where Talisman was at any given time.

Jasper Martin could have implanted a tracking device in Talisman before he was loaded on the trailer. If that were true, then Jasper was purposely trying to defraud the insurance company. But suppose Jasper *hadn't* been involved...suppose someone had targeted Talisman and had their own way of knowing his whereabouts.

Quaid quickly pulled up another file marked "Paid Claims." As he scanned the documents, anger rose in his chest. In each case where United Equine Assurance had paid claims for stolen horses, those animals had been at a horse show. Could he prove that the same people were perpetrating these crimes?

⁂

Dixie called Kim that night. "What time do you want to leave tomorrow?"

"How about seven-thirty?"

"Works for me. So, how did your show and everything go?"

"Show went okay, the rest of the stuff not so good."

"What rest of the stuff?"

"You remember that horse in Delaware that was switched out? The owner lives near Burbank where I was this weekend, so I did a little snooping."

"Kim—"

"No, hear me out. I didn't get involved. Much. Here's the interesting part. That private investigator, Garrett Quaid, was there trying to figure out if the horse owner is involved in an insurance scam."

A small pause, then Dixie said, "Huh, so that's why I haven't heard from him."

Kim's irritation surprised her. "Were you expecting to?"

Dixie didn't respond.

"Sorry, Dix, I didn't mean to sound nasty. Anyway, we shared some information and the case is really bizarre. But I'm done with it."

"Why is that?"

"I found out that Teri was murdered. She was dead before she was hanged. This is no longer a simple fraud or larceny, and I want no part of it."

As she spoke the words, Kim knew she lied, both to Dixie and to herself.

"I think that's a good thing."

Kim turned out the lights in the living room and kitchen, then moved to the deck slider. The sky to the west glowed with the lights of Columbus and, while she stood there, several displays of aerial fireworks lit up the night. She watched for a moment, then checked that the door was locked before heading down the hall.

The two days she'd spent working with Quaid had been energizing, though they'd been fraught with tension and emotion. He was an interesting man, once she got past his macho personality—a mirror of her own, only more muscled. She liked the way he took a problem by the throat and worked it until he could understand what was involved. He smiled a lot, exuding self-confidence. That would be important in his line of work. Talking to strangers about sinister or illegal circumstances could be dangerous, but a sincere smile put most people at ease.

It had certainly worked on *her.* Most of their tense conversations had ended amicably, except when she let her anger get the better of her. Even then, Quaid had been able to bring her around. The mob scene flashed into her thoughts and a tremor ran through her. Would she ever get over that fear? The moments that had robbed her of the two most important things in her life? She closed her eyes, reliving the experience of being drawn into Quaid's arms and held away from the crowd, safe from the danger. The heat of his body, the thump of his heart, his soft and reassuring voice. Kim sank into the memory, wondering if those sensations would ever be hers again.

Stepping into her studio, she gazed at the psychedelic patterns moving slowly across her computer screen, then she sat down to check her e-mail just one more time before going to bed. Nothing important, no orders, no complaints. She clicked on the news feed feature. Three stories popped up, but one caught her eye and she gasped.

Teri Fortune's burial would be the next day. Apparently, the brother had appeared to claim Teri's body.

Kim grabbed the phone.

"Dixie, I'm really sorry. Can we go a little later in the day?"

"Sure. I need to check in with my mother anyway before I leave. She's not taking kindly to the new arrangements. I'll talk to you when you get back."

Kim hung up and checked the obituary notice again. Quaid would be interested in this information. She glanced at the clock and decided she could at least leave a voice mail.

He picked up on the first ring and Kim sucked in her breath at the sound of his voice.

Don't even go there, lady.

ے

Quaid sat back in his chair. "Hey, you made it home. What's up?"

He listened to Kovak's soft voice, noticing that it had a sultry edge to it. She seemed upset, so he derailed that thought-train and paid close attention.

"Teri Fortune is being buried tomorrow. Apparently, that

brother you're looking for turned up to claim her body. Reginald, right?"

"Yeah, one of about forty. That's good news. Did the obituary give any details about him?"

"No, it was limited, but I'm going up there. Want me to find out?"

"Yes, I'm tied up at the insurance offices tomorrow, so I can't go myself."

"I'll call you when I get back. By the way, did you give the sheriff that information about Teri's affair?"

Quaid swallowed. "She wasn't in when I called, but I left a message. Haven't heard back, not that I expect to. She likes me so much."

Kovak chuckled. "Okay, I'll talk to you tomorrow."

After hanging up, Quaid thought briefly about the time spent with her. He'd enjoyed most of it, but her prickly nature squelched the idea of anything more. Dixie Davis, on the other hand... A stir moved through his gut and he had the urge to call her right then, drive all night if necessary. He could almost taste that sweet little mouth and feel that pink skin stretched over her small round body. The images shattered into a million pieces as his brain took charge, filling his head with images of the girl of his dreams entangled in the arms and legs of another woman.

He jumped up and strode out of the room. "Fuckin' Kovak."

Chapter 30

Kim dressed in the darkest colors she could find in her summer wardrobe, then looked through the closet for what she might take to Marietta. She pulled out some things and packed them in a bag on the bed. Such a somber start to what should be a relaxing and fun time, but with all that had happened to Teri, she deserved to have the people she knew at her service. Kim brushed her hair and tossed her makeup case into the bag. Besides, she wanted to find out more about Reginald Fortune. For Quaid, of course.

An hour later, she followed the GPS directions to the Oak Grove Cemetery south of Delaware. As she drove slowly past the rows of headstones, she thought about the last time she'd attended a funeral. Her grandfather's. How long had it been? She tried to count back, finding that more years had gone by than she cared to admit. A hard lump formed in her throat. She'd never been back to visit his grave or her childhood home in all that time. How could she have just abandoned her history like that? What had she been doing that was so important? What dream had she been chasing? Had she caught it?

A small knot of people gathered on a gently sloping section of the cemetery, a smaller number than she would have expected for a high profile death. As she walked toward them, she counted eight, not including the minister standing at the head of the casket. One man towered over the others. Blond hair carefully styled, trendy eyeglasses, and an expensive suit that had certainly not come off the rack. He had to be the brother. Or maybe he was the lover. But would that guy chance such a bold appearance? Sure he would, if he thought no one knew about his affair with Teri. Kim scanned the other people, noticing a couple of well-dressed women who had "horse owner" written all over them. Two men, one youngish, one old, and both dressed in barn clothes. Former farm staff? A small woman with gray hair sat in one of the folding chairs, her head bowed, her hands clasped. The tall man stepped over and laid his hand on her shoulder, leaning down to brush a kiss over her hair. *She must be Teri's mother. Which means that man is probably Reginald Fortune.* Kim turned her attention to the remaining person standing at the periphery of the group, a burly man of about 6-feet, hands stuffed into the pockets of an ill-fitting tweed jacket, an impassive expression on his square face. Kim's skin prickled.

Cop.

She looked away and moved to stand beside one of the women just as the minister began speaking.

"We are gathered here to celebrate the life of Teresa Marie Fortune, and to mourn her passing. But that, too, is a celebration, for she will have eternal life."

Kim watched Teri's brother. He stood, head bowed, hands clasped in front of his pristine jacket. She also threw a surreptitious glance at the plain-clothes cop and caught him staring at her. She quickly looked away, but not before she saw him shift his weight. Why was he watching her? Did he recognize a fellow officer, as she had? Did she still have that look?

The minister's voice cut in again. "Sisters and brothers, remember Ecclesiastes thirty-eight, verse nineteen. 'For of sadness cometh death, and it overwhelmeth the strength, and the sorrow of the heart boweth down the neck.' Do not let your sorrow prevail. Instead, remember your loved one in happiness and health. Let us say the Lord's Prayer together."

Kim tipped her head and murmured the familiar words, but her mind would not quiet. Teri's murder remained unsolved, and gathered in this place were people with possible insights that might help find the killer.

When the minister finished the service, he asked if anyone wanted to say something. No one came forward.

"Go in peace."

Kim stepped back, glancing toward Teri's brother. This would be her only chance to ask some questions of her own. The two women were moving slowly down the slope and she hurried after them.

"Excuse me? Did you have horses at Teri's barn?"

They turned in unison and the older one nodded. "Yes. Isn't this sad?"

"More than sad. Just tragic. She was doing *so* well, had such a successful business."

The women glanced at each other, then the younger one spoke. "That's what she tried to convey, but if you had horses with her, you'd know it wasn't so."

Kim nodded as though understanding exactly what the woman meant. "Oh, you noticed it too?"

She began walking slowly and the two came with her. The older woman seemed eager to discuss whatever problem they'd seen.

"Even though she put a good face on it, I noticed several times that the feed room was quite spare and the hayloft almost empty. I never mentioned it to her because I thought it was just delivery timing."

The other woman chimed in. "Yes, and the extras on my bill each month were beginning to be worrisome. My horse only needed some massage therapy for a pulled muscle. I don't know what all Teri used on him, but it seemed like a lot more than usual."

Kim pursed her lips. "I also wondered if she might be in some sort of financial trouble."

The older woman stopped walking. "I'm almost positive she was. I overheard a telephone conversation with someone about her mortgage. She was very upset."

"Have you taken your horses home?"

The younger woman opened her mouth to reply, then her gaze shifted at about the same time Kim realized someone was behind her. She turned and met the hard stare of the plain-clothes cop.

He had a deep, gravelly voice. "Excuse me, can I have a word?"

How long had he been there? How much had he heard?

The two women hurried away toward the line of parked cars.

Kim cocked her head. "About what?"

"About what you're doing here."

She blinked. "Why shouldn't I be? And who are *you?*"

He didn't smile. "I recognize you. Columbus Mounted Division, football riots. You're the officer who was shot, am I right?"

She exhaled slowly. Of all the inconvenient coincidences.

"Well, I don't recognize *you*, so if you'll excuse me..."

He flashed a badge. "The police department is working with

the county on Teri Fortune's murder."

Kim noted the badge number and filed it away, along with the interesting tidbit that, in all this exchange, he hadn't given her his name.

She affected a sad face, even managing to tear-up. "Lord, I hope you find whoever did it. She was my friend and I'll miss her terribly."

The man looked at her for a moment. "We're doing our best." He nodded. "You have a good day."

Kim watched him move toward the parked cars, then she glanced toward the gravesite. Everyone had gone. Her pulse thumped beneath her jaw as she walked toward her car. No name, no business card, no request to call if she thought of anything that might help the investigation. She slid behind the wheel and looked back up the hill. The man had disappeared. She scanned the remaining parked cars, but if he was there, he wasn't visible.

A sleek black late-model Mercedes glided past and she caught sight of the tall blonde man behind the wheel. She watched the taillights disappear around a curve, then picked up her cell phone and dialed information. A moment later, she connected to the Delaware Police Department.

"Hi, I just spoke with an officer and I've forgotten his name, but his badge number is 768."

A short silence and paper rustling on the other end of the line, then, "We don't have that badge number. Are you sure it was this department?"

Kim laughed lightly. "Oh, maybe not. Thanks anyway."

She quickly disconnected, then dialed the sheriff's office.

Ten minutes later, she laid her phone on the seat and eased the car down the lane. Mr. Detective did not officially exist.

Fortune Farms was a fifteen-minute drive from the cemetery and Kim used the time to ponder who the fake cop was and why he was at Teri's funeral. Usual procedure in most homicide cases would be to have a detective attend any event where friends or enemies of the deceased might gather, but she'd already determined that this guy wasn't connected with anything official. What was he looking for? Maybe he was a private investigator like Quaid. Looking into the murder? Someone from the mortgage company? Whoever he was, Kim didn't like the fact that he'd recognized her. From what perspective was that knowledge? Had he been part of the riot? A bystander? A police officer at the time? One who'd fallen from grace and now slunk around the periphery of crime? Could he have simply seen the gory front page photos and details of the event, and was nothing more than a freak with a taste for the sensational? Maybe the one who'd fired the shot? She shuddered, redirecting her thoughts to the conversation with the two women at the cemetery.

It was unusual for clients to have much insight into a business's inner workings, so whatever was going on with Teri and her finances must have been visible. Especially to clients who came to the barn frequently.

She turned into Teri's driveway. The same black Mercedes was parked near the doors. Perhaps she'd be able to talk to Teri's brother, and give Quaid some information he could use. And maybe get the wheels turning for Bandit's return home.

~

Quaid's voice rose a notch. "You want me to *what?*"

The insurance adjuster chuckled. "You heard me. The client says it will prove his claim. We have no choice but to follow up."

"But I already have proof that the horse at Fortune Farms is a different horse. Is the company just going to roll over and pay up? Jeezus."

"No other options, buddy. We have to follow it up. If we can't prove fraud, it's a legitimate claim."

Quaid disconnected, then tossed the phone onto the desk. He'd logged a lot of hours trying to determine this case, and now the whole thing would be over in a matter of hours. No way was Jasper Martin innocent here. He might have an angle that would fool the insurance company, but he wasn't fooling Quaid or Kovak.

He grabbed the phone again and dialed her number.

"You aren't going to believe the latest twist," he said. "Out of the blue, Jasper Martin called the insurance company and said he could prove the horse at Teri's isn't his. He wants the claim paid and closed. Remember he said there was some secret identification mark?"

"Yes, but we never found anything obvious on Bandit, other than the hoof scar."

"Apparently, the real horse has a heart-shaped blotch on...uh, on his...dick."

Kovak burst into laughter. "Are you kidding me? Oh, that is too funny! Of *course* no one would see it!"

Quaid was not as amused. "Yeah, well somehow *I* have to see it. Any suggestions?"

Kovak giggled again, then said, "You want me to get a picture for you?"

"Well, you *are* closer than I am."

"More than you know. I'm at the barn right now, just about to talk to Teri's brother."

"No point in that now. If the horse doesn't have any kinky artwork on his privates, then this case is over."

A long silence filtered through the phone, then, "And you're just going to let this go? Knowing what we do about the scope of the thefts?"

"What's the point? Neither one of us is part of an official investigation into the theory."

"Meaning you don't give a damn about all this unless you get a paycheck. Nice." Kovak's tone turned icy. "I'll get that photo and e-mail it within the next couple of hours. Talk to you later."

The line went dead and Quaid stared at the green claim folder. Easy for *her* to say, Miss Photographer-with-nothing-to-do-and-all-day-to-do-it. She hadn't driven and flown all over the friggin' country tracking down leads that went nowhere and talking to people who didn't give a damn. If Jasper's horse *was* stolen, for whatever reason, then the guy deserved to be compensated for the insurance premiums he'd paid. That's what goddamned insurance was for.

Quaid rose and paced his small study. File a claim. Prove a claim. Pay a claim. That's the way it worked. How did Kovak come off being so holier-than-thou?

⚕

Kim jammed the phone into her pocket.

Quaid was a royal ass.

She strode across the barn aisle toward Teri's office. At the door, she stopped and rapped lightly on the doorjamb.

The tall man from the cemetery looked up, his eyebrows coming together. "Yes? May I help you?"

She stepped through and held out her hand. "Are you Teri's brother? I'm Kim Kovak, a friend."

He shook her hand half-heartedly. "Reggie Fortune. Thank you for paying your respects. I'm a little busy right now. Was there something else you wanted?"

"Actually, yes. I'm working with United Equine Assurance in Cleveland. We have an open claim on one of Teri's clients and I just need to take a photograph of the horse to close the case."

Suspicion clouded Fortune's eyes. "What kind of insurance claim?"

"I'm not at liberty to say, but this photograph will end the investigation."

He gazed at her for a moment, then nodded. "Okay. Which horse are we talking about?"

"Talisman, far end stall near the tack room."

Fortune stepped out the door and looked in that direction. "I'm waiting for owners to come pick up the horses. Haven't heard back from that one."

Kim's pulse quickened. Somehow, she had to get Bandit back to his rightful owner. If no one claimed him, this guy would simply send him off to auction.

"I'll only be a minute. Is there someone here who can hold his head for me?"

"There's an old guy out back who's doing something with a tractor. Now, if you'll excuse me..."

"Thanks. Nice meeting you."

She was speaking to the back of the expensive suit. *Jerk.*

A few minutes later, she found the old man peering at the innards of a tractor engine.

"Excuse me, can you come help me with a horse?"

The man nodded and wiped his hands on a greasy rag. "You one of them horse owners?"

"No, I'm a photographer. I just need a second pair of hands."

As they approached Bandit's stall, alarms went off in Kim's

head. A wary look darkened the horse's eyes, as though things had not been good at the barn since Teri's death.

The old man stood near the horse's head. "What is it you want to do again? Take pitchers?"

"Yes, but this is a special picture and I need you to hold him real still. Can you do that?"

He snorted. "'Course I can do that! Been around horses since I was ten." He slipped a halter over Bandit's head and attached a lead rope. "Where do you want him?"

Kim adjusted the camera settings. "Right there where you are. I'm going to take pictures of his underbelly. He has some unusual markings that will help us identify him."

The old guy scratched Bandit's chin. "He's a nice horse. Hasn't had much attention since..." His voice cracked.

Kim stroked Bandit's neck and back, waiting for his muscles to relax. Getting him to drop his penis wouldn't be easy, especially if he'd been neglected for a long time. She'd just have to try a couple of tricks they'd used at the police barns at bath time. As her hands moved softly along his side, he cocked a hind foot and exhaled. *Good, he's at least in a trusting mode.* She continued stroking his body, moving slowly down his sides to his underbelly. When she reached the area just in front of his sheath, she began to gently scratch and massage, humming softly. She glanced up at his ears every so often. He was totally relaxed. The old man watched her, a quizzical look on his face. Should she have warned him? Too late now. She continued to rub, moving slowly onto the soft, furry sheath. Sure enough, Bandit dropped and Kim clicked off five shots before he pulled himself back into hiding.

Jasper had his proof. The horse's penis was as pink and unblemished as a baby's butt.

"Did you just take a pitcher of his *Johnson?*"

Kim almost laughed, but the old man's expression was unpleasant.

"Yes, I did, and I'm sorry I didn't warn you. We need it for proof of ownership." She moved toward the stall door. "Thank you for your help."

She quickly let herself out of the stall.

The old man muttered, "Dang pervert."

Kim hurried to her car, her thoughts in turmoil. She had to contact Bandit's real owner before Fortune disposed of the horse. She stopped in mid-stride. He couldn't do anything unless the insurance company closed the claim. But they couldn't close the claim without the pictures she'd just taken. Much as she hated the idea, she'd have to ask Quaid to delay his report until Bandit was safely on his way home.

Her shoulders sagged. Why would Quaid even consider doing that? As far as he was concerned, the case was over. He was no longer involved or interested.

She slid in behind the steering wheel. Quaid would just have to wait on those photographs.

Chapter 31

Dixie's patrol car was in its usual spot in front of the condos and Kim closed her eyes briefly. In the morning's excitement, she'd forgotten about her trip to Marietta. How was she going to explain all this to Dixie? Would it look like a dodge? The dashboard clock said noon, but Marietta was only two hours away. They could still leave in late afternoon and be there in time for dinner.

She hurried into the house and headed for her studio. Bandit's owners lived in Texas, so how could they get to Ohio before Quaid figured out what she was up to? It would depend on how much they wanted Bandit back. But what if they'd moved on? No longer cared, no longer wanted him?

An elderly man answered and Kim swallowed hard.

"This is Kim Kovak in Ohio. I've found your horse, Bandit."

"Oh, my goodness, oh." He fell silent for a moment. "Are you sure?"

"Yes, he's listed as missing on a stolen horse website. Didn't you know?"

The old man's voice cracked. "I guess my wife must have done that."

Kim spoke gently. "May I speak to her?"

"She passed away two weeks ago...on her 75th birthday."

Kim let out a soft breath. "I'm so sorry."

"Yes, I am too. We were married thirty-eight years. Polly, that's my wife, spent her life rescuing horses no one else wanted. Saved a lot of 'em from the killers." He sighed. "I'm not sure now what to do with them."

Kim closed her eyes, joy surging through her heart. He certainly wouldn't want Bandit back.

The man's voice became stronger. "Polly used to let the local pony club kids show the horses. It helped attract folks who might want to buy or adopt one of them. Bandit was stolen from one of those shows. Polly was devastated."

"I can imagine she was. Would you like me to arrange to send

Bandit back to you?"

Kim held her breath.

"Does he have a good home now?"

"Well, it's complicated, Sir. He's in excellent health, but–"

"I'll just ask you this, Ma'am, straight from the heart. Please find a good home for that horse. To honor my wife and her lifelong dedication. Can you do that?"

Kim's throat ached. "I'll do my best, Sir."

She hung up and began to tremble. The horse in Teri's barn was definitely Bandit, and he'd arrived there through a careful and cunning scheme. All the more reason to delay Quaid's case closure and save that horse from again becoming a pawn in a treacherous game.

She pressed star-67 to hide her number, then dialed and put the phone to her ear.

"Mr. Fortune? This is United Equine Assurance calling. Our case files on Jasper Martin won't be closed until next week. I'm calling to instruct you that the horse, Talisman, is not to be released to anyone until we send you written permission."

"Some broad from your firm was just here taking pictures. She said it would close the case. I can't keep spending money on feed for these nags, so make it fast."

I am NOT a broad!

She kept the irritation out of her tone. "We'll let you know the minute we finalize the claim. Thank you so much for your patience." She swallowed hard. "You can bill the insurance company for the board fees, if that helps." *Oh, boy, this could get me in a lot of trouble!*

Fortune's tone warmed. "Oh, alright then."

Kim almost laughed out loud. What was it with people who were so consumed by money?

She hung up, hoping Reggie Fortune would not check to see if the call was real. Why would he? He only wanted to be rid of the problems so he could sell that property for a tidy piece of change.

She glanced at her packed bag lying on the bed. She *really* needed a break. Could she afford to take a couple of days, then get back on this? Could she afford *not* to?

She grabbed the phone again and dialed Dixie. "Hey, I'm packed and ready to go. Meet you at the car."

For a moment, she gazed at the phone, recognizing an obvious solution to her dilemma. She set the phone in the charger, picked up her bag, and walked out the door.

ﻪﻠﻣ

Quaid spent some time fuming about Kovak's attitude, but eventually put it out of his mind and began thinking about his upcoming trip with Ricky. Now that the insurance case was history, Quaid could take as much time off as he wanted. He looked at a calendar. By the weekend, the Smithsonian would be a zoo and not much fun at all. If they could get to D.C. tomorrow, they'd have a more leisurely visit. He pulled up MapQuest and checked the driving time. A little over six hours.

He dialed Jenna. "I'd like to leave first thing in the morning. Is that doable?"

"Sure. He's driving me crazy he's so excited. I'll tell him to get packed. What time will you be here?"

"Six. We'll grab breakfast on the road."

"He'll be ready."

"Hey, will you be all right while we're gone?"

She laughed. "Are you kidding? A few days to myself to do anything I want?"

"Oh, yeah. Well, see you tomorrow."

He hung up and shook his head. He had no idea what mothers did with their time. They were always just *there*, handling things, keeping the wheels of familydom moving smoothly. A twinge moved through his chest. His own mother had been a rock, seemingly undaunted by everything life threw at her. He hadn't appreciated that when he lived with her, and mostly hadn't thought much about it through the years. Had she ever had a moment to herself to... to do *what?* Eat chocolates and read romance novels? Hardly. An image of her in the rocking chair with her knitting reminded him of the few times she sat still. He'd always thought the knitting was to produce socks and mittens, but maybe it was her way of dealing with everything else. A mindless, relaxing activity.

She'd been a good mother, he knew that. He just wished he'd

ever told her so.

Shaking off the melancholy thoughts, he began gathering the bits and pieces of paper and information for the Talisman investigation. Once the final decision was made, he could bill the company, then see what other business he could cook up with them. He checked his e-mail to see if Kovak had sent the photographs. Empty inbox. *It's been at least three hours, for Pete's Sake. What's the holdup?*

He looked at the notes he'd made concerning Teri Fortune's brother, and the lover, Wade Warren. The brother was accounted for, although Kovak hadn't said anything specific about the guy, other than he was at the cemetery. But what about the lover? Quaid's instinct told him the guy factored into the case somewhere, but how? And which case? The theft or the murder?

Quaid opened the Tracer Database he used for finding people. Wade Warren was a common name. Too common, with hundreds of hits all over the country. Quaid would have to refine by state and age and occupation to find the right person. Five minutes later, three matches came up for Ohio. At the same time, his e-mail alert sounded and he closed the database.

The e-mail was not from Kovak.

"This is ridiculous." He dialed her number, but it went directly to voice mail. *She must be in a dead zone.*

&

Kim stopped just inside the entrance to Marietta's beautiful Lafayette Hotel, inhaling the scent of history and remembering some wonderful times spent there as a girl. The riverboat-era hotel remained as she remembered it, the lobby filled with comfortable chairs and settees, reading lamps, gilded mirrors, and floral arrangements on the many tables in the area. Soft music played in the background and the subtle fragrance of lemony furniture polish permeated the air. Floor to ceiling windows, heavily draped with burgundy velvet and golden cord, afforded a view of the mighty Ohio River on the south side and the bustling streets to the east.

Dixie stepped up beside her. "Wow, this place is great. So charming and elegant."

"Yes, it's always been like this, even after several floods that caused extensive damage. But she always bounces back."

"Let's get checked in. I'm ready for a beer."

Inside the elevator, Dixie stuck her hands in her pockets. "I need to talk to Quaid. I've been avoiding him."

"Are you going to tell him the truth?"

"Yeah. He's a pretty neat guy, but he's not too swift, if you know what I mean."

"I do, and it's hard to believe. I mean, he was in the military and he's a private investigator. You'd think he would be a little more in tune with stuff."

Kim's thoughts churned. Now, a few hours later, she felt guilty about ditching him in order to follow her own plans for Bandit. But Quaid only cared about the job and the paycheck, not the humanitarian side of the case. In the brief time she'd known him, she'd come to believe he was a good man with honest values, but this disappointed her. *Too bad.*

"You like him, don't you?" Dixie's voice was close.

Kim started, then stammered a bit. "No, I mean, yes, of course, I mean..."

The elevator doors slid open and Dixie winked. "Come on, we've got some sightseeing to do before it gets dark."

At the end of a long, narrow hall wallpapered in vintage roses, Kim stuck the keycard into the modern lock mechanism on the old wooden door. They entered the tiny room. The air was warm and stale, and the window air conditioner was silent.

Dixie whistled softly. "Whew, this place is stuffy."

She tossed her duffel bag onto one of the twin beds, then fiddled with the AC unit. It rattled and growled, then finally settled into a low hum.

"Should be comfortable when we get back tonight."

She moved to the small dressing table and checked her reflection in the mirror, doing a quick finger-comb of her curls and straightening her shirt.

Kim got her wallet out and pocketed the keycard. "Ready?"

"Yep, but don't you need your phone?"

"That's a very long story which I will tell you when we get to the bar."

Quaid ordered a pizza and flopped down in his recliner to wait. He was pissed. Kovak had never sent the photographs and she hadn't returned any of his five calls. By now, the office was closed and he couldn't finalize the case and get on with his own plans. He'd have to delay leaving for D.C. What the hell was the matter with her, anyway? Had she been *that* angry about his attitude? Was she playing games again?

A sudden thought leaped into his brain. She was a solid, sensible ex-cop, not someone he'd expect to impede an investigation. Maybe something had happened, gone wrong at the Fortune barn. He sat forward, suddenly tense. The two of them *had* been screwing around in what looked like major criminal activity. Kovak was pretty close to Teri Fortune, and the murder had been a shock. Had Kovak stumbled into something she shouldn't have? Was she in trouble? Was that why she wasn't calling him?

The doorbell rang and Quaid leaped to his feet. While he'd been placating his ego, Kovak might be needing help.

Kim and Dixie tucked up shoulder-to-shoulder at the gleaming mahogany bar in the Riverview Lounge.

Dixie whistled softly. "What a neat place. That mirror and wood must be original."

"Probably not. When the Ohio comes over its banks, this hotel gets the brunt of it. I don't know how well the original wood would have fared."

Dixie glanced over her shoulder at the windows facing the river. "It's sure right there, isn't it?"

Kim searched her memory. "There were several floods in the eighteen-hundreds that crested at well over fifty feet." She glanced around. "This room would have been completely underwater. I'll show you the markers in the lobby when we leave."

Dixie took a long drink of beer. "So, tell me why you don't have your phone."

Kim sketched out the conversation she'd had with Quaid that morning. As she went over the details, Dixie's expression changed from curiosity to concern.

The blue in Dixie's eyes intensified with her concentration.

"Kim, I understand your concern about this horse, but what exactly do you think you can do about it? Sounds like, technically, the barn owns the horse because Jasper says it's not his. Even though you have the flyer from the website as proof, you only have verbal authority from an old man. How is this going to work?"

Couched in so many words, Dixie's assessment seemed crystal clear, but Kim couldn't accept that Reggie Fortune could just keep Bandit and do whatever with him. She couldn't let her brain go where that might be.

She ran a finger through the condensation on her beer mug. "I was thinking I could go there and say I was picking him up for the owner."

"You're thinking about *stealing* him? Are you crazy? Have you forgotten that I'm a cop?"

Kim jerked her gaze from the beer mug to Dixie's solemn expression. "You'd arrest me? Would you really do that?"

Dixie sat back and looked away. "Kim, I don't think you've thought this through. I think you're operating on emotion and knee-jerk."

Kim was stunned by the change in her friend. The compassion and love-of-life that defined Dixie had disappeared like water down a drain. Kim's chest ached. Why had she thought Dixie would understand? Dixie had never owned a horse, had no idea of the bond between horses and their owners. Most of all, Dixie had never *lost* a horse, the most horrible experience imaginable.

Dixie leaned close. "Listen, why don't you just contact this Reggie guy and tell him the situation, say you'd like to have the horse. If that's actually what you want." Her eyes narrowed a bit. "Or you might be able to bluff him into thinking you know something about his involvement in the switch. He might just let you have the animal to get you out of his hair."

Kim's eyes burned. "I wish Quaid and I had enough time to ferret out these thieves, put a stop to this madness. I feel so helpless... thanks for listening. You're right. I'm not thinking straight."

Dixie patted Kim's hand. "Come on. I'd like to see those flood marks and the river that made them."

Chapter 32

The pizza didn't taste all that great and Quaid tossed a half-eaten slice back into the box. Worry had replaced his hunger. What if Kovak had asked one too many questions of Teri's brother? Questions that threatened to reveal wrong-doing on his part. Quaid wasn't convinced that the brother was uninvolved in the insurance deal. He was, after all, apparently connected to the financial sector and, if so inclined, would know the ins and outs of working around the system.

Carrying the pizza box into the kitchen, Quaid considered the possibility that someone had gotten to Jasper and forced his hand, made him call the insurance company and give the one piece of information that would facilitate the claim to quench the spotlight. A piece of information that Jasper had carefully excluded from any conversations about the theft. Had his troubles with the IRS overridden his fear of whomever was spearheading the theft ring? No, the Feds simply took stuff and levied fines and sometimes pressed criminal charges, but none of that would be frightening enough to turn someone into a puppet.

Quaid froze in mid-step, caught up in a vision of grainy vintage mob movies, gangsters and cops racing through dark, rainy streets. Criminals with no souls. Quaid slowly laid the pizza box on the counter and exhaled. Jasper Martin had probably gotten tangled up with loan sharks and was fighting for his life.

And that danger could reach out to touch anyone with whom he was involved.

Quaid hurried into his office and booted the computer, drumming his fingers on the desk while he waited. The empty inbox sent another coil of worry through his gut. He grabbed his phone and dialed Kovak again. Still no answer. He thought for a minute, then scrolled through his phone book.

Sitting back in the chair, he almost held his breath, waiting for that magical voice to answer.

"Hi Garrett, this is a pleasant surprise."

He smiled, loving that she seemed happy to hear from him. Too bad it wasn't a social call.

"Listen, Dixie, I can't get hold of your friend, Kim Kovak. I've left several voice mails and it's extremely important that I talk to her. Do you happen to know where she might be?"

"Ahh, I do, but—"

"You *have* to tell me. She might be in danger."

Dixie's voice softened. "I don't think so, but why don't you ask her yourself."

Before he could respond, Kovak came on the line, her tone not at all friendly. "What danger, Quaid? Is this a joke, tracking me down while I'm on vacation?"

He frowned. Where was she? And with *Dixie?* Anger came on like a Bradley Fighting Vehicle. Kovak had ignored his calls, just blown him off!

"No joke, Kovak. I need those pictures, so what game are you playing anyway?"

"You didn't get them? I sent them this afternoon."

"They never got here. Would you send them again, right away?"

"I can't. I'm out of town, but I'll do it Friday after I get home. Okay?"

Quaid squeezed his eyes shut. "That won't help me. I'm headed out of town myself in the morning." He exhaled loudly. "I could go there and take some myself, but it's too late. I guess this will have to wait until next week. Sorry to *bother* you."

Her tone warmed a little. "Sorry to snap at you."

"Apology accepted. Talk to you later."

He hung up and stared at his computer. Had Kovak actually sent the photos or was she lying? Why would she dodge something like this? What could possibly be more important than evidence to close a case?

He smacked his forehead. *"Bandit!"*

She'd been all gung-ho to find the horse's rightful owner. Clearly, she knew something that *he* didn't. He sat down at the computer.

Opening the Talisman file, he scrolled through the documents to refresh his thoughts, then switched to the Tracer Database to finish what he'd started earlier. Of the three Wade Warrens, only one seemed a good probability. Married, mid-forties, rural address outside Cincinnati. Quaid recalled Kim's comment about the wife's possible involvement in the murder. Jealousy and all that. But Quaid wasn't in the homicide solving business. He simply wanted to know where the lover might fit into the horse thefts. Might be a long shot, but worth tracking down.

He drilled down through the file on Wade Warren. The guy had been in some sort of real estate venture for many years in the western regions of Ohio. Quaid squinted and leaned closer. Warren seemed to specialize in farm property. *Interesting. That would certainly give him access to horse farms where good animals were kept.* Perhaps Mr. Warren was the Ohio contact for the theft ring. They'd need someone in the various places that had large horse events. Columbus hosted the Equine Affaire every spring, and the Quarter Horse Congress in October welcomed over 300,000 people and hundreds of top-notch horses. Yes, Ohio would be prime pickings for theft.

Quaid switched from the Tracer Database to a site he used to discover police records on individuals who'd tangled with the law. Wade Warren was clean, not even a DUI.

Just for the heck of it, Quaid searched Google images and, a few seconds later, all the air whooshed out of his lungs and time stopped.

He grabbed his phone, but Dixie's number went straight to voice mail.

ﻋﻠﻰ

Summer evenings along the Ohio River were the softest, sweetest imaginable. Every care ebbed from Kim's mind as she and Dixie strolled along the promenade by the riverboat landing. Across the river, lights twinkled on the West Virginia shore and a few boats still floated lazily on the current. Music drifted from one of the bars on Ohio Street.

Dixie slipped her arm through Kim's. "I never imagined how peaceful it could be in a place like this. I've always lived near or in a city." A dimple appeared in her cheek. "I could get used to this."

"Yes, I've thought a few times about moving back down here, but it just never happened." Kim stopped walking. "I can't believe Quaid called you to track me down."

"Well, you *are* playing games. You don't think he's smart enough to figure that out?"

"Maybe, but it's actually a good thing I bought some time. You've probably saved me from a life of crime. At least I have some time to figure out what to do about Bandit. Your idea about approaching Fortune seems reasonable."

Dixie squeezed her arm. "Okay, but let's not talk about work now. This is R&R for a couple of very tired girls."

They continued along the street, taking in the sounds and sights of the riverfront before turning down a short side street.

Kim gestured toward an oddly-shaped building on the corner. "This is the Levee Café, my all-time favorite place to eat. You're gonna love it."

They entered and chose a table near a window facing the river.

Kim leaned forward and whispered, "This place was a sleazy hotel at the turn of the century, complete with riverfront whores and a scandalous murder."

Dixie looked around at the art on the walls and the dozens of plants gracing the corners and cornices. "It's so cozy." Her eyebrows suddenly came together, then she pulled out her phone. She stared at it for a moment, then put it away. "One of the disadvantages of always being connected."

"Problem?"

"No, now where were we? You were going to tell me all about your childhood in this charming town."

A waitress appeared and took orders for wine and an appetizer. As she walked away, Kim tried to remember the last time she'd been in the restaurant.

"When I turned thirteen, my grandfather brought me here to celebrate my birthday. I didn't have many friends, just one boy down the road from us who rode my bus. Grandpa wasn't keen on friends who were boys, so my birthday dinner was just the two of us. But we had a great time. Grandpa knew everyone and, by the end of the evening, a long string of folks had come by to wish me a happy birthday."

Two glasses of Malbec appeared on the table, then a plate of calamari with dipping sauce.

Dixie raised her glass. "Happy birthday."

"Thank you, but I stopped having them this year."

Dixie sipped the wine. "Yeah, me too. Excited as I am about the K-9 duty, the routine is more grueling than I'm used to. I'm taking a little heat from the other guys about being the 'senior' in the group."

Kim chortled. "What are you, forty?"

Blue eyes sparkled with delight. "Girl, you are gonna be my best friend. I'll be fifty in November."

Kim raised her glass. "Here's to old broads lookin' good!"

The wine worked its magic and Kim reveled in the warmth and comfort of being in Dixie's company.

"Tell me more about your job, and your dog."

"Saskie. He is so wonderful. So smart, and he seems to be able to read what I'm thinking and anticipate what I'm going to do."

"What kind is he?"

"Belgian shepherd, Malinois to be exact. You should come over and meet him." She grinned. "I can't wait to officially get out on patrol with him."

Kim enjoyed watching Dixie's enthusiasm for the new job, although a twinge of longing ran through her chest. She had everything she'd worked for, everything she'd thought she wanted, so why did she feel empty? Her vow to change her life seemed hollow. What would help? What, exactly, would she change if she could?

Dixie leaned forward. "Space to Earth. You okay?"

"Yeah, just thinking about life choices and how hard they are to make sometimes."

Dixie toyed with the stem of her wine glass, not looking at Kim. "Tell me why a good-looking, smart woman like you isn't married, or at least in a relationship."

Kim blew out a long breath. There it was, the demon she needed to face and put to rest.

"I came real close once, had the ring and everything." She glanced at her left hand, remembering the magnificent sparkling diamonds Peter had chosen for her. "But life offers no guarantees."

"Tell me–I want to know. It wasn't just drifting apart, was it?"

Pain crushed Kim's chest. "Hardly." She drank the last of her wine. "You remember the story I told you about the riot?"

"How could I forget?"

"It was the turning point in our relationship. From the very beginning, Peter hadn't liked the fact that I was a cop and he always acted as though, once we were married, I would quit the force. I think he actually believed it. I was awfully stubborn in those days and I saw no reason to give up my career just because it bothered him. I figured if he loved me, he'd want me to be happy."

"Sounds reasonable to me."

The waitress chose that moment to deliver the salads and bread, and Kim wondered if she wanted to continue this conversation.

Dixie must have seen the indecision.

"So did you guys fight about it?"

"Not exactly. He gave me an ultimatum to choose."

Dixie's eyes opened wide. "You mean between him or the job? Holy crap! What did you do?"

Kim pushed a crouton around the salad bowl. "I told him I'd give him an answer after the weekend." She looked up. "It was the weekend of the riots."

Dixie waited while Kim struggled to frame the words.

"After I got out of the hospital and was finally making some progress in rehab, Peter came to see me one day. He said he couldn't deal with it anymore. We argued, then he finally admitted that he felt like the default choice, that if I'd really loved him, I would have left the force. But my injury had taken the decision out of my hands. He said he'd never feel like he'd been my first choice."

Dixie's face crumpled into sympathy. "Kim, I'm so sorry. What a hell of a story. Why wouldn't he stand by your side through all that?"

She suddenly frowned and looked down again. "What the..." She stared at her phone screen, then sighed. "I'd better see what this is about...Hello?"

Dixie's expression moved from mild irritation to concern. *Oh God, I hope her mother is okay.*

Dixie took a deep breath. "You'd better tell her yourself." She held the phone out to Kim. "It's Garrett Quaid."

Kim snatched the phone, anger rising in her chest, but Dixie shook her head frantically and Kim controlled her voice.

"What's going on?"

Quaid's tone set every nerve on alert.

"Wade Warren is Bill Smith, the guy you saw in all the photographs and in California."

Chapter 33

Kim listened hard, her mind spinning as Quaid expanded on what he'd learned about the dark-eyed mystery man. The main thought running through her brain was the connection between Teri and whatever this Warren was involved in. A sickening feeling rolled through her stomach.

Quaid continued. "What bothers me most is that the guy's history doesn't go back very far. I need to dig a little deeper, 'cause his record is spotless and doesn't fit with your theory."

"Maybe he's fallen on hard times like the rest of the country. Real estate isn't exactly booming right now."

"We'll see. In the meantime, I thought you should know about this. In view of Teri Fortune's murder, Warren might consider your snooping as a threat."

Kim thought for a moment. "I doubt it, but thanks for the heads up."

"So, you're taking a little time off?"

"Yeah, my brain is fried after the California trip. I started thinking about visiting the old homestead, so here I am."

"Well, have a good time. Say hello to Dixie for me."

"Thanks, will do."

"Kovak? Don't be too complacent about this Warren guy. Just sayin'."

Quaid actually thought she might be in danger. Interesting. Why would he even be thinking about her that way?

She handed the phone back to Dixie. "Quaid says hi."

Dixie nodded. "Guess I'd better take care of that sooner than later."

As they walked toward the hotel, the lights of West Virginia reflected on the river. The night air was still soft and warm, and now the only background sounds were the hum of traffic on the bridge and the water lapping against the banks. A comfortable silence enveloped them and Kim's anxiety faded into the night air. She needed this, needed Dixie's rock-solid friendship on which to lean.

Quaid stepped outside his back door and inhaled the night air. The tree peepers were in full voice and, though the sound could be deafening at times, he loved it. Two loud bangs made him jump, then he heard laughter. Someone in the neighborhood was using up the last of the fireworks. His thoughts moved to Wade Warren. A simple scenario would be that he'd gotten involved with Teri either out of true passion or on purpose as a way to get close to the valuable horses in her barn. If the affair was simply an affair, then it stood to reason that the angry wife might have killed Teri. Quaid walked the perimeter of his small yard as he pondered. He knew nothing about Mrs. Warren, but she'd have to be one helluva big strong woman to hoist a dead body to the rafters to mimic a hanging. No, if the wife had killed Teri in a fit of jealous rage, she'd have used a gun or a blunt instrument for bashing. Teri had been strangled. Again, an action requiring strength or skill.

So, back to Wade Warren. Bedding Teri to integrate himself into her life and business was the most logical motive. He'd have had access to her barn office and client records, paperwork for horses, and who knew what else. And pillow talk could divulge a great many secrets, so he'd have had that advantage too. Women seemed so vulnerable when they were in love, often saying or doing things they'd never consider in other circumstances. Had Teri shared information with Warren that could potentially put Kovak in danger? There was no way to know, but Quaid's instincts told him that Warren would be a part of whatever the outcome of this case might be. Quaid clucked his tongue. He was supposed to be wrapping this up, not chasing suspects.

The neighbor's dog barked as he passed by. Glancing up at the dark sky, now brightened by the glow of lights in Cleveland, he headed toward the house to pack. He had a date with a little boy.

Kim hid a smile when Dixie came out of the bathroom wearing pink pajamas covered in little black Scottie dogs. Kim's own well-worn sleep-shirt was blatantly unglamorous in comparison. Dixie grabbed the TV remote, then crossed the room and climbed onto the bed near the window. Sitting cross-legged, she looked exactly like a teenager at a sleep-over.

Kim laughed. "All we need is popcorn and a pillow fight."

Dixie's eyes sparkled. "I remember those days. So much fun. All the giggling and playing with makeup. Part of the process of changing from a little girl to a woman. Getting ready for everything that means."

She flicked the remote and focused on the television screen. "You like old movies? One of these channels has some of the moldy oldies."

Kim slipped under the covers. "You choose. I see so few films I probably won't even know it's an old one."

"You need to get a life, girl."

The TV screen illuminated the room and Kim propped herself up with pillows.

Get a life. You are so right.

Sometime later, Kim woke with a start. The room was dark, the television turned off. She raised her head and looked toward Dixie's bed. A small amount of light came through the edges of the drapes, outlining Dixie's body under the covers. Kim laid her head down and stared into the darkness. Thoughts of Peter surfaced, then faded as they always did—no longer relevant, but still painful. Garrett Quaid's face drifted into her mind and she allowed her thoughts to go back to the street scene in Burbank where she'd found comfort in his arms, if only out of happenstance. Loneliness curled through her chest and her eyes suddenly burned. She couldn't imagine living like this for the rest of her life. There had to be more.

Dixie's soft whisper drifted across the room. "You awake?"

"Yeah, it's too quiet here."

Dixie chuckled softly. "Yeah, and I think this bed is the same age as the hotel."

Kim took a deep breath, taking courage in the cover of darkness. "Can I ask you a personal question?"

"Of course."

Not sure how she'd frame the words, Kim paused.

Dixie's encouraging tone helped. "I have thick skin. Shoot."

"What's it like for you? I mean, being a gay woman."

"As in, how is sex with a woman? It's very different from being with a man. Very sensual, very gentle. Suspenseful."

Images of Dixie with a faceless woman flashed through Kim's head and she felt almost embarrassed at this glimpse inside Dixie's private life.

"Did you ever go with guys?"

Dixie's musical laugh floated in the dark. "Oh, yeah, quite a few tumbles in the hay while I was in college. Nothing permanent ever developed."

Kim sat up in the bed and wrapped her arms around her knees, drawing on a surprising well of courage. "Do you have someone special? A partner?"

A long, soft sigh drifted from Dixie's bed. "I did, but she died a couple of years ago. Breast cancer."

Chapter 34

Quaid turned down the street where Jenna lived, wondering how many more times he would visit this neighborhood. If base housing opened up soon, Ricky and his mother would move to Wright-Patterson immediately. Not something Quaid wanted to think about. As he approached the house, the front door flew open and Ricky bounded down the steps, waving wildly. Quaid's chest tightened. Changes were afoot and they would involve him personally, whether he liked it or not.

Jenna appeared in the doorway, holding Ricky's bags. "You are just in the nick of time. I was about to lock him out of the house so I could think straight."

Quaid turned to his nephew. "Excited?"

Ricky nodded vigorously. "I'm gonna keep a journal of everything we do so I can tell Mom all about it when we get back."

Quaid took the duffel bag and backpack from Jenna and secured them in the back of the truck. When he turned around again, Jenna was hugging Ricky while she gave him a long list of "be-sure-to's".

He struggled to free himself. "Mom, I *will.*"

She looked toward Quaid, as though to add something, but he shook his head.

"He's gonna be just fine, aren't you, Sport?" He winked at Jenna, then waved. "See you Sunday night."

As he backed out of the driveway, he glanced at Ricky adjusting the seatbelt. This boy that Quaid had known from a distance would now be a companion for days. A perfect opportunity to get to know each other and build a true family bond.

"Can we listen to the radio?"

"Sure. What kind of music do you like?"

Ricky started twiddling the knob. "I'll find something good."

As the truck eased into the stream of traffic headed south on I-480, Quaid cringed. He wasn't sure he could stand seven hours of whatever that noise was. He glanced at Ricky, who was bobbing his head to the beat.

What the hell, this is part of knowing who he is.

احبا

Kim turned left into the road leading up to the condos, laughing at a story Dixie had just told about one of the other K-9 officers. Kim glanced at her friend, the best companion Kim had ever had. Dixie's personal pain broke Kim's heart, but she could truly understand the sorrow.

Dixie unbuckled her seat belt. "Well, party's over. Time to get back to the real world...and my mother."

"Is she doing all right?"

"Not really. I'll need to go see her every day now. Apparently, she's informed the staff that she can't eat her dinner unless her daughter has visited." A brief silence. "I never imagined this to be my future. I guess I thought she'd be strong and independent forever. Real wake-up call."

Kim patted her hand, then climbed out of the car and opened the trunk. Dixie reached in and grabbed her duffel.

"If you want company later, just call. I'm going to hang out at home."

Kim nodded. "I have to get those pictures to Quaid before he comes after me with a gun."

"Does he carry?"

Kim cocked her head. "I have no idea. I suspect he owns a weapon, but I haven't seen him with one."

"How about you?" Dixie's tone was offhand.

"Locked in a safe. I haven't touched it since the riots."

Dixie shook her head. "Seems strange. I can't imagine not having my weapon accessible."

"You're working. I'm not." Kim hoisted her case out of the trunk and turned toward the building. "Talk to you later."

Out of habit, she glanced up at the deck.

"Oh, no."

Miss Kitty peered through the railing. The door was open.

Dixie grabbed Kim's arm. "Don't go in." She unzipped her duffel and pulled out a small handgun.

Kim shivered, listening to the familiar sound of the clip sliding into place.

Dixie cocked the gun, then gestured toward the garage door. "I suspect whoever broke in is long-gone, but we won't take any chances."

Unarmed, Kim felt vulnerable, her instincts fighting to surface and direct her actions. She stayed a little behind Dixie as the door rolled up. The garage was small, but there was no place for a person to hide, so they moved toward the door to the apartment.

Dixie tried the door, then whispered, "It's still locked. I'll bet they came in through the slider. Those doors are old and easy to jimmy."

The living room and kitchen didn't show any signs of intrusion. The minute they stepped into the room, Miss Kitty came bounding toward them.

Dixie touched Kim's arm. "Stay right here while I check the other rooms."

She moved down the hallway while Kim waited, heart hammering.

A minute later, Dixie called out, "All clear, but you'd better come look at this."

Kim stopped at the door to her studio and gasped.

"Oh, my God."

Every drawer, every cupboard and closet, every bookshelf had been ransacked. Papers and books and boxes covered the floor.

Her computer and laptop were gone.

ملة

Washington, D.C.

Quaid sank into a chair in the Georgetown motel room and watched Ricky examine the television, coffee maker, and fridge.

"Hey, we can buy sodas and stuff and keep 'em in here!"

"Yeah, but how will that help while we're out sightseeing?"

Ricky looked blank for a moment. "Oh, yeah. Duh."

"What do you want to do first tomorrow?"

"Smithsonian. I want to see every part of it. Then if we have time, we can go look at old buildings and stuff."

Quaid laughed out loud. This would be a real experience.

"Okay, but right now, I'm hungry. How about you?"

"I'm in the mood for fried chicken."

"Good choice, let's go find some."

Half an hour later, they tucked into a pile of Popeye's crispy fried chicken and buttery biscuits.

Quaid smacked his lips. "Boy, I'd forgotten how good this tasted."

"Did you eat here a lot when you were in the Army?"

"Not this particular restaurant, but when the guys wanted fast food, this is what we always chose."

"What was it like, being in the Army?"

Quaid gazed at the boy, remembering his solemnity about heroes, and his almost heart-breaking stoicism at his father's funeral. Ricky might already be thinking about a future in the military, a possibility that made Quaid proud and sad at the same time.

"Just like any other job, only a lot more exciting. We all had our jobs to do, our time off, a paycheck every month."

Ricky nodded. "Yeah, it must have been neat to drive those Humvees." His eyes sparkled. "Did you ever get to drive a tank?"

Quaid grinned. The private sector had an interesting perspective of military life. Except, of course, that of the troops fighting overseas in some Godforsaken desert. Then, the public could see on television what it was all about. But the day-to-day stuff? No clue.

"Never drove a tank or a Humvee."

Ricky's face fell. "Well, what *did* you do?"

"First I was an MP, then I was transferred to Arlington to the Caisson Unit because of my experience with horses."

"Did you ever shoot anyone?"

Quaid frowned. "Jeez, Rick, why so many questions? No, I never shot anyone. Can we talk about something else?"

Ricky looked crestfallen, but nodded. He took a long drink of soda, then wiped his mouth.

"How come you never got married?"

Quaid almost dropped his drumstick.

"I just never met the right girl. Well, I did have one close call." He grinned wickedly. "My job got in the way and she decided she wanted to marry someone who came home after work."

Ricky pinned him with an earnest look. "You could marry my mom."

All the breath left Quaid's chest. The kid was serious! What else was going on in that small brain?

Quaid tempered his tone. "Listen, Rick, it's not that easy. A man and a woman have to fall in love and want to be together. They need to have something in common, and like each other too."

"You don't like my mom?"

"Of course. I like her very much. She's my sister-in-law. She's family. It's different."

Ricky's voice softened. "I don't think Dad would mind."

Quaid's throat ached. He could see that Ricky didn't understand at all, but what could he say to change that?

He stacked the trays, then stood up. "C'mon, Sport. Let's go see the lights of the city."

As Quaid drove toward the core of the nation's capital, his thoughts churned. Ricky was lonely and at an awkward age. *Maybe it would be a good idea to consider moving closer to Dayton. I could be a little more connected to him, help him through the coming years. Yeah, like I know anything about kids.* But would making that move give Ricky the idea that his uncle was interested in his mother? Not that Jenna wasn't attractive and a nice person, but Quaid couldn't imagine being romantically involved with his dead brother's wife.

Ricky pointed through the windshield. "Look! How cool!"

The Washington Monument illuminated against the black sky was breathtaking, the white obelisk mirrored perfectly in the glassy surface of the dark reflecting pool. Quaid had never tired of seeing the buildings and monuments in their night-time splendor, so much more impressive than the towering marble and stone structures of the daytime. As they drove along Constitution Avenue, Quaid pointed to the far end of the pool.

"There's the Lincoln Memorial. We'll see that tomorrow after we've done the Smithsonian. Then on Friday, we can visit the Capitol building and the Library of Congress."

"When are we going to see my dad?"

Quaid laid a hand on the boy's arm. "Whenever you want to."

ولا

The police officers finally left Kim's apartment after almost two hours. She sank onto the couch, her brain spinning. She accepted the cup of coffee Dixie offered.

"Dix, those computers are old. Why would anyone want them? It isn't like they have any pawn value."

"Maybe it wasn't the computers they were after."

"Then why take them? There's nothing but—ohmigod, I'll bet it's the guy Quaid found!"

Dixie paced back and forth, hands on her hips. "If Garrett thinks the man might be a threat, then it's a reasonable idea that the guy thinks you have something that will incriminate him." She stopped pacing and looked at Kim. "*Do* you?"

"If the photos with him in them are tied to any of the thefts, then yes. But someone would have to be quite clever to put all the pieces together based on some random photographs."

"Garrett Quaid is about as clever as they come and I suspect that, even though he says he's done with the case, he wants to know the truth. That's where the danger lies."

"I'd probably better tell him about this."

"Especially in view of the fact that he warned you about this guy. Garrett might know more about him than he's telling."

Kim snorted. "Yeah, that would be right in character. He's a game-player."

Dixie's voice softened. "And he also likes you. A lot."

Kim stood up. "I think you're wrong, but I'm too tired to think about that right now." She looked at her watch. "And it's too late to call him. I'll do it in the morning."

Dixie stepped close and slipped an arm around Kim's shoulder. "Get some sleep if you can. I'm right next door if you need me."

A few minutes later, Kim stared at the deck slider and shuddered. Someone had invaded her home, touched her things, stolen her livelihood. She could think of no more horrible feeling than the one roiling through her head at that moment. Alone and vulnerable, she didn't want company or sympathy. She scooped up her cat and headed for her bedroom.

ناه

When Kim awoke the next morning, a few seconds passed before she remembered the robbery. Nausea pooled in the pit of her stomach and she took two deep breaths, trying to dispel the feeling.

What on earth would she do? Every aspect of her photography business was stored on those two computers. Every client photograph, every commercial collection, every business transaction, all her contacts. She'd been wiped out. Why? Could Dixie be right? Had Wade Warren instigated the robbery because he knew she'd been watching him? He appeared in almost every show photo and, if he was involved in the horse thefts, then it stood to reason that the pictures might incriminate him.

Kim climbed out of bed and padded to the studio door. An involuntary shudder crawled over her body as she scanned the shambles, wondering if the police were finished with the room. She couldn't look at the mess for long. Her assessment stopped at the desk. Her phone still sat in the charger. Games. She'd been playing games and look where it had gotten her. She moved into the room and picked her way through the clutter on the floor.

As she scrolled through the phone numbers looking for Quaid's, she realized that every person she'd dealt with in the past two months was logged right there in her phone. At least she could call her clients and explain the situation. If that was any consolation.

A deep ache began in her thigh, reminding her that she'd lived through worse.

Chapter 35

Quaid's feet were killing him by noon and Ricky showed no signs of slowing down. They'd only visited half of the exhibits in the National Air and Space Museum, a process that took a long time since Ricky wanted to look at everything and read each sign.

Quaid took charge. "Okay, we need to eat. Let's grab a bite in the café, then we can finish. At this rate, we'll never see anything but this museum."

Ricky pulled out the guide he'd picked up at the motel. Poring over it, he nodded. "No, we're good. I don't wanna go to any of the art museums, so that will leave plenty of time."

Thank you, God. "How about the Arts and Industries Building, and the Castle?"

"Yeah, we can do those too."

"Then we need about twelve more hours in this day."

Ricky grinned. "Let's eat."

After waiting half an hour in a line that bordered on ridiculous, Quaid and Ricky carried their ham sandwiches to a tiny table by the window. Ricky read a brochure while he ate, and Quaid simply enjoyed the short respite. About three bites into the sandwich, his phone rang.

His work assistant sounded tense. "Hey, Garrett, admin wants to know if you got those pictures." He chuckled. "You know, the ones of the horse's—"

"Yeah, I know which ones. I wasn't able to get down there, but I'll have them by Monday."

"Why so long?"

"I'm out of town. Family emergency."

"Oh, gee, sorry. Okay, I'll talk you next week then."

Quaid disconnected, irritated by the reminder that Kovak had messed him up. And he didn't appreciate her attitude about whether Wade Warren was a threat. Certainly, her law enforcement background would—

His phone rang again. *Speak of the devil.*

"Quaid?"

Something in her tone set his alert system on high.

"I have bad news. My house was broken into while I was away and...well, those photographs you need are gone. The thieves took my computers."

"Jeezus, really? They take anything else?"

"Nope, just my entire business."

"You had it backed up somewhere, right?"

A long silence.

"I've been meaning to get one of those external hard drives to use for just that, but it never happened."

Quaid's brain was on fire. It could be no coincidence that Kim had photos of Wade Warren and Talisman and Bandit—and now everything was gone.

"I think you've shown up on our theft ring's radar."

"Dixie thinks so too. Any ideas about the next step?"

"I think I'd better advise United Equine that this case shouldn't be closed."

"What can I do to help?"

"I'm out of town right now, but when I get back, I think we need to meet and put all the cards on the table to see where we are. Deal?"

"Deal. Talk to you later."

Quaid pocketed the phone. His gut had been right about Wade Warren. If Teri's pillow talk had revealed Kovak's interest in the Talisman switch, then it stood to reason that Warren would know who Kovak was and where she lived. And if Warren could kill the woman he'd been sleeping with, he'd easily kill anyone who could link him to a crime.

"What's the matter, Uncle Garrett?"

"Huh? Oh, nothing, just work."

"What about? You look mad or worried or something."

"It's nothing you'd understand."

"Jeez, Uncle Garrett, you treat me like I'm a little kid or something. I'm almost thirteen."

Quaid laughed. "You only just turned twelve."

Ricky scowled. "That doesn't mean I wouldn't understand."

Quaid exhaled in surrender. "Okay, I've been working on this case where someone is stealing valuable horses and substituting look-alikes in their place. Then the horse owner calls the insurance company and says his horse is stolen and he wants to be paid. *Lots of money.*"

Ricky nodded, looking thoughtful. "That would take a lot of planning, wouldn't it?"

"You got that right. We think there's a network around the country that has the whole thing plotted out from the time a horse is stolen or gets transported somewhere, to the place where the switch is made. Using a look-alike buys time for the crooks and when the switch is discovered, the original horse is long gone and impossible to trace. What we can't figure out is how the thieves know *where* to pull off the switch."

"They could use a transmitter, like the ones the Air Force uses to keep track of drones."

"Yeah, I thought of that, but it would have to be implanted under the horse's skin before it left home. Which means the owner would be purposely scamming the insurance company. We don't think that's true for most of the cases, especially the horses that were stolen from horse shows."

Ricky nodded, taking another bite of sandwich. "Can just anybody plant a transmitter in the skin?"

"Most folks, no. It would require a veterinarian or a specialist trained with the technique. Which adds more people to the theft ring." Quaid grinned. "You're pretty sharp, you know that?"

"I like spy stuff."

ﬡ

As Kim listened to the New Albany police officer outlining the process for recovering stolen goods, her heart fell. If the computers were taken to a pawn shop, they'd be photographed and catalogued, then put into a safe for the required ten days. Photographs would be available to the local police, but the process could take many days before Kim could try to identify her property. That was *if* the computers were pawned. The officer thought a more likely scenario was kids, bold teenagers who'd rather have the computers than the money. In which case, thought Kim, she'd never get them back.

What's more, she'd been warned that, either way, the hard drives would probably be wiped clean.

She laid the phone down and looked at Miss Kitty.

"What should I do now? Call the Burbank show manager, or wait to see if, by some stroke of luck, I get my stuff back?"

Miss Kitty blinked her big green eyes and moved the tip of her tail ever so slightly.

"You're right, I should call my customers, get this over with."

She turned her gaze to the deck slider, thinking about the conversation with Quaid. He'd been decent about the situation, and she was glad that they would have a chance to talk about the case without sparring. One thing she needed to be careful about was revealing exactly why she'd put off sending him the photographs. He didn't need to know about her plans for Bandit, either the original one or Dixie's Plan-B.

Kim's heart warmed. Through all this mess, Dixie had been wonderful and supportive, like a good partner.

Whereas Kim had wondered about the delicate balance of their relationship, it now seemed so simple. Dixie wanted nothing more than to make Kim happy, care for her, be there for her. What more could Kim ask of a friend?

Later, as Kim climbed into her car, she glanced toward the empty spot where Dixie's vehicle usually sat. Dixie's enthusiasm for her job almost made Kim sad. Once upon a time, she'd been the same, greeting every day with joy and excitement. Why had all that changed? Shouldn't she feel the same way about what she was doing now? Did intrigue and danger have to be part of her life in order to satisfy her? She clucked her tongue. Like the past twenty-four hours hadn't been exciting. A fake cop tailing her and a home invasion seemed enough to stimulate a zest for life.

The fake cop. She'd actually forgotten about him. Was he part of the plot to steal her computers? Maybe he'd been hired by Wade Warren to follow her. Had she been so wrapped up in her own little world that she'd missed seeing him until the day of Teri's burial? She wracked her brain, trying to remember if she'd been anywhere else he could have been watching her. That coil of uneasiness crept into her gut again. *Someone* had watched her closely enough to know she'd gone out of town.

Driving through the pretty countryside toward Delaware, Kim thought about getting her hands on Bandit. Dixie's idea of asking Reggie might just work. If he agreed, she'd need to pay the outrageous board bill, but that was doable. As far as Reggie knew, she was connected to the insurance company. Was there a way to make that work for her?

Teri's barn was closed up tight and the pastures and holding pens were empty. Kim's stomach flip-flopped. What if all the horses were already gone?

She pulled up next to the black Mercedes and took a deep breath, composing her opening comments. As she reached for her shoulder bag, she spotted Bandit's flyer on the floor. Grabbing it, she grinned. The perfect reason to come back and ask questions.

If Bandit was still there.

She hurried toward the barn door, worry gnawing at her gut.

The stillness inside the barn made Kim's skin crawl. At first glance, all the stalls appeared to be empty. *Oh-no, he's gotten rid of all of them!* She walked slowly toward the office, glancing toward Bandit's stall. Without going directly to the stall door, she couldn't see if he was in there or not. Better find Fortune first before he found her snooping around.

As she approached the office door, she called out, "Hello?"

A loud whinny echoed through the building and she whirled around to see Bandit's handsome face appear over the stall door. At the same time, Reggie Fortune stepped into the aisle.

"What are you doing here?"

Kim offered her hand. "I'm from the insurance company, remember?"

His eyes narrowed. "You guys are taking your sweet time on this investigation. I need to finalize my sister's estate and get on with my own business."

Kim pretended innocence. "Oh? You're not in the horse business?"

"I'm a banker and I've been away from my office too long as it is. Are you here to finish this up?" He gestured toward the office. "I have the final board bill for the last month. Someone from your company said I could send it to the insurance company."

Kim hesitated, afraid to take her charade too far. "Shouldn't it go to the owner?"

"That asshole says the horse isn't his and he won't pay board fees. He's pissed because he says my sister lost his horse."

Kim pulled out the flyer. "Jasper Martin is not the registered owner. The horse in that stall was stolen in Texas. As for the lost horse, we have no proof that your sister had anything to do with it. More likely, this is an insurance scam."

"So *now* what do I do with him?"

Kim could barely contain herself. "I know someone who'll take him until we get this thing sorted out. How much is the bill?"

Fortune's phone hummed and he turned away, murmuring a short response, then closed the phone. He swiped a piece of paper off the desk and handed it over. Kim looked at it and sucked in her breath.

Staring him straight in the eye, she said, "This is for real? From what I remember, Teri charged about half this amount for board."

Fortune didn't miss a beat. "I could always just send him to the killer auction."

So we're playing chicken, huh? Kim's instinct told her that Reggie Fortune wouldn't hesitate to ship this horse, or any horse, off to slaughter.

A car door slammed outside and Fortune moved quickly to the desk and picked up a folder. A minute later, a man in a nondescript brown suit came into the room and flashed a badge. Kim's brain reeled with suspicion. Was he a real detective or another pretender?

"Mr. Fortune, I need you to come with me to the station to answer some questions."

"About what?"

The man turned and gave Kim a pointed look. "You'll have to excuse us, Ma'am."

She gave his look right back. "Which station are you with?"

The man's eyebrows came together. "Local PD. Homicide unit. What's your interest here?"

Kim shrugged. "Just curious."

The man escorted Reggie through the barn and, the minute

they disappeared through the door, Kim scurried over and peeked out the window. A plain-Jane gray sedan, typical of unmarked squad cars, was parked behind the Mercedes. The man in the suit opened the rear door and Reggie climbed in. As the car backed around to leave, Kim caught sight of the driver. It was the fake cop from the cemetery. Had Reggie Fortune just been thrown into the lion's den?

Kim's heart thudded and the adrenaline rush sent all sorts of wild thoughts through her head. She could be totally wrong, jumping to conclusions with no proof. She counted back to when Teri was murdered. It had been ten days. If the police had questions for Teri's brother, wouldn't they have already asked them? Surely Reggie Fortune didn't murder his own sister, but possibly he knew or suspected who did. Could he have any connection with Teri's lover, Wade Warren? Anything was possible.

She looked at the board bill again. Fifteen hundred dollars. Reggie Fortune was the real bandit here. Tucking the invoice into her bag, she moved to the desk, scanning the papers and folders strewn across the top. A phone number scrawled on the back of a business card caught her attention and she picked it up. The number had an unfamiliar area code. The printed side of the business card informed her that Reginald Fortune was an executive vice-president of Fortune Five Hundred Financial Services. She pocketed the card, then stepped out into the aisle. Bandit saw her and squealed again, bobbing his head and banging his hoof against the door.

Kim laughed as she walked toward the horse. "You miss me? Or are you just lonely being the only guy left in the barn?"

Bandit nosed her arm, then nuzzled her shoulder, chuckling deep in his throat. Kim's eyes burned and she leaned her face against his smooth cheek, inhaling the indelible scent of horseflesh. The sensation sent her reeling back to her childhood, then fast forward into her life as a mounted cop. *My God, I've missed this so much.*

She smoothed her fingers along his neck. "I'm gonna get you outta here, I promise."

A quick glance inside the stall told a sad story. The bedding hadn't been changed in days and Bandit was looking a little thin. Kim hung her shoulder bag on a halter hook, found a lead rope, and went into Bandit's stall. No way was she leaving this place without taking care of him.

She found a relatively clean stall and put him in it, then climbed into the hayloft. The large area contained only five bales of hay, confirmation of what the women at the cemetery had said. Teri had been on a shoestring.

Bandit eagerly buried his nose in the hay and Kim found a manure rake and wheelbarrow. As she settled into a steady rhythm, she thought about her conversation with Clark Jennings. He'd been most sympathetic, but of course she'd had to offer to repay the fees they'd sent her. She groaned. And now she was considering shelling out a bunch of money for Bandit. She stopped scooping.

"Where in the world am I gonna keep him?"

His whinny echoed through the barn and she grinned.

"Don't worry, I'll think of something," she called out.

An hour later, the stall was filled with fresh shavings, the water buckets scrubbed and filled with clean water, and the hay bag overflowing. Kim put the tools away and walked toward Bandit, who'd been watching her carefully for the past fifteen minutes. The connection she'd made to this horse seemed to be one that he felt, as well. They'd bonded through the sad circumstances of his theft and abandonment. Did he remember his loving lady? Kim was sure that he did, but animals were resilient and Bandit now had a chance for a new life with another loving lady.

While she waited for Reggie's doubtful return, Kim found some grooming tools and set about restoring Bandit's hygiene. The familiar movements and strokes of brushing, and picking a mane and tail soothed her beyond her wildest imagination. It had been too long and she was so ready. Again, the question of where she would keep him prodded her. There were some fancy stables in the Greater Columbus area, but with the loss of her computers and clients, Kim didn't think she could afford to consider something local. Dixie might have some ideas. Kim glanced at her watch. Dixie's hours were a little longer than normal, but she'd be home later in the evening. Maybe they could hatch a plan for Bandit's living quarters.

Thinking of Dixie took Kim back to their time in Marietta. It had been one of the best and most relaxing weekends she'd had in years. Dixie had been such good company and, as they'd roamed the town and explored the shops, it had been no different than Kim remembered spending time with girlfriends when she was younger. After a nice lunch in the hotel bar, they'd driven out to Kim's childhood home. She'd been almost panicky as they approached the road where her grandfather had lived for over sixty years. At one point, she'd told Dixie it was a mistake, she shouldn't be trying to go back, that it was going to be awful. Dixie had calmed her, saying that everything changes and people have to change, too, and move forward. Never look back, that was what she'd said.

As it turned out, the farm was well-kept and looked just the way Kim remembered it. The house was painted, the barn still a little lopsided, but in good repair, and the fences were all intact. In fact, some sheep even grazed in one of the pens at the back of the barn. It was a good homecoming.

Kim's hand stopped in mid-stroke across Bandit's rump as she remembered seeing a sign by Grandpa's driveway. "Pasture for rent"

Chapter 36

Around five o'clock, Quaid stared bleary-eyed at the rush hour traffic on Independence Avenue. He'd lost track of the time and now would pay the price. It would be at least an hour before they got back to the motel. He glanced over at Ricky. The boy's eyes were closed and he leaned against the window. Quaid turned his attention back to the sea of taillights, wishing he could do the same thing. His thoughts turned to Kim Kovak's misfortune. If she'd been robbed because of those photographs, then it stood to reason that her personal safety was no longer an issue. Or was it? Whoever took the photos had what they wanted, but could they be sure she didn't have copies?

Back at the motel, Ricky turned on the TV and Quaid ordered a pizza, then hit the shower. When he came out, Ricky was sound asleep. With any luck, they could head for Arlington in the morning. A rush of anticipation gave him gooseflesh. He hadn't seen his old unit in years. It was time to reconnect, in more ways than one.

He gently jiggled Ricky's shoulder. "Hey, Sport, better wake up before the pizza gets cold."

The boy opened one eye, then burrowed back into the pillow. "Inaminit."

Quaid sat down and took a bite of pepperoni swimming in cheese. He leaned over and pushed on the bed.

"Rick, get up. You need to eat."

Another bout of grumbling, then Ricky sat up and yawned. "Okay, okay. You sound like my mom."

Quaid ate another piece of pizza, lost in thought. Kovak was a smart gal. Maybe the photography was something she did just to keep from thinking about what she really wanted to do. She was a cop, through and through. Her analytical mind, penchant for detail, and ability to see several scenarios in a situation were qualities highly sought after in law enforcement. She also had that annoying stubborn streak—she probably thought of it as being independent—but it was intriguing in its own way. He'd never been around a woman quite like her. And why was he even thinking about this?

Glowing in the morning sun, the impressive gate façade towered above the circular ceremonial area of Arlington National Cemetery. Soft tones of gray and terra cotta contrasted against the blue sky and greenery surrounding the entrance. Quaid looked up, examining the domed ceiling of the structure, noticing for the first time the precision placement of each six-sided medallion. He'd never been through this entrance before, and though he'd spent several years there, the sight of the nation's graveyard still sent a crush of emotion through his chest.

He drove slowly along Roosevelt Drive, all his senses absorbing the perfect rows of white headstones top-stitching acres of brilliant green grass. He'd walked or ridden these roads so many times he wouldn't be able to give an exact number, but it seemed as though it had been only yesterday. He glanced over at Ricky, his small face silhouetted against the window, his eyes focused somewhere in the distance. Quaid's chest tightened. Was this a good idea? Was Ricky ready to visit his dad and refresh the pain? Quaid swallowed. Was *he?*

Ricky sat forward suddenly. "Look! The horses! Can we go over there?"

Alongside another sector, the soul-stirring sight of six white horses drawing a flag-draped caisson sent a burn to Quaid's eyelids.

His voice cracked. "We can watch from over here. This is a solemn and sad occasion for the soldier's family. We shouldn't intrude."

Ricky whispered, "Yeah, I remember, even though I was only a little kid."

Quaid smiled sadly. Four years was a long time to a child, but thank God that time would eventually heal the wounds.

They sat in silence, watching the procession wend its way along the road toward an area where a small group of people stood beneath a dark green canopy. How many times had Quaid watched this same scenario play out? Hundreds? Considering the over 300,000 burials, his own few hundred seemed hardly worth mentioning.

"Can we go see Dad now?"

Quaid eased the truck forward, the unpleasant pressure

growing in his chest.

Ricky looked out the window. "This place is huge!"

"Six hundred and twenty-four acres, to be exact."

"What will happen when they run out of room?"

Quaid closed his eyes. How long *would* it take to fill up Arlington? He let out a quiet breath. Surely someone in Washington knew the answer.

"I have no idea." He pointed to an area on Ricky's side of the truck. "Right over there is President Kennedy's grave and the Eternal Flame. It's been burning since 1963."

Ricky nodded. "I don't remember him, but my teacher talked about him."

Quaid drove back to Roosevelt Drive and headed for the amphitheatre complex.

"Do you want to see the Tomb of the Unknown Soldier?"

Ricky nodded and Quaid turned into the parking lot.

"Boy, this place is busy," said Ricky. "Are they all here for funerals?"

"No, it's a big visitor attraction to people all over the world." He dropped his voice. "Our country's fallen heroes sleep here with honor."

A few minutes later, they stood in front of the massive marble monument that honored those who'd died nameless and unclaimed, a travesty that had always made Quaid's heart ache. Ricky read the inscriptions while Quaid wondered how emotional their next stop would be.

Ricky turned and nodded solemnly. "I'm sure glad my dad isn't in this one."

"Me too," whispered Quaid.

They walked in silence back to the truck. Quaid thought about his brother and how good their bond had been. Ben had always been the responsible, sensible one—Quaid the impulsive, usually-in-trouble one. Even as adults. Ben had found the one girl for him and married her, settled down, done things right. Well, most things. Getting killed wasn't one of them.

Quaid drove toward the southeast section of the cemetery, then pulled over to the curb to allow room for another horse-drawn caisson headed toward another final chapter. He inspected the dark horses, remembering their good nature and willingness to do whatever they were asked. As always, they were sleek and shiny, perfectly groomed, and wearing the black leather harness proudly. The soldiers looked straight ahead, never distracted from their solemn duty.

"Why did you quit the Army? Was it because of Dad?"

Quaid looked over at the only living blood relative left in his life. "The hardest thing I've ever done was to walk beside that caisson that carried your father to his grave. Forever after that, I couldn't perform my duties without those images. I owed it to my comrades to be a productive member of the unit, and I wasn't."

"Are you gonna go see 'em and say hi?"

"I was thinking about it. Would you like to?"

"Yeah, that would be cool. Let's go see Dad first and then we can visit your old job."

⚓

Dixie stopped by the next morning, and laughed when Kim told her about the plan for Bandit. "Boy, you've got this all figured out, don'tcha?"

"Mostly, but I need to do something quickly before the county gets involved. I'm sure that the guys who picked up Reggie Fortune are bogus."

"I can find out, if you like. It might be that with all the funding cuts, the sheriff's department is outsourcing to PI's. It could also be the reason Quaid has had such a hard time getting information from that deputy."

"Yeah, that's a possibility. If you can find out anything, let me know. It will be handy to have some cards up my sleeve when I meet with Quaid."

Dixie set her coffee mug down. "Still playing games?"

"Hah! You should talk."

"Oh, yeah, that. I'll take care of it soon. Leave you a clear shot."

"Wha-at?" stammered Kim. "No, that's not the way it is."

Dixie chuckled. "I'm sure you'll figure it out. Gotta go, Saskie's waiting. See you tonight."

The door closed behind her and Kim sat still, trying to corral the thoughts vying for attention in her head. Before she had any luck, the phone rang.

"Ms. Kovak? This is Sergeant West with the New Albany Police Department. We found your computers."

Quaid took a deep breath and pulled up to the gate at Fort Myer. An MP stepped up to the truck window and Quaid handed over his ID card, then turned to Ricky, who already had his out. The guard examined the cards, then handed them back and saluted.

"Have a nice day, Sir."

Quaid nodded and put the truck in gear, easing forward into a world he'd never forgotten.

"Why did he salute you? You're retired."

"Protocol. Once a soldier, always a soldier."

"Do you miss it?"

"Some days more than others."

He parked the truck and turned to Ricky. "When we get inside the stables, you have to stay out of the way and be careful. These men are busy and on a tight schedule. They won't have time to chat much. And don't go near any of the horses that aren't in their stalls. They're working, and I don't want you to get hurt."

Ricky nodded, his eyes wide. "'Kay."

They walked toward the building where Quaid had spent almost four years. Would anyone he knew still be here? Not likely, and maybe it was just as well. He'd been a mess by the time he'd retired.

The clang of metal against metal rang out and Ricky craned his neck toward the open double doors of the blacksmith's workplace.

"Can we go in there?"

Quaid nodded and they walked into the large space where a brawny man was hammering a glowing horseshoe. Sparks flew like fireworks with every stroke. He glanced up and nodded, then plunged the horseshoe into a tub of water, filling the air with a hiss of steam that rose in a cloud.

"Cool!"

Ricky moved quickly toward the anvil and the farrier held up a hand.

"Watch it, son. This is no playground. Better go back over there with your dad."

The look on Ricky's face slammed through Quaid's chest. This whole idea had been wrong from the beginning.

The farrier stepped closer to Quaid. "Say, weren't you with the platoon a few years ago?"

Quaid stuck out his hand. "Yessir, Garrett Quaid. I'm surprised you remember me."

"Every single man and woman who's ever been part of this battalion is worth remembering." He turned to Ricky. "I'm gonna put this shoe on that horse. You wanna watch?"

Ricky nodded eagerly and followed the farrier to where a muscular black Percheron gelding stood patiently, ears flopped, hip cocked.

The farrier ran his hand down the back of the horse's left front leg. As his fingers touched the fetlock, the horse immediately lifted his foot. Ricky kept his distance, but maneuvered around a little so he could see everything the horseshoer did. Quaid watched in wonder at this boy who was so resilient at such a young age. Quaid wasn't yet ready to think about their visit to Ben's grave a short while before, but just the fact that Ricky seemed able to move on was a great comfort.

Once the shoe was secured, the farrier patted the horse's shoulder and turned to Ricky.

"The Heinz ketchup people donated six of these big beauties to the platoon a few years back." He looked at the horse fondly. "Yep, those horses pulled 30,000-pound Rose Parade floats without even breakin' a sweat!"

He turned back toward the anvil. "Here, let me give you a souvenir. What's your name?"

"Rick Quaid, Sir."

The farrier grinned, then handed over something small.

"You enjoy your visit. I gotta get this guy back to his stall."

Quaid nodded. "Thanks. Nice seeing you again." He steered Ricky toward the door. "What did he give you?"

The boy held up a horseshoe nail that had been twisted into the letter "R". The blacksmith probably went through hundreds of those alphabet nails a year, but it was a nice touch for young visitors.

As they stepped outside, a soldier barked, "Heads up! Horses!"

From the direction of the base gate to the cemetery, the clip-clop of hoofbeats danced a familiar and poignant rhythm. The white team approached, the uniformed soldiers walking beside them, the caisson empty. Quaid glanced at his watch. These animals were done for the day and could look forward to hay, fresh water, and a long snooze. Then tomorrow, they'd do the whole thing over again.

Once the procession passed, Quaid guided Ricky toward the doors to the stables. The soldier who'd been directing traffic came over.

"Good afternoon. Welcome to the 3rd U.S. Infantry Caisson Platoon. The stables are open, but please be careful of the horse traffic." He looked at Ricky. "These guys are pretty tuckered out. They won't hurt you on purpose, but they're big and thinking about grub right now." He looked at Quaid. "If I can answer any questions, don't hesitate to ask."

Before Quaid could respond, Ricky piped up. "We saw two different teams in the cemetery this morning. How many funerals do you guys do?"

"Right now, we're doing eight a day. We work six days a week."

Ricky's eyes widened. "Wow, that's a lot," he whispered.

The soldier's eyes clouded. "Yes, it is. These are tough times for our service men and women."

"I know. My dad's buried here."

The soldier's armor cracked for just an instant and he glanced quickly at Quaid, apology and sympathy softening the lines of his youthful face.

Ricky moved toward a stall, then reached up to pet an inquisitive nose. The rubbery lips flopped and nibbled at his fingers, sending him into fits of giggles.

The soldier moved up closer to Quaid and murmured, "Thank God for the resiliency of youth."

Ricky called out, "Can we look at the wagons?"

In the next building, the soldier's commentary held Ricky's attention.

"These wagons are called caissons. They were originally built to carry cannons, but they've been modified to accommodate the caskets."

Ricky blinked. "Cannons? Don't we use tanks now?"

The soldier chuckled. "The caissons were built in 1918."

"Oh. Duh." Ricky ran his hand along one of the spokes on the great wheels. "I can't wait to tell my teacher I touched a military vehicle from ancient times!"

Quaid grinned, then turned to their host. "I retired from the platoon four years ago. Greatest job on earth."

The soldier looked embarrassed. "You could have answered all his questions."

"Nah, this is better."

As they left the base, Quaid felt a tug in his chest. He really missed military life, the precision and order of it all. He'd been comforted by the fact that time would soothe Ricky's pain, but had he thought about the same salve for his own turmoil? Had he made a mistake bailing out as a knee-jerk reaction to Ben's death?

Ricky's voice broke into the self-defeating thoughts. "I forgot to ask that soldier why some of the horses have riders."

"It's one of those things that carried forward from the earliest war years. The horses pulled the caissons with the artillery, but instead of having a teamster, or driver, like with a regular wagon, the soldiers rode the left horse in each of the three positions to guide them. The horses on the right side of the team carried supplies and feed, like pack animals."

"Those wagons must be heavy to need six horses."

"Oh yeah. The cannons were huge. The caskets don't weigh that much, but the tradition is what's important."

"1918, huh. Was your platoon around back then?"

"The Old Guard is the U.S. Army's oldest unit, formed in 1784 as The First American Regiment."

Ricky nodded solemnly. "Cool."

He turned and gazed out the window as they passed over the Memorial Bridge and between the massive bronze horses on the other side.

A minute later, he said, "You know, I've been thinking about that transmitter."

"Oh, yeah? What about it?"

"It wouldn't have to be stuck under the skin. It could be on something else, like maybe the horse blanket or that leather thing they wear on their heads."

Quaid's jaw dropped. "You're right! Now how could I have missed thinking of that idea?"

Ricky grinned. "You're just too close to the situation. Takes an outsider to see what's really going on."

Quaid's brain was on fire. A tiny transmitter could be easily attached to a halter or blanket or even shipping boots, and it would never be noticed. However, the persons involved in the switch would know, making the horse accessible at any time. Once the thieves hooked up with the horse, they could remove the device, then disappear forever. Ricky's idea didn't preclude the owners being involved, but it certainly gave wider latitude for peripheral individuals to be involved. Stall cleaners, barn staff, even farriers or veterinary staff. The idea opened up endless possibilities.

"Uncle Garrett?"

Quaid blinked. "Yeah?"

"Wasn't that our motel back there?"

꧁

Quaid stuffed the last of his clothes into the duffel bag, then turned to Ricky.

"You got everything, Sport? We can go get some dinner, then get on the road."

Ricky pouted. "Yeah, but I thought we were gonna stay the whole weekend."

Quaid walked over and squeezed his shoulder. "I know, but you basically broke my case and now I gotta get back and work on it."

"Did I *really?* Boy, wait'll I tell Mom!"

Quaid thought about how un-thrilled Jenna would be when they showed up two days early. Couldn't be helped. Whether Jasper Martin's claim was paid or not, Quaid now had Kovak's same burning desire to root out the theft ring. There were a lot of scumbags that needed handling.

Chapter 37

Heavy dark clouds hung low in the sky, the thick air hard to breathe as Kim moved along the brick walkway toward the New Albany police station. She glanced up at the limp flag, proof there wasn't a breeze anywhere. The burnished brass door handle felt cool and the door swung open easily. Her thoughts sharpened as she entered the reception area. They'd found her computers, but no one had shared what condition they might be in. She was hoping for a miracle, but not with much confidence.

The officer who'd called was working the desk. He checked her identification, then buzzed her through to an interview room.

"Have a seat, Ms. Kovak. I'll get someone from Evidence."

Kim sat down and checked her phone for voice mail or text messages, anything to distract her from the worst scenarios racing through her head. The door opened and a woman in uniform pushed her way in with her hip, her arms full of equipment.

Kim jumped up. "Here, let me help." She slid her hands under the desktop computer to help balance the weight. "You need a cart or something for hauling this stuff around."

The officer set the machines down and smiled without humor. "Yeah, along with a lot of other stuff that costs money."

"May I look at these?"

"Before you do, would you confirm they are definitely yours? And you'll need to sign this release."

Kim scribbled her name, then gazed at the woman. "How were they found?"

"Believe it or not, some nine-year-old kid clear over in Springfield found them in a dumpster behind a school. Took them home and showed his mom. She called the local PD and they called us. Apparently, the boy didn't mess with them, but we've no way of knowing what happened before he found them."

Kim ran her fingers over the laptop, finding the dings and scratches from being thrown around. She lifted the cover and pressed the start button. Nothing.

"Oh, the battery was missing when we got it."

"Well, that's a relief. Easy to replace, but I'm more concerned about what was on the hard drive." She turned her attention to the Mac G5 she'd used as her main computer. The screen was cracked. "Looks like I'm going to be spending some serious money."

"I'll help you get these out to your car."

"Did you get any prints off them?"

The officer shook her head. "Only those of the kid who found them. They'd been wiped clean."

As Kim drove away from the station, she thought about that statement. Only a professional would go to the trouble of removing fingerprints from stolen goods. But why had the computers been thrown away? They'd only been missing for three days. Her heart sank. Almost without question, once a computer lab tried to recover the hard drives, she'd find out that fingerprints weren't the only things wiped away.

Later that afternoon, Kim called Teri's farm, hoping Reggie Fortune had returned. The answering machine picked up immediately and she disconnected without leaving a message. If she couldn't connect with someone by five o'clock, she'd drive up and feed Bandit. The thought of him standing in a stall all alone in that big barn sent a wave of sorrow through her heart. The poor guy had been a pawn in the plans of unscrupulous people and now he'd been abandoned.

Her phone chimed and Dixie's cheerful voice came through. "Hey, you got a minute? I called a friend in Columbus about that situation with the Delaware unit, and I was right. They've had terrific funding cuts, have been forced to downsize and reduce personnel hours. For sure, Quaid's contact is one unhappy deputy right now."

Annoyance prickled Kim's neck. "That doesn't mean you stop doing your job. Sorry, I don't buy the 'poor me' syndrome."

"I agree, but not everyone does. Your friend's death is still under investigation, it's just not a high priority with all the other stuff going on day to day. The drug dealers don't know there's a recession, violence is increasing, and theft is at an all-time high."

"You're telling *me?*"

"Sorry, that wasn't a good example. Did you pick up your stuff?"

"Yes, I have an appointment this afternoon with a computer lab to see if my data is still there."

"Good luck with that. Say, you have any idea when Garrett will be back?"

"He didn't say. In fact, I have no idea where he went, just that he was upset that I didn't get his photographs before he left. Now I wish I had. What a mess."

Kim paced the living room a couple of times, not sure what to do with herself until her appointment. She glanced at her watch, then called Teri's barn. Still the answering machine. Remembering Reggie Fortune's business card, she dug into her pocket. A minute later, a woman's crisp voice answered.

"R. W. Fortune's office, may I help you?"

"Hi, I met with Mr. Fortune this morning and forgot to ask him something important about a horse I'm buying. May I speak to him?"

"You must be mistaken. He's been in Mexico all week for a monthly meeting. You may leave a message, if you wish."

"No, that's okay. I'll call back next week."

She disconnected and stared at the phone. Why would Fortune tell his office he was going one place, but actually be in another?

She picked up the business card again and gazed at the handwritten number on the back. On impulse, she dialed. Four rings, then a man's voice.

"Victory Farms."

⟡

After leaving her computers at the repair shop and calling her insurance company, Kim wondered briefly if her insurer would entertain the possibility that the computer theft was bogus. She grinned, thinking about having to dance around Quaid's questions. Nope, she didn't want to be on the wrong side of *that* guy. Of course, she'd already been there several times, but it wasn't that bad. Underneath all the gruff stuff, he was actually okay.

She pondered the implications of Reggie Fortune's connection with Victory Farms. Until now, she hadn't considered him connected to anything illegal. She glanced at the clock. She hadn't heard back from him, wherever he was, and it was too late to go home if she planned to drive up to Delaware. She dialed Dixie's number and left a message.

"Hey, just so you know, I'm going up to Teri's barn to feed Bandit. No one's been around all day and I'm worried about him. I should be home about seven."

When she pulled into the entrance to Fortune Farm, she frowned at the "For Sale" sign. Reggie certainly hadn't wasted any time. She drove onto the property and climbed out of the car, standing for a moment to absorb the stillness of what had once been a busy, vibrant facility. The empty pastures in the dull evening light lent even more sobriety to the picture. The place was a prime piece of real estate and that knowledge sent Kim's mind into another round of what-if's regarding Teri's death. Suppose someone had orchestrated all the misfortunes that had befallen the girl, simply to destroy her business to make the real estate accessible. Not too far from believable. Jasper's horse, then the mare stolen off the trailer. Loss of clients followed by loss of revenue. It would have been only a matter of time before Teri had closed down and the bank seized the property. But someone had accelerated the process by taking her out of the picture.

Who would benefit from that? Was Reginald Fortune's business the one holding the note? Would he inherit? Would he really have murdered his own sister for a piece of real estate?

Kim walked into the barn and took a deep breath. "Bandit?"

The horse hung his head over the stall door and whinnied. She hurried toward him, tears burning her eyes. She had to get him out of this place, and soon.

While she fed and watered him, she thought about how easily Reggie had gone with the supposed detective. Could that have been a charade? But Why? He wouldn't have known she would be there. Maybe *that* was the problem—she'd arrived at an inopportune time. Was the man who showed up, in fact, collaborating with Reggie in some way?

Kim sucked in her breath. The Victory Farm phone number connection was too much to be coincidence. She'd bet money that Reggie was involved with the theft ring. Maybe he'd gotten in the murderer's way. Quaid seemed to think Wade Warren played a big part in this, and it stood to reason that with his wife's association with Teri, Warren might have connected with Reggie at some point. Maybe Reggie threatened to expose whatever Warren was doing. Or vice versa. Kim's head swam with ideas. Right now, a good brainstorming session with Quaid would be helpful.

His number went straight to voice mail and she left a message for him to call her back as soon as possible. She set the phone to vibrate and stuck it into her pocket. After spending a couple more minutes with Bandit, she wandered along the aisle, looking into the empty stalls. They were all in disarray, having been simply abandoned in the past few days. She stopped in front of the stall where the stolen palomino mare had once lived. The mare that had mysteriously disappeared out of the trailer. Stepping inside, Kim moved slowly around the perimeter, trying to imagine the scenario of the mare's theft. Kim kicked a mummified horse apple, then stopped to peer at something white sticking out of the shavings. She toed the bedding aside, then picked up a glass vial marked "Buscopan."

Closing her hand around it, she gazed out the window. "What was going on here, Teri?"

Kim left the stall and walked toward the office. There might be something in the file cabinet that would answer some of her questions, or at least point her in the right direction.

Unlike earlier that morning, the desktop was clear. No papers or mail, another indication that someone had come to the barn that afternoon. Kim moved to the file cabinet and opened the top drawer. It was empty. She looked in the second and third drawers. All empty. Puzzled, she stooped to open the bottom drawer and the lights went off. She jumped up, reaching for her non-existent weapon.

Suddenly, her head exploded in pain. Stars whirled through her consciousness, then faded into complete darkness.

Chapter 38

A deep throb bumped through the base of Kim's skull as she became aware of the hard chill of concrete beneath her. She struggled to open her eyes, fighting the blur and the pain roaring through her head. When her focus cleared, her heart lurched. She lay on the floor of the feed room, staring into familiar unfriendly dark eyes.

Wade Warren offered an ugly smile. "You just couldn't mind your own business, could you? Had to muck about in mine. You shoulda just kept snappin' pictures like a good little photographer and none of this would have to happen."

Kim's mouth felt like cotton. "You killed Teri."

"Excellent, Officer Kovak! I heard what a good cop you were." He sneered. "As though there's any such thing."

"Why did you kill her?"

Warren leaned against the opposite wall and contemplated Kim for a moment. "She wasn't any use to us anymore. She was what you call a loose end. And so are you."

He took a step forward and leveled a gun at her head.

Panic screamed through her brain, but years of training took over. Negotiate. Always appeal to the criminal ego.

"At least tell me how you and Reggie Fortune so cleverly organized the theft ring."

Warren's surprise would have been comical had it not been so deadly. After the initial shock of her comment, he narrowed his eyes and smiled cunningly, the typical stupid thug obviously dying to brag about his accomplishments.

"Stroke of genius, if I do say so myself. Buying time with doubles made the whole operation easy as taking sweeties from a baby. Key people in the horse industry plus a few poor sods who'll do anything for a buck. Perfect set-up."

Kim feigned awe. "Wow. But how did you get the stolen horses to the buyers?"

Warren's dark eyes flashed. "Too many questions. Say goodbye."

Terror surged through Kim's head and she shrank back, waiting for the bullet to take away all her dreams. Instead, Warren's gun butt slammed into the side of her head and fireworks exploded behind her eyes. As she spiraled downward through the darkness, an insistent vibration pressed against her thigh.

~ُ~

Quaid sat back in the booth. "That should hold you 'til we stop for breakfast, probably around six. I'll put the seat back and you can sleep all the way home."

Ricky looked a little pensive.

Quaid cleared his throat. "Listen, I'm sorry about cutting the trip short, but I do need to work on this case."

"It's okay. I didn't want to go look at a bunch of old buildings anyway. Visiting Dad and seeing where you worked was a good way to end the trip."

Quaid's chest ached with emotion. He really loved this kid and would do everything in his power to make his life happier.

He stood up. "Let's go, Sport. We have a long drive ahead of us."

His phone chimed and Dixie's name on the screen sent a jump-for-joy feeling through his head.

Her tone frightened him. "Garrett, I'm not sure what to do. Kim left me a message that she was going up to that farm in Delaware, the one where the woman was murdered..."

"What's the problem?"

"The place has been abandoned except for one horse, which is why she went. But she's alone and not answering her phone. She was supposed to be home by seven."

"Jesus, Dixie, get up there right away. We've discovered someone who's probably responsible for Teri Fortune's death, and they just might have figured that out."

"I'm fifteen minutes from there. I'll call you back."

Quaid disconnected and stared at the dark screen, noticing for the first time that he'd missed an earlier call. Kovak's voice held the excited tone of discovery. "Quaid, I have some ideas about the theft ring that won't wait until you get back. Give me a call when you get this message." He pressed the call button and his shoulders sagged as Kovak's voice mail took over. That damned Bandit horse might have put her in real danger.

He steered Ricky toward the truck, fending off the kid's questions. "Later, Rick. Right now I have to think, so just sit back and listen to your music or something."

He found the ramp to the interstate and set cruise control to 70, then let his mind work, trying not to think about the worst case scenario. The digital clock ticked off the minutes. More than fifteen passed and he was tempted to call Dixie. No, he'd give her time to find out what was going on. She'd call him when she knew something.

~ॐ~

Kim struggled up through the muck and mire of unconsciousness, thoughts tumbling through memories and recent recollections. Hard concrete, pain, horses whinnying. Where was she? Her thigh throbbed and then a memory slammed into her brain.

My God, I've been shot! Red! Where's Red?

An acrid odor burned her nostrils and her eyes flew open. She wasn't on the street, she hadn't been shot. That was a dream—no, a nightmare. She inhaled and coughed. Smoke! A high, terrified whinny echoed somewhere. She struggled to get up off the floor, but her legs wouldn't cooperate. She sank back against the wall and looked up at the ceiling. A distinctive crackle came from above, the sound of something burning at a terrific rate. *The hayloft is on fire.*

As she tried to push herself up from the floor, her hand pressed on something sharp. Despair coursed through her head as she stared at her smashed phone. She was on her own.

She attempted to stand up again and, this time, one leg supported her, but the other was limp and useless. Confusion raged through her head. Why did one leg not work? *Wade Warren!* She supported herself and hopped along the feed bins toward the door. Grabbing the handle, she pulled. Locked. Smoke curled through the crack under the door and she suddenly understood.

Warren hadn't shot her because he knew the fire wouldn't destroy the fact that she'd died earlier. No, he'd planned that the barn would burn down, the investigators would find her and think she'd been trapped in the blaze. The insurance would pay off, Reggie Fortune would be richer, and Wade Warren would still be a free man. They would both win.

Through the door, she heard the frantic cries of her beautiful Bandit.

"Over my dead body!" she screamed.

و

Quaid clenched the steering wheel so hard his knuckles hurt. Helpless didn't even begin to describe how he felt at that moment. The only saving grace was that Dixie was a cop and she was Kovak's best friend. *Or more.* Quaid took a deep breath. *Don't go there.*

The digital numbers on the dashboard clock had only advanced three minutes since the last time he'd looked. Dixie should have called by now. It had easily been more than forty minutes. To distract himself, he thought about Kovak's strange voice mail. What had she been doing that had instigated a desire to talk to *him?* Had she discovered something at the barn, or had she called before she got there?

"Uncle Garrett?"

Quaid jerked, then let out a sharp breath. "Yeah, what?"

"When we move to Dayton, will you come to visit as often?"

"I'll come *more* often, Sport. I might even do a little moving myself."

"Wow, that would be great! We can go to the air museum and I can show you all the neat stuff there."

"Absolutely. But it won't be right away. I have to organize some things first."

Ricky looked at him for a minute, then turned his attention to the night sky. Quaid scowled. He hadn't meant to reveal his plans quite so soon. What if it didn't work out? Ricky would be disappointed and Quaid would once again be the unreliable uncle.

A huge billboard welcomed them to Pennsylvania as Quaid's phone rang.

Dixie was breathless. "Jesus, Garrett, the barn's on fire!"

"Is she there? Is she okay?"

"Her car's in the lot, but I don't see her. I've called 911. I'll call you back when I have something."

Quaid felt like a man trapped in a cage.

و

Kim tried to gather her wits to figure out her next move. She examined the door. It opened inward, so kicking it down wasn't an option. As if she could do such a thing with only one functional leg. She looked down at the throbbing limb, then leaned against the wall and unzipped her jeans. As they slid down around her ankles, she saw the problem. Her knee was swollen with blue and dark red bruises leaching into the skin above and below. Without a doubt, the kneecap was either broken or dislocated. Warren had guaranteed that she wouldn't be able to function when she regained consciousness. She gritted her teeth as she pulled her jeans back up.

"You only *think* so, asshole."

She examined the door again, trying to remember what it looked like on the other side. The door handle looked like an ordinary lock mechanism, not a deadbolt. Or there might be a latch and padlock. If she could find a crowbar or something similar, she might be able to pry the door open. She turned and scanned the room. Bags of supplement, salt blocks, buckets and scoops, a broom, and a ladder to the loft. As her graze traveled up the rungs, she saw smoke seeping around the edges of the trap door. She didn't have much time. In the background, Bandit's frantic neighs tore through her heart.

The room suddenly became brighter for a moment and Kim wheeled around to focus on the small oblong window near the ceiling. A flash of lightning zagged beneath the heavy plank of dark clouds, the brilliant rays lighting up the room and giving her an idea. If she could climb up on the grain bin, she might be able to hoist herself out the window. She grimaced. Now would be a good time to be about twenty pounds lighter.

She hopped over to a shelf laden with supplies and hefted a shrink-wrapped salt block the size of a brick. Calling on her high school days of softball, she threw it as hard as she could. It arced up toward the window and she held her breath. The block fell short and tumbled to the floor. She grabbed another one and moved closer to try again. The block hit the window and disappeared through the shattered glass.

Taking a deep breath, Kim hopped over to the grain bin. Would she be able to hoist herself up there? A sudden roar caught her by surprise and she looked toward the door. Smoke poured under the door, moving quickly in a deadly blanket across the floor.

"Oh God, I've just made it worse."

Eyes burning, she placed both hands on the grain bin and pushed up, managing to get her good knee over the edge. She lay there for a moment, panting and gritting her teeth against the excruciating pain in her right leg. *No time for this, no time. Get up! You have to get Bandit. Go!*

She managed to push herself upright and roll onto her thigh. As she looked up at the window three feet away, a loud pounding sound reverberated through the room.

"Kim! Kim, are you in there?"

Smoke choked Kim's throat and she closed her eyes tightly against the sting of the smoke. She tried to answer, but no sound came out. Her arms began to tremble, then gave out and she rolled over the edge of the grain bin, hitting the floor hard. Pain seared through every part of her body and tears coursed down her cheeks as she listened to Dixie's frantic voice on the other side of the door.

"Kim, stand back from the door. I'm gonna shoot it open!"

Wood fragments flew everywhere as three bullets shattered the lock. In a heartbeat, Dixie was through the door and on her knees.

"Kim! Oh God, come on!" Her voice sounded strangled. "We've got to get out of here!"

She slid her arm under Kim's shoulders and helped her sit up. Kim pointed to her knee, making croaking sounds, but no words.

Dixie nodded, then grabbed Kim under the armpits and pulled her up. Holding her around the waist, Dixie headed toward the door, but Kim's battered body wouldn't function. She started to slump.

"No! Kim, you have to try or we're both going to die!"

A man's voice broke in. "I've got 'er."

Strong arms curled around Kim's body, scooping her off the ground. Kim struggled to talk, tears of panic and frustration blinding her, but all she could do was point toward the stalls.

The fireman's voice was gruff. "We got the horse out. He's fine."

Kim closed her eyes and succumbed to the pain raging through her body.

Chapter 39

Quaid looked at the clock again, then scowled through the windshield. *That does it—I'm calling.* As he reached for the connect button on his Bluetooth, his phone chimed and Dixie's voice came through.

"She's safe, we got her out. God, Garrett, this was awful!"

"What the hell happened?"

"When I arrived, the far end of the barn roof was engulfed. As I got out of my unit, something crashed through a window and that's how I knew where to look for her."

"Let me talk to her."

"No one's talking to her right now. She's in an ambulance on her way to the OSU trauma center." Dixie's voice broke. "She's hurt bad."

"The fire?"

"No, someone beat her up. Head wounds look like a pistol-whipping, and I think her leg might be broken."

Quaid couldn't speak. Of all the scenarios both he and Kovak had dreamed up, the worst ones were clearly right on. Maybe he was partly responsible for her circumstances. If he'd been less worried about his ego and more in-tune with her passion for solving the mystery of the theft ring, perhaps this wouldn't have happened.

"Garrett, I have to go now. I'm following the ambulance and we're almost there. And I've got my police dog with me. I need to walk him and get him some water. Can I call you later?"

"Sure, Dix. I'm gonna be driving all night."

The phone went silent and Quaid lined up all the players in his mind. He had plenty of time to assess each one and figure out who had the most to lose by Kovak's knowledge. And the most to gain by her death.

He took a deep breath and looked over at his nephew, sound asleep as only a child could manage. Then he stared out the windshield into the dark and let his thoughts run.

Around two in the morning, his Bluetooth hummed.

Dixie sounded exhausted. "Hey, it's me. Where are you?"

"About an hour from home. How is she?"

"Out of surgery and heavily sedated. The doctor said she'd probably have a full recovery. No skull fractures, but the damaged knee will probably give her problems for the rest of her life."

Quaid let out a long breath, surprised he'd been holding it.

Dixie said, "What in the world did you guys uncover that got her into this mess?"

"Let's just say that what looked like a simple insurance scam turned out to be a lot bigger. We hadn't worked out the details yet. I'm surprised she didn't tell you all about it."

"She's been more focused on the plight of the horses than the bad guys."

"Did Bandit—"

"He's fine, they got him out."

"What about the barn?"

"Pretty bad, but the firemen got it doused before it was a complete loss."

"Good, 'cause I'm guessing there'll be something there that will help us figure out who attacked Kim."

Quaid blinked as he heard her name roll off his tongue. He rather liked the way it sounded.

"My money's on the brother," said Dixie "The insurance payoff on that place should be huge."

"I'm not so sure. I think Wade Warren is at the bottom of this. I'm going to do some digging later this morning, see if I can find out anything more about him other than what he wants us to know."

Dixie yawned. "I'm beat. Thank God I'm off tomorrow. Saskie and I can just stay in bed all day."

Quaid's vision of adorable Dixie, lounging on silk sheets with a beautiful dog by her side, sent a sharp tug through his groin.

He lowered his voice to a suggestive level. "Mmm, that sounds good to me."

Dixie's tone was soft. "Oh, Garrett. You and I need to talk. Soon."

Bandit nuzzled Kim's cheek, chuckling in his throat and searching her pockets for treats. She laughed and stroked his beautiful neck, admiring his large muscled body and thinking about how much fun they'd have together. Suddenly, he wheeled and headed toward the blazing barn, tail high, kicking up his heels. Kim gasped and started after him.

"No!" she screamed.

Strong hands grabbed her shoulders. She struggled for a moment, then looked around in confusion. Everything was white or cream, it smelled funny, and she became aware of a deep throb in her knee. She focused on the person next to the bed.

"Who are you? Where's my horse?"

The man smiled, his dark eyes warm with compassion. "You're in the best hospital in the state. I'm the physicians' assistant for this ward, but I don't know anything about your horse."

Kim tried to get out of the bed, but he held her back. "No, you can't get up yet. Your friend is here, though. Maybe she knows."

Dixie's face appeared in Kim's line of vision and, suddenly, some of it came back.

Dixie picked up Kim's hand. "How you feelin'? Like a tank ran over you, I suspect."

Kim nodded, unleashing a bowling ball to crash around inside her skull. "Where's Bandit?"

"Animal Control picked him up. He'll be well cared for until you've recovered."

Kim sank back into the pillow and closed her eyes. "Thank God," she whispered.

"I talked to Garrett. He was worried about you. He's coming down later today. Maybe you can tell us both exactly what happened."

Kim refrained from nodding this time. "I'll try, but everything seems a little disconnected right now." She gazed at Dixie for a moment. "You know if Quaid has any family? He seems to be a real loner."

"He mentioned a nephew, so there must be someone." Dixie smiled sweetly. "Why do you ask?"

Kim looked away. "Just curious."

"Mm-hmm."

♆

Tired as he was, Quaid couldn't sleep after they got back to Cleveland. He had put Ricky on the couch and gone into his own room to unwind, but the long drive coupled with the drama unfolding through the night had sent his adrenaline levels to an all-time high. He rolled out of bed and went into his office. Wade Warren was the pivotal figure in this mess. The fact that the guy was so clean made it even more obvious. With some digging, Quaid knew he would discover that Wade Warren was someone else, someone capable of doing evil things.

Reviewing the information he already had, Quaid again tried to fit the pieces together of how the whole theft operation had worked. He was reasonably sure that the slaughter auction was the key factor in the disappearance of Talisman. And Kim—*there it is again*— had pretty much proven that Wade Warren was present at every location where horses were stolen. Unfortunately, all her proof had disappeared with her computers. But that was another problem for another time. The only out-of-step incident in the scenario was Teri Fortune's murder. Was that just coincidental? Quaid hardly thought so. The woman had been too closely associated with Warren.

Just for the heck of it, Quaid brought up the international criminal database he seldom used. It was a long shot, but no stone unturned and all that. The name Wade Warren did not register in the files, and Quaid couldn't even think about how difficult it would be to look up someone named Bill Smith. Quaid's eyelids grew heavy and he headed back toward the bedroom. He'd have to deliver Ricky home in a couple hours. Quaid would be a basket case himself by the time he got to the hospital in Columbus.

Kim woke up with a start, again briefly confused by her surroundings. She looked at the IV running from her arm to the bag hanging next to the bed. Whatever was in that drip seemed to control the pain. She looked down at the tent over her right leg. She didn't even know yet what they'd done. She closed her eyes, remembering the grueling physical therapy after her gunshot injury. This would be worse. The physician's assistant had said the surgeon would come by sometime during the day to explain everything. One thing was sure, she wouldn't be riding Bandit any time soon.

A small sound caught her attention and she looked across the room at Dixie, sound asleep in a large chair. Without being told, Kim knew that her friend had been there all night, been there for her the whole time. Dixie had saved her life. How could she ever repay that debt? Did she need to? Wouldn't she have done the same for Dixie? Of course she would.

Thinking about Bandit brought to mind a number of problematic questions. First, even though pasturage was available at her grandfather's old farm, Marietta was two hours from home—not exactly convenient. Owning a horse involved more than just "owning a horse." The day-to-day communion and bond-building required closer proximity, not to mention the cost of gas to do all that driving. No, Bandit would have to live closer to Kim, and that would require some money. But after all they'd been through together, it would be money happily spent.

A moment later, the reality of the situation sank in. Kim did not own Bandit. On the surface, he belonged to Reggie Fortune. Until she sorted out some official arrangements with the real owner, there was no point in making boarding plans.

Dixie sat up suddenly and stretched. "Oh, good, you're awake." She looked at the clock on the wall. "Garrett will be here in about a half hour."

"I hope I can remember everything," said Kim. "Seems like days ago."

She pulled the rolling bed tray toward her and opened the top. As she caught sight of herself in the mirror, she gasped.

A wide swath of gauze circled her head, a dark blood stain marring the white fabric over her left eyebrow. Half of her face was the color of hematite, a melange of black and brown and blue and dark red. Dark circles hung below both eyes, and the swelling gave her the look of one of those nylon stocking craft dolls. Her lower lip was cracked and scabbed over, and her hair was stringy with who-knew-what.

She looked up at Dixie. "Can you call him and tell him to come tomorrow?"

Dixie grinned. "Well, aren't we just being a girl. I don't think he'd pay attention. If he hadn't had his nephew with him last night, he'd have driven straight here."

Kim pushed a hank of hair off her cheek. "Crap."

ۮ

Quaid waved at Ricky and Jenna, then backed out of the driveway. In the rearview mirror, he watched Jenna give her son a big hug. Deep satisfaction rolled through Quaid's head. The trip had been both painful and wonderful at the same time. Connecting with Ricky was the best thing Quaid could have done for himself, and it was clear that it had been good for the boy too. Jenna had been tickled to see them, admitting that she'd really missed him, that the house felt too empty. Quaid knew that feeling, the emptiness of a dwelling when an important person disappears. The empty place at the table, listening for the footfall that would never come, the longing to hear a familiar voice.

Had he purposely avoided commitments to prevent that from ever happening again?

The trip to Ohio State University Medical Center took less time than he'd expected and, as he pulled into the parking garage, he started organizing his thoughts. Kovak would have key information that would help them solve this case, but she also might be in such distress that some of it might not be accessible. He'd have to take it slowly.

The elevator rose to the fourth floor, the doors whispered open, and Quaid stepped into the wide hallway. To his left, framed watercolors hung on walls painted in muted colors and, to the right, a large nurse's station hummed with activity.

He approached the counter. "Kim Kovak? She was brought in last night."

The woman pointed down the hall to the right. "She's in 457A."

As he walked toward the room, Quaid's chest tightened, whether from anxiety over her condition or the prospect of seeing Dixie again, he didn't know, but it was a feeling he did *not* like. At the door, he knocked lightly, then stepped inside. Dixie was standing beside the bed and she turned, flashing him a smile that would have brightened the darkest room. His heart thumped. Then he looked at the woman in the bed. *Oh, my God.* His heart did another spin around his chest and he almost felt sick. Anger surged up out of the emotion. *Whoever you are, you bastard, I will find you and I will make you pay!*

Dixie tilted her head. "Garrett, you look like you haven't slept in a week."

"Pretty close. I'm gettin' too old for these all-nighters. Uh, drives." He turned to Kovak, trying not to let her see how upset he was, trying not to stare at the kaleidoscope of colors flowing across her cheeks and forehead.

"Hey, how are you doing?"

She gingerly licked her battered lower lip. "I could be better, but you should see the other guy."

The old joke fell flat.

"So tell us about the *other guy.*"

She tried to scoot up to a sitting position, without much luck. Dixie darted forward to help and, with much scrunching about, Kovak finally leaned back against a pile of pillows.

She exhaled slowly. "Wade Warren."

"I knew it!" Quaid punched the air with his fist. "That son-of-a-bitch has been on my radar from the beginning."

Dixie murmured, "You might want to lower your voice or we'll have the security people in here with us."

Kovak took a deep breath. "I went up to the barn to check on Bandit because this morning Reggie Fortune was escorted away by a guy flashing a badge. I don't for a minute think he was legitimate, but that's not important. I was worried that Bandit didn't have food. Someone had cleared the office desk of everything, but I just figured Reggie had come back at some point."

She took a sip of water, then continued. "Since I had the place to myself, I decided to snoop around a bit." She grinned sheepishly. "I do that a lot. Anyway, the file cabinet had been cleaned out, too, but before I could look at anything else, the lights went off and someone hit me on the head."

"You didn't hear them come up behind you?"

She started to shake her head, then winced. "I think he was right there in the office the whole time. I was concentrating on my snooping."

Dixie sat on the edge of the bed. "What happened next?"

"I woke up on the floor in the feed room, with a splitting headache. And there he was, Wade Warren, just leaning against the wall, watching me. Then he started giving me a hard time about minding my own business." She grinned. "But you know me..."

"Did he tell you anything useful?"

"He admitted to killing Teri because—get this—she was a loose end. Then he got agitated and started threatening me. I pretended to be impressed by his theft organization, and his ego bought right into it. When I asked about how they got the stolen horses to buyers, he lost it. That's when he knocked me out again." She took a deep breath. "When I woke up, the place was on fire and I had a knee the size of a football."

Quaid paced the floor at the end of the bed. "We've got him. You can identify him and we've got him."

"But no proof he was ever there, Quaid, other than my word."

He stopped pacing and turned to Dixie. "Was the barn completely destroyed?"

"Only some parts."

Quaid headed for the door and Kovak called out, "Hey, where are you going?"

"Fortune Farms to collect some fingerprints."

"Quaid, that's dangerous!"

He turned, grinning like a Cheshire cat. "Yeah, but unlike you, I have a gun."

Dixie's voice followed him down the hall. "Garrett, wait!" She trotted up to him, eyes flashing. "I should go with you."

He hesitated for just moment, his thoughts torn between getting evidence for the case or spending time with Dixie. The case won out and he shook his head.

"Not a good idea. She needs you here."

Dixie's tone became wheedling. "I can help you. I can get the prints run by one of my friends at the department. Otherwise, you'll have to ask the sheriff's department and they won't appreciate your meddling." She grinned. "You remember Deputy Dexton, don't you?"

Damn. This is why women always get the upper hand. They don't play fair.

"Okay. Your car or mine?"

"Yours. I still have the squad car and the dog. Let me go tell Kim what's going on. Be right back."

Quaid watched her small, trim body saunter down the hall and disappear into Kovak's room. This would be interesting.

Chapter 40

Quaid waited in the garage while Dixie parked her vehicle and put the dog on a leash. The animal was magnificent, muscular and masculine, covered in shiny mahogany-colored fur. His muzzle and ears were black and his intelligent eyes took in every detail as he approached. He glanced up at Dixie, adoration and respect reflected in every movement.

Dixie stopped about four feet away. "Sit."

The dog obeyed immediately. Dixie leaned down and stroked the top of his head.

"Saskie, this is my friend. Say hello and play nice."

The dog's tail thumped once and he looked up at Dixie, clearly making sure he understood her tone. Dixie stepped forward and the dog rose to his feet, his tail waving softly from side to side.

"Saskie is a Belgian Shepherd Malinois. Just stand there and let him get your scent. When he noses your hand, you can pet him on the head. Then we can go."

Saskie checked out Quaid's shoes and pant leg, then shoved a cold, wet nose into his fingers. Quaid grinned, pleased that he'd passed inspection.

A few minutes later, Quaid drove the truck out of the parking garage and turned onto the street that would take them to Route 23. Saskie sat in the middle of the bench seat, an effective chaperone for his handler.

Quaid grinned. "I guess no one has to worry about *your* safety any more."

She ruffled the dog's ears. "It's an amazing feeling, even though I carry a weapon."

Saturday traffic was heavy and they managed to hit every other red light. Quaid didn't mind, though, because he had Dixie's full attention. As far as he was concerned, the trip could take forever. The feeling was short-lived.

"Garrett, I really need to talk to you seriously."

He waited a beat before answering. "About what?"

"Us. I've just been being selfish, enjoying your attention and company."

He glanced over at her solemn face. "So what's wrong with that? Isn't that what relationships are all about?" He gulped at his use of the word "relationship."

"Exactly. But I haven't been completely honest with you."

Quaid gripped the wheel. *Here it comes.*

Just then, a car shot out of a side street, slithering into the small space in front of them and clipping a car that waited at the light. Quaid slammed on the brakes, nearly knocking Saskie off the seat.

Dixie jumped out of the truck and strode toward the culprit, unsnapping her holster as she walked. Saskie put his front feet on the dashboard, eyes riveted to his handler, ears rigidly upright. He whined, then let out a yip.

"It's okay, boy."

The dog turned his large head, pinning Quaid with unfriendly eyes.

Oh my God, I'm mixed up with a woman who packs heat and a vicious dog. Good choice, Quaid.

He immediately broke eye contact with the dog, turning his attention back to Dixie. She was on the phone while she examined the driver's papers. Three minutes later, a city patrol car rolled up. Dixie spoke briefly to the officers, then walked back to Quaid's truck.

"Damned smart-mouthed kid. I'm so glad I don't do traffic anymore."

The police directed the backed-up traffic around the fender-bender, and Quaid relaxed as they left the urban area and rolled into the more rural part of Columbus.

"I think maybe you shouldn't bring Saskie on our next date."

Dixie was quiet for a moment. "That won't be a problem. Say, could you find a place to pull over so we can talk?"

Quaid didn't like the direction this was headed, but there wasn't much he could do about it. A few miles up the road, he saw signs for a public park. He pulled into the deserted parking lot, then turned to Dixie, trying to peer around the dog.

"Okay. What's going on?"

She told Saskie to get down on the floor, then she scooted over to sit closer.

Touching his hand, she smiled sadly. "Garrett, I'm gay. I should have told you right from the beginning, but I *like* you. A lot. I wanted to be able to spend time with you and laugh the way we did the night we met. So, I kept putting it off and putting it off."

He gazed at the woman who'd finally penetrated his armor, wondering why his choices were always so wrong. She was so beautiful, so nice. So unavailable.

Apology reflected in her blue eyes. "Can you forgive me? Can we still be friends?"

He smiled wryly. "I think I knew, but didn't want to admit it. You were just too easy to be with, not like any other woman I've ever tried to date. They all turned me into a blithering idiot."

She chuckled. "Some of my best friends are men, for the very same reason."

What the hell, go for it.

"So, are you and Kovak..."

"In a perfect world, yes—realistically, no. I'm crazy about her, but she plays for a different team."

Why this made Quaid feel better, he didn't know, but suddenly his life seemed a little less confusing.

"Thanks for telling me before I made a complete fool of myself." He grinned and put the truck in gear. "Let's go catch some bad guys!"

∽♐∼

Quaid sucked in a sharp breath as they turned into the driveway leading to Teri Fortune's barn. Only two-thirds of the structure remained standing, rising above piles of charred wood and debris. The ground was saturated with thousands of gallons of water, and the heavy fire equipment had left cavernous ruts in the mud. Yellow caution tape surrounded the site, draped from fences to the corner of the building and tied off on a burned-out tractor parked by the back of the structure. Even with the truck windows closed, Quaid could smell the acrid odor of disaster.

"At least no one's here to run us off," said Dixie.

She opened the door and stood aside while Saskie jumped down. He sniffed the ground, lifted his head and tested the air, then looked at her expectantly.

"He's been trained as a rescue dog, so he probably thinks that's what we're doing." She led him over to a grassy spot by the fence and waited while he peed, then put him back in the truck. "Good boy. I'll be right back."

Quaid watched her, thinking about their earlier conversation. What he didn't understand was why a beautiful, intelligent woman like Dixie would be a lesbian. She could have any guy on the planet. Had she always been this way, or had some unhappy event in her past driven her in that direction? It didn't matter. He liked her and if the only way he could spend time with her was in a platonic relationship, he'd take it.

She gestured toward the door. "You first. I'm just along for the ride."

"Hang on." He opened the truck door and reached into the glove compartment to grab a small blue box. "Okay, we're all set."

He ducked under the yellow tape. "You found her in the feed room?"

"Yeah, down at the end there. I hope I didn't destroy any evidence when I shot off the lock."

"Warren had to touch both sides of the doorknob, so we're probably okay. He would never dream that the fire wouldn't take the whole building, so I'd be willing to bet money he didn't wipe his fingerprints."

At the door to the feed room, Quaid hesitated, his brain churning with images of how terrified Kovak must have been, crippled and trapped inside a burning building. He tried to discard the thoughts.

The door jamb and edge of the door were shattered, but the handle itself was intact. From the blue box, Quaid removed a small brush, a jar of powder, and a roll of fingerprint tape. A few moments later, he held the tape up to the light.

"I'd say we've got him. There are some smudges, too, and I'm sure others have touched this handle, but we shall see."

He went through the same procedure with the inside handle, then looked around for anything else Warren might have touched.

Dixie said, "He probably left prints in the office, too, although I think it's badly damaged from the fire."

"We can take a look."

Quaid left the feed room, glancing toward the stall where Bandit had once stood. The horse that had started it all. *What a mess.*

They walked across the aisle toward the fire-razed portion of the barn. In the silence, the building suffered softly, stressed timbers creaking and groaning.

The office no longer had a roof, and two of the interior walls were gone, looking as though they'd been knocked down by the fire fighters looking for embers. Quaid shuddered and his step faltered.

"Garrett, you okay?"

"Yeah, just had a nasty flashback to a fire I investigated in Kentucky a few years back."

"Barn?"

He nodded, trying to disperse the old images. "I still have nightmares about it."

She touched his arm. "That's because you have a heart."

He cleared his throat, suddenly uncomfortable with the conversation. Stepping into the office space, he looked around.

"Kovak said the file cabinet was empty. You think Warren did that?"

"Could be. Depends on what he was trying to hide, but from the looks of it, I suspect you won't get any prints."

Quaid pulled out the fingerprint tape again. "Never pass up an opportunity."

When he'd finished with the file cabinet, he did the same with the desk drawer.

"Warren would have looked for the feed room key and it's logical that Fortune kept it in here."

Outside, Saskie barked twice and Dixie turned. "I'd better go to him."

Another series of groans and creaks emanated from above.

"I think we should get out of here. This can't be a safe situation."

As she spoke, another loud groan, then a resounding crack

from out in the main area.

Quaid grabbed her arm and propelled her toward the big doors. As they dived through the yellow tape, a section of roof crashed to the floor, spraying shards and splinters everywhere. Dixie slipped in the mud and went down.

"Damn it! I just had this uniform cleaned."

Quaid tried not to laugh, but she looked cute sitting there with mud on her cheeks and indignation flashing in her blue eyes. He held out his hand.

"I might have some sweats in the truck."

She grasped his hand and stood up, grinning with embarrassment. "Oh, *those* should fit really well."

Quaid climbed into the driver's seat and gazed out the windshield, listening to the sounds of Dixie shedding her muddy pants. Maybe this platonic thing could work. It was nice to be able to relax around a woman, have that softness and compassion they all seemed to possess, without him needing to play the games that seemed necessary to function in an intimate relationship. He let out a soft breath. In just a matter of a few hours, he'd told Dixie about his ineptness with women, and revealed his emotions about his job. Yeah, this could work. If he moved closer to Jenna and Ricky, he'd also be closer to Dixie and Kim. He shook his head, startled by the way the photographer kept getting into his head.

Dixie climbed into the truck. "Okay, I'm all set. What's next?"

"How soon can you get the prints run?"

"After I pick up my vehicle from the hospital, I'll drop the prints off at my friend's place. She'll do them first thing in the morning."

"I appreciate this. I'm not officially investigating this thing, but I want to know for my own peace of mind."

"And for Kim's. She's been a hundred percent dedicated to routing out these guys and making them pay."

Quaid turned and draped an arm across the back of the seat. "You have any idea why she never went back to the force? I know she was shot, but she's *such* a cop."

Dixie looked pensive. "Sometimes our fears consume us, the

self-preservation response overwhelms reason and the vicious circle spins out of control. I think that's what happened with Kim. Plus there were some relationship issues right in the middle of it."

Quaid lifted his eyebrows. "Such as?"

"It's not my place to tell you. Kim's an extremely private person and I will respect what she told me in confidence." A sweet smile curled the corners of Dixie's mouth. "Of course, if you get to know her better, she might just tell you herself."

Uh-oh. Matchmaking.

Quaid slipped the gear shift into first and eased out of the parking area, trying to think of a way to direct the conversation elsewhere. He turned onto the highway and glanced in the rearview mirror.

"Hmm, someone just drove into the farm. Looks like a black Mercedes. Maybe we should..."

"Should nothing. We have no business snooping around there. Let's just get back to the hospital."

Dixie's phone rang and her face brightened. "Hey, Kim, how're you feeling?...that's great. If you want me to pick them up, I can... Okay, yeah, we're on our way back right now...no, we can talk when I get there." She closed the phone. "The computer geek was able to retrieve all Kim's data."

"Great." Quaid was unable to suppress a yawn. "Sorry."

"You look beat. When was the last time you slept all night?"

"Um, must have been Thursday, but I don't sleep all that great in a strange bed."

"Where were you, anyway? If I may ask."

"I took my nephew down to Arlington to visit his dad's grave."

The words hung in the air, surprising Quaid with their impact.

"Oh, Garrett," she said on a soft breath. "That must have been tough."

"It was, in some respects. He's such a trooper, but he's still just a little boy who lost the hero in his life. Watching him at the cemetery was almost harder than the day we buried my brother."

"You want to talk about it?"

Quaid stared out the windshield at the yellow line ribboning off through the countryside. Yes, he did. He'd not been able to talk to Jenna, not wanted to open the wounds again. Ricky would tell her and that would be better. Yes, talking to Dixie would be good for his soul.

"We visited all the famous graves in the cemetery before going to the section where Ben is buried. I really worried that the whole idea was a mistake, but Ricky actually was strong enough for both of us. When we got there, he sat down on the grass beside the marker and ran his hands over the letters. He said 'Hi, Dad,' at which point I almost lost it. He was so brave, so intent on making the visit a good one. He continued talking to the gravestone, telling Ben about school and some bullies, and how his mother was doing better, but still missed him. At that point, I had to turn away. I had my own thoughts that I wanted to share with my brother, but not in front of his son."

Quaid stopped talking for a moment, thinking back over the events of that day. Dixie, in her womanly wisdom, remained silent.

A few moments later, he continued. "Before we left, Ricky dug into his backpack and pulled out a little statue of a mounted soldier. Ben was with the 1st Cavalry Division known as the War Horse Soldiers. Anyway, Ricky set the statue on the marker, then stepped back and saluted."

Quaid's eyes burned with the memory.

Dixie reached out and squeezed his hand. "That's a beautiful story. Thank you for sharing something so special with me."

He met her gaze and knew that, for as long as he wanted her friendship, Dixie would be there for him.

Chapter 41

Kim gazed at her full leg cast, then stared at the crutches. "This should be interesting."

The nurse's aide grinned. "You'll get the hang of it in no time, I promise."

He took hold of her arm, steadying her as she rose to her feet. She grasped the crutch handles and eased the padded tops into her armpits, then took her first step forward.

"Use your hands and arms for support or you'll be sore."

She took three more steps, realizing immediately that a lot of things in her day-to-day life would have to change to accommodate these contraptions. She galumped through the door into the hall, then stopped to catch her breath.

Quaid sauntered toward her with that charming lopsided grin. "Don't you ever relax?"

His voice sent a ripple of pleasure through Kim's head and she laughed.

"Look who's talking. Did you get any prints?"

"We did and they are on their way to Dixie's lab friend as we speak."

"Is she coming back here?"

"I don't know. She had a little altercation with a mud puddle, so she was headed home to change clothes. And she had the dog with her."

The nurse's aide spoke up. "Let's get you back to your room. Don't overdo working with the crutches. You can practice again later tonight."

Kim turned with some difficulty and hobbled back into the room, Quaid close beside her. She sank onto the bed, stunned by how exhausted she felt. This sure threw a monkey-wrench into her life.

Quaid pulled a chair closer to the bed, then sat back and crossed his legs.

"Looks like we stirred up a hornet's nest. I spoke briefly with the fire department and they are considering arson. Of course, you and I know that, but at least they're on the case, and looking at Reggie Fortune as the person with the most to gain from the fire. With your identification of Warren and the fingerprints that will put him in the barn, the fire marshal will probably nail him."

"Maybe Reggie sent Warren there to torch the place and I just happened to get in the way. Warren definitely wasn't expecting to have a conversation with *me.*"

"Could be, but I can't find a connection between Fortune and Warren."

"Maybe Fortune financed some horses for Warren's wife. Most of the animals in Teri's barn were top-dollar breeds. That would give Reggie the introduction to Warren."

"Yes, but unless Fortune is dealing in shady loans, he'd have no reason to be involved with a thug."

Quaid's face suddenly blanched, and Kim knew exactly what thought had just surfaced.

They both said it at the same time. "Loan sharking!"

Kim's excitement grew. "Jasper was in deep trouble with the Feds. If Teri knew it and told her trusted lover, Warren, he might have collaborated with Reggie to put the squeeze on Jasper to coordinate the theft."

Quaid nodded. "And Warren told too much to Teri, which put him in a dangerous position."

Kim thought for a moment. "She was very unhappy for those couple of weeks before she died. I thought she was just worried about her reputation, but looks like there was a lot more to it. Poor Teri." Kim sagged back onto the pillow. "Lord, I'm tired. Sorry."

Quaid stood up. "You need a ride home tomorrow?"

She looked up at the man who'd been both adversary and partner. Regardless of their personality differences, she knew she could count on him for support.

She nodded. "Thanks, that would be good. I think Dixie's working through the weekend, and I've already taken too much of her time."

Quaid gazed down at her, a knowing smile playing about the corners of his mouth. "She thinks you're worth it."

The next morning, Kim watched while Quaid fiddled with knobs and levers, then shoved the passenger seat as far back as it would go.

He stepped away from the truck. "That should work." He threw her a mischievous grin. "If it doesn't, you can ride in the back."

"I might have to. This cast is gonna be like trying to accommodate a two-by-four everywhere I go."

With the help of a hospital staffer and Quaid, Kim managed to get up from the wheelchair and hoist herself into the truck. Her armpits ached and her arms were wobbly as muscles protested against the unusual exercise she'd put them through on the crutches. She closed her eyes briefly. This could only get better in the coming days.

With light Sunday morning traffic, the ride home took less than thirty minutes. Kim thought about some of the things she needed to tell Quaid, beginning with her foolish attempt to keep him from closing the Talisman case.

"Are you in a hurry to get back to Cleveland?"

"No, why?"

"I have a few more insights about our case."

Quaid glanced at her, his expression hard to read. Was he irritated? Surprised? Already knew something?

"Yeah, I figured. You feel up to it right now?"

"I'm fine, just a little bed-weary."

He pulled up in front of the condos and Kim leaned forward. "How did my car get back?"

"Dixie and I picked it up last night. She took your camera stuff into the house."

"You know, at some point in this mess, I thought about that, but they had me so doped up I couldn't keep a thought in my head for more than two minutes. Thanks for doing that. The last thing I need right now is to shell out a couple thousand bucks for a new camera."

"Dixie picked up your computers too. Oh, and fed the cat."

"She takes good care of me." Kim cocked her head. "So you guys spent the evening together?"

The lopsided smile appeared. "Yeah. She's great. Just like one of the guys." He glanced over at Kim. "And yes, she told me. No further discussion needed."

In her newly-found wisdom of fifty years, Kim kept her mouth shut.

Quaid helped her out of the truck, then stayed close by as she made her way to the door.

"Come on in," she said. "We'll get some coffee going and figure out this whole debacle."

Quaid walked past her into the kitchen and began filling the coffee maker with water. Kim eased onto a stool at the breakfast bar and let out a long sigh of relief. Miss Kitty effortlessly leaped up to Kim's lap and peered at the strange man making himself at home in the kitchen. She watched for a moment, then butted her head against Kim's chin, purring loudly.

Kim glanced at the two computers sitting on the counter, then picked up a sheet of paper with Dixie's distinctive script rolling across the pale blue lines.

The computer guy said the desktop is not fixable, but he did get all the data. Your photos and files are stored on the external drive. The laptop only needed a battery. He put one in. He said you could just transfer the backed-up files to your laptop.

I'm working until seven today, but I'll be over as soon as I get home. There's food in the fridge and a pizza in the freezer. And plenty of beer.

Love, Dixie

Kim's eyes burned. How did she rate such a wonderful friend?

Another sheet of paper lay beneath Dixie's note. An invoice for the computer work. Kim sucked in a breath. Her snooping had cost her plenty. She opened the laptop and pressed the start button. The machine whirred softly and the screen began to brighten.

Quaid set two mugs of coffee on the counter and sat down next to her. "You back in business?"

"We'll see shortly. Thanks for the coffee." She took a sip, gingerly testing the temperature.

Setting it down, she turned to face Quaid. "I'd better start with the pictures you wanted for the insurance company. I did get them, and I *was* going to send them to you. When I told Reggie the horse didn't belong to Jasper, he threatened to send him to the killers. I couldn't let that happen. I had to contact the real owner first. I needed time, so I didn't send the photos to you."

Quaid looked at her long and hard, then nodded.

"How did that all work out?"

"The real owner knew that Bandit had been stolen at a horse show, but his wife had just died and he really had no heart for the whole mess."

She took a deep breath, wondering if she should tell Quaid the rest of it.

He whistled softly. "So the Talisman theft *was* carefully orchestrated, right down to finding the perfect look-alike. So what happened after you talked to Bandit's owner?"

Kim squirmed. *Here comes the bad part.* "I called Reggie, pretending to be from your insurance company..."

"You *what?* Kovak, you—"

"Let me finish. I just told him the horse couldn't be moved until the file was closed. I needed some time to figure out what to do next."

Quaid stared at her. "You had no business posing as a company employee."

"I didn't have a choice. Reggie Fortune had no qualms about sending Bandit off to the auction. It's—"

"I know, I know. It's all about the horse. And look where *that* got you."

He took a deep breath, as though to say something more, then he looked away.

Taking advantage of his change in mood, Kim busied herself setting up the external drive to transfer files to her laptop, then sat back.

"This will take about twenty minutes. As soon as I can access them, I'll e-mail Bandit's identification photos to you. You can watch me do it, just to be sure."

Quaid got up, poured himself another cup of coffee, then stood on the other side of the breakfast bar, his expression solemn.

"Listen, I think I understand. I'm as confounded as you are

about this whole situation. But when it comes down to reality, neither you nor I have any authority to do anything more than turn our evidence over to the investigating organizations. I have to provide the photos to the insurance company, even though I'm certain Jasper is not totally innocent in this deal. Whatever we find—or *think* we find—about Teri's murder or your near-death experience has to go through proper channels. We are *not* law enforcement, no matter how invested we are in this situation."

"I know. I just can't believe that poor horse has been abandoned."

"Dixie told me that you want him."

Kim gazed at Quaid's sincere expression. Should she just tell him the truth? Once he'd closed his case, did the disposition of Bandit even concern him?

Quaid grinned. "Well, here's a news flash. The fire marshal said the fire was started with a pile of file folders and papers doused in gasoline. You said the filing cabinet was empty. I suspect there's no record anywhere of who really owns Bandit. He might just be yours for the taking."

Chapter 42   *Cleveland*

Quaid opened Kim's e-mail and downloaded the photographs to his Talisman folder. He'd go over all his notes and evidence one more time before writing up the report for United Equine. He hated seeing Jasper profit from this deal, but there seemed no way to prove his involvement.

The phone rang and Dixie's voice warmed his heart, as usual.

"Morning, Garrett. How you doin'?"

"Excellent, as always. Got home about seven last night, had a burger on the way, and was in my bed by nine."

"Lucky you. I was late getting off shift and by the time I got home, Kim was in bed. We talked for a little while. You can't imagine how happy she is about that horse being up for grabs."

"Oh, yes I can. She lit up like a Christmas tree when I told her."

"I believe it. Okay, my lab friend called awhile ago. She said there were quite a few smudges and partials, but she got a couple of hits on the prints you lifted, both the ones from the feed room door handle and the desk drawer. Reggie Fortune popped up as a result of a routine bonding investigation, and the other print belongs to a William "Willie" Shank. He's in the system for petty larceny about fifteen years ago."

Quaid's shoulders sagged. "Crap. I was hoping to nail Warren. Why the hell was this Shank person at Fortune's barn? Unless..."

"He was hired by Warren to set the fire?" said Dixie.

"That's the only explanation, unless he was a barn client."

"Sorry the news isn't better. Listen, I need to get going. I'm on again at three and I need to check on Kim, then swing by and see my mother."

"How's she doing?"

Dixie sounded pensive. "Some days are better than others. I never know what to expect."

"Call me any time if you need to talk."

"Thanks, Garrett. I definitely will."

Quaid hung up and stared at the name on the notepad. *William*

"Willie" Shank. The man was somehow connected with Warren or Fortune, maybe both, but in what capacity? Recalling the brief conversation with the fire marshal, Quaid considered calling the guy back to see if they'd located this Shank person. Surely the arson investigators had checked the scene for fingerprints. Or maybe in a fire, they didn't do that because of the smoke, heat, and water damage. Quaid scribbled a note to himself to make that call today.

Jenna phoned a few minutes later. "You busy?"

"Not at all. Everything okay?"

"Yes, we're just fine. Ricky's starting to come down from Cloud Nine. I can't thank you enough for taking him to Arlington. He's talked about nothing else. I actually feel like he's going to be okay."

"It was as good for me as it was for him. I had lots of time to think about stuff."

Jenna's voice changed slightly. "I got a call this morning from Wright-Patterson. A house became available unexpectedly and we can move in two weeks."

"Wow, that was fast! Congratulations."

Quaid didn't feel quite as pleased as he tried to sound. Things were moving quickly and now he'd have to make some important decisions.

"How did you get bumped to the front of the line?"

Jenna chuckled. "Friends in high places. No, actually, the psychologist who interviewed Ricky recommended that we relocate as soon as possible. I was as surprised as you. But, oh Lord, now I have to start packing and figure out what to do with the stuff I'm not keeping."

"Just give me a holler and I can come help you."

"Thank you for that. I don't think we can do it by ourselves." Her voice cracked. "This will be the first house move I've made without Ben."

After Quaid hung up, he thought about the new life that Jenna and Ricky would have. A new home, new friends, a break with the painful past and all the reminders of the way things had been. Ben would always be in their hearts, but Quaid was sure that, wherever his brother was right then, he was happy that his family was going to find peace.

ॐ

Kim sat on the couch, a pillow propping her leg on the coffee table. Miss Kitty seemed to think the whole arrangement was for her benefit. She walked all over Kim's lap and chest, paraded down the cast to the table and back, tail held high. But even her feline antics didn't raise Kim's spirits.

"This is the absolute pits. Glad I'm not booked to do a horse show any time soon."

Which was both good news and bad news. The expense of replacing her stolen equipment and any medical costs not covered by her insurance would make a significant dent in her bank account. And for the time being, she had no way to refill the coffers. She stared out the deck doors, feeling sorry for herself.

The doorknob rattled and her punk mood disappeared as Dixie came in, carrying a white bakery bag.

"Thought you could use a little sugar jolt." She came over and set the bag on the couch beside Kim, then leaned down and examined her face. "Your bruising is already starting to fade. You'll be good as new in a couple of days."

"The bruises I can live with. The cast, not so much."

Dixie pulled a plump blueberry muffin out of the bag, placed it on a napkin, and handed it over. "Consider the time as a resource. How often do you have the opportunity to do nothing but think and ponder things?"

"I've tried real hard not to let that happen."

Dixie sat down and rested her hand lightly on Kim's arm. "You can't run forever. Use this time to face whatever demons you're battling and bring them to task. Don't dwell on the past—you don't live there anymore."

"Thanks, you're right. I'm just being a big baby. I do have some things I can do while I'm immobilized. Would you bring my laptop over here? I have about ten thousand photographs to sort and store."

Dixie set the computer on the couch next to Kim, then put her hands on her hips. "I have to go now. Mom's having a good day, according to the staff, so I'd like to see her before I go to work. You call me if you need anything, okay? I'm in the car with Saskie today, so I can get here if need be."

Kim's throat tightened and her voice cracked. "Thank you for everything. I—"

Dixie put a finger to her lips and shook her head.

Kim listened to the soft thud of the door against the frame and the sound of Dixie's footsteps. An ache grew in Kim's chest. The time had come to face the things that paralyzed her.

رله

Quaid typed the final summary of the Talisman case, then printed it out and sat back to read through it. The whole thing was pretty basic. With the photographs of Bandit's unblemished penis to support Jasper's claim of non-ownership, plus the identification flyer for Bandit's legal owner, United Equine would have no option other than full payment. Irritation prickled Quaid's neck. Jasper Martin would be a hundred grand richer at the expense of hundreds of other customers. Equine insurance was not cheap, and those honest horse owners who protected their investments in good faith would end up paying higher premiums because of people like Martin.

Had the guy hired someone to steal the horse? Or had he simply gotten tangled up with the wrong people and become a victim? Would Quaid ever know? Probably not.

He fixed two typos in the report, then transferred the whole file to the FTP server at headquarters. A feeling of disappointment washed over him as he hit the upload button. This hadn't been one of his better cases.

He rose from his chair and wandered out into the living room. The place was a mess, just like he'd left it. Had he expected the housekeeper fairy to come during his absence? He opened the drapes and basked for a moment in the sunshine pouring through, then started picking up newspapers and magazines. As he tidied the room, he thought about Kim Kovak's unfortunate situation. She'd be laid up for at least four weeks, maybe more, and that could put a dangerous crimp in her pocketbook. All that time with no work and nothing to do. And what about Bandit? How would that turn out?

A nice memory worked its way into Quaid's head, long-ago rides through the pastures on a spunky Quarter Horse named "Spark." At the time, in his disdain for country life, Quaid had taken his horse for granted. Every kid who lived in the sticks had a horse. Not a car or a good bike, but a horse. And yet, those solitary treks over the rolling hills and through knee-high rye grass had been Quaid's salvation, though he hadn't known it at the time. He hadn't been on a horse since his platoon days.

He walked into his office and sat down at the computer. A window informed him that the file transfer had been successful. He opened a browser and, grabbing a pen, pulled his notebook closer to focus on William Shank's name. Who *was* this guy, anyway?

A Google search turned up nothing. Opening the Tracer Database, he plugged in the name and waited while the search engines worked. Sure enough, William Shank was in there. In fact, he had more than just a petty theft arrest. He'd been involved in gambling and some investment scams. It appeared that Willie Shank might have had a reason to be in Teri Fortune's barn after all.

Switching to Google images, Quaid again used the man's name to search the files. The screen loaded and Quaid jumped out of his chair, punching the air.

"Yesss!"

William "Willie" Shank was none other than Wade Warren.

Chapter 43

Kim picked up the phone and gazed at Quaid's number for a moment, surprised at the mixed emotions churning through her head. With the final piece of evidence for the Talisman case, Garrett Quaid would end his involvement, making it unlikely that Kim would ever see him again.

"Hi, Quaid. What's up?"

"I just wanted to bring you up to speed on those fingerprints. Remember we wondered why Wade Warren seemed to have no apparent history? Well, I just discovered that he's someone else, a transplanted thug from London by the name of Willie Shank. Came over here—or rather escaped from the law in the UK—about twenty years ago. Apparently, he was heavily involved in some nasty racing scandals. He's on Interpol's wanted list."

"Wow, just like a Dick Francis novel."

"Pretty close, and Shank's just written a few more chapters here in the States. Did you ever talk to the police while you were in the hospital?"

"Yes, they came and took my statement, but they didn't stay long. At least, I don't think they did. Whatever pain killer I was on did a number on my memory. The whole thing seems like a dream, except for the cast. That's for real."

"I suspect they'll question you again, give you some time to remember the events. So, if the arson team ran fingerprints, Warren's going to get caught. At least for the fire. I'm sure the Fire Department shares information with the police, so it's only a matter of time before Wade Warren is arrested. Right?"

"Possibly, although things don't usually move as fast as in the movies."

Quaid thought a moment. "You know, if the police pursue the assault aspect, you might have some more involvement."

"That suits me just fine. I'd like to nail the bastard for anything that will take him out of circulation in the horse industry." She shifted her hips, trying to relieve the cramp that was starting in her thigh.

"Any more info on Jasper?"

"No, but I suspect he's still trying to dig himself out of whatever financial sinkhole he's in. I'll tell you one thing, though, if he was even remotely involved in the thefts in any way, he could go to jail. I checked with an FBI friend of mine. Transporting stolen goods across state lines is a federal crime. I just wish we could figure out who organized this. It has to be someone with connections and a lot of knowledge about both horses and international law, someone who can mix comfortably with both the legitimate community and the lowlifes."

Kim nodded thoughtfully, then suddenly jerked so hard she made her head hurt. "Wait a minute! I called Reggie Fortune's office Friday afternoon and his secretary told me he was out of town, but I'd been with him face-to-face early that morning."

"Out of town, like where?"

"Mexico. She said he goes there every month for—"

"That's it! He's the connection!"

"Quaid, what are you talking about? Slow down."

"I never got a chance to tell you about my trip through Texas, but after I put some pieces together, it looks like the horse auctions near the Mexican border might be the key."

Kim blinked. "You're going to have to spell this out for me."

"There is some paperwork required to transport horses across the border, but papers are easy to manipulate. Horses bound for slaughter must have a number-coded microchip, as well as paperwork. I think our stolen horses are tracked by tiny transmitters attached to their halters, then loaded at the auction site onto Mexico-bound trucks, and taken to a holding area for the slaughter house. The contact for the buyers is waiting on the other side to collect the animals that don't have microchips. You did say that there's a hot market for good horses in other countries. With his financial background, Fortune would be a perfect person to coordinate this thing."

"The ban on slaughterhouses in this country provided the perfect environment for such a plan. Quaid, you are a genius."

"It's only a theory and without some bad guys, who would believe us?"

"I think we need to talk to your Deputy Dexton, give her what we know and what we think. Maybe this thing will turn out the way we want it to after all."

Quaid sounded resigned. "Let's hope so. Listen, I have to run. You take care of yourself. I'll see about setting up a meeting with Dexton when you feel up to it. You keep me posted if you hear anything more."

Kim spent some time thinking about all that had transpired in such a short time. With any luck, the loose ends would be tied up soon. Except for the mare stolen from Teri's trailer and the possible switch of Robidoux.

Remembering the items she'd found in the palomino's stall, Kim did a quick search on Buscopan. The drug was used for control of colic pain, but Teri had said she didn't give anything to the mare. Kim read further through the pharmacological data, then sat back, cold realization sweeping over her. When administered to a perfectly healthy horse, the side effects mimicked colic: dilated pupils, increased heart rate, no gut sounds. Someone had set up Teri to take the mare off the property.

Kim dug through her bag and found David Craig's card.

"Mr. Craig? This is Kim Kovak. We met at the show in Burbank..."

"Oh, yeah, the show photographer. I hope you got some good shots of Robidoux 'cause we lost him on the trip home."

Kim's chest caved in. "Oh, I am *so* sorry!"

"So are we. Apparently, one of the grooms gave him too much sedative and he had heart failure." Craig's voice cracked. "He was the best horse I ever had."

Kim slowly closed her phone. The beautiful Robidoux was undoubtedly now living in another country, and some poor look-alike had been killed to cover up the theft. Feelings of helplessness crashed over her. This thing had a life of its own.

Quaid sat back and reviewed everything he'd just learned. Why would a small Ohio financial company have monthly dealings in Mexico unless there was something shady going on? First thought would be drugs, but Reggie Fortune's involvement with the horses and the mess at Teri's barn made theft-for-profit a more likely reason. Time to make some calls.

"Delaware County Sheriff's Department."

"Deputy Dexton, please."

"She's not in until tomorrow. Do you want to leave a call-back, or can someone else help you?"

"No, just ask her call me when she comes in."

He gave his number, then immediately dialed the City of Delaware Fire Department.

"Good afternoon, this is Garrett Quaid with United Equine Assurance. I understand the barn fire last week is being looked at as arson. May I speak to the investigator on the case?"

"He isn't here today, but maybe I can help you. What do you need to know?"

Quaid smiled. It was always helpful to get hold of someone who had no idea that they shouldn't be giving out information.

"Did the arson crew get any fingerprints, or was the place a complete loss?"

"I think they did take some prints, but of course getting the results back takes a long time. Your company the one to contact with information?"

"Yes, but we haven't started the paperwork yet. Someone will get back to you in a day or two, and I'll call back later when your arson guy is in."

Quaid hung up. He was venturing into dangerous territory here, planning to reveal criminal information that he shouldn't even have. Deputy Dexton would probably eat him for lunch, and who knew how the fire department people would react. Nevertheless, it was the right thing to do. Both he and Kovak needed closure on this, and soon.

The insurance case was wrapped up, the perpetrator of the fire and Kim's assault soon to be under arrest, and Teri Fortune's murderer identified. So why did he feel this way? He stood up and walked into the living room. All the really bad stuff was more or less under control, but the theft network—the reason he'd become more involved—was still out there, slithering through an unsuspecting horse community. And he could think of no way to stop it.

Chapter 44

Kim's armpits ached from the pressure of the crutches. More painful was the pressure in her chest as she stared at the small Kahr 9mm handgun lying on the sofa cushion. It would take her awhile to get used to having it in plain sight, but common sense had finally overridden her painful memories. She ran a finger lightly over the smooth steel and a shiver sluiced through her body.

She'd been hobbling around the house for the past half-hour, thinking about all of Quaid's revelations. The connection between Reggie Fortune and the theory about the Mexican slaughterhouses made perfect sense, but how would they prove it? Or even get the authorities to take a look? She stopped at the deck slider and gazed at the trees shading the tennis courts. The FBI would be more likely to get on this case than the locals. Maybe that was the answer—alert the Feds that there might be a case of interest.

She picked up her phone to call Quaid. He had FBI connections, so he'd be the person to instigate the heads-up. The phone chimed and she squinted at the name on the screen. "Delaware County Sheriff's Department."

"Ms. Kovak? This is Detective Green. I spoke to you in the hospital. How are you doing?"

"Better, thank you."

"I'd like to come by and ask you some more questions about your assault. When would be convenient?"

"Any time. I'm sure not going anywhere."

"Okay, I can be there in about an hour."

He verified Kim's address and hung up, leaving her wondering if she could contribute anything of value to the case. She began a detailed mental replay of everything that had happened from the morning she'd first visited Reggie Fortune until she'd awakened in the hospital. Surely somewhere in that mess she had important information.

An hour later, Detective Green arrived. He had a nice smile and a friendly manner, but Kim was Old School.

She smiled. "Badge?"

A small flicker of irritation passed over his features, but he pulled out his identification. Kim nodded and gestured toward a chair opposite the couch.

He sat down and pulled out a little notebook. "I understand you're retired from the Columbus force."

"Yes, over five years now."

"Ms. Kovak, I know I asked you some of these questions before, but you were a little fuzzy."

"I don't remember much of anything about our conversation."

"What were you doing at the Fortune barn that day?"

"I went there to check on my horse."

Kim almost smiled at how easily the words slipped from her lips. *My horse.*

"Who else was there?"

"No one. I had talked to the owner, or rather the owner's brother, earlier in the day, but he wasn't around when I came back."

"How long were you in the barn before you were attacked?"

Kim thought a moment. "About an hour."

A cold knot formed in her stomach, remembering how quickly her visit had deteriorated.

"And all that time, you never heard or saw anyone else in the building or on the premises?"

She shook her head.

"Tell me again what happened. How you ended up locked in the feed room."

Kim related the events as she remembered them, from the time she'd been knocked out until she'd awakened to the smell of smoke.

"You say you recognized your assailant, a Wade Warren. How do you know him?"

"I've had a few encounters with him at horse shows, but it's my understanding that he was intimately involved with Teri Fortune."

"The woman who was murdered there?"

Kim nodded, her throat tightening. "Warren admitted killing her."

Detective Green's eyebrows shot up. "Describe exactly what he said and what he was doing at the time."

The detective's pen moved furiously over the notepad as she related the painful conversation, wishing Quaid were there to help out. Should she mention to the detective that Warren was actually someone else? No, that would reveal that she and Quaid had been meddling in an official investigation. But if she withheld the information, would Warren elude apprehension and disappear into the fabric of the population, never to be held accountable for Teri's death?

She took a deep breath. "And that's all I remember."

The detective nodded, then looked her straight in the eyes. "Can you tell me why your fingerprints were all over the file cabinet in the barn office?"

Kim met his direct gaze without wavering. "I was looking for horse health records to send back to the owners, but all the file drawers were empty."

A sharp rap on the door preceded Dixie's bright smile. She stopped suddenly, then came into the room.

"Sorry, I didn't know you had company."

The detective stood up and held out a hand. "Detective Green, Delaware County."

Dixie shook his hand. "K-9 Deputy Davis, Franklin County Sheriff's Office."

Kim watched Dixie in a role she'd never seen, brisk and all business in her crisp uniform.

Green's expression showed a hint of irritation. "I'm investigating Ms. Kovak's assault. We're just about finished here, if you'll excuse us."

Dixie looked at Kim. "I think I'll stay. I might be able to contribute something."

The detective's jaw tightened, but he nodded and looked down at his notebook. "You were going to tell me about your fingerprints in the office."

Dixie stepped forward. "Wait a minute, if this is the line of questioning, then Ms. Kovak needs her lawyer present."

Green gave her a hard look, then pocketed the notebook. "Okay, I'll be back in touch."

He strode toward the door, then turned. "Don't leave town."

Kim stared at the door as it closed, then burst into laughter. "That was like something out of a bad movie."

Dixie nodded. "So, how much did you tell this guy? I mean, about what you and Quaid are doing."

"Nothing. Quaid's arranging a meeting with the deputy working on Teri's case. We'll try to get all the information out on the table and hope for an arrest. Lord, I'll be glad when this is over."

"You'd better call Quaid right away and give him a heads up on this guy's visit. But listen, I just stopped by to see if you need anything. Saskie's in the car and I need to get back on the road."

"I'm good. Thanks for bailing me out."

⁓

The following morning, Kim leaned against the wall to take the pressure off her arms while Quaid talked to the Delaware County deputy behind the glass partition. As he turned away from the counter, a door opened and a tall woman stepped out. She filled out her uniform in a way that should have been illegal, and her features were classically beautiful. Large blue eyes, warm brown skin, and black hair sleeked back into a bun at the nape of her neck.

"Mr. Quaid?"

Kim choked back her laughter at Quaid's reaction. Clearly, he'd never met Deputy Dexton. *This should be fun.*

Quaid managed to compose himself and said, "This is my partner, Kim Kovak. We've been working an insurance case together." He brought on his charming smile. "Figured it was time to bring you up to speed on what we've learned."

Dexton looked mildly surprised, but didn't smile. "We can talk in the conference room."

Quaid pulled out a chair and waited while Kim fumbled with the crutches and sat down. He took the seat next to her and they both faced Deputy Dexton across the shiny table.

She laced her long fingers together and looked at Kim. "You're the woman who was involved in that assault and barn fire, right? So what is this about?"

Quaid answered. "We were investigating a horse theft at that barn at the time the owner, Teri Fortune, was murdered. Kovak knew her quite well and, over the course of the last few weeks, uncovered some information that might have significance in the case. You interested?"

A brief flicker of anger tightened Dexton's features. "I believe I told you, Mr. Quaid, that if you had any information about the case, you were to report it immediately. I can arrest you for interfering—"

"We're telling you now. So are you interested or not?"

Quaid didn't wait for a response, just dived right in.

"We believe that Teri Fortune's brother, Reginald, is involved in a horse theft ring and it ties into his sister's death."

Dexton's eyes widened at the mention of Reggie Fortune and she leaned forward. "What do you know about Mr. Fortune?"

"What do *you* know about him? We came here to trade information and see if justice can be done, not to play games."

The deputy studied Quaid for a few seconds, clearly trying to decide whether to play the heavy, or take advantage of information she might possibly need for her investigation.

Finally, she nodded. "Okay, that's fair. We've been keeping tabs on Fortune for awhile because he's being investigated by the FAA for some flight plan discrepancies that might tie into another case."

Kim leaned forward eagerly. "Like flights to foreign countries?"

Dexton's fine eyebrows arched. "Yes, how did you know that?"

"A fluke phone call to his office."

Kim related the conversation she'd had with Reggie's secretary, all the while taking great pleasure in the excitement she'd kindled in Deputy Dexton.

Kim continued, "For our own case, his regular flights to Mexico might be the key to where the stolen horses are ending up. And I think he might have hired someone to burn the barn to destroy evidence." Kim glanced down at her knee and grimaced. "I was unfortunate enough to be in the wrong place at the wrong time."

Dexton looked up and, for the first time since they'd met, her stern expression softened. "You must have been terrified."

"I was, but the result was worth it, knowing who killed my friend Teri."

The woman nodded. "Yes, I read the detective's report. You

named a Wade Warren, but our fingerprint report came back with only Reginald Fortune and an unknown person named William Shank."

Quaid cleared his throat. "Ah, yes, well Warren and Shank are the same person. And Shank is really bad news."

Dexton's tone became menacing. "And you know this *how?*"

Quaid offered his best lopsided grin. "I'm a private detective, Deputy. I detect stuff."

Dexton snatched up the telephone, pushed a button, and spoke into the mouthpiece as she glowered across the table at Quaid.

"Pick up Wade Warren. The file is on my desk."

She hung up the phone and looked down at her notes. "I appreciate you two coming in to share. What I don't appreciate is amateur sleuths mucking around in my business. I should charge you both, but in view of the fact that this could close the case, I won't." She stood up and turned to Kim. "Detective Green says you were at the barn to visit your horse. The county took him to Animal Control. I suggest you arrange to take him home. They can't keep him much longer."

Kim's heart swelled with joy. "That's our next stop."

"I'll tell them you're on your way." She opened the conference room door and stood aside. "Thanks again for coming in."

She met Kim's gaze. "Good luck," she said softly.

᯼

Quaid turned the key in the ignition. "Whew! She is some piece of work."

Kim chuckled. "You're just surrounded by lady law enforcement, aren't you?"

"Yeah. Sure is different from the good ol' days."

"Okay, don't go there. Welcome to the twenty-first century."

Quaid backed out of the parking space. "We've sure dug up a load of manure, haven't we? Basically closed Dexton's case for her, identified Teri's killer, possibly nailed Warren for the barn fire. At least got a good handle on how the thefts are being done. Identified Bandit. Too bad we can't hang Jasper Martin on all this."

"He'll hang himself on something, you can be sure of that." Kim sighed. "There's still a lot that we don't know. How did those fake cops figure in? Were they part of Reggie's theft ring? Was Wade Warren's wife involved? Was she the woman with him at the horse shows?"

Quaid glanced over and grinned. "I guess you can take the cop out of the force, but you can't take the force out of the cop."

Kim glowered back. "Yeah, well *this* cop is out."

"Yeah, right. Say, how about we consider our case closed and let the law figure out the rest?"

"Yes, indeed."

"Ready to go see Bandit?"

"Yes, indeed."

Chapter 45

As they drove, Kim gazed at the beautiful green countryside, painfully aware of how close she'd come to never seeing it again. An uncontrollable shudder ran through her body.

"You okay?" Quaid sounded concerned.

"I'm fine, it will just take some time to erase the images from my brain, but I should be pretty good at that by now."

"Turning off the voices in one's head isn't the easiest thing in the world."

They rode along in silence for a few more miles, then Quaid pointed through the windshield.

"I think that's the place."

Fenced kennels ran the length of one side of a sprawling, flat-roofed building. At the back of the property, electric ribbon fenced a small pasture. Even from a distance, Kim could see a lone horse standing by the run-in shed. Her heart thumped.

Ten minutes later, a rosy-cheeked woman wearing a county uniform beamed at them.

"You're here about that horse? Glad someone finally claimed him. He's a real sweetie."

Kim's emotion choked her, so Quaid took over.

"We're just here to check on him. We still need to make some arrangements for his transfer. How much longer can you keep him?"

The woman's smile disappeared. "We don't have funding to keep large animals for longer than a few days. They cost a fortune to feed. If you can't move him by tomorrow night, we'll have to transfer him to one of the rescues. I don't know what their policies are for releasing a horse once they've accepted it."

"Not a problem. We'll have him out of here tomorrow. Can we see him?"

"Sure thing. Follow me." She glanced at Kim's crutches. "Be careful, the ground's pretty rough."

Kim focused on each step, making sure the crutch tips didn't slip into a hole or catch on a high spot. Her arms ached from the work and her brain ached from the concentration. She exhaled sharply when they reached the fencing.

A long, loud whinny pierced the air and thundering hooves beat a rhythmic accompaniment to Bandit's cries. He raced across the pasture toward them, tail up, mane flying.

The woman chuckled. "No doubt about who his mommy is!"

Tears burned Kim's eyes as Bandit slid to a stop just short of touching the electric ribbon. The animal control officer opened the gate and they all entered the pasture. Bandit moved immediately to Kim's side, snuffling her clothes, inspecting the crutches, and making little noises in his throat. Kim smoothed her hand along his neck, savoring the sleek smoothness of the rich brown hair, the warmth of his huge body, and the indescribable horse scent that was indelibly stamped on her psyche.

⁕

Quaid helped Kim into the truck, trying to wrap his brain around her emotional reunion with Bandit.

He climbed behind the wheel and she gazed at him. "*Now* what? You've promised the horse will be out of there tomorrow and I've made no plans or arrangements."

He put on his best grin. "Well, I've been thinking about it for a couple of days. You're going to be out of commission for quite awhile and I thought I might pick up Bandit and keep him up by me. I could take care of him, keep him happy until you're ready to take him."

Her jaw dropped. "You'd do that for me? I've been wracking my brain trying to figure this out. But do you have a place for him? Boarding a horse is not a cheap exercise, and I do have some income limitations right now. To say the least."

"I have a couple of friends who might be able to help. I'll make some calls tonight." He glanced over at her. "Really, I'd love to do it. I can catch up on my riding and grooming skills, and I can have my nephew over on weekends. He'd love it."

The reminder of Jenna's move hit Quaid suddenly and he gripped the steering wheel hard. Where the hell was his life headed? At forty-eight, he had no family, no roots, no plans other than getting through each day. And now he was taking on a horse. *Time to prepare Plan B.*

Kovak gazed at him. "I don't know what to say, other than thank you."

Her smile sent a surprising jolt through his chest.

He grinned. "That'll do."

و

Quaid's brain was on fast-forward all the way back to Cleveland. Surely he could find a place to board Bandit for a few weeks. Finding a horse trailer to rent or borrow was quite another matter. He mentally searched his long list of acquaintances in the area. Did he know anyone with horses? He grinned, feeling a little foolish. He'd sure jumped into this without thinking it through, other than being the hero with Bandit.

His phone rang and he turned on his Bluetooth.

Jenna's voice held a lightness he hadn't heard in years. "Hi, Garrett. You busy?"

"Nope, just driving. I'm almost home. What's up?"

"I'm going to take you up on your offer to help us pack. Can you come over tomorrow?"

"Aw jeez, Jen, I have something to do that can't be put off. I might be able to come in the evening, though. Especially if you'll feed me."

She chuckled. "I can always feed you. What's going on tomorrow?"

He blew out a long breath. "You won't believe what I've gotten myself into."

He went on to detail Bandit and Kim's story, finishing with his own intervention.

His sister-in-law's voice softened. "Garrett, I think that's wonderful. This Kim must be a very nice person for you to go to all that trouble."

Quaid thought he caught an innuendo in her tone, but decided to ignore it. He didn't need to be explaining why he'd done what he'd done. Actually, he wasn't exactly sure himself.

"Yeah, well the sticky part is finding a way to get the horse up here. Any suggestions?"

"Yes! One of my friends has a horse-crazy daughter about Ricky's age. She has two horses at a barn not far from here and I think she owns a horse trailer. Want me to call her?"

"*Absolutely.* Jenna, I love you!"

꒰ℓ꒱

Clearly, all the exercise and excitement had drained Kim's energy. A dull pain throbbed at the base of her skull as she settled onto the couch. Miss Kitty immediately settled into a furry ball in her lap. Kim let her thoughts return to the reunion with Bandit, images that tightened her throat and brought a sting to her eyelids. She and that beautiful animal had a bond forged through trauma and tragedy, and nothing could ever change their connection. A surge of excitement ran through her head at the prospect of spending time with Bandit, being on his back, returning to a part of her life forsaken by circumstances she'd never controlled. Bandit would be her healer and she would be his protector.

Mostly made possible by Garrett Quaid.

Kim reviewed his actions and their conversations, searching for any hint that she might have misinterpreted his intentions. Why would he do such a thing for her? They hadn't gotten along all that well most of the time they'd known each other. True, they worked okay together when they weren't playing games. But that was over and this was now. The man lived on the other side of the state. Other than helping her out because of their work connection, he was out of her life. The unsettling thought tightened her chest.

Shareen telephoned awhile later. "Kim? How *are* you? We haven't talked in a long time."

Kim glanced at her cast. "I'm just fine. How are *you?*"

"I'm good, God willing. Working hard to prepare for the nationals in October. Will you be there?"

"I don't think so, Shareen. I have some other things going on and, of course, I want to save my money to come to Cairo in December."

"Oh, yes! We are so excited about that. We will be leaving for home directly after the national show, and I'm having the guest house redecorated for you."

"Oh my, that's certainly not necessary, but thank you."

Shareen's tone changed. "You know, I wanted to tell you something we heard recently. One of our friends in Alexandria told Albert that some beautiful horses had been purchased by one of the Saudi sheiks, horses from America. One of them, especially, is a fabulous show jumper. I thought you might want to look into that to see if the horse is one of those you think was stolen."

All the breath left Kim's lungs. If Talisman had made his way to Saudi Arabia, then Quaid's theory was correct. Her shoulders sagged. But they still had no way to prove any of it.

"That's very interesting, Shareen. Thank you for telling me. I'll see what I can find out."

"Well, I must say goodbye. Albert wants to go for a trail ride and I'm holding things up. Stay well, my friend."

"God willing, and same to you, Shareen."

Kim laid the phone down and stared out the deck doors. Could Talisman be the horse Shareen had heard about? How could Kim find out? A soft throb moved through the scar on her thigh, followed by a sharp pain in her knee. Even if she could determine that the horse in question was indeed Talisman, at this point, there seemed no reason to pursue it. The insurance case was closed. Jasper had been paid. At least once, maybe twice. It was over. Kim simply didn't have any more energy to expend on it.

She picked up the laptop, heaved a sigh, and turned it on. She still had hundreds of photographs to sort and file. When she was again mobile and able to work, she wanted to concentrate on new work, not fiddle with old stuff.

She gently moved Miss Kitty to the cushion beside her. "Sorry, baby, I need my lap now. You know, just for the heck of it, I think I'll work on the oldest pictures first."

She opened a photo folder dated October of the previous year. Four hundred picture thumbnails appeared on the screen and she began looking at each one. She'd taken pictures at four different major horse shows that month and most of the candid shots could probably be deleted. One by one, she opened the photographs to full size, inspected them, checked the meta data, wrote captions if needed, then saved them.

Two hours later, she opened the last folder in the November

batch, photographs taken at the Washington National Horse Show. All the shots of Talisman came up first since Kim had worked on them recently. She looked through them again, feeling sad that the wonderful equine athlete had been a pawn in someone's money game. More valuable than Bandit, but nonetheless, nothing more than a commodity in someone's eyes.

Chapter 46

Quaid listened to Deputy Dexton's clipped speech.

"This is just a courtesy call, since you provided us with some information that made a difference. We talked to Reginald Fortune and he has an alibi for the barn fire. He was on his way to Mexico. We have a copy of his flight plan and his passenger list. He was also willing to give us some details on Wade Warren. You were correct. Warren is actually a displaced Brit who's wanted for several major crimes. We have him in custody and I'll be calling Ms. Kovak to come identify him in a lineup. That's all I have right now, but I thought you'd want to know."

"I appreciate it, Deputy. I just wish I could tie Warren into my insurance case, but it's closed now, so I'll just have to always wonder."

After saying goodbye, Quaid wandered around his house, thinking about all the connections and interconnections in the case. His gut told him that he had all the pieces, but his logic said they were useless at this point.

His phone rang and Kovak's number appeared.

Her voice shook with excitement. "Quaid! Go to your email! You will never believe what I found!"

He started up his computer. "Must be pretty amazing to get *you* so revved up."

She sounded smug. "You'll see."

His mail program took forever to load and then he scrolled through several messages before hers popped up.

He clicked on the attachment, then let out a sharp breath.

"Holy Moley!"

A photograph of Talisman sailing over a jump in a large public arena. Grandstand seats rising in the background. Two lone men sat with heads together, deep in conversation.

Wade Warren and Jasper Martin.

ele ele ele

Raves for Toni Leland

Rescue Me~"The story was capturing, intriguing, and hard to put down characters were believable with strengths, weaknesses, emotions, longings, needs, uncertainties, and goals that seemed to elude them throughout the story...a terrific mystery that keeps the reader in suspense and in constant fear for Julia's survival!"
~Janet Lukas, Gray Horse Trading Company

"...explores two painfully similar worlds and, through deft storytelling, gives a better understanding of both." ~ Robbie Huseth, Blue Ribbon Books

Deadly Heritage~ "This book was a great read! Toni Leland is the best for any horse lover. Just can't wait for the next one!" ~Gail Nettles, Amazon.com

"...combines elements of romance with a well told story of mystery and intrigue...a fast paced page-turner that characterizes the writer's indepth knowledge of horses. The characters are real and believable, and the circumstances they find themselves in are typical of many American family situations today...the writer's fast paced style keeps the reader glued to the pages until the very last sentence."
~ Robert Bennett, author of the Lanny O'Brian mystery series

"I inhaled *Garden of Secrets* in two dark-and-stormy Pacific Northwest evenings, ... This is one seriously atmospheric piece. Shadowy things flitting at eye's edge... the tendency of inanimate objects to loom...evasively scarce Winterwood staffers... tricks of the eye (or are they?) woven throughout the vast, enviable gardens...a great read...and, oh-that-ending!" ~R.K. Lindh-Wilson, Amazon.com

Gambling With the Enemy~ "...a fast paced book that's part romance, part thriller, and part the kind of horsey book you grew up reading."
~Carolyn Banks, author of *A Horse To Die For*

"...I could not put it down...I really felt the story unfolding in what astrologers call a 'conspiracy of energy'..." ~Robbie Huseth, Blue Ribbon Books

Hearts Over Fences~ "...a charming and clean love story set in the heart of horse country and the horse industry. .." ~Midwest Book Review, June 2005

"...Ms. Leland weaves a fascinating tale of horses, business, and romance...*Hearts Over Fences* is a great read that I highly recommend."
~Coffee Time Review, June 2005

Winning Ways~ "...this book took me on an exciting journey of how cutthroat the show world can be...a roller coaster ride from start to finish..."
~Rebecca, *Horsemen's Yankee Pedlar*, June 2004

"...all great reads that I could hardly put down. I just wanted you to know how much I enjoy your books..." ~MP at ArabianExperts.com

"...Toni Leland presents us with a sensitive, well written story. Her knowledge of horses and the people who care for them is impressive."
~Luvada White, *Ohioana Quarterly*, Fall 2004

CPSIA information can be obtained at www.ICGtesting.com
Printed in the USA
BVOW071741240912

301137BV00006B/1/P